Praise for Jane Rubino and Caitle[n]

Lady Vernon and Her Daughter

"Cleverly inverts the premise of Austen's *Lady Susan*, with a richness

any Austen aficionado."

—MARSHA ALTMAN, author of *The Darcys & The Bingleys*

"A delightfully clever resculpting of Austen's youthful *Lady Susan*. Jane Rubino and Caitlen Rubino-Bradway have rewarded honesty and perseverance in the style of *Sense and Sensibility*. Good fun!"

—KATHRYN L. NELSON, author of *Pemberley Manor*

...of background and detail that enlivens the original epistolary novel. Should delight the most acute Austen fans."

—STEPHANIE BARRON, national bestselling author of the Jane Austen Mysteries

"A captivating read with a charmingly redeemed heroine—Jane Austen fans will love it!"

—SYRIE JAMES, author of the bestselling The Lost Memoirs of Jane Austen

"Austen devotees will appreciate the authenticity of language and setting as well as the many witty allusions to the canon."

—LAURIE VIERA RIGLER, author of Rude Awakenings of a Jane Austen Addict

"This solid retelling of Lady Susan deserves a place on the shelf of...

A Novel of Jane Austen's Lady Susan

Lady Vernon

and

Her Daughter

JANE RUBINO *and*

CAITLEN RUBINO-BRADWAY

THREE RIVERS PRESS

NEW YORK

Originally published in hardcover in the United States by Crown Publishers, an imprint of
the Crown Publishing Group, a division of Random House, Inc., New York, in 2009.

Excerpts from Lady Susan by Jane Austen, originally published in Great Britain in 1871,
appear throughout Lady Vernon and Her Daughter and following the novel.

Library of Congress Cataloging-in-Publication Data

Rubino, Jane.
Lady Vernon and her daughter / Jane Rubino.—1st ed.
p.   cm.
1. Austen, Jane, 1775–1817. Lady Susan—Fiction.   2. Widows—Fiction.
3. Mate selection—Fiction.   4. England—Fiction.   I. Title.

PS3568U1835L33 2009
813'.54—dc22   2008051999

ISBN 978-0-307-46167-4

Printed in the United States of America

Design by Lauren Dong

10 9 8 7 6 5 4 3 2 1

First Paperback Edition

For Professor Mary Ann Macartney,

with thanks for her wonderful Jane Austen seminar

BATH

The
Martin ❦ Vernon ❦ de Courcy
Family Tree

Sir William Martin ❦ Lady Martin

Elinor ❦ William
Metcalfe Martin

John ❦ Susannah
Martin Osbourne

James William
Martin

Susan ❦ Sir Frederick
Martin Vernon

Frederica
Susannah
Vernon

Ealing Park

PARKLANDS

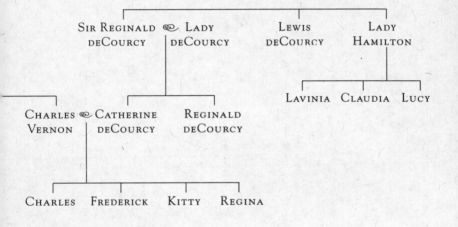

SIR REGINALD deCOURCY ❧ LADY deCOURCY LEWIS deCOURCY LADY HAMILTON

LAVINIA CLAUDIA LUCY

CHARLES VERNON ❧ CATHERINE deCOURCY REGINALD deCOURCY

CHARLES FREDERICK KITTY REGINA

CHURCHILL MANOR

VOLUME I

Town and Country

Vernon Castle

A WOMAN WITH NEITHER PROPERTY NOR FORTUNE MUST ward off this affliction by cultivating the beauty, brilliance, and accomplishment that will blind a promising suitor to the want of a dowry. When she is securely married, she may suspend her own improvement and turn her energies toward the domestication of her husband and the acquisition of wealthy suitors for their daughters. Still, she must never sink to complacency, but always keep sharp, for it may be her unfortunate lot to survive her spouse and she will be thrown back upon her wits once more.

This principle became the subject of debate one evening between Sir William Martin and his lady. He observed that a young woman of marriageable age must always be accomplished and handsome, while a gentleman was under no such obligation.

"I cannot agree with you, Sir William," protested his lady. "It is not nature but circumstance that determines how far one must exert. Personal advantages are no less necessary to a male than to a female, save in the case of a firstborn son. *He* may be as coarse as he likes, but unless he is quite sickly, his younger brothers will be obliged to cultivate a superior mind, a pleasing manner, and a handsome face."

"Well, if you are right," answered her husband, who was too good-humored to argue long with his wife, "then it is a fortunate thing for our John that he has them all."

Lady Martin could not disagree. She favored John over her elder son, William, for the latter was a plain, dry, serious sort of person, while John Martin was a young man of extraordinary good looks and captivating manners.

Upon the death of Sir William, the elder son succeeded to the title and the handsome estate in Derbyshire; he married Miss Elinor Metcalfe, who dutifully presented him with an heir, christened James William, after her father and his. John Martin, meanwhile, was left to secure his future as well as he could, and for some time he deliberated whether he must look to the law, the Navy, the clergy, or marriage to a woman of fortune.

Alas, John Martin had neither talent nor inclination for the law, the sea, or the church. He was not averse to a good match, but he wanted to be happy as much as he wanted to be rich, and while there were many young ladies who were pretty and many who were rich, there were few who were both, and *those* did not have to settle for a second son.

An introduction to the lovely daughter of a merchant named Osbourne persuaded John Martin that he wanted to be happy *more* than he wanted to be rich. Miss Susannah Osbourne possessed a beautiful face, an elegant bearing, and a lively wit, and John Martin fell so thoroughly in love as to conclude that they might do very well on his modest fortune and her five thousand pounds. The lady's affectionate father took a more practical view of the matter and introduced John Martin to an enterprising young man who was connected with a prominent banking house. Lewis deCourcy was a second son himself; his elder brother, Sir Reginald deCourcy, had inherited a large fortune and considerable property, while the younger had to make do with an excellent understanding, diligence, and an acumen for business. Lewis deCourcy was favorably impressed with Martin's cleverness and handsome manners and had no trouble in securing him a place where he had to do little more than be agreeable to gentlemen of fortune and persuade them to relinquish their money.

Into this happy union came one child, a daughter. Susan Martin was a beautiful girl who became a beautiful young woman without suffering those years of awkward transition. An active mind, a fondness for reading, and acute powers of observation gave her a precocious understanding of the world and supported a respectable measure of accomplishment. She learned to read German, speak French, and sing in Italian. She played the fortepiano in a style that was more emphatic than lyrical, but she was shrewd enough to play only those pieces that suited her spirited fingers. She possessed a keen eye for contour and expression, though her sketches were confined to caricatures of anyone she did not like. To these were added the quickest tongue in repartee, the surest seat on a saddle, the lightest foot on a ballroom floor, and most important of all, an inimitable charm of presence that livened a room when she entered it and left its mark in the dullness that followed upon her retreat.

Susan Martin's beauty was particularly gratifying to her father, for his natural liberality and want of economy had them always living in a style just above what they could afford and leaving nothing over for her future. "She will have her pick of rich men," he consoled himself. "For I do not think there is a prettier girl in all of England!"

Well before Miss Martin might express her inclination for anyone, however, her parents settled upon their nephew, James, for their future son-in-law. Although their daughter's affection for her cousin was expressed in nothing more than the teasing fondness of a sister for a brother, the Martins were not discouraged, for their designs were promoted by Lady Martin who believed that her impetuous son would feel the want of cleverness in a wife more than he would feel a want of fortune.

Sir William was of an opposite opinion and resolved to do what he could to get rid of his niece before his son lost all sense of obligation to unite his fortune to one of equal measure and tendered his proposal to his fair cousin. As soon as Miss Martin was out, her uncle gave a grand private ball in order to bring his niece together with several single gentlemen who ought to be married and wanted only a few more dances and a few more charming smiles to fix them.

James Martin secured his cousin for the first two dances, which allowed the pair to turn their wit upon the party. "Is this not superior company, Susan?" asked he. "I did not know that my excellent father had so many vain and empty-headed acquaintance! There are three fools to every sensible fellow. Among so many peacocks I will certainly appear to advantage."

"Or perhaps you can only take pleasure in the company of equals," she replied archly.

"I take pleasure in whatever is before me, *that* is my particular talent."

"To think of nothing beyond the present?"

"Indeed, yes! The past cannot be altered, and the future cannot be known—to dwell upon either will turn one into a fright or a bore."

"We cannot all enjoy such agreeable indifference, James."

"You reproach me wrongly," protested her cousin. "You may think me a fool or a reprobate, but you must never think me indifferent."

Sir William had been observing this repartee with some apprehension, and at the first opportunity he approached the young cousins with the outward motive of complimenting their dancing. "But you must allow the other gentlemen their share of pleasure or they will feel themselves slighted," Sir William said to his son. "When your set is done, bring Susan to me, for some acquaintances have just arrived whom I particularly wish her to know."

These candidates were the brothers Vernon. Frederick Vernon, the elder, was a good-natured gentleman of thirty. He had, some years earlier, rescued an impulsive young duke who had jumped into a pond on a challenge only moments before recollecting that he did not swim. A knighthood had been the result, and the conversion from Mr. Frederick Vernon to Sir Frederick Vernon had been effected without injuring the young man's kindhearted civility. He had a great fondness for society but had lately been kept from the enjoyment of it out of filial obligation. His father had suffered a prolonged illness, and Sir Frederick sacrificed his own pleasures to remain at the family property in Sussex, attending his father with great devotion until his demise.

It was the younger Vernon, however, who immediately petitioned Miss Martin for the next two dances, and she was obliged to consent. Charles Vernon was six years his brother's junior, and very different in appearance and disposition. He was handsomer of figure and face, more ingratiating in his manner, and livelier in his conversation. An unsophisticated observer would find him the more pleasing of the two, but the more cautious eye would detect the sort of high spirits that were the result of habitual indulgence in all of the license that a young man of good family can lay claim to. When Miss Martin expressed her condolences upon his recent loss, his remarks displayed a want of feeling and propriety that not even his handsome face and ingratiating conduct could disguise. While his father lived, Charles Vernon did not scruple to forfeit principle to pleasure, and when his father lay ill, he continued to amuse himself in London and Bath, arguing himself into the conviction that his father's health would not hang upon his going to Sussex and making a show of concern. If the old gentleman lived, Charles would have sacrificed his diversion for nothing, and if he died, Charles would be scarcely a penny better off. Mr. Vernon had always held the opinion there was no wisdom in assigning large portions to younger children; it was the heir who must keep up the family property and he must have the money to do it.

Having neither property nor profession, and only the five thousand pounds through his mother's marriage settlement and another five that was left by his father's will, Charles had resolved upon marrying a rich woman—yet when he laid eyes upon Susan Martin, even this principle began to give way. She was, beyond anything, the most beautiful woman he had ever beheld, and to her personal advantages was added the material one of being a near relation to Sir William and Lady Martin. The affection of Lady Martin for her niece was particularly promising as it was rumored that she had something in her own right that might be disposed of at her discretion, and Vernon wanted only the assurance that the "something" was in the neighborhood of ten or twelve thousand pounds before he applied for Miss Martin's hand.

Charles Vernon's pretension was not the result of any display of reciprocal feeling on the part of Miss Martin, for she was far too clever to be drawn in by a charming facade, and she perceived that although Sir Frederick was not as handsome or animated as his younger brother, in manners and understanding he was far superior.

Sir Frederick's disposition was not at all like his brother's. While Charles Vernon had been all artificial politeness and cold selfishness, every expression of Sir Frederick's revealed his affability, understanding, and taste, and she concluded their dance with the wish to know him better.

Sir William observed these symptoms of compatibility and devised many subsequent occasions for bringing them together. Charles Vernon could not be excluded, and he was invariably charming, but he could not declare himself before he was assured that Susan Martin would have something more than a mere five thousand pounds, and he held back long enough for Sir Frederick to overcome his natural diffidence and make Susan Martin an offer of marriage.

The lady's parents offered no objection; Sir Frederick was an excellent man and very much in love with their daughter, and Susan's happiness was motive enough for them to moderate their ambitions for rank and connections. As for Sir William, he was so relieved that he had divided his niece from his son that he succumbed to a plan of Lady Martin's to add to Miss Martin's settlement. "Our brother has been an excellent father in everything but prudence," said she. "He can settle nothing on Susan but five thousand pounds. We have only our son, who is provided for, and I have always regarded Susan as a daughter. May we not do something for her?"

"Indeed, yes," declared Sir William. "I will settle another five thousand upon her and buy her wedding clothes as well."

"It is no less than I would have expected of you—but I ask for something more. Everybody exerts on a woman's behalf when she is to be married, but it is when she is widowed that she most wants some consideration, for a woman who is predeceased by her husband is often left with no place to go. We have not gone to London above one winter in four—why may we not settle the house in town upon her? The diversions of town, though not to *our* liking, will be very agreeable to *them*—it will allow Susan to spend part of the year near her family, and she will be assured of having someplace to go if she should find herself a widow."

"It is a very strange thing to put her in weeds upon the eve of her wedding," remarked Sir William, and yet he saw the prudence of her suggestion and consented to settle their fine house on Portland Place upon his niece.

Everyone was delighted except for Charles Vernon, who began to be angry that—as Susan Martin was to have *ten* thousand pounds rather than five *and* a fine house in town—he had not pressed his suit.

The necessity of being on amicable terms with his brother, however, obliged him to make a show of goodwill, yet he did not scruple to mention to all of his acquaintance that Miss Martin's affections had been overruled by ambition, that she had set her cap for the brother who could make her mistress of an estate with an income of four thousand a year rather than the one who, at present, had no prospects at all.

And so, before her eighteenth year, Miss Susan Martin became Lady Vernon.

chapter two

L ADY VERNON'S FIRST OPINION OF THE VERNON FAMILY
property was highly favorable as it was formed as they passed
through the village of Churchill, which was yet five miles
from the estate. Nothing of the manor was visible but for an imposing
pair of stone turrets, and the high ground gave a picturesque aspect to
the farms and tenant cottages and to the parsonage and churchyard
beyond. As they approached the steward's lodge, however, Lady Vernon observed that the smooth roads became rutted, and their carriage
was rattled by furrows and potholes that would invite mud when the
weather was wet and dust when it was dry (for the late Mr. Vernon
had always been of the opinion that the tenants and cottagers must be
able to get round to one another, while it was not at all necessary that
they wait upon him).

The manor house lay at the end of a long avenue bordered by
lichen-covered oaks that formed a dense canopy that rendered the
passage oppressive and dim on all but the brightest of summer days.
The house itself had begun as a handsome edifice of old gray stone,
rising turrets, and looming gargoyles, but it had been handed down to
master after master who made only those improvements necessary to
ensure his immediate comfort. While the parsonage and farms and
tenant cottages were always kept in good order, the manor house fell
into such a state of disrepair that it could only be made habitable by
appending an entirely new dwelling onto the old one.

Sir Frederick apologized to his bride for the property's neglected
state. "There is not a better library in four counties," he declared, "but

I am afraid that my honored father's illness did not allow him to exert as far as he ought. But I assure you, my dear Susan, you shall have the liberty and funds to do as you like."

Improvements were talked of—the kitchen garden and green-houses were to be restored, the bedchambers would need considerable refurbishment, the arrangement of the rooms modified so as to take full advantage of the view offered by the hedgerows, the park, and Churchill Pond. Plans were resolved upon quickly, yet Sir Frederick was compelled to acknowledge that the aged steward, retained for so many years out of the late master's benevolence and affection rather than the man's capability, was quite unequal to the undertaking. Sir Frederick prevailed upon the steward to accept a comfortable cottage and a handsome sum of money with such great diplomacy that the old man believed he had been elevated in his station and yielded his post to a successor.

Mr. Deane had been given a very good character by John Martin's friend Mr. Lewis deCourcy, and to his own accomplishments was added the advantage of a young daughter who was suited in every way to the post of Lady Vernon's maid. Sir Frederick reviewed the number of improvements with Mr. Deane, and the two agreed that the best plan would be for the newlyweds to quit the house in order to give the carpenters and glaziers and upholsterers a free rein. They were at Churchill Manor, therefore, only long enough to be introduced to the neighbors and tenants, to give a half-dozen dinners, and for Sir Frederick to have some shooting before they consigned the property to Mr. Deane and repaired to London for the season.

UPON THE DEATH of Sir William Martin, at the end of the winter season, Sir Frederick and Lady Vernon, accompanied by her parents, traveled to Ealing Park, the Martin estate in Derbyshire. The family circle was so compatible, and of such comfort to Lady Martin and Sir James, that they were all urged to prolong their visit as long as they could. Sir Frederick readily consented; he was very fond of Lady Martin and her son, and his kindness, his steadiness, and his good humor were so pleasing to them that if Lady Martin ever did sigh, "Ah, if only she had married my James!" it was quickly followed by "But I daresay she could not have done *much* better."

The Vernons did not return to Churchill Manor until December and found that owing to some delays in the procurement of materials and laborers (for many had been hired from the local population and could only be enlisted when they were not wanted on their own properties and farms), their improvements were but half-finished. They remained, therefore, only to give a few informal balls and dinners for the neighbors and to pass out shillings to the carol singers and presents of money and mince pies to the servants. Once the slice of twelfth cake was eaten, they again removed to London. An appeal from Lady Martin (who was, at her son's insistence, to remain at Ealing Park) that she not be abandoned to James and his merry set of friends for the entire summer persuaded them to put off Churchill Manor once again. A visit to Mr. Lewis deCourcy at Bath was followed by a long stay in Derbyshire, where Sir James's succession of balls, water parties, and picnics kept them well into the beginning of autumn.

It was in the middle of this visit that Sir Frederick received a letter from Mr. Deane, giving a favorable report of his progress and yet acknowledging that it would be many months more before the renovations were complete. Sir Frederick was content to give his steward all the time that was necessary; his lady, however, confided to him a very particular reason that they must be settled well before the date that Mr. Deane had proposed.

Sir Frederick's delight in the prospect of an addition to their family was exceedingly great, and when their visit at Ealing Park was concluded, they repaired immediately to London, where they would remain until Lady Vernon was confined.

In the early part of spring, they welcomed into their family a daughter, christened Frederica Susannah, and the matter of a fixed residence now acquired some urgency.

"A child must be given the advantage of open space and fresh air," Sir Frederick decided. "Churchill Manor will not be ready for another six months at least and—I am sure you will forgive me—I do not think that Ealing Park would suit, at least not for the coming summer."

"Why may we not find another purchase?" suggested Lady Vernon. "We have fortune enough, and it will be something that we may settle upon Frederica, as she will have no claim upon Churchill Manor."

"An excellent scheme!" declared Sir Frederick. "I will leave the choice entirely to you. Only let it have some fishing and some grouse or pheasant or woodcock to shoot, and whatever you like for yourself, and I will be content."

Lady Vernon turned up an excellent property in Staffordshire. The manor house had been built within the last century, and both the grounds and the interior were laid out in a style that combined elegance with comfort and sense, while the extensive woods offered some of the finest sport in the country. The neighbors were said to be as agreeable a collection of folk as one would meet anywhere, with the nearest of them being the Clarkes, an affable couple who, despite dissimilar natures, were admired through all of Staffordshire as models of conjugal felicity. He was a quiet gentleman who enjoyed a morning stroll with his dogs and the remainder of the day among his books, and his wife was a lively woman who must spend part of every day visiting the neighbors or walking into town. There were also the Misses Clarke, two little girls a few years older than Frederica, who, Lady Vernon and Sir Frederick hoped, might be companions for their daughter.

Sir Frederick was so pleased with his lady's choice that he left all of the bargaining to her as well. Lady Vernon did justice to his confidence and got a price that was three thousand less than he would have paid, and Sir Frederick rewarded her cleverness by settling the difference upon her.

The dwelling was christened Vernon Castle, and they were so delighted with it that it became their country home, and Churchill Manor was only opened for a fortnight every Christmas.

chapter three

T HE VERNONS WERE AS ENTHUSIASTICALLY COURTED AS
any couple will be when they are handsome, clever, and
have plenty of money. Every picnic and shooting party at
Vernon Castle added to Sir Frederick's affability, and every reception
at Portland Place added to his wife's brilliance. Even little Frederica,
who was not seen enough to give any material impression of her character or appearance, was said to be the prettiest and most well-
behaved child who ever lived.

Alas, after ten years of universal goodwill, there came a decline
in their fortunes, for which Sir Frederick's brother bore no small
responsibility.

Charles Vernon's pride had sustained a blow when Susan Martin
chose Frederick over himself, but he knew that the surest way to preserve Sir Frederick's trust and liberality was to keep up a facade of
family affection. When he was not imposing upon his brother's hospitality, he was in the company of a very fast set who had a love of gaming and a reliance upon speculation rather than employment. Charles
introduced some of these acquaintances to Sir Frederick, who found
them so personable and their manners so engaging that he set down
their impulsiveness and indiscretion to affability and allowed them to
lure him into an ill-fated speculation. The result of this was a considerable financial loss. To Sir Frederick's credit, he blamed no one but
himself for the error of judgment, nor did he allow self-reproach to
embitter his warm and openhearted nature. Charles Vernon was
equally complacent; he had no conscience to provoke embarrassment
or remorse. If he did experience any anxiety, it was only when he

wondered whether his brother's situation would affect his own invitations to shoot at Staffordshire and to dine at Portland Place.

Lady Vernon would surely have advised against the scheme, but these associates had imposed upon Sir Frederick at a time when she had been obliged to spend several weeks in town, to attend to her ailing father. His untimely death, followed in a fortnight by her mother's demise, deprived Sir Frederick of his most prudent counsel, and Lady Vernon learned nothing of the predicament until it was irrevocable and the money was lost.

Sir Frederick's creditors were kept at bay until the disposition of his father-in-law's fortune was known, as his daughter's bequest might be equal to what they were owed and spare them the embarrassment of having to go to the duns. The will was read, and as with almost every other will, it brought more disappointment than consolation. John Martin had been so confident in his daughter's security that he never ceased to indulge his own extravagance, and what modest fortune he had managed to set aside (as his wife had not long survived him) was to be divided among his faithful servants, with the remainder settled upon Frederica. The latter portion allowed her parents a life interest, but this amount was too little to materially relieve their present distress, and Sir Frederick decided that they must settle their debts by finding a tenant for their house in town or a purchaser for Vernon Castle.

"Churchill Manor has long been ready for our tenancy," declared Sir Frederick, "and it would not do to keep two country houses and have nothing in town, as Frederica will be out in a few years, and it would be greatly to her advantage if we retained Portland Place."

"I confess, my love, I am more concerned that Freddie be left with no place at all," his lady replied. "Vernon Castle was to be settled upon her."

"You are quite right, my dear, but a good match will make Freddie her own mistress, and if we sell Vernon Castle and are frugal for the next few years, I may mend my affairs and add considerably to her portion. There is something else in its favor, as I have the advantage of an immediate offer. Charles has written that if we find ourselves compelled to give up Vernon Castle, he will take it off our hands. You know that Charles has always wanted a property of his own and he is particularly anxious to settle on something quickly."

Lady Vernon could not conceal her surprise. Where had Charles Vernon, always in want of ready money, got the funds to purchase any property at all? Had he profited from his brother's loss and having deprived Sir Frederick of money now meant to take his property as well?

"And why is he so eager to settle now, pray?"

"He is engaged to be married."

"Charles? Engaged?"

"Yes, it all happened only in the last fortnight, it seems. Even our friend Mr. Lewis deCourcy has written to me of his surprise at how speedily it all took place. But Charles is nearly five and thirty, you know, and ought to have settled before now."

"But how is Mr. deCourcy involved in the matter?"

"It is his niece, the daughter of Mr. deCourcy's elder brother, Sir Reginald, whom Charles means to marry. Their sister is Lady Hamilton, so the connection is an excellent one for my brother. I have been told that Mr. deCourcy means to extend to Charles the same patronage he did to your father."

"To place him in a banking house?" Lady Vernon inquired with some surprise. She did not add that *she* would not have put Charles Vernon where he might have a free hand over other people's money. "I wonder, then, that Charles would purchase an estate so far from town. And what sort of offer has he made you for Vernon Castle?"

Sir Frederick named a price that seemed so shockingly low to Lady Vernon that it took all of her self-command to keep from expressing her indignation. "And what do you mean to do?" she asked Sir Frederick.

"My dear Susan!" he cried. "It was through your efforts that we found Vernon Castle and I would not let it go to anybody without your consent. Our affection for the place, and our intimacy with our good neighbors, the Clarkes, would make it very difficult to surrender entirely. I thought that it might be of some comfort for you to know that Vernon Castle has not gone to strangers."

Lady Vernon wisely refrained from remarking that she would *not* be comforted to see a property that was to be settled on their daughter pass down to Charles Vernon and his children. After a moment's consideration, Lady Vernon observed, "My dear Frederick, it is not always wise to enter into business with family. If matters go wrong, there is so much ill feeling, and you would not want to risk that, particularly when the occasion of Charles's marriage may bring us all together more. Surely Miss deCourcy will bring something of a fortune into the marriage, which ought to allow them to purchase. Let us look elsewhere. My Aunt Martin has a very wide acquaintance, and I am certain that she can help us find a purchaser, and if she cannot, we may reconsider your brother's offer."

"Your advice is excellent!" agreed the amiable Sir Frederick. "I am quite of your opinion. When you next write to your aunt, lay our situation before her, and I will wait upon her reply before I give Charles my answer."

LADY VERNON TO LADY MARTIN

Portland Place, London
My dear Aunt Martin,

I know that some word of our circumstances will have preceded this letter, for it seems that anything in the way of misfortune can never be kept to one's self. To be sure, it would have been more interesting if I had run off with the groom, or some natural son of Frederick's had turned up at our door, but alas, it is only money that distresses us, or the lack of it at least.

We must, it seems, give up Vernon Castle if we are to remain above water, and will be compelled to spend our country months at Churchill Manor. I can only hope that you and James will overlook the informality of the neighborhood and come to visit us there. You need not worry about its being too lively, or of falling into a crowd that demands that you always appear to advantage—those people will certainly drop us, and the only excitement that is likely to occur will be for someone to be mistook for a stag or a grouse and to be shot by another in his hunting party.

In the meantime, if you or my cousin happen to know of a pur-
chaser for Vernon Castle, one who would give us a price that would
be fair enough to alleviate our present distress, I hope that you will be
the means of an introduction. We have had one offer made to us, one
that is so small as to be insulting, and I cannot allow Frederick to be
taken advantage of, not even out of <u>fraternal affection</u>. But of that, I
will say no more.

I remain,
Your affectionate niece,
Etc. etc.

Lady Martin gave this letter to her son, who immediately responded with an offer to forward whatever money was necessary to
ease Sir Frederick's distress. A succession of letters followed in which
the matter was argued back and forth with all of the lively antagonism
that had marked the youthful quarrels of the cousins, for Lady Vernon
had a strong aversion to accepting charity while Sir James was determined to bestow it. The genteel arrangements between her father and
his creditors, and the more vulgar maneuvers by which Charles Vernon had remained solvent, had given Lady Vernon a thorough disgust
of indebtedness.

Convinced that his cousin would not yield, Sir James wrote to Sir
Frederick.

If you are determined upon the sale of Vernon Castle, allow me to
be your surrogate. I promise that I will find you a purchaser who will
not offer a penny less than what is fair. Devote your energies to my
dear cousin, whose recent loss must make your obligation to her up-
permost in your consideration. Give me the power to act for you in all
the rest.

To this Sir Frederick consented and Sir James acted with discretion and speed. Before a month had passed, Sir Frederick was informed that a gentleman named Edwards, with a wife and two sons,
had taken a fancy to Vernon Castle. Sir Frederick gave his wife's

cousin power to act in his stead and the business was concluded without the necessity of Sir Frederick even going to Staffordshire.

Charles Vernon was very angry when he heard that he had been cheated out of Vernon Castle, and he confided to Miss deCourcy that it had all been Lady Vernon's doing, implying that she had come to regret her choice and as she could not bear to see Charles happily married to another, she meant to thwart him in everything. This left Miss deCourcy with no fond feelings toward her future sister-in-law, and with no desire to ever know her.

chapter four

REDERICA VERNON HAD NOT REACHED HER ELEVENTH year when her family was obliged to give up Vernon Castle. Still, she possessed the strength of understanding and superior abilities that supported her in the loss of all that was familiar and reconciled her to the move from Staffordshire to Sussex.

She was not disheartened by the prospect of a quieter style of living, for she had never been easy in any company outside her family circle. She had not yet learned to feign an interest in conversation or mask her desire to retreat to a book. Under the tuition of her mother and an excellent governess, she became diligent and accomplished, but nothing was acquired for praise or show. She learned to play upon the harp and the pianoforte with considerable proficiency, though never with the élan of one who means to perform before company. She learned to paint and sketch but confined her subjects to flowers and wildlife, for she would not impose upon a human subject to sit for her. When the weather was poor, she was happy to pass the day in Churchill's superior library, and when it was fair, she was equally pleased to explore the grounds for some curious specimen of moss or leaf, or to attempt to improve the flower beds and greenhouses.

Her parents and governess approved this activity, which was particularly suited to Frederica's patience and curiosity, and given complete liberty to do as she liked, she brought the forcing garden back to use, laid out a convenient kitchen garden, cultivated a variety of flowers, and coaxed the pear trees into bloom and yield.

That winter, the Vernons went up to town with every expectation that their society would not be as eagerly sought as when they did not have to practice anything like economy. Sir James Martin, however, had resolved that his cousins should not be slighted by anybody, and they were not two nights in London before he gave a grand party in their honor. He had a spirited set of companions to supply the gaiety, ladies and gentlemen picked up before he had come into his title and who could not be got rid of afterward; the elegance was furnished by the distinguished families who had a sister or daughter of marriageable age, for Sir James was considered to be one of the most eligible young men in England.

At this gathering, Lady Vernon was introduced to a Mrs. Johnson. Mr. Johnson had made his fortune in trade, which had put him at variance with his lady. She believed that her husband's wealth entitled them to know everyone of distinction, while Mr. Johnson was of the opinion that it relieved him of the necessity of knowing anyone at all. He contrived to be at his club when his lady received visitors, and sent her to balls and parties when he wanted to spend a quiet evening among his books. Her accounts of gaiety and noise, meant to tempt him out of his misanthropy, had the reverse effect and always left him very glad that he had stayed at home.

"What an agreeable party!" Mrs. Johnson began. "Sir James brings together such lively company. I am sure that Mr. Johnson, if only he would come out, would not find it at all tedious."

"Does Mr. Johnson not like dancing?"

"He would like it well enough if it could be accomplished alone and in silence and with a book in one hand! And if I tease him for being so dull, he will threaten to give up London altogether and move to the country! Perhaps he would come out if Robert Manwaring would stay away," she declared with a nod in that gentleman's direction. "But *that* will never happen, for Manwaring is as determined to seek pleasure as my *bon mari* is to avoid it."

Robert Manwaring was a comely and engaging fellow whose attraction toward lively company had drawn him into Sir James's circle. He was ruled by impulse and too readily led by sentiment rather than sense, and the most grievous effect of this was his marriage to a very dull wife. It was rumored that he would never have proposed if there had not been some opposition on the part of the lady's guardian, which had inflamed Manwaring's romantic nature. He had pled his case to the lady with energy, won his point, and now lived to regret it. He was not the first man to err in his choice of a partner, and he would not be the last, and in the meantime he sought relief in society where he played at cards with men more imprudent than he and flirted with women who were prettier and more pleasing than his wife.

"How do you like Manwaring?" Mrs. Johnson persisted. "His manners are very handsome, are they not? You must be aware, for he will flirt with you if you are not on your guard, but he means nothing by it."

"If he means nothing by it, then I need not be on my guard," Lady Vernon replied with a smile. "He was giving me an account of his estate in Somerset."

"Oh, it is a pretty little bit of property, but not as great as my *bon mari* wished."

"Does Mr. Johnson have an interest in Mr. Manwaring's property?"

"Oh, yes! My *bon mari* was Eliza Manwaring's guardian and a very great friend of her father. Mr. Johnson was entrusted with the administration of Eliza's fortune, and when she married Manwaring against his wishes, he withheld all but an allowance—fifteen hundred per annum. He was very angry that she married Manwaring, when she might have done so much better, but if Manwaring's sister catches Sir James, perhaps there may be some ground for *rapprochement*. Of course, Maria Manwaring is only seventeen, but she has no older sisters to hold her back. I met my *bon mari* when I was seventeen and I caught him before he had the time to look elsewhere! What is Miss Vernon's age?"

"Frederica is not yet in her teens."

"Well, it is not too early to start looking," Mrs. Johnson advised. "The best matches will often be set up well before a young lady is out, particularly since young men nowadays are so fickle and teasing. They will put young ladies of good family through the trial and expense of season upon season and then run to the altar with the governess!"

Sir James approached the two with a smile and an outstretched hand. "Ladies, I come to separate you. I am obliged to begin the dancing and must have a partner."

"There is Maria Manwaring, sitting with her sister-in-law, and I am sure that you and she will open the dance very prettily," Lady Vernon replied archly.

"But she is such a figure of quiet and tranquillity, it would be quite a shame to animate her. You two, however, appear to be engaged in the sort of *tête-à-tête* that always bodes ill for my sex. No, I must put an end to it. Come, Susan, you are the guest of honor, after all."

Lady Vernon glanced across the room toward her husband, who wore the contented smile of a man who enjoys seeing his wife distinguished, and accepted her cousin's hand. The pair took their place amid many expressions of surprise at his choice.

"And how do you like Alicia Johnson?" inquired Sir James. "Are you not grateful to me for the introduction? She is just the sort of incorrigible busybody that makes for a diverting acquaintance and an indispensable correspondent. You will be very glad to know her. Only see how quickly she hurries over to Eliza Manwaring in order to gossip about us!"

"Gossip cannot abide a delay," agreed Lady Vernon. "It will risk being disproven and lose all of the delights of prejudice and error."

"And what can be the nature of their delightful conjecture?"

"Mrs. Johnson will declare that you pronounced Maria Manwaring quiet and tranquil and Mrs. Manwaring will wonder whether you meant that you find her husband's sister to be refined and gentle or tedious and dull—and from *there* they will wonder how soon Freddie can be out, and whether you have not married because you delay on her account."

"I honor your imagination!" Sir James laughed heartily. "If I could not suit you, Susan, I cannot hope to please Freddie!"

"You suited me quite well when you were not in the way," replied she. "But you invariably bothered me for conversation when I was in the middle of a book, and wanted to read your newspaper when I was of a mind to converse."

"That is the advantage of the dance, you see." He smiled. "You must lay down the book and I put aside the newspaper. And, as we are out of everyone's hearing, we may talk nonsense and give the appearance of engaging in conversation that is very artful and deep."

"I may not be as satisfied as you are, cousin, to suggest only a *pretense* of understanding."

"That is because you are not a man, Susan. A man is all the happier for having the world make him out to be more interesting than he knows himself to be, and his character will suffer rumor and offense more easily than a woman's."

"Beware, James—you begin to sound artful and deep."

"I mean only to give you a word of caution."

"Against the rumors of Alicia Johnson and Eliza Manwaring?"

"No—but against the offense taken by a brother, I would have you be on your guard."

"Is Charles still angry that we would not let him have Vernon Castle for next to nothing?"

"Charles Vernon has not forgotten that you preferred Sir Frederick to him," replied Sir James.

"He evidently has, as he is to marry Miss deCourcy."

"Well, he could not wait forever to catch you as a widow."

"James! You will retract that, else I will wish with all my heart to see Maria Manwaring catch you as a husband."

"I do retract it," he said with a laugh. "Perhaps the inconceivable will come to pass and marriage will make Vernon amiable and prudent."

"And does Miss deCourcy have the power to effect such a change? Is she of an amiable and prudent disposition?"

"Miss Catherine deCourcy has got to three and twenty without finding a suitor she liked, or that Lady deCourcy liked, which is much the same thing, and so she decided to take the one who was most adept at flattering her vanity. Vernon can be very pleasing when he exerts himself, and Catherine deCourcy likes to be pleased."

"But is it a love match?"

Sir James laughed. "Love does not rank high when choosing a wife. Marriage is always a business transaction. One invests in a partner with the expectation that the investment will produce a return."

"I do not think that Frederick would agree with you," his cousin replied when the steps of the dance brought them together once more. "He might have contracted far more advantageously."

"Frederick has made the best bargain of any man that I know. If you had come with twenty thousand pounds he would not have loved you one whit less," Sir James declared with mock earnestness. "At any rate, I understand that Miss deCourcy's twenty thousand will settle some very pressing debts of honor, and many gentlemen rank the good opinion of their creditors above that of their wives."

"And does Miss deCourcy offer no better return than the reconciliation of debts and the goodwill of the wine dealer and the tailor?"

"No more *immediate* return, but a little ill fortune could work greatly to his advantage, as the deCourcy entail is somewhat vulnerable."

"In what way? Is there not an heir? I have heard that Miss deCourcy has a brother."

"Yes, but he is not above seventeen or eighteen, so it will be some years before he can marry and produce an heir of his own. Other than this young man, there is Sir Reginald's brother, Mr. Lewis deCourcy, who is a bachelor and past fifty. After *that*, the writ provides for the entail to pass through the female line, which would put a son of Charles Vernon in the way of considerable property."

"And yet something very dire would have to occur to remove *both* gentlemen from the succession."

"Well," replied Sir James cheerfully, "a bit of avarice often brings out the resourcefulness in all but the best of us."

"You see what comes of entailing fortunes entirely from the female line," Lady Vernon observed. "You will begin to look upon your male relations as a necessity to your happiness—or an impediment to it."

"I hope that I shall never give you cause to think of me as an impediment to yours," he replied with grave sincerity.

chapter five

ALICIA JOHNSON AND ELIZA MANWARING WERE OF THE same age, for Eliza's husband was some years her junior and Alicia had taken a husband many years her senior. A similarity in the narrowness of their minds, a love of society, and a penchant for disparaging the finery of others and exhibiting their own had persuaded them that their husbands' differences ought not to prevent them from being better acquainted.

"What an elegant couple!" exclaimed Mrs. Johnson, as she and Mrs. Manwaring observed Lady Vernon dancing with her cousin. "It is said that Lady Martin attempted a match between them, but her husband opposed it. It turned out well enough, for Sir Frederick Vernon seems a very amiable man."

"There is only one daughter, is there not?" inquired Mrs. Manwaring. "They ought to have had a son. Mr. Manwaring says that Sir Frederick has been very imprudent—a son would keep a roof over their heads, at least. But I daresay they look toward making an advantageous match for Miss Vernon."

"*That* cannot be for many years."

"And yet," replied Mrs. Manwaring with a troubled look, "if Miss Vernon is as pretty as her mother, she will have her pick of beaux. Perhaps, having lost the mother to Sir Frederick, Sir James means to marry the daughter. How often have you heard of a gentleman who lives the bachelor life for many years and then settles upon a girl he had known as a child?"

The conversation continued in this vein through supper until Mrs.

Manwaring was consumed with a desire to have a look at the young girl she regarded as Maria Manwaring's rival. The two ladies resolved to call on Lady Vernon the next day with the express purpose of getting a look at her daughter.

To their very great disappointment, they were informed that Miss Vernon was not at home.

"We do not bring Frederica to London as a rule," said Lady Vernon. "She is much happier in the country, but Sir Frederick was able to gain admission to the apothecaries' garden and brought her to town on purpose to spend an entire day there, for she has a keen interest in anything to do with plants and flowers."

"La, is she scientific?" inquired Mrs. Johnson. "I am not scientific in the least, though it is said to be quite the *ton*, so long as it is confined to leaves and petals, which may be pressed into a book. But surely Sir Frederick does not direct her education? Has she a governess?"

"She has an excellent governess, but education is not confined to the nursery and the classroom."

"I must compliment you on your dancing," said Mrs. Manwaring. "But I suppose that you and Sir James have had a great deal of practice. I daresay you grew up quite as close as brother and sister."

"Well, I can go so far as to say that James was such a companion as ensured that I would never want for a brother," Lady Vernon agreed with a smile.

"And how is Lady Martin? Does she never come to London?"

"Not if it can be avoided. She much prefers the quiet of the country."

"And yet Ealing Park cannot always be quiet when Sir James is in residence," remarked Mrs. Johnson. "Lady Martin must often be pressed into service as his hostess. It is a very convenient arrangement for both of them, and one that accounts for the fact that he is in no hurry to marry."

"I cannot answer for my cousin, but I think that Lady Martin would be very happy to see James married," replied Lady Vernon. "I would venture to say that the event cannot occur too soon for her."

That brought a smile to the face of Mrs. Manwaring, who saw a better chance for Maria if Sir James was encouraged to marry soon. Before she could reply, however, Sir James Martin himself was ushered into the room.

"My dear cousin!" Lady Vernon exclaimed. "I would have thought that you would still be in bed—it is not yet four o'clock."

Sir James bowed to the visitors. "I have got a present for Freddie." He drew a pamphlet from his pocket and handed it around. " 'An Introduction to Botany.' It is written by a gentlewoman who proposes that our leisure be given over to mental improvement! What do you say to that, ladies?"

Lady Vernon's visitors looked at each other. To promote the idea would be to declare oneself the most tiresome sort of bluestocking, but to reject it might be taken by Sir James as an affront to his generosity. At last, Mrs. Manwaring ventured to say, "I am sure that too much study can be as bad as too little."

"I am quite of the same opinion," declared Mrs. Johnson. "Leisure hours are necessary to one's tranquillity and temperament. Excessive study may put one out of sorts."

"I cannot disagree with you," Sir James replied. "I do not think that you will find a more thorough idler than myself and I am never out of sorts. What is your opinion, cousin?"

Lady Vernon was very near to laughing at her cousin's show of sincerity and managed to say only, "I have never been an advocate of throwing time away," to which her two visitors nodded in such emphatic agreement that she was forced to turn her face away to hide her mirth.

Sir James observed his cousin's predicament and hastened to make inquiries after Mr. and Miss Manwaring and Mr. Johnson until Lady Vernon was once again mistress of herself.

After a few more minutes of conversation, the ladies rose to depart, and when they had settled in their carriage, Mrs. Johnson declared, "What very good luck for Maria! Miss Vernon—encouraged to be scientific! *That* will only teach her to be the sort of dull, bookish girl that men do not like at all."

Mrs. Manwaring was so delighted with this notion that she invited her guardian's wife to drink tea with her and urged her to give Mr.

Johnson her warmest regards and to beg his pardon yet again that she had married against his wishes.

LADY VERNON REPAID the call to Mrs. Johnson the following day and brought Frederica with her. The little girl made her curtsy and then sat quietly on an ottoman, turning the pages of the pamphlet that Sir James had given her.

"What a delightful child," Mrs. Johnson remarked to Lady Vernon. "What a keen interest she has in her book! La, you would not see me so transfixed by a book when I was her age! What a pity she was not a boy."

"Do you not think that science might be of interest to a girl?"

"La, yes! Children will fill their heads with knowledge that does them no good whatsoever, but we all grow out of it in time. No, I meant that a son would secure your family property, for else it will go to your husband's brother. And that does not often work to advantage, as a brother who has his own wife and family might overlook those occasions to be generous—unless his wife is of a particularly charitable nature."

"I must hope, then, that Miss deCourcy's disposition is a generous one."

"Have you never met her?"

"No, never. The news of Charles's engagement took Sir Frederick and me quite by surprise. Charles has been a bachelor for so many years that we had concluded he was content to be so. He had never mentioned any acquaintance with Miss deCourcy at all until after the engagement had been formed."

The visit did not last long beyond this exchange, and when Mrs. Johnson next spoke to Eliza Manwaring, she repeated it with blithe inaccuracy, and Mrs. Manwaring did not hesitate to add embellishments of her own when *she* conveyed it, and soon it was all around London that Lady Vernon disapproved of her brother-in-law's union with Miss deCourcy, that she had likely expected Charles Vernon to pine away for her forever, and that she was the worst sort of hardened coquette, who could bear for no one to be admired but herself.

chapter six

THE MARRIAGE OF CHARLES VERNON TO CATHERINE deCourcy was celebrated in so exclusive a fashion that among those excluded were the groom's own brother and sister-in-law. Charles Vernon wrote to Sir Frederick, explaining that the ceremony was to be held very near the deCourcy estate and that the indifferent health of Sir Reginald would not allow for much company and commotion. Sir Frederick was sorry to miss the ceremony, as weddings were such happy gatherings, but he wrote to his brother offering kind congratulations, and Lady Vernon likewise dispatched her very best wishes to her new sister-in-law. The replies they received were civil and completely lacking in warmth, for Miss deCourcy had been informed by her mother, who had heard from her husband's sister, Lady Hamilton, who had been told by Lady Millbanke, who had it on very good authority from Eliza Manwaring that Lady Vernon was said to have heard something so ill of Catherine deCourcy as to make her positively set against Charles Vernon's marriage.

As for Charles Vernon, he had got a handsome dowry, a position in a banking establishment, and a wife. Another man would have been contented, but Charles was of a temperament that dwelt less upon what he had attained than what he had been denied. An alliance with one of the oldest families in England did not do away with the knowledge that his first choice had preferred his brother, and a position with a respectable establishment only served to remind him that he was obliged to do something to keep himself, while Frederick had to do nothing at all. But what rankled most was the fact that Frederick would not sell Vernon Castle for what Charles was willing to pay, which left him unable to purchase an establishment of his own, as he had been compelled to apply the greater part of his wife's dowry toward reconciling his debts. He and his bride, therefore, had no alternative but to settle in Parklands Cottage on the deCourcy estate.

Parklands Cottage was far less humble than the term *cottage* generally implied. The residence was modern and roomy and the gardens and copses were so cunningly laid out as to almost make one forget that it was only separated from the great house by a quarter-mile lane. Unfortunately, Charles Vernon could not forget it. Mrs. Vernon felt herself obliged to visit her parents every day, and these visits often concluded with Lady deCourcy walking back to the cottage with her daughter and staying to tea. Visitors to Parklands were rare, and there was no sport at all, as Sir Reginald's frail health would not permit the commotion. They dined with fewer than half a dozen families, people who had no conversation and little interest in anything beyond the neighborhood. Charles was not long married when he was persuaded that if he could put a greater distance between his wife and her parents, he might *almost* be willing to sacrifice one or two of his private vices to accomplish it.

A situation in the banking house had the material advantage of taking him often to town. There, in the livelier society of gentlemen who had amassed fortunes in India or Antigua, or who had been the happy beneficiary of a relation's premature demise, and free from the scrutiny of his wife and her mother, Charles gave way to indulgence. When these visits concluded, he would return to Parklands less contented and more in debt than when he had left it, and he would half resolve to live frugally. But whenever a surplus of money came his way, it was spent.

In due course, they were blessed with a young Charles, who was followed by Frederick, Kitty, and Regina. With each addition to her family, Mrs. Vernon was more content to remain as they were, while Vernon became impatient for change, an impatience that had him always eager to accept his affectionate brother's invitations to visit Churchill Manor. Mrs. Vernon, persuaded as she was that Lady Vernon had opposed her marriage, would never consent to going, but her mother had advised that a gentleman must have some diversion, and Churchill was a better bargain than London, where Charles was wont to spend too freely.

And yet Vernon's visits to his brother were not entirely without cost, for they had a very adverse effect upon his equanimity and contentment. The family property, which in his youth Vernon had found to be very dull and insignificant, had become one to be coveted. Vernon did not consider how far Sir Frederick's affability and Lady Vernon's refinement and taste had effected Churchill Manor's rehabilitation. He saw only that *there* it was all liveliness, elegance, and good company, which was a sharp contrast to the dull routine of Parklands Cottage and the insipidity of the deCourcy family circle.

Inevitably, Charles Vernon would come away from Churchill Manor, dwelling upon the accident of birth that had given Sir Frederick precedence, and lament, "What an excellent thing it is to have an estate of one's own! Why would they not sell Vernon Castle to us! How well situated we should have been if I had been the elder!"

His wife did not share his feeling; she longed for no change in circumstance, as there would be no other situation where she might be both a pampered daughter and a complacent wife. "We must not be downcast, my dear, but look to the future and hope for the best. Sir Frederick is already past forty, and he cannot live forever. We will have Churchill Manor in time, or our son shall."

Charles could not be encouraged by the latter prospect, as it could not take place until his own demise, and soon all of his waking hours were entirely consumed with schemes and contrivances directed toward improving his situation—imaginings that, more often than not, were reliant upon Sir Frederick being put in his grave.

chapter seven

IN FREDERICA'S FIFTEENTH YEAR, A SPELL OF EXCELLENT weather persuaded Sir Frederick to bring together a small hunting party to Churchill Manor after Michaelmas. A matter of business kept Sir James Martin at Ealing Park, and as there were no other single gentlemen in the party, many of the marriageable ladies and their mothers had stayed at home as well. On a morning that was too damp for the ladies to take exercise out of doors, Lady Vernon sat with Eliza Manwaring and Frederica's governess, Miss Wilson, in the parlor that overlooked the hedgerows and lawns.

"Maria and I enjoyed our month at Bath so much that we may do it again in the coming year," Mrs. Manwaring remarked. "I recommend it for Miss Vernon, as there were a great many plants and grasses that grow nowhere but in that climate. And the public rooms are filled with a very lively set of young people. I think she would like it far better than London."

"I think that she would like to stay here in the country better than either of them, but we must bring Frederica to town for the season," replied Lady Vernon. "She has been to London only once, and my Aunt Martin means to come down on purpose to see Frederica presented at court."

"Well, you must not have any great expectations for her first season, and if nothing comes of it, you will have time for a few weeks at Bath. I am certain that Mr. Lewis deCourcy will be happy to have you come, particularly now that there is a family connection that brings you even closer."

"My fondness for Mr. deCourcy cannot be improved upon. I will always be grateful to him for his many kindnesses to my father."

"He is truly the gentleman, to be sure, and quite distinguished looking for a man of his age. His nephew must resemble him, for it is said that Sir Reginald is quite frail and sickly. Have you met Mrs. Vernon's brother?"

"Mr. Reginald deCourcy? Why, no. Do you know him?"

"We very nearly met him at Bath," said Eliza. "He was at an assembly with our mutual acquaintance Mr. Charles Smith—a very high-spirited, forward sort of young man. I had hoped that he would introduce us, but Mr. Reginald deCourcy did not seem inclined toward talking much to anybody, and he did not stay above an hour, though Mr. Smith remained until the very last."

"And what is Mr. deCourcy like?"

"He is certainly a handsome fellow, tall and a bit imposing in his bearing and countenance, but I suppose he has every reason to think well of himself, for there are few young men in England who will come into a better fortune. Try as we might, we did not see Mr. deCourcy again before we left Bath. Mr. Smith told us that his friend spent nearly all of his time at the library and declared that Mr. deCourcy was a very dull fellow, though I am certain that he exaggerates, for Charles Smith is the sort who always takes it upon himself to amend the truth."

"Then perhaps in amending Mr. deCourcy's character, he improves it, and in truth Mr. deCourcy is much duller than his friend reports."

Eliza was about to make her reply when Frederica flew into the room with her hair disheveled and her apron strings flying loose. "Mama! Come at once! Father has been injured!"

Miss Wilson threw aside her needlework and rang the bell while Lady Vernon and Frederica dashed out of the house and tumbled down the sloping meadow to the wood. The two women had just reached the trees when they were met by a party of men who were carrying the senseless Sir Frederick. His forehead and one forearm were wounded and bleeding.

"Good God, what has happened to him!" Lady Vernon cried in great distress.

"I found him on the ground with his boot caught in a large tree root," Charles Vernon stammered. "It must have tripped him up, and he struck his head when he fell."

Lady Vernon took command at once and ordered one of the men to send for the surgeon while Sir Frederick was carried to his chamber. She then called for water and bandages, and with the assistance of her daughter and her maid, dressed her husband's wounds while the others paced and asked each other if there was something more to be done.

The surgeon arrived, examined the patient, and praised Lady Vernon for her skill, declaring, "You must summon me at once if he regains consciousness, but until that time, you can only make him as comfortable as possible." He then departed with a promise to return that evening.

Lady Vernon remained at her husband's side, leaving Miss Wilson and Deane to perform her offices. Mrs. Manwaring suggested that a house full of company would only add to Lady Vernon's burden and advised that they make preparations to depart. Manwaring argued against his wife's proposal—they must remain, he was certain that Sir Frederick would wish them to remain—but the rest of the party was of the mind that they must defer to Sir Frederick's brother, and Charles Vernon seemed very eager to have them go.

His presence proved to be more of a trial than a relief to Lady Vernon. His excessive agitation did nothing to promote an atmosphere of confidence and calm, and his attempts to take Frederica's place at her father's bedside were so persistent that they were an irritation rather than a comfort. Lady Vernon rebuffed him with as much civility as she could, but she could spare little attention for anyone but her husband.

Frederica would not yield her place to her uncle, but when Sir Frederick appeared to be sleeping comfortably, she slipped into his dressing room and, taking up a sheet of paper and pen, she wrote to Sir James.

MISS VERNON TO SIR JAMES MARTIN

Churchill Manor, Sussex
My dear cousin,

I would not trouble you when the business that has kept you from coming to us must be pressing, but a terrible situation has risen that compels me to beg for your immediate assistance. My father has been gravely injured and I know that my mother would be grateful for your counsel. She cannot leave my father's bedside, or she would write to you herself.

Do come to us, but only if it can be managed to your convenience and without distressing my dear Aunt Martin.

Your affectionate cousin,
Frederica Vernon

Sir James was at Churchill Manor within twenty-four hours of the receipt of the letter, with a prominent Derbyshire physician in tow.

Charles Vernon was visibly alarmed when Sir James arrived, and his greeting was barely civil. "My niece was very wrong to distress you and Lady Martin."

"She meant no offense, I am sure," Sir James declared. "I am certain that Frederica's only desire was to prevent Mother from hearing this unhappy news from another."

"There is nothing at all to be done that the servants and my sister's kind neighbors cannot do."

"If that is the case, then you must not prolong your absence from Parklands," declared Sir James coldly. "It may be days, or even weeks, before there is a change for the better or worse. You cannot be spared from your family for so long."

Vernon struggled to conceal his chagrin. To endure days or weeks until his brother's fate was known was a great hardship. If Sir Frederick was to succumb, would it not be better that it happened immediately, rather than eventually, and spare everyone the pain of agonized suspense?

Two days after Vernon's departure, Lady Vernon and her daughter were sitting at Sir Frederick's bedside when he opened his eyes and declared in a very weak voice, "Ah, what a fright you gave me. I thought at first that I had gone to the angels, but here it is my dear wife and little Freddie beside me."

Lady Vernon wept with relief when she heard his words, and Frederica was so overcome that she began to sob and ran from the room. Sir James found her sitting in the garden, giving vent to her emotions, and he began to babble something about the grounds, mistaking a fir for a spruce and debating whether moss grew in the sun or the shade until Frederica was obliged to calm herself far enough to set him to rights.

Sir Frederick improved and soon was able to leave his chamber and sit with the family for part of each day. Sir James remained at Churchill, and his brilliant cheerfulness, when added to the gentle solicitation of Lady Vernon and her daughter, and the diversion of Alicia Johnson's chatty missives, had a beneficial effect upon Sir Frederick's health and spirits.

MRS. JOHNSON TO LADY VERNON

Edward Street, London
My dear Susan,

It grieves me immensely to think that Sir Frederick's situation must keep you from coming to London at all. I cannot take pleasure in anything nor delight in going anywhere if there is not the possibility that we should meet. I dined with the Carrs two nights ago—they were very happy to take your house for the season, and I daresay they pay a generous rent, as they are come back from Antigua with a great deal of money! They had thirty at the table, but the conversation was exceedingly dull. She wore a gown of sarcenet beaded all over and pearls *wrapped about her head—her gown was <u>green</u>, which did not suit her complexion at all, as she has gone very brown. Your husband's brother was among the company and he was very attentive to Mr. Carr in the way that a banker <u>will</u> be toward anyone who has come into plenty of money. The evening was a very late one, with most of the gentlemen still at cards when I was obliged to leave. Bye the bye, Mr. Vernon was quite cool toward me, but I put that down to the fact that he was unsuccessful in getting Mr. Johnson to put money into some sort of scheme. Surely he cannot blame <u>me</u> if Mr. Johnson would not open his purse—it is all that I can do to get a few new gowns out of him every year.*

I was obliged to drink tea with Colonel and Mrs. Beresford on account of their leaving London for Newcastle, and to go to the Millbankes' on account of their son's getting engaged to Miss Reed, and we had Mr. Lewis deCourcy to dine, as he was in town to direct some matters of business for the Parkers. They have got more money than is good for them, and I expect that they will soon look to purchasing something in the country. Mr. deCourcy has taken Sir James Martin's house for part of the winter; he declares that Sir James does not mean to come to town at all for the season.

It is a great pity that Miss Vernon will miss her season in town, but if she would like some relief from the country, you may send her to me, and I will stand up with her. There are a fine crop of naval officers come through London, and they make for good husbands as they are like to spend much of their time at sea. How I wish that Mr. Johnson had gone into the Navy, though I cannot think that I would see any less of him than I do with him upon dry land.

There is a little something in the way of a dance at the Younges' tomorrow night, but as they have taken a very cramped set of apartments on Argyll Street, I cannot think that I will take any pleasure in it.

Your devoted friend,
Alicia Johnson

WHEN AT LAST SIR FREDERICK WAS WELL ENOUGH TO dine with the family, and walk with Frederica to the greenhouse and back again, Lady Vernon insisted that Sir James could no longer be spared from Ealing Park and sent him away with a vow to bring Sir Frederick to Derbyshire when he was able to stand the journey.

Sir James's departure was followed, to Lady Vernon's great displeasure, by the arrival of Charles Vernon. She could not account for his wanting to come to them, for she had heard that when his own father had lain ill at Churchill, Charles had demonstrated no patience for the sickbed or desire to be anyplace that could not promise him company and diversion.

Lady Vernon set down his parade of fraternal affection to some mercenary motive. She suspected that perhaps Charles hoped to have some gambling losses in London offset with money cajoled out of his brother, for Mrs. Johnson's letters had given an odious picture of Charles's want of discretion when he was in town.

Sir Frederick was more trusting; his propensity to think well of everybody had him contend that if the gravity of his situation brought out the best in Charles, he was quite content to be an invalid.

As for Frederica, she regarded her uncle with civility but avoided him whenever she could. The severity of her father's injury had left him with no memory of the accident, but she could not forget the sight of Mr. Vernon standing motionless beside his fallen brother and afterward wondered what would have become of her father if she had not happened upon them. She had not read enough novels to convert her uncle into a certain scoundrel, but in her study of nature she had observed that from the same ground, one tree may grow up straight and sound while another may stand upright but within be all corruption and decay.

Had Lady Vernon or her daughter suspected that Charles had a very particular motive in forfeiting the pleasures of London, one or the other would have insisted upon being a third party to their meetings. Instead, they left Sir Frederick entirely under his brother's influence, and Charles did not hesitate to use every moment to his advantage.

He would begin by engaging his brother's sympathy and affection with some diverting anecdotes of the children, in which the cunning expressions and boyish tricks of Sir Frederick's namesake played the principal role. These sentimental parables were invariably followed by some flattering observations upon Churchill Manor's material improvement. "The property is quite superior to what it was," he remarked. "I confess that I now understand our father's decision to keep fortune and property together—though I may have harbored some youthful resentment at the time. What is the value of an entail if one has not the means to keep the estate in good order? How often have we seen a gentleman in possession of a good property carve up his fortune in such a way as to make it impossible for his heir to make even the smallest improvement? If that heir should be a single gentleman who brings some income of his own into the arrangement, all may be well, but if he should be a gentleman with a large family to provide for, either they or the property must suffer, unless some very particular provision enables him to maintain it."

He returned to this subject whenever they had an opportunity for a *tête-à-tête* until Sir Frederick was compelled to consider that if anything *should* happen to him (though he would never consider this prospect as imminent), Charles, with a wife and four children, might find the family property to be an encumbrance if he had not the money to keep it up.

Sir Frederick's will had been drawn some time before his marriage and had been influenced, in the disposition of his fortune, by the principles of his father, and stipulated that "all of my remaining fortune,

exclusive of any portions assigned by marriage settlement and indi-
vidual bequests named herein, is bequeathed to my Heir," but of late
he had given some thought to making a more equitable division of his
fortune. "When we were first obliged to retrench," he said to Charles,
with no shade of reproach in his voice, "there was no possibility of en-
riching them beyond what had previously been settled. But in the
years since, my circumstances have so much improved that I think I
must set aside some portion that would ensure the comfort of my wife
and settle something beyond two thousand pounds upon Frederica."

"There will be leisure to attend to business when you are completely well," urged his brother. "Remember that if some dire circumstance should leave my sister a widow, she would never be without a
home, for the house in town is settled upon her."

"Yes, very true," replied Sir Frederick. "And yet a house in town
can no more be kept up than a house in the country if one has not the
means."

Charles hastened to relieve his brother on this point with promises
of liberality and assistance, though keeping to very general terms and
avoiding the mention of any fixed sum. "What more pressing obligation can a gentleman have than to see that his brother's widow and
child are provided for? You must not suppose for an instant that I
would ever neglect my obligation *there*—do not think for an instant
that you must go to the trouble of setting anything down, for is not
the word of a brother as firm as pen to paper? You have only to think
what you would do for Catherine and my children to comprehend
what I would do for Lady Vernon and my niece."

This declaration rendered Sir Frederick easy—he likened his
brother's exertions to what his own would be, and so believed that the
comfort of his wife and daughter were assured. Charles Vernon could
not be unaffected by how readily Sir Frederick was lulled back into
complacency and trust, which produced an unfamiliar warmth of feeling that persuaded him that he was *almost* capable of generosity.

$\mathcal{S}$IR JAMES WAS A VERY FAITHFUL CORRESPONDENT, AND AS
winter gave way to spring, he reminded Lady Vernon of her
promise to bring the family to Ealing Park. *All arrangements for
Frederick's particular comfort will be made ready as soon as you name the
date*, he wrote to his cousin.

*For our tenants' sake, it cannot be too soon. All of them who have
had the goodness to fall ill over the winter have got better and Mother
is left without anyone to put on the mend. If you do not come, I fear
that she will give a pinch of bane to the groom for the pleasure of nursing him back to health.*

Lady Martin's letters were more direct.

*I cannot abide James lolling about anymore. He ought to have
gone to London and got into mischief. And what do you mean to do
with Frederica? What do you say to placing her in a good school for a
term? Miss Wilson has been an excellent governess, but Frederica has
got to the age where a governess has done all she can.*

Lady Vernon read the last portion of this letter to Frederica. "I am
inclined to agree with my aunt, Frederica. You have been so little in
society. At school, you would learn to be more at ease among people
of your own age and better able to deal with those who are different or
difficult."

"It is too much trouble to meet people who are different and best to avoid those who are difficult," replied Frederica.

"You cannot always be at Churchill."

"What a great pity it is that I was not a boy. Then our property would be secure, and I should not have to go anywhere at all."

"It is not a pity," Lady Vernon replied with a smile. "We would not exchange you for a dozen sons. But the day will come when Churchill is no longer your home. You will be well married, and I will come to your grand estate and take possession of some little set of rooms and spoil your children and plague your husband."

At last, Frederica was compelled to smile. "But what of Miss Wilson? I should be very sorry to think of her being cast out into the world."

"And so would I, but it seems that Dr. Bentley has tended to other matters while he has been with us. He has made his proposals to Deane and my dear Deane has accepted him. If Miss Wilson will not think it a very great degradation to go from your governess to my lady's maid, she may condescend to remain. Her steadiness and good character have been a great comfort to me these many months."

In the first week in April, Dr. Bentley and the surgeon determined that Sir Frederick was strong enough to travel, and a party consisting of Sir Frederick, Lady Vernon, Miss Vernon, Dr. Bentley, and Miss Deane left Sussex for Derbyshire.

When the carriage drew up to the great house, Lady Martin herself came out to greet them, and looking over Sir Frederick with a sharp eye, she declared, "Why, you are worn to nothing! You must go right to your chamber and I will have a dish of beef tea sent up to you at once!"

When Sir Frederick had been dispatched, Lady Martin looked over Lady Vernon and her daughter. "Ah," she said to the former, "it is a blessing that you have your mother's looks. *Her* family were Osbournes and the Osbourne looks would stand up to any trial! Frederica, go to the greenhouse and have the gardener show you the geraniums that you helped him get into bloom—they have got as big as cabbages!"

"I would prefer to go up to my father, if you please, ma'am."

"Well, go then. I will have Cook send up a portion of plum cake and you may toast a slice of it for your father. One slice will do him no harm."

Frederica made a hasty curtsy and hurried off to her father's chamber.

Lady Martin took her niece into the parlor and scrutinized her thoroughly. "And what is the true state of Frederick's health? Dr. Bentley had written that he had no illness of an infectious nature—why does he not improve more rapidly?"

"I do not mind if he improves slowly, Aunt, so long as he gets back his strength in the end."

"And what do you think of my scheme to place Frederica in school? There are some excellent schools in town that are just the place to meet well-connected girls with single brothers. She will not find a husband in a greenhouse. Ah, me, it is such a trial to see that everybody makes a good match. When I think of how it may have turned out if my husband had not introduced you to Frederick—you might have taken James off my hands."

"There might have been even more dire consequences, Aunt. I might have married Charles Vernon."

"No, you would not, for I would have stepped forward to prevent it," Lady Martin averred. "You were far too clever for Charles Vernon and he would not have liked you for it."

"Then we must hope that he has got a wife who is not too clever to suit him."

"I think his wife would suit him better still if she did not come with a mother."

"Charles told Sir Frederick that Lady deCourcy was a most attentive mother-in-law."

"Hah!" exclaimed Lady Martin. "*That* is what your dear husband said because he has the provoking habit of making people out to be pleasing when they have neither the talent nor the inclination to live up to his good opinion! I have no doubt that what Charles Vernon *said* was that Lady deCourcy is a meddlesome busybody who is at Parklands Cottage with her daughter far more than she is at Parklands Manor with her own husband."

"Is her husband's company so tedious? His brother, Lewis de-Courcy, is a most amiable gentleman."

"Well, brothers are not always like, as you no doubt have learned," replied Lady Martin. "Sir Reginald was the first son, and they do not have to be agreeable if they are not inclined. The marriage was arranged by their families when they were children, and women who are sure of a husband do not bother to cultivate any talents. If she had learned to play or paint or enjoy a book, she might be good for something other than prying into her daughter's affairs, and Charles Vernon has no patience for a mother's meddling."

"Who does not like a mother's meddling?" inquired Sir James, who entered the room in time to overhear the remark. "Not I, surely! Do I not come down every fortnight during the season so that you may tell me that I have attended too many parties and lost too much at cards?"

"You play too well to have suffered any loss of significance." Lady Vernon smiled.

"I have lost only once, and then because I held my hand and did not play it when I should have," he replied gravely.

"That will teach you to play high when you cannot afford to lose," his mother said briskly. "You and your cousin have confidences to exchange, no doubt. You may take Susan for a turn about the grounds."

Sir James gave his arm to his cousin and they set out toward the park.

"I went up to welcome Frederick and I must say that, while I mean no offense to Dr. Bentley—for I understand that his interest was diverted at Churchill, and that there is to be a Mrs. Bentley ere long—I had hoped to see Frederick in better color. I have all due confidence in the efficacy of Mother's marrow pie, but if your time with us does not improve him, you may want to consult with a specialist in London or Bath. So Vernon has been with you a good deal, has he?"

"Yes."

"I am not fond of Vernon, but perhaps I have not done him justice. Does not a willingness to forgo so many weeks of diversion in

London in order to attend Frederick—which is very different from what his conduct was toward his invalid father—bespeak an encouraging change of heart?"

"I would be easier in my mind if his partiality had come in easy stages, for I am always wary of a swift reversal of sentiment," was Lady Vernon's response. "A sudden change of heart is never to be trusted."

chapter ten

IR FREDERICK RETURNED TO CHURCHILL MANOR much stronger than when he had left it, and encouraged by any small symptom of energy or well-being, he disregarded the cautions of Dr. Bentley and the surgeon and resumed all of his former pursuits.

One afternoon, as summer was nearing an end, Sir Frederick and Lady Vernon made their way, in a leisurely fashion, around Churchill Pond to a point of rising ground that gave them a pleasant view of the scattering of fields and tenants' cottages below. The sight seemed to inspire Sir Frederick anew with his obligation as husband, landlord, and master, and as they turned back, he raised the matter of amending his will and resolved that Mr. Barrett, the attorney from Churchill, would be sent for on the following morning.

He related, for the first time, Charles's many pledges and promises regarding their legacy. "For Charles's sake, as well as for your own, I was very pleased with his voluntary assurances—it does credit to his heart, for a man who has a wife and four children can have no motive other than goodness and affection to be liberal with mine."

Lady Vernon could not share his complacency on this point, and she might have been sorry that she had allowed Charles to engage so much of her husband's undivided interest if she were not certain that another day would legally preserve, from the profligacy of Charles Vernon, what was necessary for her security and Frederica's future.

They discussed the particulars of how Sir Frederick's wealth should be disposed of with the security that came from the conviction that they now had many more years before any of these contingencies would come to pass. With a tragic irony that will occur sometimes in life and always in novels, they had no sooner resolved upon the amount of their daughter's fortune than Sir Frederick fell to the ground, and within an hour, he was dead.

Lady Vernon collapsed in a state of shock and was carried to her bed. Frederica remained steadfastly at her side while Wilson composed the necessary communications to the family and assisted the housekeeper in preparations for the arrival of visitors and in hastily dyeing garments for mourning.

THE PARTY THAT assembled at Churchill Manor was very small, consisting only of the Martins, the Manwarings, Mr. Lewis deCourcy, and Mr. and Mrs. Clarke, their neighbors from Staffordshire. Charles Vernon came alone, presenting to Lady Vernon a very pretty note of condolence from Mrs. Vernon and an apology that she could not be spared from Parklands and the children.

"How very unfeeling!" declared Lady Martin to her son. "Such incivility toward poor Susan! And as for Vernon, he struts about as though he is quite the master."

"He is the master," Sir James replied with more composure than he felt. "As for Mrs. Vernon, we must excuse her—perhaps she feared that there would have been as much indelicacy in her coming as incivility in staying away."

Every household for ten miles around was represented at the funeral service, for Sir Frederick had been held in very high regard; and many side glances were cast toward Charles Vernon by the servants and tenants, who fervently hoped that the new master would be as quick to dispense alms and provisions and as tardy in the collection of his rents.

The Reverend Mr. Chapman read the service with feeling, as he had lost a great patron and friend in Sir Frederick. They had enjoyed many hours of backgammon in Churchill's library, partaking of the excellent dark ale that Dr. Bentley had prescribed for Sir Frederick's health, and every Sunday there seemed to be some point of theology that could not be resolved upon the parish steps and so obliged Mr.

Chapman and his wife to dine with the Vernons in order to settle their differences.

The party returned to Churchill Manor to dine, and Charles Vernon did not scruple to take his brother's place at the table, which gave such distress to Frederica that she burst into tears and ran out of the room. Lady Vernon followed her daughter and the rest sat down to awkward silence and more awkward conversation, and before the ladies withdrew, Vernon excused himself from the table and shut himself up in the library to write a letter to his wife.

Mr. Vernon to Mrs. Vernon

Churchill Manor, Sussex
My dear wife,

As circumstances have not permitted you to acquaint yourself with Churchill Manor and the surrounding property, I will have the pleasure of accompanying you on your first tour of the estate, and while it is nothing to Parklands, I do not think that you will be disappointed. The society will not be what you were accustomed to in Kent, but except for one or two families that we will be obliged to notice, the neighboring estates are just far enough to make the distance a convenient excuse for not always visiting back and forth.

As for how matters have been left, I congratulate myself that they are so far to our advantage, and that my time spent attending my brother was not done in vain. I believe that had I not sacrificed so many hours to his company and diversion, he might have dwelt upon his infirmity in a manner that may have persuaded him to amend his will and leave his fortune to Lady Vernon and her daughter. This I was able to forestall by some very general assurances that, in the event of his demise, I would always see that my sister and niece were comfortable. Be assured that no particular sum was ever stipulated, nor (though my brother spoke of the advantage of allowances and annuities) was any promised—and a very good thing it was for us, as my brother had so far recovered from the imprudence that compelled him to give up Vernon Castle, and laid aside a good savings—as much as thirty thousand pounds, perhaps—which will make a very fine addition to Churchill's comfortable income.

Feel no distress, my dear Catherine, over what is to become of Lady Vernon and her daughter—recall that the house in town will be Lady Vernon's outright, and that the sum settled upon her at the time of her marriage (to which my brother had added some three thousand pounds) will give her something to live on. If she wants anything more, I am certain that she need only apply to the Martins, as they are very rich.

My sister talks of placing Miss Vernon at school—yet while her education has certainly been neglected, I must think that such a place can do her no good. A temperament that is already weak will only fall prey to the giddy imaginations of those about her, and rather than attaining some measure of education, she will only incur permanent defects in understanding. She would greatly benefit from your example, and might be of some use to you in looking after the children and providing something of companionship to you when I am obliged to be in town. If you are at leisure to write, therefore, I would hope that you will send a few lines to Lady Vernon and encourage her to leave Miss Vernon with us.

Prepare our children for the change that they are to undergo and console your dear parents as far as you can. Sir Reginald and Lady deCourcy will be sorry to see us leave Parklands, but it is only a good day's journey to Churchill, and when Sir Reginald's health allows, I have every confidence that they will attempt it.

Our Uncle deCourcy is of the party assembled here, and I took the liberty of giving him your warmest regards, and those of your father and mother.

We shall need to purchase our own silver, as the service used at Churchill, as well as some other effects, were bequeathed to Lady Vernon and I am sure that she will take them away with her when she goes.

Your devoted husband,
Charles Vernon

THE FOLLOWING MORNING THE PARTY ASSEMBLED AT breakfast, but Lady Vernon rose feeling so ill that she was obliged to return to her bed and send Wilson down with apologies to her guests. In their presence, Vernon made a great show of concern and gave orders that everything was to be done to make Lady Vernon comfortable and that the servants need not defer to him before offering her any small amenity or service that her situation warranted. He then expressed his hope that the guests *might* remain at least long enough to see Lady Vernon once more, but if they were compelled to go *sooner*, he would convey to his sister-in-law their sincere apologies and regrets. This declaration could only make his company acutely conscious of their host's desire for them to be off and so they all agreed that orders should be given for their carriages to be ready at two o'clock.

Vernon then went to his sister-in-law's apartments, where she was sitting with Frederica and Wilson. Frederica avoided his gaze and looked as if she would like to run away, but her mother answered his inquiries after her health with as much composure as she could summon.

He then assured them that they were welcome to remain at Churchill Manor as long as they liked, and they were not to think for a moment that they might be in anybody's way. Mrs. Vernon would not take it amiss if they were there *still* when she arrived. "I am certain that your kind friends have all quarreled over who is to take you away, and I know that you will not wish to be in a household with four active children, but if my niece is of the opposite opinion, she is very welcome to remain with us. You find yourself very low now, Frederica, but I think that the company of your cousins and the comfort of familiar surroundings will raise your spirits, will they not?"

Frederica would make no answer, and Lady Vernon replied, "My dear brother, Frederica and I are grateful for your kindness, but it would be too great a sacrifice for me to be deprived of both husband and daughter. I know that Mrs. Vernon, who is said to be the best of mothers, will understand why we would not wish to be separated just now. As for our removal, I do not think that more than two or three weeks will be necessary. I must beg you and Mrs. Vernon for your forbearance until then."

Vernon did not believe that it was of any consequence to Lady Vernon whether her daughter remained at Churchill or was sent to a school in town. But he bowed and murmured, "Mrs. Vernon and I will always be happy to receive you at Churchill, should you find yourself left with no better place to go," and took his leave, saying that he must see that all had been made ready for their visitors' departure.

"My uncle talks as though our visitors leave today!" cried Frederica. "Surely they will remain a week at least! The Clarkes have had a long journey, and it will be very difficult for Mr. deCourcy to return so immediately to Bath."

Lady Vernon dispatched Wilson to the servants' quarters, and she returned in a matter of minutes, declaring, "So it is! They are all to leave this afternoon! Mr. Vernon has ordered the carriages for two o'clock."

Frederica was shocked into silence at her uncle's selfish inhospitality. Lady Vernon rose immediately. "Help me with my dress, Wilson. I must go down. I hope that they do not hasten their departure on our account. They cannot think that it is *we* who want them gone." Quickly submitting to the arranging of her hair and her gown, she accompanied Frederica to the drawing room, where the party had assembled.

Sir James approached as soon as they were seated. "My dear Susan," he began in a low voice, "my situation here is tenuous, for

Vernon wants us gone, and I cannot impose myself upon him. Come away with us to Ealing Park. You may stay as long as you like, and you will not be hurried into a decision as to where you will settle."

Eliza Manwaring spied a vacant chair beside Sir James and hurried Maria into it. (For she had brought the girl to the unhappy gathering expressly to throw her at the gentleman.) "My dear Lady Vernon, we hope that you and Miss Vernon will come to us at Langford. There may be some sport, but it will keep the men out of the way, and there will be some young people to keep Miss Vernon company. And you may be sure, Sir James, that you and Lady Martin will always be welcome to visit." Mrs. Manwaring then solicited the support of Mr. Lewis deCourcy, who had drawn his chair up to the group. "Do you not think, sir, that it would be the best plan for Lady Vernon and her daughter to come to Somerset? I am sure that you would not have her open her house in town at this time of year."

"Indeed, no, but I hope that you, Lady Vernon, and your daughter will give me a share of your time and come to Bath," replied Mr. deCourcy. "I do nothing but ramble about in that large house upon the Crescent, with a barouche that sits idle while my footman and horses go to fat! The air and the waters would put some roses back into your cheeks, Miss Vernon, and you might help me determine what can be grown in my garden—I can do nothing with it."

"I thank you for your offer, sir," murmured Frederica.

"Will you not take a turn with me now?" continued the gentleman as he rose from his chair. "I have heard so much about the forcing gardens at Churchill and the groundsmen give you all the credit for it. I would be very sorry to be off without seeing what you have done. Come, I will take you both," he added, offering one arm to Frederica and the other to Miss Manwaring. "I do not have the opportunity to parade about with two such elegant young ladies. I am sure that you can indulge an old gentleman for a quarter of an hour."

The two girls exchanged shy smiles as they allowed themselves to be escorted from the room by Mr. deCourcy.

"My dear Susan, will you let me sit with you for a few minutes?" asked Mrs. Clarke, and Sir James yielded his chair to her and walked over to the window, where he gazed out with a look of sober concentration while Eliza Manwaring endeavored to determine whether Miss Vernon or Miss Manwaring was the object of his attention.

"How much time will it take you to settle your affairs here, my poor Susan?" inquired Mrs. Clarke.

"Much of that will depend upon Mr. and Mrs. Vernon."

"I hope that you will think of coming to us—you would be put to no expense there, I assure you, and would it not be comforting to be in a place where you and Sir Frederick were once so happy? Unless the business of weddings will give you pain. It seems that neighborliness has done its work, and the sons of Colonel Edwards have asked for our girls. Anne is to marry Phillip and Mary will take Frank, and the Colonel only waits upon the weddings to be off to a more congenial climate, for he is very much afflicted with rheumatism and pleurisy."

Lady Vernon knew that Colonel Edwards was the gentleman who had purchased Vernon Castle, and Mrs. Clarke had occasionally mentioned him in her letters as a genteel and solicitous neighbor.

"I believe he told Sir James that he means to be gone by January at the very latest, and then—why may Sir James not give Vernon Castle back to you?"

"How can my cousin give me Vernon Castle?" inquired Lady Vernon, puzzled.

"Oh, dear!" cried Mrs. Clarke. "I quite forgot! I was not to speak of it. Mr. Clarke will be so angry! But he knows that he ought not to tell me anything he does not want repeated! Yes, it is all his fault—oh, Mr. Clarke, see what you have done!" she called across the room, which caused that gentleman to duck his head in embarrassment, although he did not know why.

"Pray, what interest does my cousin have in the Edwardses' property?" entreated Lady Vernon.

"But it is *not* the Edwardses'! Of course, I would know nothing of the matter had not Miss Drake mentioned something to me. She is the daughter of the solicitor in Sudbury, the one who arranged it all for Sir James. It was done with great discretion, but of course when Miss Drake heard of it, she could not keep it to herself. There are *some* who cannot be trusted with a secret! But, of course, it was not such a secret, for when I mentioned it to Mr. Clarke, he told me that *he* had known of it from the first! *He* who goes nowhere and takes no interest at all in gossip! How provoking! And, of course, Colonel and Mrs. Edwards were such a well-bred couple and dressed so fine, and their horses and carriage were so handsome that everyone took it as a matter of course that they were not mere tenants. I cannot imagine why Sir James wanted it to be kept such a secret, unless he did not wish for Lady Martin to think that he had bought the property as a place to put her after he marries. And though we much preferred to have *you* at Vernon Castle, the Edwardses have turned out to be a blessing, for I have got two sons-in-law out of it. But why do you look so distressed?"

Lady Vernon could not conceal her mortification. "When we were obliged to sell the property, I asked my cousin only to assist us in finding a purchaser. It was not ever our intention to solicit relief. We were quite determined against taking any charity from my cousin or Lady Martin."

"Oh, I am sure it was not done out of charity. I am sure that Sir James acted from the very best of motives."

Lady Vernon's grief over the loss of her husband could not bear even the possibility that her cousin's actions had cast Sir Frederick as a beggar. "My dear Phoebe, I am afraid that I am not equal to company," she declared, rising from her chair. "If you would be so kind as to make my excuses, I will avail myself of Mr. deCourcy's excellent advice and take a turn in the air."

Lady Vernon slipped outside and walked down the avenue under the canopy of heavy shade. She had got as far as the steward's lodge and was about to strike out into the road when she heard a quick step and a voice calling out her name. She turned to see Robert Manwaring hurrying toward her.

"I have found you!" he said as he fell into step beside her. "We had supposed that you meant to walk with Miss Vernon and Mr. deCourcy and Maria. I am very glad to find you alone, as I have not had the opportunity to express to you personally how deeply I feel for your loss."

He offered her his arm with easy gallantry. "I know that all of your friends have petitioned for a share of your time, but you must allow me to add to Eliza's arguments in favor of Langford. Think of the advantage to Miss Vernon—at Langford, she will have Maria for company, and there may be some young people about who will keep her from dwelling upon her sorrow. You may come as soon as you like and go away at once if the situation does not please you. Indeed, there will be nothing to hold you, but for . . ."

Here he broke off with a glance that held too much meaning to be directed toward a new widow.

Lady Vernon had never encouraged Manwaring's flirtation unless to ignore it entirely had been encouragement. Still, she did not reject his proposal immediately. A departure from Churchill was inevitable and she and Frederica must go somewhere. Until the matter of her income was addressed and she knew what she would have to live on, she must accept the hospitality of one of her friends. She could not consider going to Ealing Park while the thought of Sir James's deception was still fresh in her mind. She might go to the Clarkes', and in fact, that seemed the pleasantest and most comforting option, but to be in the vicinity of Vernon Castle might aggravate her emotions rather than compose them. Bath would be hot and desolate at this time of year, and though Lady Vernon knew that Mr. deCourcy's invitation was well intentioned and sincere, she believed that the arrival of two ladies and their necessary attendants would be too great a disruption for a quiet bachelor household. No one was in town save for Alicia Johnson, and Lady Vernon believed that Mr. Johnson was the sort of misanthrope whose hospitality could not be depended upon, even by a mother and daughter in mourning.

Langford, for all its drawbacks, seemed the least unfavorable situation for her, and the most favorable for Frederica, and as they returned to the house, Lady Vernon gave Manwaring her consent. He was so delighted to win his point that the first words uttered were improperly joyous before he remembered the occasion that had prompted the invitation and became somber once more.

Sir James did his best to conceal his surprise when his cousin announced that upon leaving Churchill Manor, she and Frederica would go to Langford. He could not address her privately until the carriages were ordered and the party were saying their farewells. "I did not think you would seriously consider going to Langford, Susan. I do not like the scheme at all. The Manwarings keep a great deal of company and—forgive me—Manwaring admires you too much for a married man. Your situation will not protect you, for he may think that you are all the more susceptible for being unencumbered and may behave in a way that will distress you and embarrass Freddie."

"Forgive *me*, cousin," she returned with some warmth, "but I am no longer certain that you have ever understood what will distress or embarrass me or my family."

"I understand enough to know how Vernon's rudeness must make you uneasy—to send your friends and relations away—he has a very strange notion of hospitality and charity."

"I neither expect nor desire charity, cousin, as any of my acquaintance *ought* to understand. Nothing could be so offensive to my husband's memory as to have his wife and daughter become the objects of charity."

Sir James looked upon her with bewilderment and made no reply. He concluded that it was too early to expect any moderation in her grief. Within a few weeks, he would no doubt receive a letter from her expressing a change of heart and a desire to come to Derbyshire.

Lady Martin bustled up to them and gave her niece a hearty embrace. "If they do not suit you at Langford, you will always have a home with us. Come, James, we cannot delay or we will be on the road after sunset and then who knows what will befall us!"

Sir James kissed his cousin's hand and then addressed Frederica, insisting that she be a faithful correspondent and assuring her that it would take only a line from her to bring him to their aid.

The carriages departed, the women retired to their rooms. They did not come down to dine, and so Charles Vernon dined alone, eating little and drinking a good deal of Sir Frederick's excellent port.

chapter twelve

ON THE FOLLOWING DAY, LADY VERNON ROSE FROM HER BED and went directly to her writing desk, where she sat down to calculate how little of her husband's debt was outstanding, how far his rents had increased, and how frugally they had lived over the last half-dozen years. By these tallies, she determined that Sir Frederick may have left as much as thirty thousand pounds with his estate.

Lady Vernon resolved to address Charles at the earliest opportunity on the matter of how she was to be recompensed; she was sensible of the indelicacy of raising the subject so soon after her husband's funeral, but she could not trust the firmness of his promises as far as Sir Frederick had. If his memory of them was not fixed while she and Frederica were before him, it must dissipate when they were out of his sight.

Vernon steadily avoided all discourse by keeping himself away from the house as much as possible. For the first days after his brother's funeral, he rode out very early or found some concern that took him into Churchill, and at last, with no notice whatsoever, he departed for London, where the unhappy presence of his sister and niece were not always before him. There, the society and its diversions soon eased him into the conviction that whatever assurances he *may have* given his brother had only been the sort of necessary lies one is compelled to give to an invalid. Would not a gentleman who had a wife and four young children to maintain (and who must keep himself in *some* style when he was in town) need far more than a widow who was not without rich relations, and a daughter who was of an age when she would soon marry?

Soon Vernon was persuaded that there had been no *promise* at all, only an informal understanding that Lady Vernon and her daughter would not starve.

Lady Vernon could not believe that Charles meant to stay away from Churchill Manor until after she and Frederica departed, but when a week passed with no word from him, she dispatched a letter to his address in town.

I understand that your new responsibilities, as well as settling the matter of appraisals and outstanding debt (of which there cannot be more than a hundred pounds), may be the cause of some delay in fulfilling the promises upon which my husband, your brother, faithfully relied. The business of establishing yourself and Mrs. Vernon will be uppermost in your mind, but may I plead, on behalf of myself and my daughter, for something like expedience in fulfilling any assurances that you made to my husband in regard to the disposition of his fortune?

She did not post this letter but sent it with the housekeeper who was to take charge of the Portland Place residence, and instructed her to carry it directly to Mr. Vernon's lodgings in town. She would dearly have loved to send the portrait of Sir Frederick to Portland Place as well, but she conceded that its place was in the gallery at Churchill among those of his forebears, and so contented herself with a likeness of him set into her locket.

She then turned her attention to separating her personal possessions from what property belonged to Churchill and distributing Sir Frederick's clothing to the menservants and the poor. There were gloves to be dyed and bonnets to be divested of trimming and swansdown and lined with crepe. She and Frederica took leave of the neighborhood, exchanging particularly affectionate farewells with the Chapmans.

Instead of any reply from Charles, Lady Vernon received a visit from Mr. Barrett, the attorney from the village of Churchill. He hemmed and hawed a great deal and presented Mrs. Barrett's compliments and after making every possible observation upon her loss and

the weather and what a pretty note their housekeeper had got from
Mrs. Bentley, who had married Lady Martin's doctor, and how Mrs.
Barrett had so often joked that she had rather married a doctor or an
apothecary at least, "as seven children will go through so many ill-
nesses and sprains and fevers that it would be a great savings if their
father were in the trade, while the cost of bringing them all up upon
the earnings of a country lawyer would leave them nothing left over
to bequeath to any of them," he got around to the purpose of his visit.

"It would have been a great benefit to address the family together,
but Mr. Vernon was obliged to be in town and he was most particular
that you know how matters stand before you depart." He then gave
her the dubious satisfaction of knowing that her calculations had
been quite on the mark, and that Sir Frederick had, indeed, left a fortune of some thirty thousand pounds—which, owing to the language
of his will, was to be disposed entirely upon Churchill's heir.

"The generosity of your relations, in adding to your settlement at
the time of your marriage, when added to the three thousand pounds
given over to you by Sir Frederick at the time that Vernon Castle was
first purchased . . ." He groped about for words, which trailed off into
something like ". . . your house in town . . . the kindness of your relations . . . the Martins may always be depended upon . . ."

This remark served only to call up Lady Vernon's aversion to
charity—she would not allow Mr. Barrett to suppose that she was left
so indigent as to have to beseech the Martins' aid. She assured him
that she would be able to manage very well and conveyed her warmest
regards to Mrs. Barrett.

The following day Lady Vernon and Frederica walked to the
churchyard to lay flowers upon Sir Frederick's grave, and the day after,
with a last, unhappy glance at her family home, Lady Vernon, accompanied by her daughter and Wilson, set off for Langford.

VOLUME II

Langford and Churchill

LANGFORD

T HE JOURNEY FROM CHURCHILL TO LANGFORD WAS TO take the ladies through Bath, where they would stop for the night at the home of Lewis deCourcy.

When they had dined, Wilson retired to her sewing and Miss Vernon was invited to form her opinion of the rose garden. Lady Vernon took the opportunity to discuss the matter of her finances with Mr. deCourcy. He listened carefully and asked a good many questions about the particulars of the language of Sir Frederick's will, then made every attempt to alleviate her anxiety.

"I am not ready to believe that you have any real need for concern yet," said he, "though your acquaintance with Mrs. Manwaring's situation must make you sensible of the evils of having your money under the control of one who deliberately withholds it from the intended object. There may be some working of the law that must take place before Charles can make good on any promises given to Sir Frederick. An inheritance will always come with some matters of unfinished business, and in my experience, the law does nothing so well as prolonging what ought to be swift. I advise you to wait a little longer— once Mrs. Vernon and the family are settled, Charles will be at leisure to address those points of honor that his more pressing obligations have deferred. In another month or very shortly thereafter, this will all be resolved, and if it is not, I will be more than happy to intercede on your behalf."

Lady Vernon was sensible of the delicacy of his situation in being her particular friend and Charles's uncle through marriage. She assured him that no intercession would be wanted and thanked him for his counsel, and the remainder of the evening was spent in discussing the pleasures of Somerset and Mr. deCourcy's hopes that Miss Vernon might find a friend and confidante in Miss Manwaring.

At Langford, they were received with a great deal of effusion and ceremony. The business of welcome took above an hour, for the Vernon ladies must be embraced and exclaimed over, and relate how they had traveled, and how they had left Mr. deCourcy, and whether the roads had been very hot and dirty, and whether the dust had soiled their gowns. This brought on a brief embarrassment, as the remarks must draw attention to the Vernon ladies' black dresses and remind the Manwaring ladies of the tragedy that had brought about the invitation.

At last, it was supposed that the travelers would want to rest, and they were shown to their chambers. Lady Vernon permitted herself to be taken out of her traveling dress, and when Wilson left them, she sat down to explain the state of their affairs to Frederica.

"I will not wait for my uncle to be honorable," declared Frederica. "My father was always inclined to be fond of Mr. Vernon and I would not dare to contradict him, but from the day of my father's accident, I have had cause to think very ill of my uncle."

"What cause?" her mother asked, bewildered.

"On the day of my father's accident, I was in the wood—oh, I know that I have always been cautioned to keep away when the men were shooting, but I did not think there was any harm in going just to the edge, for I had seen a small growth of hepatia upon some of the trees, and I was certain that I could obtain a sample without getting anywhere near their party. I passed through a little copse and immediately spied my father lying upon the ground and my uncle standing motionless beside him. No alarm had been raised—and it was only when my uncle spied me that he affected anything like concern and ordered me to go for help. I cannot accuse my uncle of anything worse than the shock of discovering my father in such a state," Frederica hastened to add. "And yet—I *do* think that it is his nature to at least *consider* how far a little delay might work to his advantage!"

As certain as Lady Vernon was of her daughter's integrity and her brother-in-law's want of it, she was shocked to think that Charles

Vernon might have withheld assistance from his brother. One is always willing to believe that one's relations are lying, grasping, or vain, but a suggestion of iniquity will strain all but the most forbearing nature.

"How I wish that I had arrived a minute sooner," Frederica lamented, "or said something to Papa when he recovered his health! But I could not bring myself to introduce a matter that would raise suspicion and anxiety toward one who my father always regarded with affection—oh, if only I had spoken!"

"If you had spoken, you would only have put at variance one with whom your father had the misfortune to be on good terms. It is better that your father was never obliged to think ill of his brother. He could not have done justice to the task."

chapter fourteen

LANGFORD ENJOYED A PLEASING SITUATION IN THE EAST-
ern part of Somerset. The estate was not large, but the manor
house was spacious and modern. The common rooms, however, were furnished in a manner that annulled every advantage of
size and light, for there was not a single settee nor table where two or
three might be crammed into the space, not a solitary drapery where
shades and valances might be laid on as well. The lawns were likewise
cluttered with statuary and fountains, and the walks were overhung
with trellises. Inside and out, nothing was left alone where more could
be done to it, which kept the Manwaring property in a state of habitual clutter and chronic improvement.

Such disorder did not impose upon Lady Vernon or her daughter
during their first fortnight at Langford; but the Manwarings considered two weeks to be a sufficient period of deep mourning. They must
have some company and noise, and soon the house was filled up with
young men who came in quest of some shooting and young ladies in
quest of young men.

Among the latter were the Misses Hamilton, who were brought by
their mother. Lady Hamilton was secure of her eldest, but there were
the two younger girls to be disposed of, and though Miss Claudia was
but eighteen and Miss Lucy a year younger, they had already been
launched upon a round of visits and balls and assemblies, wherever
there were eligible men to be found. They had been four months in
town and six weeks at Bath before they were obliged to return to the
family estate only long enough for them to remind Lord Hamilton of

their affection and to coax another hundred pounds of pocket money from him before they laid siege to Somersetshire.

They had not gone immediately to Langford, for while in Bath, Lady Hamilton happened upon an old friend who introduced Sir Walter Elliot to her acquaintance. This gentleman was a widower whose middle daughter had been a schoolfellow of Miss Lucy Hamilton's, so there was an additional source of intimacy, and before they left Bath, an engagement had been formed for Lady Hamilton and her daughters to come to the Elliots for a month or two at the end of the summer. Before the superior society of Kellynch Hall, Langford must give way. Lady Hamilton very soon understood, however, that Sir Walter Elliot's motive had been to make a very unreasonable application for her eldest daughter, and promptly recollected an absolute promise to go to her dear friends the Manwarings. "No, Sir Walter, it cannot be put off . . . No, I do not think we can come back again from Langford, as I mean to have Lucy try school again, in town . . . Eliza Manwaring has invited my nephew Reginald deCourcy on purpose for Lavinia—I am certain you must understand what *that* means." And, mortified by this rejection, Sir Walter was very happy to have them go from *his* quarter of Somersetshire to one that, he was certain, was very much inferior.

The elder Misses Hamilton were slight, conceited, and no more than handsome, while Miss Lucy Hamilton was high-spirited, plump, and pretty. "But, la," she declared right after she and Frederica had been introduced, "we are very near related, are we not? *Our* mother is the sister of Sir Reginald deCourcy, and his daughter has married *your* uncle, Mr. Vernon! And we may be even more closely connected in the future, will we not, Livvy?"

This caused Miss Hamilton to simper and blush and declare that she did not know what Lucy's meaning was in a manner that implied that she did.

Frederica was drawn aside by Maria Manwaring, who said in a low voice, "It has long been decided that Lavinia Hamilton will marry her cousin Reginald deCourcy, your Aunt Vernon's younger brother. Have you ever met him?"

"No, never."

"Eliza and I saw him at Bath, with his friend, Charles Smith, but we were never introduced. Mr. Lewis deCourcy twice invited us to dine on purpose to make his nephew's acquaintance, but alas, both times he was dining elsewhere. My brother means to invite him and Mr. Smith to Langford."

"What sort of person is Mr. Smith?" inquired Frederica.

"Oh, he is not half as good-looking as Mr. deCourcy, but he is twice as lively to make up for it," Maria replied. "I am afraid that my brother insists upon everyone being very lively here at Langford. I hope that you do not mind it."

"No, I do not mind it, for if that is the case, you will all be too engaged to notice if we are quiet."

The liveliness began that evening as soon as the gentlemen joined the ladies after dinner. Lady Hamilton began to nudge and wink at her youngest daughter. Miss Lucy took the hint and immediately coaxed Maria to ask her brother's leave for some dancing. "There is your brother and Mr. Reed and Mr. Blake and Lord Whitby for partners— and you or Miss Vernon and my sisters and me. We can make up four couples!"

Maria, who was not without feeling, reminded her friends that Miss Vernon was in mourning.

"Yes," agreed Miss Claudia Hamilton. "Miss Vernon cannot dance, but if she can play tolerably well, there is no reason she cannot oblige *us*. We do not expect anything like superiority of performance, only that she give us a minuet and a few lighter dances, and perhaps a reel to finish the evening. There can be no impropriety in that."

Frederica deferred to her mother, who gave a nod of consent, and then sat down at the instrument, not at all sorry to be employed and very glad that she might oblige them without having to sing or dance.

To the chagrin of these fair petitioners, Miss Vernon performed so charmingly that the gentlemen began to compliment her upon the skill and expression of her playing when they ought to have been praising their partners' grace and smiles.

Lady Vernon soon observed that to call Langford "lively" did not do it justice; each day was a perpetual quest for diversion. While the gentlemen were shooting, the ladies were obliged to set out on walking parties or picnics, or to drive the pair of phaetons round the park, or to join Eliza Manwaring when she called upon the neighbors and coaxed them back to Langford to drink tea or dine or partake of the evening's *tableaux vivants* or dancing or music or card parties.

Lady Vernon concluded that the Manwarings must be very discontented with each other if they could not bear the prospect of dining *en famille* or passing an evening in quiet conversation, and she began to feel pity for Maria Manwaring. The uneasy union of her brother and his wife must give the poor girl a divided outlook toward matrimony; she could anticipate no pleasure in the prospect, and yet it was the only one that would remove her from a household where her brother paid court to every woman but his wife and a sister-in-law who urged the necessity of marrying upon her without exhibiting any pleasure in the state herself. Yet, to Miss Manwaring's credit, she had not been made cynical or ill-tempered by living with her incompatible relations. Her disposition was resigned and gentle, her understanding was good, and a similarity in their natures began to draw her and Miss Vernon together. Maria found Frederica Vernon a far pleasanter companion than the Misses Hamilton, who desired to appear genteel and accomplished without either talent or application, and whose mother's excessive flattery gave them a high degree of assurance without perfecting their abilities or refining their taste.

Maria and Frederica soon discovered that the subject of Sir James Martin was never a point of rivalry between them. Miss Manwaring had been persuaded that she *ought* to regard him as her object, though she had never thought of him with more than polite indifference. Frederica held her cousin in the highest esteem and yet laughed at the notion that anyone might think that he had never married because he meant to make *her* an offer of his hand.

As it was resolved between them that Sir James Martin was at liberty to marry anybody but themselves or each other, there was no obstacle to the two girls forming a sincere friendship.

chapter fifteen

LADY VERNON TO LADY MARTIN

Langford, Somerset
My dear Aunt,

I am very sorry if you perceived any coldness from me in our last parting. Toward you, Aunt, there is no reproach or blame, for I know that you could not have prevented James from buying Vernon Castle. Upon further reflection, I have come to understand that a gentleman may do far worse to his family than to make them the objects of his generosity—but of that I will write no more, for you will be eager to hear how Frederica and I fare at Langford. Be assured that we have not been allowed to dwell upon the past or to contemplate the precarious state of our future. The <u>present</u> occupies the Manwarings completely, and they keep their company so caught up in parties and amusements and paying calls and receiving visitors, and cards and charades and dancing, that there is not a moment to reflect or to pine.

We have been no fewer than twelve at dinner every night, and on occasion as many as thirty! The society and to-do suit me only in one respect—they prevent Frederica's spirits from sinking further. The oppression that marked her last weeks at Churchill Manor has lifted, chiefly through the attentions of Maria Manwaring. Her kindness and solicitude are very much to her credit, and her reward is a companion who is far superior to the Misses Hamilton, who have come to Somerset for a long visit.

At this time of year, Langford is the place to meet young men, and

Lady Hamilton is determined that her daughters will not suffer Miss Manwaring's fate—to be nearly two and twenty and not married. They have thirty thousand apiece, so I think that Lady Hamilton will let them go for as little as two thousand per annum if a bit of property, or the prospect of it, is thrown in. In disposition, the two eldest are conceited and above being pleased, and the youngest is so excessively pleased with everything that she is often restless and always noisy—the elder ones cannot bear exertion and the youngest has not the patience to sit still; their conversation is tiresome, when it is not silly, and it is not only the prejudice of a parent that leads me to think that any gentleman of worth and sense would sooner take Frederica for nothing than any of them with their thirty thousand pounds!

I want for nothing, save, perhaps, some relief from the attentions of Mr. Manwaring. For some weeks, he had been prudent, but now all reserve is gone and he is often unguarded. In the mornings, he can be avoided, as he must take the gentlemen out shooting or go into Taunton on business, but in the evenings, his attentions are so marked that they begin to kindle Eliza's jealousy. When he addresses me directly, I keep the discourse from becoming a tête-à-tête by inquiring, "Are you of the same opinion as Mr. Manwaring, Lord Whitby?" or "Do you agree with our host that the summer was a very dry one, Mr. Reed?" until one of the Hamilton girls engages his conversation or he falls victim to their mother's passion for cards.

Tomorrow, we will have another addition to the party—Alicia Johnson comes from London. Mr. Johnson, who generally confines his infirmities to home, had the ill luck to become afflicted while he was away, and will be laid up long enough to allow his wife to slip into Somerset for some diversion. If he were at home, he would likely oppose the visit, as he has not forgiven Eliza Manwaring for marrying against his wishes.

Frederica sends you her very best love and promises to write to you soon. In the meantime, I am commissioned to tell you, however, that the tuberoses at Langford are nothing at all beside those at Ealing Park.

Your affectionate niece,
Susan Vernon

It was not for many days after Mrs. Johnson's arrival that she and Lady Vernon were able to take a turn around the park without Mrs. Manwaring converting their twosome into a walking party of five or six.

Mrs. Johnson immediately began to apologize for not coming down to Sussex for Sir Frederick's funeral. "Mr. Johnson insisted that he was laid up with gout," she declared. "I am persuaded that his gout is brought on or kept off at his pleasure. Three years ago, when I wanted him to try the waters at Bath, nothing would induce him to have a gouty symptom, and yet when the Hamiltons invited me to the Lakes, he was so laid up that I was obliged to remain in London to nurse him. And—tedious man!—he bears it all with such patience that I have not even the common excuse for losing my temper! But, my dear, how pale you look! Why, you have been here six weeks and you have not got back your color. Manwaring tells me that he means to keep you here until they go to town in February."

"That may be his intention, but I do not know if I can withstand the Langford notion of tranquillity for so long. Frederica and the youngest Miss Hamilton are to be enrolled in school in December, and I have offered to chaperone them to town so that I can have the opportunity to look in on the house on Portland Place, and once there, I may decide to remain."

"It will be a delightful thing to have you in town so soon, and a good school will throw Miss Vernon in the path of rich young men by way of their sisters, which is Lady Hamilton's object for Miss Lucy. But if Manwaring *will* have you back *here*, I shall always be happy to stand up with Miss Vernon in town and to take her wherever she likes."

Lady Vernon murmured her thanks, knowing full well that Alicia Johnson was of that class of women who had always cared too much for their own comfort and pleasure to be inconvenienced by little children, but who would be very glad to have one or two fine grown girls to parade about London and Bath.

"Miss Vernon has grown into such a beauty—the Hamilton girls are nothing at all beside her. Of course, it is settled that the eldest will marry Reginald deCourcy. Your brother-in-law must have said something of it, I am sure."

"He has said nothing at all about it."

"I am very surprised, for it is said that the deCourcys talk of nothing else. They are very determined on both sides that the fortunes ought to be united," continued Mrs. Johnson, "and I know that Miss Hamilton is willing and Mr. deCourcy has never expressed any objection or shown any inclination toward anyone else."

"His disinclination toward any other lady does not mean that he is inclined toward his cousin."

"Very true. It is why Lady Hamilton throws them together at every opportunity. She has encouraged Eliza to invite him here on purpose to hurry matters along. She is very angry that he stays away, and if she is cool toward you, it is because she blames you that he does not come."

"How can Lady Hamilton think that *I* decide whether Mr. de-Courcy will come and go?" cried Lady Vernon. "I am wholly unacquainted with that young man!"

"*They* are all of the opinion that you objected to Miss deCourcy's marriage to Mr. Vernon. Mr. deCourcy feels the insult on his sister's behalf and so he stays away."

"He must be a very foolish young man to take such offense at a rumor—and even if it *were* true that I objected to the Vernons' marriage, Mr. deCourcy's affection for Miss Hamilton ought to overrule his resentment against *me*."

"Ah, well, his friend Mr. Smith will not be kept away—he takes offense at nothing if there is the promise of diversion."

When they entered the house, Eliza Manwaring met them with a letter in her hand and proclaimed, with great delight, that they were to have an addition to their party. Lady Vernon supposed that Reginald deCourcy's affection for his family *had* overcome his prejudice against her, but to her very great surprise, Eliza announced, "Sir James Martin comes to Taunton on a matter of business, and he will stop at Langford."

The news affected the ladies very differently. Lady Vernon immediately withdrew to see if she had also received a letter from her cousin; Mrs. Johnson declared that Sir James must have a *very particular* reason for coming; and Lady Hamilton hurried off to write to her mantua maker, charging her to hurry up Miss Lucy's white crepe gown, and then summoned the housekeeper to know where she might send for someone to dress Miss Claudia's hair.

chapter sixteen

WHEN SIR JAMES ARRIVED AT LANGFORD, HE GAVE NO indication of what interest had brought him from Ealing Park. He received no businesslike correspondence and never rode into town. He would as often sit with the ladies as go shooting with the gentlemen, attending them all with good humor and unfailing gallantry. Toward Lady Vernon, however, he was especially solicitous, and toward Miss Vernon so attentive and gentle that everyone at Langford was persuaded that his purpose in coming was to apply for Miss Vernon's hand (a rumor started by Alicia Johnson). Having delayed so long until she came of age, Mrs. Johnson assured them all, Sir James was too impatient to wait out the customary term of bereavement and meant to entreat Lady Vernon's consent to an immediate engagement.

The Hamilton girls and their mother were affronted; the elder girls maintained that Miss Vernon had no conversation, no style, and no fortune, and their mother was contemptuous of Lady Vernon for encouraging the suit when her own husband was not cold in the ground. "I must say, I do not think that she ought to partake of any company at all," she remarked to Mrs. Manwaring and Mrs. Johnson one evening, after Lady Vernon had retired. "If Lord Hamilton died, I would not allow myself to be seen by anybody but my maid for a twelvemonth!"

"Lady Vernon," declared Eliza Manwaring, "is the sort of person who will do everything in her own fashion." She spoke with some bitterness, for Manwaring's admiration of Lady Vernon had not been overlooked by his wife.

"That sort of fashion, which throws all propriety aside, I do not care for at all!" replied Lady Hamilton. "All of her smiles and leaning upon the family connection will not make Miss Vernon one whit less insipid and dull, nor add a penny to her fortune." She lowered her voice and glanced toward Frederica Vernon, who sat at the instrument, while the other young people were dancing. "I have heard by way of my niece that Miss Vernon was left only two thousand by her mother's parents and that Sir Frederick left her nothing at all. That sum *might* get her a clergyman—and indeed she would suit our Mr. Heywood. He is like to be a widower, as I do not believe that his wife can survive another lying-in, and it would be good to have someone at hand. I cannot bear a single clergyman. But to aim higher! Lady Martin! For Lady Vernon to grasp at that match is the sort of vulgar ambition that I do not like at all."

Unfortunately, these last remarks were uttered at a break in the music and the pianoforte was near enough to allow Miss Vernon to overhear the latter part of Lady Hamilton's speech. Her fingers stumbled upon the keys and she rose from the instrument, stammering an apology and begging to be excused. The young ladies pleaded with her to remain, but only for want of a musician. Sir James, fearing that she had been taken ill, went to her side and offered to fetch her some water or wine with great solicitation, which only added to Miss Vernon's embarrassment.

"How very ill-mannered!" Lady Hamilton declared when Miss Vernon had left the room. "To stop before the young people have had a reel, when she must see how much the gentlemen were enjoying the dancing. Lavinia, my love!" she cried out. "You must sit down and continue the music. She does not play at all badly," she told the others, "and since her future is settled, she cannot wish for her sisters' partners."

Mrs. Johnson and Mrs. Manwaring congratulated Lady Hamilton, declaring what a fortunate thing it was for a girl when an early engagement relieved her of the tedious business of accomplishment.

chapter seventeen

LADY VERNON WALKED OUT THE FOLLOWING MORNING with Frederica and heard her account of what had been said. "You must not trouble yourself," she consoled her daughter. "I will not urge you upon Lady Hamilton's clergyman. She is all presumption and vanity—she is persuaded that no gentleman of fortune can be content without a wife, and therefore marriage *must* be your cousin's object. And if James does not court any of *her* daughters, she concludes that he means to address *mine*."

"Yet they have only to look to their own family to see the error of their premise. What of Mr. Lewis deCourcy? He is wealthy and unmarried and as amiable and contented a gentleman as I have ever met."

"Perhaps the example of Sir Reginald's marriage persuaded his brother that a good character, an honorable occupation, and the pleasure of never having to give an account of himself to anyone were all the domestic comfort he wished for."

"And yet," said Frederica gravely, "a gentleman may seek comfort as readily with vice as with virtue, if he is never called to account for himself."

"Not every gentleman can enjoy such liberty," declared a masculine voice. "I must account to Mother for my vices and virtues as rigorously as a cook must account for the spoons."

Sir James Martin had come up behind them. He stepped between the two ladies and offered an arm to each.

"And what account will you give my aunt for your time at Langford, cousin?" asked Frederica. "I have not seen you attend to anything like business since you arrived."

"Nonsense, my dear Freddie. I have killed three dozen birds and danced as many dances, and I have read the newspaper every morning and played at billiards in the afternoon and at cards every night. I have admired Miss Claudia's new spencer and Miss Lucy's fashion plates and Lady Hamilton's pug and Mrs. Manwaring's geraniums. I have written letters to both my mother and my tailor every day. I do not think there is a gentleman at Langford who has been hálf so industrious."

"Then perhaps you ought to go back to Ealing Park, where you might recover from your exertions," declared Lady Vernon.

"I will go today, if you will both come with me."

"It would please me very much to see my Aunt Martin," Lady Vernon replied. "But the *master* of Ealing Park is the sort of deceitful, giddy person that I do not like at all."

"And what do you say to that, Freddie?" inquired her cousin.

"I do not think that you are deceitful."

"There!" Sir James laughed. "If a young lady of such sound and analytical mind cannot think me deceitful, then her mother must be mistaken. What is your opinion, Freddie?"

Frederica reflected upon the question. "In science, if our conclusions do not prove true, we must go back to the premise."

"Very sound! So what is the foundation of your mother's displeasure?"

"I can think of nothing that you have done to offend my mother. I am sure that the great kindness you have shown us both places us greatly in your debt."

"And what is your reply to that?" Sir James asked Lady Vernon.

"That it is the very notion of *indebtedness* that offends me" was his cousin's reply.

"I think that 'indebtedness' is a term for business or to be used among strangers," observed Sir James. "Surely among relations there is only generosity and regard."

"You did not regard my instructions concerning Vernon Castle. I had asked for advice and assistance, not for alms. I am grateful that it was not more generally known that you were the purchaser," she added.

"It would have been very ungenerous indeed to have Sir Frederick exposed as the object of his relations' charity."

"You asked for assistance in finding a purchaser, which is precisely what I did. You did not ask that you *approve* the purchaser—you and Sir Frederick gave me leave to manage all. Come, my dear cousin, we must not quarrel. Give me your opinion, Freddie, for you are a very sensible girl. Was I wrong to buy Vernon Castle? If you tell me that I have done wrong, I will beg forgiveness."

Frederica pondered his question. "I think that you deliberately withheld information from my mother that she ought to have had."

"There!" Lady Vernon declared.

"But," her daughter added, "my cousin's motives were for the best, and he acted out of generosity, so as not to let dear Vernon Castle go to strangers. If he *has* offended you, I think he ought to have been forgiven."

"A very sound answer," Sir James replied. "What goodness and compassion! Can you have acquired it without any encouragement from your parents? Surely something must be attributed to maternal influence."

Lady Vernon found herself smiling and realized that she had *believed* that she ought to be angry with her cousin after all sensation of anger had gone. She had never been able to remain cross with him for very long. His liveliness, good humor, and wit were the sort that might test one's patience but never provoke a permanent ill will.

"Come, Susan, sit down on this bench here in the sun—you are far too pale. Freddie, walk to the greenhouse and let me talk to your mother alone. Then I will come join you and cut one of the roses for you on purpose to vex the Misses Hamilton."

"It is wrong to encourage discord, cousin."

"It is worse to encourage hope."

Frederica gave him a reproving smile and left them alone.

"It is good to see her smile," Sir James remarked.

"She has had little enough to smile about."

"Do you still mean to send her off to school?"

"Frederica can have no better opportunity to acquaint herself with the advantages and manners of London," Lady Vernon replied. "She has seen too little of the world."

"Perhaps she is all the better for it." After a moment's reflection, Sir James added, "Susan, I do ask you to forgive me and offer you Vernon Castle if you like. The Edwardses are very genteel, unimaginative folk who did not move a chair nor trim a hedge—it will all be as you remember it. They depart after the Christmas season. It can be yours on the first of January."

"I do not wish to be as far from Freddie as Staffordshire. Not every mother can be like my Aunt, who looks to the first of the year when she can send you off to London and enjoy Derbyshire in peace and quiet."

"Too much peace and quiet will dull the mind—think what Mother would be if she had no troublesome son to whet her better nature and to sharpen her wits upon! She might have sunk to an Eliza Manwaring or a Lady Hamilton. Every mother should have such a son, do you not agree?"

"We all have our share of maternal pride, cousin. I think as well of my daughter as any mother does of her son—I wish for nothing more, except perhaps some assurance that it will be in her power to attract a husband of consequence."

"How can you say so when everyone whispers that she is being sent to London in order to be *finished* for me?"

"You may laugh as much as you like, but I cannot afford to be diverted where Freddie's future is concerned."

"I will not laugh, I cannot laugh, if you cannot afford to share my mirth. Come, Susan—we are not good at keeping secrets from one another—what allowance will you have for your diversion?"

"Per annum?" she returned with a renewal of spirit. "I think that it will be something more than you paid for the new mantelpiece at Cavendish Square and considerably less than the annual bill from your tailor. Now, do not look grim, cousin, and do not think of making us the object of your charity once more. We will not want for a roof over our heads."

"I do not like that it is Manwaring's roof," replied he. "I like it even less than I did when I left you at Churchill. Manwaring's attentions have made you the object of some very unpleasant talk—the gentlemen, of course, can say nothing offensive in my presence, but the ladies do not have to be so circumspect. They may cast as many winks and allusions as they like and have no fear of a calling-out."

"I am not wounded, cousin. Lady Hamilton's wit makes for a dull weapon."

"She is not to be taken lightly, Susan. Her connection with the deCourcy family means that everything she sees here will find its way to Mrs. Charles Vernon."

"I am convinced that Mrs. Vernon cannot dislike me more than she does already. I am grateful to Lady Hamilton for giving her niece some foundation for her aversion. I would not want to be hated for nothing."

"My dear cousin, I beg you to bring your visit to an end when you take Freddie to London. *That* is my only business here. If you do not wish to come to Derbyshire and do not like to open your house in town, you may have mine on Cavendish Square, and I will take a set of rooms somewhere. Everyone will anticipate that we are planning my engagement to Freddie and she will become such an object of interest that some rich, headstrong young man will hurry to address her just for the fun of cutting me out. Every party will come out the winner."

"Save for you. You will be as idle and giddy and *single* as ever. Go to Freddie, James, and let her tell you how many uses she has found for the Manwarings' lovage leaf and archangelica. Let me sit and enjoy a few moments of tranquillity—that is such a rarity at Langford."

He laughed and went off to walk with Frederica, while Lady Vernon sat down on a bench to reflect upon her cousin's advice. She *had* erred in coming to Langford, not because she had encouraged Manwaring's flirtation, but because she had removed from Charles Vernon's consciousness the discomfort that her presence must have wrought. She could not dispute his *right* to deprive her and Frederica of all that Sir Frederick meant for them to have, but she might not have allowed him to be so easy.

Although Frederica, in her account of Sir Frederick's injury, had suggested that her uncle had not acted as promptly as he might have,

Lady Vernon was willing to concede that his hesitation may have come from shock and dismay rather than a malicious desire to see his brother perish. Yet, however pardonable his motives may have been *then*, his subsequent visits to Churchill Manor and his continual attendance upon his brother must now be seen as hopelessly, heartlessly mercenary. In persuading Sir Frederick against assigning any part of his fortune to Lady Vernon and her daughter, he had eased his brother into complacency and indefinite delay in the hope that it would be to his advantage, and with that as his object, could he do other than rejoice at its fulfillment?

The sound of horsemen aroused Lady Vernon from her reverie and she looked up to see Manwaring alight from his horse and hand the reins over to his groom.

"How fortunate that I should find you without a party of a half-dozen to act the chaperone! Which walk do you take? Do you prefer the park or a country lane?"

"I came out only to meet the post," she replied, turning back toward the house. "I am expecting a letter from Miss Summers's Academy—the arrangements for Frederica's placement must be completed before we go to town."

"But you go only to get Miss Vernon settled. You must give me your word that you will return to Langford, for we quite expected you to be with us for many weeks longer."

"I may be obliged to stay on in London to attend to some business of my own. My housekeeper at Portland Place is anxious for some direction as to what I mean to do."

"Oh, but you need not be in town for that—correspondence will do as well. Or you may send your instructions with Sir James, who goes to town from here. Something *very particular* must take him to town so early, and *that* interest will make him happy to oblige you."

Manwaring viewed the prospect of an engagement between Miss Vernon and Sir James Martin with complaisance. He liked his sister well enough, but he was resigned to the fact that if Maria had not caught Sir James when she was seventeen, eighteen, or nineteen, she could have no hope of him at twenty-two. "And," he continued, offering Lady Vernon his arm, "if it is money matters, you can leave it all to Charles Vernon, can you not? You are not left as Eliza was, with her fortune in the hands of one who regards her right to it as *conditional only*, and with no one to come forward and dispute it. Sir Frederick's intentions were so well known that his brother must abide by them. It is excessively diverting to hear Lady Hamilton talk about Miss Vernon as though she were penniless. To be sure, Miss Vernon's ten thousand pounds may be nothing when compared to the thirty thousand of *her* daughters, and I daresay Sir James will not even ask for *that*, so you will be all the richer! If I had been able to settle ten thousand upon Maria, I would have got her off my hands before now!"

"You have a very happy opinion of my prosperity, and my daughter's fortune."

"My opinions can only be drawn from Sir Frederick. Why, the very day we were all a-shooting at Churchill, he spoke of the matter, for Vernon had been trying to coax us both into some speculation. I quite forget what it was, something that involved a great deal of risk, I daresay, for Vernon always had a touch of the gamester about him. I could put nothing into the venture, and Sir Frederick *would* not and declared that he had learned his lesson from the last scheme and that he must be prudent for Miss Vernon's sake. It was then that he said he meant to settle as much as ten thousand upon her and very likely more."

"And was Charles disappointed?"

"I daresay he was—and I confess that I teased him a good deal about what a poor sort of banker he must be! How could he expect to coax strangers out of their money when he could not succeed with his own brother, said I! I am sorry to think what sport I made of him when the day ended so badly, but I understand that Vernon was often at Churchill while Sir Frederick was on the mend, so between *them* there was no ill feeling. *You* will not be left at the mercy of one who regards your claims as provisional or who will drag his feet where any money but his own is at stake—a brother will be conscientious out of family feeling."

"I don't believe that I ever gave Charles his due in regard to his family feeling," Lady Vernon replied coolly.

"Indeed. I don't think I love Maria half so much!" Manwaring laughed. "How I wish that Eliza had been left to a brother instead of in the guardianship of Mr. Johnson. She was left quite as handsome as you, after all, but Mr. Johnson withholds all but a very insignificant allowance. Yes, you will always be better served by family than by friends."

He continued to congratulate her on how well off she had been left until Lady Vernon began to think that Manwaring's pursuit of her had been motivated, in some part, by supposing her to be a woman of fortune.

chapter eighteen

LADY VERNON TO MR. VERNON

Langford, Somerset
My dear brother,

I find that I can no longer refuse myself the pleasure of profiting by your kind invitation when we last parted, of being received by you and Mrs. Vernon at Churchill Manor, and therefore, if it is quite convenient, I hope that I shall very soon be introduced to a sister whom I have so long desired to know.

Though my kind friends here are most affectionately urgent that I prolong my stay until they go to town in February, their hospitable and cheerful dispositions lead them too much into society for my present situation and state of mind.

It is my plan to leave Langford for London upon the first of December. Frederica is to be placed in one of the best private schools in town, and I shall leave her there myself, which will allow me to be of use as a chaperone to Miss Lucy Hamilton, who is to be enrolled as well. As Frederick's long illness prevented us from opening the house on Portland Place last season, this journey will also allow me to see to Mrs. Forrester's management of it and to determine whether I will be equal to its continued maintenance.

The separation from my only child must make the prospect of familiar surroundings and a family circle my only comfort, and it would pain me to learn that it will not be in your power to receive me.

*Indeed, I am determined not to be denied, for I truly long to be made
known to your dear little children, in whose hearts I shall be very eager
to secure an interest, and to be introduced at last to my sister.*

Your most obliged and affectionate sister,
Susan Vernon

Lady Vernon showed this letter to Frederica before it was sent
to post.

Frederica confessed herself astonished and doubtful. "If, when the
grief of my father's passing was immediately before him, my uncle
would not admit of any duty to us, he will not be any more obliging
after so many weeks have passed. And why to Churchill? My uncle is
so often in town that he cannot avoid you if you settle there."

"Nobody is so easily avoided anywhere as in town. But in his family home, in the presence of his wife and children, your uncle will be
forced to appear hospitable and obliging, which may kindle something like a sense of duty. If I had any hope of legal redress, I would
not put myself in his way—even for my own welfare, I would not do
it, as I might sell the Portland Place house and live very comfortably.
But if, as Mr. Manwaring attests, your father expressed how much
he meant to settle on you, I must make some attempt to call him to
account."

"I do not wish, for my sake, that you expose yourself to the duplic-
ity of my uncle. I will not forget how he came to us at Churchill
Manor while my father was in frail health, preying upon family feeling
in a very underhanded manner, and to a most mercenary end! How
the brother of a man as kindhearted and generous as my father can be
so selfish and wicked! To have the same mother and father and yet to
turn out so unlike! I pity my aunt and cousins—to have such a vile
man for their husband and father!"

"You may be as liberal as you like with your pity," replied Lady Vernon. "I will reserve mine for us."

"But what of the Manwarings? They talk of you returning to them
after I go to London. Maria says that they quite depend upon it."

"I think that Mr. Manwaring does, but I cannot think that Eliza is feeling as charitable as she did when the invitation to Langford was first given. Eliza was willing to tolerate me as an object of pity, but a woman can never be charitable for long when she believes—however wrongly!—that she has a rival for any man's attentions, even if that man is only her husband."

chapter nineteen

S<small>IR</small> J<small>AMES</small> M<small>ARTIN</small>, <small>HAVING EXHAUSTED HIS APPEALS TO</small>
bring his cousins to Ealing Park, departed from Langford on
the following day. His absence was but briefly felt; four gentlemen, eager for gaiety and diversion, came to fill his place, so that there
was no time to lament the absence of one. Indeed, they began to be
sorry that Lady Vernon had not followed her cousin to town, for she
seemed resolved upon making herself so charming that, when she announced her decision to leave them some weeks before her proposed
departure, nobody was sorry save for Manwaring and his sister. Manwaring's defense of her was in proportion to what he supposed her fortune to be, and Maria would not join in the censure of one whose
conduct she had never observed to be improper and whose daughter
had become her closest friend. The other ladies, however, began to resent that Lady Vernon managed to be more elegant in bombazine and
crepe than they could manage in velvet and silk, and the gentlemen
pronounced her "monstrous pretty"—too pretty for a widow—and
they would not want their own wives to be so gay after *they* were cold
in the ground. "I daresay everything I ever heard about her is quite
true!" declared Charles Smith, a lively, forward young man who had
come to Langford with a friend. "She is too much the coquette for my
taste," he determined, though Lady Vernon had said little more to
him than a polite "Good morning" when she came down to breakfast
and an equally civil "Good evening, sir" when she retired at night.
"And her daughter, entirely the reverse!" he continued. "So dull and
bookish—so entirely without style or elegance!"

Lady Hamilton approved these speeches and declared that Mr.

Smith was a very sensible young man and not one to be fooled by appearances. *She* would not scruple to set down all of Lady Vernon's coquetry and impropriety in her letters to Lady deCourcy and to her niece at Churchill Manor—indeed, *every* letter posted from Langford had something of Lady Vernon in it.

Mrs. Manwaring to Mrs. Johnson

Langford, Somerset
My dear friend,

You were mistaken, my dear Alicia, in supposing that Lady Vernon and her daughter would be with us for the rest of the winter. Had I not been so overcome with pity for her situation, I would never have had her come to Langford. Though she was so recent a widow, I was not without apprehension, and she had not been here very long before she began to invite the attentions of every gentleman present, not excluding those of my own husband! Upon Sir James Martin, she bestowed what notice was necessary to detach him from Maria, and now it appears that, though Sir Frederick has been gone for scarcely three months, Sir James has every intention of making his proposals for Miss Vernon. I have learned from Maria that Miss Vernon is not at all inclined toward the match, which, if that is true, must make her the greatest simpleton on earth! I have no doubt, however, that her mother will be rewarded for her exertions as wicked people so often are, and that the scheme of placing her in the care of Miss Summers's Academy on Wigmore Street is only done to give the girl a bit of polish before entering into the engagement.

We are in a sad state, but that will soon be relieved as Lady Vernon leaves us at the beginning of December. It is said that she will not open her house in town but only install Miss Vernon in school and then go down to Churchill Manor. I cannot think that she would go to them unless there were truly no place in England open to her—to Churchill she is to go, however, until something better comes into view, and so she may plague Mrs. Charles Vernon and flirt with her husband—who was once Lady Vernon's beau. What an abhorrent thing for Mrs. Vernon to have to receive her!

Adieu. I beg you, my dear Alicia, to give my warmest regards to Mr. Johnson and tell him that I do not at all resent his throwing me off upon my marriage, which—considering the conduct of my husband— showed a greater affection for me than I gave credit. If I had been one degree less contemptibly weak, I should never have married him, for you know that I was applied to by more than one title above baronet—yet I was foolish and romantic and would not be satisfied by riches alone. If Lady Vernon were not to leave us very soon, I might find myself so desperate as to appeal to Mr. Johnson—but I will not impose upon your domestic tranquillity just yet. I will know better how things stand after we are relieved of Lady Vernon's presence.

Yours, etc.,
Eliza Manwaring

Lady Vernon, accompanied by her daughter and Miss Lucy Hamilton, quit Langford in the first week of December. Mrs. Manwaring was so overcome with joy at seeing them go that she was almost restored to cordiality. Manwaring, on the other hand, was so despondent that Lady Vernon might have felt sorry for him had she not believed that the Christmas season would bring him many more visitors who had pretty wives and sisters, and that he would not want for somebody to flirt with. Miss Manwaring was genuinely unhappy at the loss of a pleasant companion, but the promise of a steady correspondence and the prospect of being in London within a few months herself reconciled her to the loss of Miss Vernon's company.

In London, there was nobody to receive Lady Vernon except for Alicia Johnson, who could only invite her to drink tea at Edward Street when Mr. Johnson was at his club. Rumors of Lady Vernon's scandalous conduct while at Langford had reached him, and though he was not prepared to forgive his ward for marrying against his wishes and was gratified that her husband's immoderate conduct had proven his objections to be justified, he did not think that it would be quite

respectable to meet the woman who had added to the Manwarings'
discord.

"He does not *hate* you," Mrs. Johnson assured her friend. "Mr.
Johnson cannot hate anybody, he has not the heart for it. But you see
how it is. *We* are intimate friends and your brother-in-law is very high
in the banking house now, and your cousin is Sir James Martin, so
slighting you would have an awkward look—yet as Eliza was his ward,
something is due her. He cannot bring himself to approve of one connection, nor to insult the other, and so he takes himself to his club to
avoid the situation altogether. So, how did you leave them all at
Langford? Eliza is very angry at Maria for not fixing Sir James while he
was there. Poor Maria will never catch anybody with such a placid
and reserved disposition—artlessness will never do in love matters!"

"The truth of *that* matter is," replied Lady Vernon with candor,
"Maria Manwaring does not care for Sir James at all and looks to marriage only in a very general way, as the means by which she may escape from the unhappiness at home. Poor girl, she might have made a
suitable match by this time if Eliza had not been so determined that
she *must* marry Sir James."

"Ah, but one cannot blame her—he is so very handsome and rich.
Eliza might be almost forgiven for aiming so high, and Miss Vernon, if
I may say so, cannot be forgiven for resisting the idea of a match with
her cousin. What will you do if she continues to refuse him?"

"I suppose I shall have to marry him myself!" Lady Vernon
laughed.

"Well, Miss Summers's young ladies will make her more reasonable. *They* know the importance of husbands, and their influence will
do what a mother's cannot. So you are really to go to Churchill? How
long must we postpone the pleasure of seeing one another again?"

"Alas, if it were in my power to invite you, I would, but I have
no standing there. We must wait and see how far I can win over Mrs.
Vernon."

"I will not depend upon her hospitality. The Parkers have just
come back from a fortnight in Sussex. They mean to take Billingshurst after the new year, and Mrs. Parker said that they dined with a

half-dozen families in the neighborhood and yet did not once see any-thing of the Vernons. She says that Mr. Vernon and his wife go nowhere and keep no company—it is quite as bad as Mr. Johnson! But if I cannot visit you in the country, I can at least be a friend to Miss Vernon in town."

"YOU WILL HAVE to suffer Mrs. Johnson's invitations—that cannot be avoided," Lady Vernon told her daughter at the time of their part-ing. "The sacrifice of an hour or two a week will not be too trying."

"And if it is," Frederica replied, "I will introduce her to one of the girls at Miss Summers's—a nice orphan girl from a good family ought to satisfy all of her maternal ambitions."

chapter twenty

Mrs. Charles Vernon took a great deal of pleasure from living in as unvarying a style as a marriage and
four children would permit. She never traveled from her
home and took no delight in society beyond that of her family circle
at Parklands. She had a natural complacency about everything around
her, and had her circle been wider, and her routine more varied, she
might have felt compelled to acquire something by way of accomplishment or education that would have justified her good opinion of
herself. This good opinion, however, rested solely on her being the
daughter of Sir Reginald deCourcy, and the niece of Lady Hamilton,
which she could cultivate very well by going nowhere and doing as little as possible.

Her husband's frequent engagements in London, his attachment to
a very fast set, his penchant for gaming and cards, his coolness toward
her parents, and his indifference to their children were less troublesome to her than the prospect of any alteration in her routine, and the
acquisition of Churchill Manor, therefore, was not entirely welcome.
She had known that it must come someday, but had always hoped that
it would not be until after her husband was dead, when the property
would pass to their eldest son and spare her the trouble of uprooting
herself from Kent.

To be sure, the distance from Parklands Manor to Churchill was
not great, but it was very far to one who had never lived a quarter-
mile from two very indulgent parents. At Churchill, there would be
no fond mother to bring her gossip and hear her complaints, and she

would have to be hospitable to strangers rather than pampered by her parents.

Regarding Churchill itself, she could find little fault and wrote to her mother the very day of her arrival:

> I confess, madam, that while the wooded areas are quite somber, and the grounds nothing at all when compared to Parklands, the house is a good one, the furniture fashionable, and everything is fitted out with elegance and taste. I cannot think that a woman of my sister-in-law's reputation can have had the refinement to effect such an improvement in the property over what it must have been, for Mr. Vernon's accounts of his youth had made Churchill Manor out to be a very uninviting place. We shall have to get a new housekeeper and cook at once, but I think that we may wait until after our visit to you at Christmas to engage the rest of the household—for many of the former staff left Churchill Manor after Sir Frederick's death. I shall be anxious to hear your advice on how the business will best be managed.

Lady deCourcy responded to her daughter's letter with a great deal of advice on how she was to direct her household, how thoroughly she must go over the cook's accounts and how few dishes she might get by on when only the clergyman and his wife came to dine, expressing her confidence that anything she had forgot would be resolved when the Vernons came back to Parklands for Christmas.

This plan was at the heart of all of their succeeding letters, which invariably concluded with *when we return to Kent at Christmastime* or *when you and my dear grandchildren come to us at Christmas*. It was, therefore, particularly irksome to Mrs. Vernon when her husband showed her Lady Vernon's letter. Mrs. Vernon was all astonishment and immediately protested. "After all that we have heard from my Aunt Hamilton of her conduct at Langford! Conduct that showed no regard for the feelings of her hostess or the memory of her late husband! Can you think of bringing such a woman into our home? To expose our children to her! I am certain that my mother would never approve such a plan."

Charles Vernon was no more eager to receive Lady Vernon than his wife, but the prospect of going back to the dull festivities of Park-lands and the oppressive meddling of Lady deCourcy was even less inviting than receiving his brother's widow. The reports of Lady Vernon's improper conduct at Langford persuaded him that she could not make any appeal to him that was based upon a claim of rectitude, nor would she find an ally to defend her in the wake of the scandalous rumors that had come out of Somerset. "Lady Vernon can exert no influence that your own excellent character will not offset, my dear," her husband replied. "It need not prevent us from spending our Christmas with your family. You may invite them here."

That suggestion was put forth in the full knowledge that Sir Reginald's frail health would not permit him to travel, which gave Vernon the advantage of appearing liberal without actually having to put himself out. An unsettling discomfort—the beginnings of dissatisfaction with his new responsibilities—had begun to diminish the triumph of acquisition, and his chief enjoyment of it came from the distance he had put between himself and his mother-in-law.

Mrs. Vernon to Lady deCourcy

Churchill Manor, Sussex
My dear Mother,

I am very sorry to tell you that it will not be in our power to keep our promise of spending this Christmas with you; and we are prevented that happiness by a circumstance that is not likely to give us any pleasure. Lady Vernon, in a letter to her brother, has declared her intention of visiting us. I was by no means prepared for such an event, nor can I account for her desire to come to us when she has a perfectly suitable house in town. I can only suspect that her extravagant manner of living and her determination to have Miss Vernon schooled in London at great expense has left her in narrow circumstances, and that she wishes to have my husband render her some pecuniary assistance.

I can think of no other reason for her coming to us, and though she

expresses a most eager desire of being acquainted with me and makes
very generous mention of my children, I am not weak enough to sup-
pose that she disposes her own child in town so that she may engage the
affections of mine. I cannot forgive her artful and ungenerous opposi-
tion to my marriage—no one could overlook it, save for one as ami-
able as Mr. Vernon. Mr. Vernon will think kindly of her, but he is
disposed to think well of everyone, and I have no doubt that his own
grief has softened his heart toward his late brother's widow.

I am very glad to hear that my father's health has not declined to
any great degree and I am, with best love, etc.,

Catherine Vernon

When Lady deCourcy heard of the alteration in plans, she wrote
to her daughter in language that could not conceal her anger and frus-
tration, directing all of her resentment against Lady Vernon. *We shall*
at least have Reginald with us, she added.

And Lord and Lady Hamilton will come with your cousins, which
will bring your brother together with Lavinia. Reginald has been so
provoking of late—going here and going there, and behaving as though
all of our expectations are of no significance. If we get them together
for a few weeks, I have no doubt that matters will be settled before the
new year.

Mrs. Vernon read this letter to her husband and expressed her relief that her parents would not be *completely* alone at Christmas, and
said how likely it was that it would be the last Christmas season her
father would see, which would make the presence of at least *one* of his
children a great source of pleasure.

Vernon was not equally pleased. Sir Reginald's frail health had
been among his wife's most amiable attractions, as it was likely that
the demise of so fond a father would bring them something in the way
of a bequest. That he would have hung on into the seventh year of
the Vernons' marriage was, to Vernon's thinking, an example of the
deCourcy obstinacy.

Vernon had other reasons to reflect upon his father-in-law's demise, for the deCourcy estate had not been entailed entirely from the female line. Only Sir Reginald's son and brother barred Parklands from going to Vernon's eldest son. As far as Lewis deCourcy was concerned, Vernon had no anxiety. He was a bachelor of long standing and it was inconceivable that in his middle fifties he would marry, or bring forth an heir if he did. Reginald, however, was a more troublesome prospect. A union with Lavinia Hamilton was being urged upon him, one that would likely put a succession of deCourcys between Vernon's son and a property worth a clear twelve thousand per annum. To have Reginald single, therefore, was a matter of some consequence to Vernon, and if the burden of responsibility had lessened the charms of his present situation, it had not kept him from wanting more.

To Reginald's credit, he had thus far avoided matrimony as deftly as any young man will when he has plenty of money and no reason to hurry himself into wedlock, but Vernon imagined that a family Christmas at Parklands, with all of the warmth of feeling that the season will generally produce, would weaken Reginald's resolve and end with an engagement.

Vernon was determined to thwart such a prospect by inviting Reginald to Churchill Manor. Charles wrote:

> *We must receive my sister, Lady Vernon. As the necessity of this will keep us at Churchill, I hope that you will not deny your sister the pleasure of having you with us. I would not deprive my good in-laws of your company had I not been assured that they will have Lord and Lady Hamilton and the Misses Hamilton with them. The weather has been so remarkably mild that I ride out every day. The countryside is excellent for a gallop if one's mount is not timid, and there will be some excellent pheasant shooting for many weeks more.*

Charles was fairly certain that Reginald's fondness for sport, and his attachment to Catherine and the children, would bring him to Churchill Manor, but when Mrs. Vernon next received a letter from her brother, there was mention of the particular inducement that had persuaded the young man to make the journey to Sussex.

MR. deCOURCY TO MRS. VERNON

Bennet Street, Bath
My dear sister,

I congratulate you and Mr. Vernon on receiving into your family the most accomplished coquette in England. I can have no kind feelings toward one who so energetically opposed your marriage to Mr. Vernon, and it has lately fallen in my way to hear some particulars of her conduct at Langford, which proves that she does not confine herself to that sort of honest flirtation that satisfies most people but aspires to the more delicious gratification of making a whole family miserable. By her behavior to Manwaring, she gave jealousy and wretchedness to his wife, and by her attentions to Sir James Martin, she deprived Miss Manwaring of a suitor. I learned all of this from Charles Smith, who passed a fortnight at Langford, and who is therefore well qualified to communicate the particulars of Lady Vernon's conduct.

I shall certainly accept your kind invitation, for though I had resolved against any introduction to Lady Vernon, I confess that I long to see her so that I may form my own idea of the sort of bewitching powers that can engage, at the same time and in the same house, the interest of two so very different men as Robert Manwaring and Sir James Martin (though, in the latter case, her motivation was to secure him for Miss Vernon).

I am glad that <u>she</u> does not come with her mother to Churchill, as, according to Charles Smith, she is dull and proud and has not even manners to recommend her. When pride and stupidity are united, they will inspire such unrelenting contempt that even the simulation of notice is too great an exertion, but where pride is joined with the sort of captivating deceit as Lady Vernon is said to possess, the opportunity to witness it cannot be declined.

I shall be with you very soon, and am,

Your affectionate brother,
Reginald deCourcy

This letter was the first information that Mrs. Vernon had of her husband's invitation to Reginald. She was very surprised, but she was so used to being indulged that she supposed Charles's real motive was to console her for the loss of a Christmas at Parklands, and to appease her for having to put up with Lady Vernon. This absolute assurance that affection for her had been uppermost in everyone's mind very nearly reconciled Mrs. Vernon to the inconvenience of hospitality.

chapter twenty-one

ATHERINE VERNON HAD BEEN BRED TO THINK OF HERSELF as a woman of fashion, but a weak understanding and the indulgence of a fond mother had left her susceptible to think too well of herself and too meanly of others.

She went down to meet Lady Vernon's carriage with a determination to be perfectly civil, and yet her greeting was lacking in the warmth and cordiality that might persuade Lady Vernon that they sprang from any genuine feeling. Persuaded as she was that Lady Vernon had objected to her marriage, Catherine might be excused for some coolness, and yet where there is a disposition to dislike, a motive will never be wanting.

Catherine anticipated that her own coolness would be reciprocated, for she quite expected to find Lady Vernon to be a dangerous, cold, and forbidding sort of creature, and was very surprised to find her excessively pretty, with such a union of symmetry, brilliance, and grace that she might have been taken for a woman of no more than five and twenty.

When Catherine ushered Lady Vernon into the sitting room, Lady Vernon made mention of some minor alteration in furnishings and complimented her sister-in-law's taste. She then thanked Catherine for receiving her and added, "I am not apt, my dear Mrs. Vernon, to affect sensations unfamiliar to my heart, and therefore I trust that you will believe me when I declare that as much as I had heard in your praise before this meeting, I see that it was very short of the truth. I am gratified by your kind welcome, particularly as I have reason to believe that some attempts were made to prejudice you against me. I only wish—but upon that subject, let us say no more! I will only thank you for your goodness and Mr. Vernon for his generosity—but I know that he was always the fondest of brothers and I never doubted that he would receive me for dear Frederick's sake."

Catherine Vernon could not be insensible to the effect of Lady Vernon's sweet voice and winning manner. It must be a superior deceit, she decided, and wondered how a disposition that could temper *her* resentful heart might work on her husband's generosity.

"I cannot think where Mr. Vernon has gone to," declared Catherine, and she repeated the phrase whenever the conversation sank into a lull until the appearance of the children relieved her of the exertion.

To Catherine's surprise, Lady Vernon addressed the children in a tone that was frank, gentle, and even affectionate, greeting each child by name and exclaiming over the younger of the two boys, who was her late husband's namesake. "You must be dear little Frederick!" she cried, and careless of her gown, she took the child into her arms and gave him a kiss, and then distributed presents to all of them.

Charles Vernon appeared at last, and summoning a smile of welcome, he cried, "My dear sister!" and took her hands and kissed her cheek in an awkward show of affection.

He then sat down and began to speak very quickly, running from subject to subject and barely pausing to allow for any response, stopping only to turn upon the children and reprimand them for the untidy manner in which they had thrown their wrappings and boxes on the carpet and then to attempt a jovial remark about how the children would make Lady Vernon "long for the everyday commotion of Langford," adding that the Manwarings must have been very sorry to have her leave them so soon.

"I cannot tell if they regretted or welcomed my departure," replied Lady Vernon with a smile, "but Mr. Manwaring supposed that there must be a matter of business that could only be resolved by my coming to Churchill."

Vernon stammered something about Manwaring being a very glib fellow who talked a great deal of nonsense. "He is amiable enough, but if he knew half as much as he ought about business, he would have made a better marriage," he added with a laugh.

"Oh, I believe it was a very businesslike proposal on his part, for he had not a shilling and Eliza had a great deal of money settled upon her. It was Mr. Manwaring's ill fortune that the custodian of her money withheld it from spite—a very ignoble thing for Mr. Johnson to do, do you not agree? Mrs. Manwaring's father had intended for her to have the money and depended upon Mr. Johnson to carry out his wishes. No man of honor could have doubted the *intent*, but perhaps there was just such an informality in the arrangement that allowed Eliza's guardian to withhold it. But I fear this subject does not interest Mrs. Vernon—indeed, the subject of business often becomes either too dull or too heated for many people, and she is not acquainted with any of the principals."

Charles Vernon attempted some weak humor about women and business, and Mrs. Vernon agreed that business was better left to men and that her children gave her all that she needed to think about.

At last, Lady Vernon begged her relations to excuse her, pleading the fatigue of her journey and the desire to rest and refresh herself before dinner. She was shown to her apartments, which were in a very inferior situation that would expose her to all of the noise and traffic of the nursery and the back stair. The rooms themselves were large and well furnished, however, and the windows opened to the back, upon the crisscrossed hedgerow and a portion of the park, with enough of the forcing garden and greenhouses within view for Lady Vernon to observe that they had fallen into disrepair.

"I know nobody in the servants' quarters," Wilson told her mistress. "Even Cook—dear Cook—has been sent away, and I cannot think that the woman who has come to replace her is half so good, though she may do well enough for the family. It is said in the kitchen that it is rare for Mr. and Mrs. Vernon to have anyone to dine, and that they accept very few invitations. The neighborhood must feel such a very great change from Sir Frederick's open hospitality."

"And yet the house itself is unchanged. There has been almost no alteration to the furnishings or in the arrangement of the rooms, no adornments that would have put the Vernons' own stamp upon the property or pronounced their good fortune to the world—nothing save for one change that I do *not* like," added Lady Vernon warmly.

"Sir Frederick's portrait has been removed from the gallery and has been replaced with one of Mrs. Vernon's grandfather."

She was all composure, however, when she went down to dinner and took her place below Mrs. Vernon. Catherine experienced no discomfort until her sister-in-law declined the pheasant curry and the sweetbreads. Lady Vernon apologized for her poor appetite, attributing it to the parting from her daughter and an uncomfortable carriage ride, and declared that a day or two of exercise and fresh air would allow her to do justice to Mrs. Vernon's excellent table. Mrs. Vernon was not consoled; she believed that for all her sweetness of address, Lady Vernon meant to express her contempt for her sister-in-law by taking no more than a plain breast of chicken and a boiled potato.

chapter twenty-two

LADY VERNON HAD DETERMINED, WHEN SHE CAME TO Churchill, that she would make a direct appeal to Charles and the morning after her arrival, she waited until Catherine excused herself from the breakfast table to go up to the nursery. "Stay, if you please, brother," said she, for Charles had made a move to depart. "As happy as I am to be introduced to Mrs. Vernon and my nieces and nephews, I must tell you with all candor that I have other motivations for coming here."

Charles appeared distressed, and glanced at his watch and made some remark about having to ride into the village. "I hope that your apartments are to your liking—they are very near the children, and the children are very lively. They will soon come to an age where some renovation will have to be thought of, and there will be the expense of governesses and masters—yes, it is a costly thing to raise a large family."

"It can be more difficult to provide for one child than four, if you have not the income."

"Yes, but that is not the case with you, as you were left a very fine house in town—a house in town, so handsomely furnished, may be let or sold for a very good price, and there is your own income, which must be above seven hundred pounds per annum. That ought to keep you and my niece quite comfortably until she marries, and she has two thousand settled upon her, has she not? That is very handsome."

"It cannot be said to be handsome, if it is only a portion of what she was intended to have. Charles, I must be frank. If my husband's injury and ill health prevented him from carrying out his wishes as far as Frederica was concerned, is it not for you, his heir and brother, to see that they are fulfilled? You know that he intended to settle ten thousand upon her."

"My dear sister, you suppose that I was in my brother's confidence to a greater degree than was the case. If his motives for leaving matters as he did are obscure to you, who lived with him daily, how much more so must they be to me? All I can know of his intentions were set down in his will, and as this was influenced by the manner of provision favored by our honored father, I must take it to be a genuine expression of my brother's desire. And if that is the case, how can I contradict it?"

Until that moment, Lady Vernon did not know how far she had continued to hope, for the sake of her husband's memory as well as her own comfort and Frederica's future, that her ill opinion of Charles might have been undeserved.

With as much dignity as she could command, Lady Vernon rose from the table and left the room.

They did not meet again until dinnertime, and although the ladies sat for nearly two hours after dinner, the dullness of Mrs. Vernon's company was only relieved by the appearance of the children for half an hour. Charles did not join them.

The next day and the next were much the same—Charles kept himself very much engaged, and though Lady Vernon saw no evidence of anything that could so completely occupy his time, and some very disheartening indications that the property was not being attended to as it ought, he did not appear again at breakfast, nor did he sit with them after dinner. Catherine, without accomplishments or conversation, spared Lady Vernon the pain she might have felt for detesting the husband of an amiable woman. Only the company of her little nieces and nephews gave her any pleasure. They were still too young to have had their tempers impaired by the indulgence of their mother or the neglect of their father.

Thus did the first week of Lady Vernon's return to Churchill Manor pass away.

chapter twenty-three

WITH THE FOOLHARDINESS OF MANY SELFISH MEN, Charles Vernon had thought only of the pleasures of acquisition without the sting of conscience. He was entitled to all that his brother's will had assigned him, and had been in a fair way to arguing himself out of any reproach. Yet while Lady Vernon's reproving gazes could be avoided, the quantity of letters she received could not. Vernon began to put a troubling construction upon each letter she sent off to the post and each one she perused at the breakfast table. He imagined her confiding her situation to the Martins, to Lewis deCourcy, or to one of the gentlemen at the banking house, and although Vernon knew that the law was on his side, they might be prevailed upon to aggravate him with appeals for charity or compassion.

One morning, a week into her visit, Lady Vernon descended much earlier than usual and espied Vernon in the passage, examining the mail that had just been brought in, giving particular attention to the direction on several of the letters.

"Are there any letters for me, brother?" Lady Vernon asked.

He turned upon her with a start and a guilty flush spread over his cheeks. He muttered something about Mrs. Vernon's expecting a letter from her mother that morning. "Why, yes, here are three—no, four!" said he as he handed them over. "So many letters, and so soon after your arrival, but I expect at least two or three of them are from my niece. Catherine and I shall be very eager to hear how she gets on in town."

Lady Vernon made no reply and took her letters to the breakfast table, sensible of the reason for her brother-in-law's discomfort. If he was anxious that she had confided the particulars of their conversation abroad, she was not inclined to make him comfortable by correcting him.

The first letter she opened was from Sir James. She had not sent him any word that she meant to go to Sussex until after she had left Frederica at school. Her letter to him had begun:

> *You will be very happy to know that I have taken your advice and brought my time at Langford to an end. You will be surprised to learn that I do not remain in London to be near Freddie, and you will be angry when you learn where I have gone. I pray you, cousin, do not take up your pen to reply until you have reconciled these incompatible sensations and are capable of making a rational reply.*

Sir James, however, was too impetuous—upon receiving her letter, he immediately dashed off a reply full of astonishment and anger; Lady Vernon found herself smiling at his excessive expressions, certain that the next day's post would bring a retraction that was equally immoderate in its remorse and affection. Lady Martin's letter was more resigned.

> *I am excessively disappointed that you did not come to us. I shall have to put up with James until the new year, with nobody to relieve me of his company. But do not be alarmed for me—if he becomes too troublesome, I have only to remark upon the shabbiness of his attire to get him off to his tailor in London. That is always sure to get me a fortnight of peace and quiet.*

The next letter had her address penned with all of the loops and flourishes of a female hand, but when Lady Vernon opened the sheet, she saw that it was from Manwaring. She read, not without amusement, his dismal accounts of the tedium of Langford and his eagerness to quit it for London.

And when I get to town, you may write to me under the cover of our mutual friend, Alicia Johnson. You need have no fear of our correspondence being intercepted, as Alicia tells me that Mr. Johnson has accepted an invitation from Mr. Lewis deCourcy to pass a few weeks at Bath. Mr. Johnson continues to hate me for taking away his ward when he was so opposed to the match, and I confess that I begin to be on his side. Alicia, however, likes to be on the side of whoever gives her the greater share of participation in a romance. We must not disappoint her.

The last letter was from Mrs. Johnson.

MRS. JOHNSON TO LADY VERNON

Edward Street, London
My dear friend,

We have been very dull here, but it promises to be more exciting, as Manwaring (who has contrived, in spite of Mr. Johnson, to get a letter to me) will come to town before Christmas. He is in a deplorable state and laments over your premature departure from Langford as fervently as Eliza delights in it. I advise you to be as firm with him as you can, lest he commit the grave impudence of attempting to come to you at Churchill. It is said that he will take rooms on Bond Street, and leave Maria and Eliza to shift for themselves. Everything points to a strong desire on both sides to part, and it is only the mutual ambition to get Maria married that keeps them from acting upon it.

Mr. Johnson leaves London next Tuesday. He is going for his health to Bath. He will stay with Mr. Lewis deCourcy, and during his absence I will be able to choose my own society and receive Manwaring without Mr. Johnson reminding me that I had once made some sort of promise never to invite him to our home. Nothing but my being in the utmost distress for a new gown and some ready money could have extorted such a pledge from me, but I consider my promise to Mr. Johnson as comprehending only that I do not invite

Manwaring to sleep in the house or to eat anything beyond a cold luncheon or tea.

Poor Manwaring! In his letter, he gives me such histories of his wife's jealousy! Silly woman, to expect constancy from so charming a man! But she was always silly; intolerably so, in marrying him at all. She was the heiress to a large fortune and nothing else—neither looks, nor good humor, nor sense—she might have had a title and instead settled for a man without a shilling to his name!

I do not in general share the feelings of Mr. Johnson, but when I heard of what she threw away, I quite understand his resolve never to forgive her.

I have had Miss Vernon twice to tea and once to dine—a difficult enterprise, as the conditions under which Miss Summers's charges are permitted to leave the premises are very strict. Your daughter bade me to send you her love and says that she has directed a letter to you by way of the parsonage.

Your affectionate friend,
Alicia Johnson

Lady Vernon had been anxious that she had received no word from Frederica, and rising from the table, she announced her intention to walk to the parsonage and call upon Mrs. Chapman.

Charles Vernon seemed very much alarmed. Though he was not comfortable in his sister-in-law's presence, he did not like to think of her running all over the county and engaging the sympathy of the neighbors. "But see how dark the sky is!" he protested. "It will surely rain."

"It is only a passing cloud or two."

"Then perhaps Catherine will accompany you. Do you not wish to call upon Mrs. Chapman, Catherine?"

"Indeed, no," replied his wife. "I called upon her only last week—my mother does not call upon the parsonage at Parklands Manor above twice a month."

"I would not take Mrs. Vernon away from her more pressing obligations," said Lady Vernon mildly. "I will take Wilson with me."

"If you will wait, I will call for the gig and drive you myself," Charles offered.

"That will not accommodate three of us," Lady Vernon reminded him. "But you are most welcome to walk with us, brother, and we may stop at the churchyard on the way. I ought to have visited Frederick's gravesite upon my arrival. I must not neglect it any longer."

Charles immediately recollected some urgent letters of business that must be written that morning, and stammering an apology for withdrawing his offer, he hurried from the room.

Lady Vernon and Wilson made their way along the neglected road, where it was passable, and crossed lawns and fields, where it was not, until the white fence surrounding the graveyard was in view, and when Lady Vernon saw the stone marker, with nothing upon it but a few humble blossoms, tokens that must have been left by some kindly tenant or villager, she began to weep. Wilson waited patiently while her mistress had her cry and then helped Lady Vernon to wipe her eyes and adjust her veil before they continued on to the parsonage.

Mrs. Chapman was delighted to see them both but declared that she was very surprised to hear that they had walked from Churchill Manor. "For Mrs. Barrett and I called at Churchill Manor not two days ago, and Mr. Vernon informed us that you were too fatigued from your parting from Miss Vernon and your travels for any visiting at all."

Lady Vernon did her best to conceal her astonishment. "I am sure that you misunderstood—I will always be happy to see my old friends while I am at Churchill. I quite depend upon it."

Mrs. Chapman then produced a letter from Miss Vernon. "I got a very pretty note from Frederica—how handsomely she expresses herself—and she enclosed this sheet for you. How I do miss her! Only last year she got my little hothouse going so well that Mr. Chapman and I shall have strawberries into January. What a pity Mr. Vernon has lost most of your groundsmen—I am afraid that Miss Vernon's gardens and greenhouses have quite gone down since your departure."

Lady Vernon took her leave soon after this exchange, but not before she had got Mrs. Chapman's promise to wait upon her at Churchill Manor.

As they walked back, Lady Vernon opened her letter and read it aloud to Wilson.

Miss Vernon to Lady Vernon

Wigmore Street, London
My dear Madam,

You will forgive this expedient for sending my letter, but I do not know who takes in the post at my uncle's house—I do not think that he would scruple to open my letters.

I am getting along well enough here. Each morning we are tutored in deportment and elocution, French, arithmetic, and music, and in the afternoon it is needlework, drawing, and handwriting, after which we are left alone until tea. The other girls employ this time in gossip or trimming bonnets or filigree work, or practicing the new steps taught by the dancing master, who visits once a week. The library is a very poor one, and I do not think I have seen any of the girls take up a book unless it is one of their own novels, which they read aloud and exchange among one another.

We may receive visitors in the open salon but may not go out on our own, and if we are invited anywhere, a carriage must be sent for us. I have been to the theater once with several of the other young ladies, and have gone to Edward Street twice to drink tea and once to dine tête-à-tête with Mrs. Johnson. She laid down a good many hints about Sir James and myself and asked questions that I did not know how to answer. I turned the conversation aside as well as I could, and fortunately there is enough going on at Miss Summers's to supply the diversion.

Lucy Hamilton is immensely popular and receives many invitations, but the only ones she accepts are those where she expects to meet with Mr. Charles Smith, who, it is said, has come to London on purpose to pursue her. It seems that Mr. Smith has been very much in the company of Mr. Reginald deCourcy, which cannot speak well for that gentleman—at Langford, Mr. Smith was so artificial and vain that his friends must be equally so. I do not envy Miss Lavinia Hamilton her prospective husband.

Lucy teases me a great deal about my "beau," and will call me "Lady Martin," and the other girls follow suit. They are all convinced that I have been sent here because I have refused Sir James and think that I am a great fool to set myself against someone who is so handsome and rich.

Please give my warmest affection to Miss Wilson. When you write to me again, you must let me know how my forcing garden and greenhouse fare.

Your obedient daughter,
Frederica Vernon

Wilson listened and then remarked sagely, "If Sir James knows how far everyone thinks of him as Miss Vernon's suitor, it may give him another cause to be angry."

"My cousin has always been rumored to be marrying some young lady or another. He laughed at the gossip regarding Frederica and himself when we were all at Langford—indeed, he encouraged it— and I am glad for anything that reminds Charles Vernon that we have an influential relation who takes our welfare to heart, particularly when he tries to keep us from old friends like Mrs. Chapman and Mrs. Barrett. Why, look! There he is now in his gig, waiting for us upon the road."

Vernon was, indeed, sitting in his vehicle, and when he caught sight of the two women, he slapped the reins and drew up beside them.

"How long you have been gone! Come, take the place beside me— Miss Wilson will excuse you, I am sure, and you look very tired."

"We are almost at the avenue, and the walking does me good."

Vernon was not content to leave them alone and so he reined in the vehicle and walked the horse beside the two women. "You must tell me who you saw. Did you see the Reverend Mr. Chapman?"

"Only Mrs. Chapman."

"And no one else?"

"No one. I took the liberty of asking her to wait upon us at Churchill. I understand that she and Mrs. Barrett attempted to visit and were turned away."

"Oh, surely not! I am sure that I only told them that you were still fatigued from your journey. There will always be time for visiting."

Lady Vernon was spared the necessity of a reply, for as they had got to the drive, a curricle raced toward the house at such an impossible speed that the women were forced to step away for fear of being caught under its wheels. Lady Vernon wondered at a person who drove with such disregard for those in his path.

"Reginald!" cried Vernon.

"It is Mrs. Vernon's brother, Mr. deCourcy," Wilson said in a low voice to her mistress.

The driver, observing the lady standing behind his brother, jumped down and handed the reins to the little groom who had struggled to keep pace with his master.

Reginald deCourcy was a very handsome young man. His eyes were the same color as his sister's, but where Mrs. Vernon's gaze was languid and indifferent, Reginald's was penetrating and lively. He was taller than Vernon, and he moved with the assurance of one who was very pleased with himself and defied anyone else to be displeased with him.

The gentlemen greeted each other formally, and Reginald was introduced to Lady Vernon. She observed that Reginald's bow was somewhat frosty and his address just short of outright impertinence. Her own curtsy was perfectly graceful and polite, which had the desired effect of making him conscious of his incivility, and he seemed close to making some sort of apology when his attention was diverted by his two nephews, who came running down the avenue. He was obliged to take each one in turn and toss him into the air and exclaim at how heavy and tall he had got since he had last seen him. He then lifted them both into the curricle and made a place for himself, and allowing each boy to put a hand on the reins, he guided the carriage, at a more moderate pace, down the drive.

Vernon excused himself and scrambled back into the gig, hurrying it after Reginald's curricle in a manner that brought the women very near to laughter.

"He is quite handsome," Wilson observed as she accompanied Lady Vernon down the drive.

"Yes, and he thinks well of himself, to be sure," Lady Vernon replied. "His greeting was certainly very cool. I imagine that his sister has given him a very pretty opinion of me."

The observation was soon confirmed in a conversation that Lady Vernon overheard not long after. She went up to her apartments to write a reply to her daughter and had got as far as

> You are very good in suffering Mrs. Johnson's notice. We must take it as a mark of her friendship for me, and I ask you to sacrifice a little of your time on my account. A reprieve from Miss Summers's education can do you no harm. For the first week, we were very quiet. Now, however, our party is enlarged by Mrs. Vernon's brother. He is very handsome

when, as the room had got quite warm, she paused to open the casement window above her little writing table. Directly below was a network of slate paths that ran beside the hedgerow, and Mrs. Vernon and her brother walked up and down in earnest conversation.

"We were obliged to receive her, Reginald," Mrs. Vernon was saying. "What else could we do? Charles was always so attentive to his brother, always spending more effort than he ought in trying to keep up the relationship, and now extending his generosity to his brother's widow. In my opinion, money is at the root of her coming to Churchill—she cannot live within her income and so means to impose upon Charles."

"And by his act of charity, your husband admits into your household the most accomplished flirt in all of England. I know from Charles Smith that at Langford she behaved so atrociously that every woman in the household was miserable and wishing her gone."

"You are mistaken there, I think. Eliza Manwaring would not keep up a correspondence if that were so."

"Well, you do not see the letters. They may be from Manwaring himself, for it is said that he is quite smitten with her. Smith tells me that Mrs. Manwaring was made utterly wretched, and that Miss Manwaring, who was in a fair way to catching Sir James Martin, was thwarted by Lady Vernon's determination to attach him to her daughter. Have you met her?"

"No. Lady Vernon has placed her in school in London. Oh, if you could but see her attentions to my children! The hypocrisy of interest and affection from a woman who has neglected her own child—but I am not deceived."

"I must say," Reginald said, somewhat reluctantly, "that as much as I have heard of Lady Vernon's beauty, I was ill prepared for how close it came to truth. But it is what allows her to deceive so many—people will always be taken in by a beautiful woman but never by a plain one."

After this remark, the pair moved out of Lady Vernon's hearing, and she took up her pen once more with a mixture of satisfaction and anger. The latter emotion overwhelmed the former. A lady will always take pleasure in a compliment, particularly if she was not meant to hear it, as such a remark would be more genuine than one made to her face. The insult to Frederica, however, annulled any satisfaction, and it was in an ill humor that she continued her letter to her daughter.

and lively, but insolent; perhaps when I have inspired him with a greater respect for <u>us</u> than the kind opinions of his sister and his friends have encouraged, he <u>may</u> become agreeable. There is an exquisite pleasure in making a person acknowledge his prejudices—it is just the project to occupy my time and to prevent my feeling so acutely the separation from those whom I love.

chapter twenty-four

EGINALD DECOURCY CAME TO CHURCHILL MANOR WITH a premeditated aversion toward Lady Vernon, expressed in a certain condescension, which the lady answered with calmness and reserve. Her manner was so free of vanity, pretension, or levity that Reginald began to wonder whether he might have placed an improper degree of confidence in Lady Hamilton's assertions and Charles Smith's gossip. He resolved to make out her character for himself and began to seek opportunities to engage her in conversation.

A few days after his arrival, he came upon Lady Vernon and his elder niece, a girl of about three years in age. The two were sitting on the ground in a little copse not far from the border of Churchill Wood. Lady Vernon had been showing young Kitty how to collect dried stalks and grass and to weave them into baskets.

"Good morning, Lady Vernon," Reginald greeted her.

She replied with an inviting smile, and so he made some general remark about the mildness of the weather and added, "It is excellent for a sportsman. I have never had the pleasure of shooting in this part of Sussex."

Lady Vernon hesitated just long enough to make the young man recognize his clumsiness. To his credit, he did recognize it and began to apologize.

"Say no more, Mr. deCourcy," she said gravely. "If I have been brave enough to return to the scene of my husband's accident, I cannot shrink from any allusion to it. You have come from Bath, I believe? I hope that you left your uncle in good health?"

"Yes, I thank you."

"I was so very grateful to him for traveling all the way from Bath last summer. My husband's death was so sudden that I am certain many people who *wished* to come were unable to make the journey." She paused just long enough for him to recollect that his own sister had stayed away.

"It would not be in my uncle's nature to do less," said Reginald. "Particularly as he always spoke of your family in terms of such high esteem." He realized as he uttered this remark that he ought to have given as much credit to his uncle's opinion as he had to that of Charles Smith.

Lady Vernon took pity on him and raised another subject. "And how do you like this part of Sussex? You will find it very quiet, I think."

"A household with four children can only be quiet when compared to the animated society of Langford."

"The Manwarings are very fond of company," Lady Vernon agreed. "It was at Langford that I was introduced to a particular acquaintance of yours, Mr. Charles Smith."

"And did you like him?" he said after a moment's hesitation.

"If I did *not*, I would not say so to one with whom he professed a strong and steadfast friendship. It might get back to him in a way that would not do justice to my abuse and then I would be obliged to think ill of both of you."

Reginald deCourcy laughed and perched on a tree stump beside them. "He has very lively manners."

"Yes, very lively. But gentlemen who are not rich cannot afford to be solemn if they want to mix with people of fashion. Such people like to be amused."

"And do you not like to be amused?" he asked.

"I think that reading and a little music and some good conversation are the only diversions that are suitable to my present situation," she replied with perfect composure. "So it is fortunate that they are the ones that I prefer. I understand that you are a great reader."

"Whoever told you so said too much."

"Mr. Smith told the Manwarings that when you were at Bath you spent a great deal of time at the library."

"When he is at Bath, Smith reads only *the* book. To him, anything more would be too much and any time away from the Pump Room would be too long. I am enough of a reader to see that Churchill Manor has a very superior library."

"The late Mr. Vernon laid out a very good foundation, and my husband added to it considerably. Our daughter has always been a great reader, and the mere mention of this title or that from her would have my husband sending around to every bookseller in England."

"Such devotion between father and daughter is remarkable. She must miss him all the more for it."

"Yes, her spirits have been greatly depressed," Lady Vernon replied. "Those who have only known her since her father's accident will find her to be quiet and aloof, I am sure, but they do not know what she was before. I hope that in the company of other young ladies, she will become herself once more. She is very fond of your cousin, Miss Lucy Hamilton, who is all liveliness and good humor—her high spirits can only raise Frederica's."

"Yes, Lucy is very far from quiet and aloof." Reginald laughed. "She will make Miss Vernon more cheerful, and Miss Vernon will, perhaps, make Lucy more prudent. I cannot speak for Miss Vernon, but for Lucy it will be a very great improvement."

"That is because you are only a cousin." Lady Vernon smiled. "A fond mother will always think her child is beyond any improvement."

chapter twenty-five

L ADY VERNON CONCLUDED THAT THERE WAS NO GREAT
mystery to winning over Reginald deCourcy. He only wanted
to be listened to. His parents dictated, his sister criticized, his
friends gossiped, but none of them paid heed to any of his replies.
With Lady Vernon, he experienced the novelty of being asked for his
opinion and the satisfaction of giving an uninterrupted response.

She observed that his education had been thorough, his understanding was sound, and his tendency to think well of himself had not
predisposed him to think meanly of others. His gentleness with his
young nieces and nephews, his regard for his uncle Lewis deCourcy,
and his very handsome countenance and figure were all to his advantage, and Lady Vernon's opinion of him had improved by the time she
next wrote to Mrs. Johnson.

> Mr. deCourcy is certainly a very handsome young man. He is less
> insinuating in his manner than Robert Manwaring, and not as teasing
> as Sir James. He is lively and clever; his mind has not been idle, and
> he has a natural curiosity that makes his conversation more to my
> taste than Mr. Vernon's or his wife's.

Her good friend, always eager to find romance and intrigue in
every situation, immediately dispatched a reply filled with the sort
of errant good wishes which indicated that Lady Vernon's praise of
Reginald had been thoroughly misunderstood.

MRS. JOHNSON TO LADY VERNON

Edward Street, London
My dear friend,

I congratulate you on Mr. deCourcy's arrival and advise you by all means to marry him. I hear the young man well spoken of and though no one can really deserve you, my dear Susan, there are reasons that he may be worth having. His father is very infirm and not likely to stand in your way long, and the estate is considerable and entailed upon Mr. deCourcy—after that, only his uncle Lewis deCourcy keeps Parklands from passing to the issue of the female line. Charles Vernon has got enough out of the deCourcys, and if he has squandered it, it is nobody's fault but his own. Mark my word, he will want to keep Reginald at Churchill Manor as long as the Hamiltons remain at Parklands, as he cannot look forward to a marriage that will put another half-dozen deCourcys between himself and so valuable an estate. How diverting to think that his efforts to keep deCourcy from one wife have thrown him in the way of another!

By all means, engage the affections of young deCourcy as quick as you can. You will be very little benefited by the match until the old gentleman's death, except for the enjoyment of Mrs. Vernon's distress. Her ability to influence her brother's opinions has always been a point of pride with her, and she will be rightly humbled to see how little the advice of a sister can go to prevent a young man's being in love if he chooses it. Lady Hamilton and Miss Hamilton will storm, and poor Manwaring will not be easily consoled, for ever since you were left so rich there have been whispers that he is scheming to effect his emancipation from Eliza on purpose to ask for your hand. I am convinced that there is no true affection anywhere—everything is all about money!

I have seen Sir James, who has come to town to visit his tailor. I gave him what hopes I could of Miss Vernon's relenting and told him a great deal of her improvements, and yet he would speak of nobody but

you—indeed I was persuaded that he would marry either of you with
pleasure. He is as silly and agreeable as ever.

Your faithful friend,
Alicia Johnson

Mrs. Johnson was so far persuaded that an engagement between
her friend and Reginald deCourcy was probable that she did not wait
for her friend to contradict it before she began circulating around
London that, despite a tacit understanding with Miss Lavinia Hamilton, young deCourcy had fallen entirely under the spell of Lady
Vernon.

The rumor was well established by the time Charles Vernon was
obliged to go to town for two days in order to attend to some matters
at the banking house and collect his dividends. He departed in high
spirits—a respite from the agitation that Lady Vernon's presence had
produced and the prospect of getting his hands on money and spending it at cards made him very happy to quit Churchill Manor for London. Men, however, must talk about something when they are at
cards, and polite inquiries after Lady Vernon's health and spirits were
followed by congratulations upon the likelihood of her being an even
nearer relation.

Vernon was astonished and disbelieving—Lady Vernon and Reginald had scarcely a fortnight's acquaintance. He imagined the effect
that such a rumor would have upon Lady deCourcy and would *almost*
have been willing to return to Parklands if he might have the pleasure
of hearing the first vehement expression of her disapprobation.

And yet . . . The thirty miles from London to Churchill Manor
were just enough to allow Vernon to consider what might be the advantage to him if such a rumor *were* true.

A new and very rich husband would surely divert Lady Vernon
from any contemplation of what was due from the former one. The
acquisition of Parklands for his line would be more secure than if
Reginald married Lavinia Hamilton, as Lady Vernon had brought
only one daughter into a union of sixteen years.

By the time he alighted from the carriage, Charles Vernon had decided that it would be an excellent scheme to have Reginald marry Lady Vernon, and he began his campaign to promote it upon his first evening home. Though it was Christmas Eve, Catherine had invited nobody to dine and so Vernon was able to address Reginald as soon as the ladies withdrew. He began by remarking that nobody had been in town—"Nobody at all!"—and set it down to the mildness of the weather, which kept everyone in the country. He urged Reginald to think of extending his visit into January and to send to Kent for his horses and hunters so that they might try for foxes when the pheasants gave out. "Catherine and the children will be very happy to have you prolong your stay, and my sister is in such better looks than when she first came that I must think your company does her a great deal of good."

This invitation was accepted with an alacrity that Charles attributed to Reginald's desire to further his acquaintance with Lady Vernon. When they entered the drawing room, Vernon announced, "My love, I have asked Reginald to continue with us a few more weeks. You and the children have been so happy to have him here that I know you will plead his case when you next write to your mother."

Mrs. Vernon's countenance hovered between a smile and a frown. She was very gratified that her husband wished to keep Reginald at Churchill Manor, as she supposed that it was done entirely to please her, but she had, in her husband's absence, seen such marks of a growing intimacy between her brother and Lady Vernon that she was willing to forgo the pleasure of having him remain at Churchill Manor to prevent him from becoming another object of Lady Vernon's idle flirtation. When she next wrote to her mother, therefore, she appealed to Lady deCourcy to hurry Reginald's departure rather than give him leave to stay.

Mrs. Vernon to Lady deCourcy

Churchill Manor, Sussex
My dear Mother,

It is with great reluctance that I communicate anything that might depress my father's health and spirits, madam, but unless something is done to prevent it, you will be deprived of Reginald for more than a holiday season. Charles has invited my brother to prolong his visit, and while I am confident that my husband thinks of nothing but my pleasure, I grow uneasy in witnessing the very rapid increase of Lady Vernon's influence over Reginald. I always regarded her coming with some uneasiness, but very far was it from originating in any anxiety for Reginald—I could not imagine that my brother would be in the smallest danger of being captivated by her after hearing Mr. Smith's account of her proceedings at Langford.

I did not wonder at his being struck with the gentleness and delicacy of her manners, and she is altogether so attractive that I should not wonder at his being delighted with her, had he known nothing of her previous conduct. But now her powers have so offset the accounts of Mr. Smith that Reginald is persuaded that they were all scandalous invention. Only yesterday he actually said that her loveliness and abilities were such that he could almost excuse Mr. Manwaring's feeling the effect of them.

I can hardly suppose that Lady Vernon's desires extend to marriage. She must know that though no formal engagement exists between my brother and my cousin, both families look forward to their union. I am convinced that her object is that of any hardened coquette, namely, the assurance that she is universally loved and admired. But Reginald is young and of such a warm nature that he may not understand that she regards him only as an instrument of her vanity.

I wish you could get Reginald home again under any pretense. I believe that a few hints of my father's precarious state of health, and of Reginald's duty to be at Parklands when the Hamiltons are there, must come from you.

How sincerely do I grieve that she ever entered this house! I wish she would leave us, but Mr. Vernon will not send his brother's widow away. Therefore, if you can get Reginald back to Parklands, it would be for the best.

Your affectionate daughter,
Catherine Vernon

chapter twenty-six

THE NEXT WEEK PASSED IN A SERIES OF QUIET DINNERS and subdued family gatherings. The Chapmans were invited to dine along with another couple or two from the neighborhood, the children sang carols in the servants' hall, the servants assembled to toast the health of their master and mistress, and the mince pies were distributed, but these were the highlights of the season's festivities. Lady Vernon supposed that Charles and Catherine kept the occasion quiet out of respect for Sir Frederick's memory, but Reginald gave her to understand that the Vernons' holiday was quite in keeping with what had been usual at Parklands, and all of his experience with Bullet Pudding and Hunt-the-Slipper had come about when he spent a Christmas season with one or another of his friends.

Much to her dismay, Catherine Vernon realized that, in the wake of Christmas Day, she was obliged to undertake a role for which she had been ill prepared and toward which she was disinclined. She must visit the tenants, and distribute gifts and assistance to the poor, and pay calls to her neighbors and receive them in return, and assure them all that she and Mr. Vernon wished them health and happiness in the coming year. She had never accompanied her mother on such rounds when at Parklands, and all that she had gathered from Lady deCourcy was that one ought not to dispense too much in the way of shillings and sympathy and hot soup as it would only encourage idleness and ill health. When Catherine asked Lady Vernon to accompany her, therefore, it was not only to keep her from Reginald as much as possible but also to catch some hint as to how she was to conduct herself as mistress of the Vernon estate.

Though Catherine did not know how much ought to be given, she had no doubt of getting a warm and grateful reception. She had, for so long, been the beneficiary of flattery and approbation that she had come to expect it as her due. It distressed her, therefore, to see her tenants' smiles bestowed upon Lady Vernon, to hear them inquire after Miss Frederica Vernon before they extended the best wishes of the season to Mrs. Vernon's household, and in the end, she was sorry that she had not left Lady Vernon at home.

On the third day of visiting, Lady Vernon returned to her apartments to find a letter from Sir James. His anger at her going to Churchill was all forgotten—he was all good cheer and gossip.

> *Eliza Manwaring and Miss Manwaring have come to town, the former in pursuit of her errant husband and the latter in pursuit of any husband <u>but one</u>. Prepare yourself for something very shocking—Miss Manwaring <u>does not love me</u>! This I learned from Freddie, who is Miss Manwaring's fast friend. I must reconcile myself to the fact that one who has been thrown at me for so many years has no desire at all to become my wife! To be rejected by the object of one's affection is a terrible thing, but to be rebuffed by one whom a fellow never meant to marry is far more humiliating. And yet—poor Eliza Manwaring is not ready to admit that spinsterhood is a kinder fate than the degree of misery she enjoys as a married woman.*

Lady Vernon had folded up the letter and took up her pen to write a reply when she was startled by a sharp knock upon the nursery door, which was opposite that of her own apartments. The passage was a narrow one, and the nursery door was left ajar, allowing her to overhear a heated exchange between Reginald and his sister. "You do wrong to make our parents uneasy by apprehending an event that no one can think possible," declared Reginald.

"My letter was intended for our mother only," protested Catherine. "A cold that affected her eyes prevented her from reading my letter, which she then placed into our father's hands. Do you now take Lady Vernon's part? Do you forget how strenuously she objected to my marriage?"

"So we have been told—and yet what motive could Lady Vernon possibly have had for preventing a marriage that was materially to Charles's benefit? His family could only welcome a connection with ours."

"It was said that she believed me to be unsuitable and that a union with Charles could not possibly be a happy one."

"But your marriage *has* been a happy one, Catherine, so you must either forgive Lady Vernon if *she* was in error or admit that *you* may have been. If you, who have lived in such retirement, have been the subject of rumor, think how those who live in the world will fall victim simply because it is in their *power* to do wrong. No character, however upright, can escape the possibility of misunderstanding."

"And is that how you account for what was said of her behavior at Langford? You were ready enough, before you came to us, to credit Mr. Smith's word."

"And I blame myself for so readily believing him. You know what Charles Smith is. Though his company is lively and entertaining, he is given to exaggeration and susceptible to gossip. Lady Vernon is exceptionally clever and charming, which will always be an affront to ladies who are less so. As for Mrs. Manwaring, it is said that she has a very jealous nature, and it is likely that Manwaring often gives his wife reason to be resentful of his conduct."

Here some interruption and demand for attention from one of the children put the conversation at an end, and soon after Reginald's steps were heard in the passage.

Lady Vernon spied him from her window as he strode across the park, and rapidly donning her spencer and bonnet, she hurried down the stairs.

She came upon him, pacing up and down between the hedgerows in great agitation, rereading the letter that had been the subject of his quarrel with his sister.

"I beg your pardon," Lady Vernon apologized. "I will not intrude upon you. I will take another path."

"You do not intrude. I have just received a very distressing communication from my father."

"Are your parents well?" Lady Vernon inquired.

"Yes, although I fear that Catherine's last letter to my mother has agitated them both."

"What can she have written that might trouble them? Mrs. Vernon and the children are in good health, and she does not seem to be displeased with Sussex."

"It is not her situation but our friendship that alarms her," replied Reginald. "She communicated to our father a belief that I am taken in by your influence and by her husband's determination always to represent your faults—which my father claims are widely known—in the most softened colors."

"Charles has done a very poor job of defending me, then, if my errors are widely known. Will you tell me a part of what your father writes? I cannot contradict a charge if I am ignorant of it."

"Hear what he says, then." Unfolding the letter, Reginald read:

> "You must be sensible that as an only son and the representative of an ancient family, more than your own happiness is at stake in your choice of a partner. Her family and character must be unexceptionable.
>
> "I cannot help fearing that you may be drawn in by one whose behavior toward you arises from her own vanity, because it is not impossible that she may now aim higher than simply to gain the admiration of a man whom she imagined to be prejudiced against her. Lady Vernon is poor and may naturally seek an alliance which may be advantageous to herself. I have been informed that this person has attached herself to you and that your own partiality for her is no secret. If the accounts of your friends have not persuaded you of this woman's extravagance and dissipation, a father cannot hope to prevail, but I think that your affection for your sister should have been a very strong argument against anything like intimacy with a woman who did, from the most selfish motives, take all possible pains to prevent her marriage to Mr. Vernon.
>
> "If you can give me your assurance of having no design beyond enjoying the conversation of a beautiful and clever woman, I may be restored to some measure of ease while you are away from us.
>
> "I do not wish to work on your fears but on your sense of duty

when I say that it would destroy every comfort of my life if you were
so foolish as to form an attachment to Lady Vernon. Even if you were
at liberty to enter into an engagement, as the husband of such a
person, I should blush to see you, to hear of you, and even to think
of you."

Lady Vernon met this insult with equanimity. "This is a very strange opinion of me, indeed, and I must confess that I cannot hope to do it justice. To be at once poor and extravagant, dissipated and clever, is more than I can manage, I assure you."

"You make light of the situation?"

"Can I do otherwise? How would anger and hostility serve me, particularly when they are directed at a man of Sir Reginald deCourcy's reputation? I would only appear the worse for expressing resentment against a gentleman who is so universally respected. But how can your father, a man to whom I have never even been introduced, have come to these conclusions, particularly if Charles has always represented me in the best light?"

"Something must come from my father's sister, Lady Hamilton. It was she who informed him that you strongly objected to Mr. Vernon's marriage to my sister, and that this opposition was widely known."

"It cannot have been widely known if Sir Frederick and I were ignorant of it," Lady Vernon replied. "We were not even aware that Charles was acquainted with your sister until we were informed of their engagement, and we learned of it *then* only when he made us an offer for Vernon Castle. Our only objection to *anything* was to *that*, for his offer was very low and our circumstances obliged us to get as fair a price as we could. We might have yielded, even at the expense to ourselves, had we not been confident that a marriage to Miss deCourcy would give Charles the ability to purchase wherever he liked and that he would not even have to depend upon coming in to Churchill Manor in order to be well settled. As for the rest of your father's letter, I cannot account for it. I can only conclude that whenever an unmarried woman and a single gentleman are under the same roof, someone or other will have them at the altar. Still, your family cannot believe *that*, as you are engaged to Miss Hamilton."

A troubled look passed over Reginald's countenance. "There is no engagement. Since we were children, my parents and the Hamiltons intended us for each other, but I have made no proposal to my cousin."

"When you do address her, your father will be more at ease."

Reginald made no reply.

"But," Lady Vernon added with great perception, "if you are *not* inclined to marry her, you only prolong your family's groundless hopes and the expectations of Miss Hamilton when you do not make your wishes plain."

"It is not an easy thing to disappoint one's family."

Lady Vernon smiled. "You must think better of your family. My family had settled on someone other than Sir Frederick for me, yet when inclination drew me to another, no estrangement from my parents resulted from it."

"Because they yielded to your preference," he remarked. "And perhaps my own would do the same if there was any young lady I preferred to my cousin, but alas, I cannot even argue that I am partial to another."

"Still, you must not delay a response to your father. If you cannot bring yourself to disappoint him in his *hopes* just yet, you must at least tell him plainly that there is no foundation for his present *fears*. You must not allow gossip to injure his peace of mind."

He admitted to the soundness of her advice, which was given without any of the attendant arguments and sermonizing that Catherine would have thought necessary. They returned to the house and parted in the hallway, he to write to his father, and she to reflect upon how different her opinion was of Reginald deCourcy than it had been only a fortnight earlier. As they advanced toward something like confidence, she discovered a thoughtfulness of manner and expression that she liked very much, and though he was not without faults, they were principally the faults of youth rather than understanding. If he was too quick to form an opinion, he was always ready to admit his error, and if he was often too inquisitive and demanding of particulars, he was never uncivil.

She could no longer disallow Alicia Johnson's expectations—

indeed, Lady Vernon now *was* thinking of Reginald and marriage together, but the partner she had chosen for him was not herself (however flattered by her friend's conviction that it was in her power) but Frederica. Though little exposed to society, her daughter was Reginald's equal in education and refinement, and though her fortune was insignificant, she was the daughter of Sir Frederick Vernon and the niece of Lady Martin. If Reginald was not bound by honor or promise to his cousin, and if his father asked only that he choose a woman of unexceptionable family and character, was not Frederica a worthy choice?

"He appears a willful young man," declared Wilson, "but there is something to be said for a spirit that has borne up against Mrs. Vernon and Lady deCourcy. The right young lady might take away that last bit of conceit in his manner, and then I will like him almost as well as I do Sir James. But," she added, "if he believes that Miss Frederica is intended for Sir James, he will not put himself forward."

"I think he would put himself forward *because* he believes she is intended for another, and if he is persuaded that she is opposed to the match, so much the better. He has the deCourcy stubbornness after all, and will go after what he thinks he cannot get."

chapter twenty-seven

MRS. JOHNSON TO LADY VERNON

Edward Street, London
My dear Susan,

I wish you the very best greetings of the season and suspect that this may be among the last letters in which I will address you in the name of "Vernon," as, despite your protestations, you are likely to take up another name in the coming year. Until that time I caution you to be on your guard against Manwaring. He is so determined to avoid Eliza in town that he talks of accompanying Maria when she goes to Billingshurst in January—he will take any excuse that brings him down to Sussex, and if he comes as far as Billingshurst, he will be teasing you to get him admitted to Churchill. A little jealousy is a good thing, but Manwaring's may lead him to press his suit in a manner that will strain your understanding with Mr. deCourcy.

Miss Vernon continues as obstinate as ever, and her opposition to marrying Sir James—which is talked of everywhere—ought to be very provoking to Maria Manwaring, who has tried to get him for so many years. And yet they are fast friends! What a perverse world it is!

Until *that* union can be accomplished, we are all diverted by a courtship of another sort. The youngest Miss Hamilton gave up her Christmas visit to Parklands Manor on purpose to stay in town and carry on a flirtation with Charles Smith! His wooing is copied out of the worst sort of romantic novel, but as she never can read two pages *before she is overcome with boredom, she finds his flattery quite original and is silly enough to think that he would take her if she did <u>not</u> come with thirty thousand!*

If nobody intervenes to prevent it, I suspect she will do something foolish. What a delicious scandal it would be to have the eldest Miss Hamilton cheated out of a match with deCourcy and the youngest throw herself away on Mr. Smith.

Adieu!
Your affectionate friend,
Alicia Johnson

Lady Vernon could only shake her head at her friend's stubborn conviction that a marriage with Reginald deCourcy was her object.

"Is your letter from Miss Vernon?" inquired Reginald politely (as they were at the breakfast table).

"No, it is from my friend Mrs. Johnson."

"I do not think that you have had one letter from Miss Vernon in *all the time* you have been with us," observed Catherine. "Our mother writes to me that Lady Hamilton has had a half dozen letters from Lucy since she has been at school."

"Perhaps," Reginald said with a smile, "Miss Vernon does not possess our cousin's freedom of expression and quantity of paper."

"I am sure that anything Frederica would like to say will keep until I go to London," said Lady Vernon.

"Oh, but it is too early to talk of your departure!" cried Charles, who did not wish her gone until she had got Reginald to make her an offer. "We will not think of your leaving us, do you not agree, my dear?"

Catherine did *not* agree. She looked eagerly toward the date when Lady Vernon and Reginald would be divided before any real harm was done. She said nothing until Lady Vernon left the room and then immediately exclaimed, "How very deficient our niece must be in her education! Not one letter all this month! Such a negligent correspondent! Such indifference to duty and decorum does not speak well for the manner in which she was brought up."

"You judge the custom of all daughters by your own, Catherine," said Reginald. "Perhaps it is not that Miss Vernon writes too seldom but that you write too often."

Catherine favored him with a reproving glance. "Indeed, one cannot write too often," she replied. "I begin to understand Lady Vernon's eagerness to hurry along her daughter's engagement. It is likely that Miss Vernon is so wanting in character that she is past reform, and Lady Vernon may want her married before Sir James can find it out."

"And yet," protested Reginald, "a cousin who has known her since she was a child must be more sensible of Miss Vernon's defects than we, who have never met her. So we must hope for Sir James's sake that she is *not* beyond reform."

"And let us hope that other gentlemen of fortune know better what is due to their families," Catherine replied.

"I will go upstairs and write to our mother this minute." He laughed and left the table.

Catherine could not conceal her chagrin. She had suffered her husband's affection for his brother, which had him always running up to Portland Place or off to the country at Sir Frederick's invitation, but it was exasperating to have him imposed upon by Lady Vernon and to see Reginald apprehended in her coldhearted ambition.

"Reginald is too blind, and you are too little in Lady Vernon's company to see how artful she is," Catherine protested to her husband. "One is too apt not to look beyond a gentle, frank, and even affectionate manner to see the deception beneath it."

"And what would be the purpose of such deception?" inquired Charles.

"To reverse all that Reginald has heard of her. With that happy command of the language which is so often used to make black appear white, she has even persuaded him that she is fond of her daughter—and yet why does she come to us and leave Miss Vernon in London? How many successive springs did *she* divert herself in town while Miss Vernon was left in Staffordshire to the care of her governess and servants? Oh, if only she had been left rich! She would have been the object of so many lovers that she would not think to engage in a flirtation with one who is ten years younger than herself!"

Charles could make no reply, for what would his wife have said if she knew how far he had exerted to keep Lady Vernon from being left rich, and that he was attempting to promote the very union to which Catherine so strenuously objected?

chapter twenty-eight

W HILE LADY VERNON WAS BEING ABUSED BY HER SISTER-in-law, she and Wilson walked to the parsonage and retrieved a long letter from Frederica.

MISS VERNON TO LADY VERNON

Wigmore Street, London
My dear Madam,

The separation from you, at this particular time of the year, is made bearable by the company of some friends from Staffordshire. I have had the pleasure of seeing Anne and Mary Clarke, who are now Mrs. Frank Edwards and Mrs. Phillip Edwards; they were married only two days ago, and were in town to pass a few days before departing for a honeymoon in Brighton.

Mrs. Johnson, upon learning that I had been visited by acquaintances from Staffordshire, pressed me to introduce them to her, and she invited all of us to drink tea at Edward Street. Her latest scheme is to have the sort of salon where people of fashion come together. She fills up her drawing room with people and Mr. Johnson hides away in his library. It is not my notion of conjugal felicity, but for them it appears to be a very effective arrangement.

She is as silly as ever, but I have discovered that Mr. Johnson is not the ogre that he was made out to be. On my most recent visit, Mrs. Johnson invited me to examine the library, as her husband was not at home. I was looking over an edition of Mr. Darwin's <u>The Botanic Garden</u> when Mr. Johnson appeared. I immediately begged pardon, and I remarked upon the excellence of his collection, which is far superior to the library at Miss Summers's. He made some gruff reply. "Mrs. Johnson tells me that Sir Frederick left you enough to get all the books you like—of course, there is no sum that will replace an excellent parent." He then hemmed a bit and said that I may borrow any of his books if I promised to return them in good time, and that if Mrs. Johnson ever had more people than I could bear to put up with in her parlor, I was welcome to make use of his library.

I confess that I do not find him an ill-looking man, and if a gentleman's taste and refinement can be inferred from his library, Mr. Johnson is a very superior person. His efforts to make some sort of conversation with me were awkward, but not at all coarse or ill bred, and after inquiring how I passed my time at Miss Summers's, he asked whether I had any particular friends.

"I am particularly friendly with Maria Manwaring. She does not go to school, but I hope to see her now that she has accompanied her sister-in-law to town." I did not realize my error until I had uttered the words. The gentleman gave a sort of sigh and made some remark about the evils of making a bad match.

I replied that a bad match may have been formed with the very best intentions, and that it was an unhappy situation when the penitence that the errant party must feel was aggravated by a more general censure. "And in any case," I added (though I cannot believe my boldness in speaking so), "I do not think that the censure ought to comprehend someone who was only a child at the time of her brother's marriage."

Mr. Johnson hemmed once again and then said, "If this person—Miss Manwaring—is a particular friend of yours, I cannot object—indeed, I do not object to anything at all. I keep out of the way entirely. Mrs. Manwaring was a very good sort of girl at one time, but nothing will ruin a good disposition like a bad match."

I did not think that I ought to give an opinion on the subject, so I merely thanked him again for the offer of his library and joined Mrs. Johnson once more.

*My uncle was in town last week on some matter of business, and
he called at Wigmore Street, but I saw nothing of him. I dare not hope
that his business was anything that might benefit us or that he has had
any change of heart where we are concerned—or any heart at all.*

Please give my warmest regards to Miss Wilson.

Your obedient daughter,
Frederica Vernon

From the window of his study, Charles Vernon spied Lady Vernon
walking slowly down the avenue, leaning upon Wilson for support.
Her regular visits to Sir Frederick's grave were becoming a source of irritation to Vernon, as he was persuaded that they were done as a reproach to him. If, he reasoned, Lady Vernon would not so regularly
indulge her misery she might turn all of her energies toward the heir
to Parklands, who was one of the richest young men in all of England.
Her beauty had been proof against her trials, and when she exerted
her full powers, there was no lady more charming. Lately, however,
she chose not to exert; instead, she would spend much of the morning
in her apartments or walking to the churchyard, often not joining the
family until dinnertime. In the evening, her spirits did revive, but it
would take more than a few hours of clever conversation after dinner
to reverse the effects of many hours' seclusion. Vernon did not doubt
that Reginald admired her, but that admiration must be hurried apace
to love if an offer of marriage was to be made before one or the other
of them took leave of Churchill.

Lady Vernon's lassitude was not affected to plague Charles Vernon,
but rather it rose from a perplexing fatigue, which often left her not
well enough to leave her apartments until after noon and with no appetite at all until dinner. She concluded that the return to a place that
held both the happiest and unhappiest of memories must have the
sort of violent effect upon her emotions, which, in turn, put a drain
upon her health.

It was a visit to the parsonage that suggested to Lady Vernon that
her symptoms might have a more astonishing origin. While she was
there, Mrs. Barrett happened to call, accompanied by her eldest

daughter, who was two or three years older than Frederica, and her youngest, who was a lively boy of six. As the other five Barrett children had remained at home, Lady Vernon found herself particularly struck by the great disparity in the ages of the eldest and youngest Barretts, and she began to wonder whether the enervating symptoms that had distressed her for so many weeks might be set down to something more than unhappiness and exertion.

Her first impulse was to reject the notion as impossible, and then to wonder whether it *might* be possible, and at last to acknowledge that it *must* be—that after so many years of wishing for, and at last despairing of, an addition to Sir Frederick's family, this hope was to be fulfilled at the most incongruous time!

The emotions that must necessarily be attendant upon such a discovery overwhelmed her and many hours passed before Lady Vernon could compose herself sufficiently to calculate, with any degree of assurance, when the anticipated event might take place, and how completely her situation would change if the child should be a son, for a son would displace Charles Vernon as the heir to all of Sir Frederick's property and fortune.

chapter twenty-nine

UPON THE SIXTH OF JANUARY, WHILE THE CHILDREN WERE exclaiming over their gifts and Mrs. Vernon was expressing her satisfaction that they had all "got through Christmas," an express was handed in to Lady Vernon. She immediately opened it and read it in a great hurry.

MISS SUMMERS TO LADY VERNON

Wigmore Street, London
My dear Lady Vernon,

Do not be alarmed by any thought that Miss Vernon has come to harm, but I regret to inform you that your daughter must be removed from my institution at once. I deeply regret the necessity of this, but as the misconduct of any pupil may injure the reputation of my establishment, I cannot do otherwise.

The incident that compels me to take this action was the following: Miss Vernon left the premises without seeking permission or enlisting a chaperone. Fortunately, she was intercepted before she had got far from Wigmore Street. Although our rules may be somewhat relaxed for the holiday season, our <u>standards</u> cannot be. To run away in this fashion was a serious infraction, and one that I cannot overlook, particularly since I could not compel Miss Vernon to acknowledge any cause for her extraordinary conduct. When I sought a private explanation of it from the other pupils, they maintained that an engagement has been formed between your daughter and Sir James Martin, and that Miss Vernon is strongly opposed to the match and meant to run away from an enforced union.

At the present, Miss Vernon is with the Johnsons on Edward Street, who have agreed to keep her until you can make your arrangements to retrieve her. I deeply regret this circumstance as, until this serious breach and despite her excessive propensity for intellectual pursuits, Miss Vernon had been a model of deportment.

Yours most sincerely,
H. Summers

Lady Vernon uttered an exclamation of dismay.

"What news?" Charles Vernon cried.

His wife prudently dismissed the servants and Lady Vernon waited for the door to close upon them before she would speak. "The letter is from Miss Summers. She claims that Frederica left the school without permission, and Miss Summers considers this a very serious infraction and says that Frederica must be removed at once."

"Removed?" exclaimed Charles. "Do you mean to say that my niece tried to run away? Where is she now?"

"She has been taken in by my friend Mrs. Johnson."

"What can have compelled her to act in such a manner?" Catherine asked.

"I am certain that it is all a simple misunderstanding. The daughters of our friends from Staffordshire had passed through London, and I am sure that Frederica did not think that she must ask leave only to call upon them. If you will excuse me, I will write to Miss Summers immediately. I must prevail upon her to take Frederica back until I can make arrangements to go to town."

"No," declared Reginald. "A personal address is more effective than a letter, and more expedient, for the horses and carriage can be ready in under half an hour and it is only thirty miles to town. Charles, you are her uncle—you must go and set matters right."

Charles Vernon was dumbfounded at this suggestion and Catherine protested the exertion, but Reginald stood firm. "If Miss Vernon did nothing but to pay a visit without proper dispensation, an uncle's address can defend her as ably as a mother's letter, and perhaps better, for you, Charles, are known about London as a man of business and your connection with the deCourcy family must bring some influence to bear."

Reginald may well have meant to flatter his brother-in-law, but it did not please Charles to be reminded that he owed much of his importance in the world to his wife's family.

Lady Vernon did not yield easily to this plan. She would rather have made the journey herself, but reason prevailed, for a gentleman might travel the thirty miles more speedily and with less encumbrance than a woman who was in a delicate state. "Very well," she said at last. "But delay, I pray you, so that I may write a note for you to carry to Miss Summers."

Lady Vernon wrote a letter that laid out all of the arguments in favor of Frederica's remaining at Miss Summers's Academy. Her daughter's tractable and helpful disposition, her amiable conduct, her excellent progress in her studies, all spoke in favor of this being a lapse that had more of the *appearance* of misconduct than the *substance* of it.

> I must think that this must all weigh heavily in my daughter's favor—however, if you will not return her to school, I will ask you to keep her only long enough for me to make my preparations to come up to London.

When Vernon had departed, Lady Vernon addressed her sister-in-law. "Have no fear that you will be imposed upon by this very distressing turn of events. I am certain that Miss Summers will see reason."

"If you will forgive me," Catherine replied coolly, "it may be more to the point to understand why Miss Vernon acted as she did, lest she be returned to school only to run away again. I cannot blame you for wanting to improve her abilities, but it may be that Miss Vernon is too used to doing as she likes to accommodate herself to the rigors of instruction, particularly when they are forced upon her by the ambitions of a parent."

"Ambitions?" cried Lady Vernon.

"My cousin, Miss Lucy Hamilton, has written to her mother of your desire to promote a marriage between Miss Vernon and Sir James Martin, and that your daughter is not at all inclined toward the match."

Lady Vernon would have denied this assertion if she thought that there was any possibility of her being believed, and so she replied in more general terms. "What mother would not regard it as the highest compliment to have her daughter the object of a gentleman who is so eligible in terms of family and fortune? I know that you do not mean to reproach me, sister. You will comprehend my feelings better on that day, many years hence, when you have the happiness of bestowing dear little Kitty and Regina upon gentlemen of excellent connections and unexceptionable character."

Lady Vernon then excused herself, saying that she had letters to write before the next post. She had no sooner left the room than Catherine declared, "If Lady Vernon had not neglected her daughter for so many years, Miss Vernon would not find the rigors of school so far above her ability and inclination."

"Perhaps it is marriage rather than education toward which she is disinclined," suggested Reginald. "I understand that she has been left nothing in the way of fortune and *that* neglect will affect her future more than a want of schooling."

"You are wrong, Reginald. Charles has told me that both Miss Vernon and her mother have been left quite independent, and certainly Lady Vernon has friends enough to enable her to live in comfort at no expense to herself for as long as she likes."

"We cannot agree here, Catherine, for your notion of comfort is *my* notion of dependence. I could not call Lady Vernon independent unless she had the resources to live well *without* imposing upon her friends or relations. Her own marriage was said to be such a contented one that I cannot think she would encourage Miss Vernon into an unhappy union if she was able to make an entirely disinterested choice."

Catherine said no more, as she had no wish to add to Reginald's attachment to Lady Vernon by portraying her circumstances to be desperate; yet, when he excused himself, she began to reflect, more thoroughly than she ever had before, on how much Charles meant to settle upon Kitty and Regina. If Sir Frederick Vernon had not sufficiently provided for *one* daughter, could her husband (whom, she must privately acknowledge, had been less than prudent in matters of money) be more capable of providing for two?

chapter thirty

CATHERINE VERNON WITHDREW TO HER DRESSING ROOM, and sat down to pour out her feelings in a letter to her mother.

MRS. VERNON TO LADY DECOURCY

Churchill Manor, Sussex
My dear Mother,

We have all been stirred up by a scandal here. Miss Vernon has been apprehended in some flagrant infraction, and she has been dismissed from Miss Summers's Academy. It seems that Miss Vernon attempted to flee from the school, and while Lady Vernon makes it out to be an innocent error, I must think from some communication with my Aunt Hamilton that the real motive for this conduct is her mother's determination to force the girl into a marriage with Sir James Martin, much against Miss Vernon's inclination and before she has even had time to mourn her father, to whom she was, I understand, very much attached.

It is fortunate that there was an acquaintance in London to take her in, or she would have nowhere to go. Mr. Vernon set off for town in order to prevail upon Miss Summers to allow Miss Vernon to continue with her and, indeed, when one considers her connection to our family, I cannot understand Miss Summers being nice upon any point of propriety unless, perhaps, Lady Vernon has been as flagrant in

*money matters as in all else. If Miss Summers has not been paid in an
orderly fashion, she may look for a reason to discharge a pupil whose
tuition cannot be depended upon.*

*If it is only that which prevents her from retaining Miss Vernon, I
would not be surprised if my husband supplied what is wanting, as
befits his generous nature.*

*I fear that her ladyship may call upon this occasion to stir up Regi-
nald's most tender feelings. Her distress upon the receipt of Miss Summers's letter had every appearance of being genuine, but for my own
part, I cannot think that anyone who has treated her daughter so
heartlessly can feel anything deeply.*

*Lady Vernon appears reluctant to have her daughter brought here
to Churchill, and justly enough, as it would reward, with our hospitality and the appearance of approbation, behavior that deserves our dis-
approval. If, therefore, she cannot be returned to school, her mother
will be compelled to end her visit with us immediately and settle in
town—if I could be certain that this would bring about a permanent
separation between her and Reginald, I would be grateful for Miss
Vernon's expulsion.*

Yours ever, etc.,
Catherine Vernon

Lady Vernon's composure lasted only long enough for her to reach
her apartments before she gave way to all of her pent-up emotions.
Wilson did her best to soothe her mistress and defend her former
charge. "We must not judge before we hear from Miss Frederica. We
have never known her to act rashly, so we have no reason to think
that she has done so in this case. If Miss Summers will not take her
back, she may remain with the Johnsons or even be sent to Lady Martin in Derbyshire."

"There is one household where she must not come," Lady Vernon
replied. "I do not want her here. Mrs. Vernon's hospitality has been
stretched as far as it will go, and I fear that the addition of another
Vernon will break it."

Their discussion was interrupted by the arrival of a second express from town. Lady Vernon broke the seal eagerly and read it aloud.

Mrs. Johnson to Lady Vernon

Edward Street, London
My dear friend,

I know that you have heard of the unfortunate turn of events from Miss Summers. Have no fear, Miss Vernon is safe with me at Edward Street, but prepare yourself for delightful scandal! You will never guess—Miss Lucy Hamilton has eloped with Charles Smith! Such a foolish, romantic, impractical pair! I think that they are very well suited to each other.

Here is how it all came about: Miss Lucy, having agreed to the elopement, left no word but for a note to one of her little protéges, Miss Mary Elliot, who, I understand, is even sillier than Miss Lucy. Not knowing what to do, Miss Elliot gave the letter to Miss Vernon, and she immediately ran after her friend to reason her out of her folly. Alas, Miss Hamilton leapt into a waiting carriage—a hack chaise!—and escaped, and Miss Vernon, knowing nothing of London, wandered about quite lost until she was at last overtaken, not two streets from Miss Summers's.

The hardest part of the matter is that I was to learn all of this from <u>*Mr. Johnson*</u>. *Miss Vernon was so frightened and ashamed at being sent away that she would not say a word to me, but there has been a sort of camaraderie between them that baffles me exceedingly! He invited her to sit in his library until she was calm, and she confided all. To think that I must be indebted to* <u>*him*</u> *for my information, and he would only disclose the matter to me on the pledge that I say nothing to anybody. Silly man! What is the use of having such delicious news if one cannot have the fun of revealing it? All that comes of* <u>*that*</u> *is that everybody puts another motive to her conduct—they believe that she ran away from school in order to escape a forced union with Sir James*

Martin! She will be a laughingstock if nothing is done to prevent it. Would it not be better if she married Sir James at once? Nothing can wipe away a little folly like a fortunate marriage.

You must write as soon as you can, and tell me how they take the news at Churchill and Parklands. Miss Lucy's imprudence can only extinguish any lingering desire Reginald deCourcy may have for a union with her sister, which will leave the way free and clear for you.

Yours, etc.,
Alicia Johnson

Lady Vernon dropped the letter in amazement. Wilson immediately began to praise her charge. "I *knew* that there must be some generous and rational motive for her conduct."

"I am only sorry for the motive that has been *assigned* to her conduct." Lady Vernon sighed. "I must write to my Aunt Martin at once, lest it reach her that Frederica ran away from a forced marriage with James."

LADY VERNON TO LADY MARTIN

Churchill Manor, Sussex
My dear Aunt,

I have been so negligent a correspondent that you will come to think that I never mean to write unless something has gone terribly wrong. Be assured that we are well, but a misunderstanding has resulted in Frederica's dismissal from school. I beg you, Aunt, if you have no choice but to laugh or to be angry, please laugh, for those who will come out ridiculous in the end do not bear the name "Vernon" or "Martin," so we may yet hold out the hope of some diversion at their expense. It is said that Frederica fled from school in order to escape an enforced marriage to James—I give you permission to laugh here.

The truth does Freddie far more credit. It seems that she ran away in an attempt to intercept Miss Lucy Hamilton before Miss Lucy could elope with Mr. Charles Smith. Alas, she failed to overtake the foolish pair; they made their escape and Frederica was apprehended. She would say nothing of the matter—perhaps in some mistaken desire to preserve Miss Lucy's reputation as far as she could—and so the giddy young ladies at Miss Summers's have set her up as the heroine in a novel, who flees from a forced marriage.

All of the family here are ignorant of Miss Lucy's situation. I daresay they will hear from Parklands soon enough, but in the meantime, they all believe that Frederica is entirely in the wrong, and Mrs. Vernon does not hesitate to attribute it to my failure as a parent.

Frederica is with Mrs. Johnson (who has been of some use as a friend and correspondent) and Mr. Vernon has gone to London to persuade Miss Summers to allow Frederica to remain—but if she cannot, I will go up to London as soon as I can make preparations to leave Sussex.

As much as you detest London, my dear Aunt, can I prevail upon you to pass a few months with me at Portland Place? When I tell you the nature of my request, I do not think you will refuse me—but you must prepare yourself for a very great shock. I have very lately come to realize that the happy event that Frederick and I continued to hope for in the years following Frederica's birth will occur after her father's death. The significance of this, most particularly if the child should be a son, makes me wish to be safely in town, and in the care of one upon whose counsel and protection I can unreservedly rely. If I believed that I could tolerate the journey to Derbyshire, I would impose upon the hospitality of Ealing Park. I do not think that I am quite strong enough to go beyond London, however, and though Mrs. Forrester manages the household with discretion and skill, and Wilson has been an invaluable companion, your presence would be of immeasurable help and comfort.

I will take no one into my confidence save for Frederica and Wilson, and I beg you, say nothing to James. I will leave Churchill before it can become evident to Charles, who cannot rejoice in the possibility that he might be deposed and thrown back upon the *deCourcys' charity once more. Yet a daughter would be no sacrifice to me. If Freddie is any example, she will be a superior creature in every respect, and, if that should be the case, may I be so bold as to bestow upon her the name of Elinor?*

Your affectionate niece,
Susan Vernon

chapter thirty-one

WHEN THE FIRST COMMUNICATION FROM CHARLES arrived, Lady Vernon was certain that it must bring word of
Lucy Hamilton's elopement. Catherine read through the
letter with composure, however, and announced only that Charles
had arrived safely in town. Lady Vernon decided that Charles meant
to delay, perhaps hoping that someone else would write to his wife and
spare him the unpleasant task of communicating the news. She said
nothing, therefore, although it was difficult to remain silent while her
sister-in-law made pointed allusions to *parental neglect* and *youthful
misconduct.*

On the second morning after Charles Vernon's departure, Catherine was handed a letter, which Lady Vernon believed *must* contain
news of Miss Hamilton.

"Is it from my brother?" inquired Reginald.

Catherine's expression had settled into a puzzled frown. "He writes
that Miss Summers will not take Miss Vernon back and that he is
bringing her here to Churchill."

Lady Vernon protested that Charles could not have proposed a
scheme that was contrary to her wishes and instructions.

"Perhaps Miss Vernon does not like to remain in London if Sir
James Martin is there," suggested Reginald.

Lady Vernon did not trust herself to reply and rose from the table.
From the breakfast-room window, Catherine and Reginald saw her
walking away from the house in considerable agitation.

"Such a false show of distress!" cried Catherine in disgust. "What can one say of such a mother! How inexcusable are those women who forget what is due to family and to the opinion of the world!"

"I can only suppose that it distresses Lady Vernon to burden you and my brother with her daughter," Reginald replied.

"She did not hesitate to burden us with herself when we would rather have gone to Parklands for Christmas. She is only sorry to have Miss Vernon come to us because she would rather have her daughter where she might be thrown together with Sir James. But that is Charles's way—he is far too generous and compassionate to compel his niece to remain where she must often meet with a suitor toward whom she is evidently opposed."

"It must always be considered an unpleasant thing to be pushed into a marriage against one's inclination" was all that Reginald would reply before he excused himself and went outside to find Lady Vernon.

She had walked almost to the boundary of Churchill Pond and was pacing to and fro.

"You must come back to the house. You are very distraught."

"I am distraught only on my daughter's behalf."

"Yet would you have Miss Vernon be tranquil? If she has acted imprudently, it is *right* that she *should* feel something like distress."

"Indeed, she has no cause to feel *anything* like it," Lady Vernon replied with some warmth. "She can be blamed for no more than having so little understanding of the world as to be ignorant of how even the most generous impulse can go wrong."

"What generosity?" Reginald inquired. "She has shown no generosity toward her mother by causing you such anxiety by running away from school."

"I am very sorry, Mr. deCourcy. There are people who delight in being the bearers of bad news, but *I* am not one of them—yet my daughter's conduct must be defended. I have it on very sound authority that Frederica's motive in running away was to apprehend your cousin, Miss Lucy Hamilton, before Miss Hamilton could elope with Mr. Charles Smith. Frederica was not able to intercept them, and only succeeded in being comprehended in her friend's folly."

"What?" he demanded. "Lucy and Charles Smith? It cannot be

true! Smith would not impose upon his friendship with our family in such a manner!"

Lady Vernon endeavored to speak more calmly. "Mr. Smith has *imposed* upon the connection, to be sure, but I cannot think that he would *abuse* it by inducing Miss Lucy Hamilton to elope with any intention other than marriage."

"My poor Aunt Hamilton! She will be shocked beyond words!"

Lady Vernon refrained from observing that she did not believe Lady Hamilton had ever experienced any emotion that had put her beyond words. "Lady Hamilton will be very distressed, to be sure, but upon reflection I cannot think that she will be surprised. Even when we were all at Langford, your cousin and Mr. Smith seemed very much attached to one another."

"Her family wished a much more advantageous union for her," he said.

"We all wish our daughters to marry advantageously, but at least there is fortune on one side and affection on both. However impulsive her conduct, with so large a fortune, your cousin can afford to marry where she likes."

"If my cousin and Charles Smith were so resolved upon their course, how can Miss Vernon have hoped to intervene?"

"It is likely that Frederica ran after them with no other thought than how wrong it would be of her to do nothing. My daughter has a very tender heart and would have been very hard upon herself if some harm had come to Miss Hamilton that her intervention might have prevented—from the day of her father's injury, Frederica had been very conscious of the advantage of immediate action and the consequence of delay. When she came upon her father, to find him lying senseless upon the ground, with Charles rooted in shock and incapable of any exertion, the incident left her very mindful of the necessity for immediate action in any emergency. I can only hope that Charles will not take the opportunity of their journey to resurrect *that* subject, as it is a very painful one for Frederica and can only stir up unpleasant memories and speculation."

"What speculation can there be?"

"Every tragedy gives rise to conjecture," replied she. "There is too little diversion in a common accident—some feature of it will inevitably be attributed to villainy or vice. As Charles was my husband's successor, it would not take many rounds of gossip to attribute his inaction to gaining *immediately* what would be his *eventually*."

She wisely said no more and allowed his imagination to go to work.

They walked back to the house in silence.

chapter thirty-two

CATHERINE VERNON FELT HERSELF VERY MUCH IMPOSED upon by the necessity of receiving Lady Vernon's daughter. Lady Vernon attempted to soften her sister's humor and to engage her sympathy for Frederica by the most effective method of persuading Catherine to do anything, which was to urge her in the opposite direction.

"I am very sorry that you should be imposed upon," she said to Catherine when they had all sat down to tea. "Though Mr. Vernon has taken it upon himself to bring Frederica to Churchill, I will not ask *you* to put yourself out any more than you like. Whatever the motive for her conduct, she has caused a disturbance in your household, which cannot be treated with leniency. I assure you that I mean to impress this upon my daughter, and if I am too indulgent, I know that I may count on your sensible reproof, and if you are severe upon her, you will hear no word of blame from me."

Catherine was surprised at this address and immediately began to ponder whether the addition of one more to the household would be a *very* great burden—whether she ought to think a *bit* more kindly of Miss Vernon—and, too, she recollected that Charles had once said something of Miss Vernon's usefulness in household duties and tending to the children.

They had just sat down to tea when the carriage was observed coming down the avenue, and after a few moments' delay, the door was thrown open and Miss Vernon entered and threw herself into her mother's embrace.

Reginald did not have any opportunity to form an opinion of Miss

Vernon other than concluding that her mother's apprehensions had been rightly felt, for he had never in his life beheld a more timid creature. She attempted to meet Mrs. Vernon and her brother with courtesy—she made a very pretty effort to give a kiss to one and a curtsy to them both—but after sitting only a few minutes in their presence, she abruptly burst into tears and was hastily escorted from the room by her mother. Reginald had only sufficient time to observe that, though not at all like her mother, Miss Vernon was a pretty enough girl, with large dark eyes and a complexion that promised very fair, had not her distress drained it of all color.

"How very timid she is!" Catherine Vernon remarked. "She did not say above three words—and her dress was very plain. What is your opinion of her, Reginald? She is very different from Lady Vernon."

"I must attribute her plain dress to the fact that she is in mourning, Catherine. But, yes, they are not at all alike. Miss Vernon is not nearly so handsome as her mother. Her complexion is not as vivid and her eyes have no brilliancy at all."

Catherine, determined to contradict any commendation of Lady Vernon, replied, "She had been crying, Reginald. Her complexion is not as radiant as her mother's, yet there is a delicacy about it that I rather like, and though she said so little, her manner was perfectly genteel. How did you find her, Charles, for you had the advantage of her company for thirty miles and can give us a better understanding of her mind and her conversation."

"I did not have much opportunity to address her openly—we were obliged to have Miss Manwaring with us for much of the journey. When I did attempt to speak to her, her responses were so simple as to be almost childish. I confess that I saw no indication that she is the equal of any young ladies of quality. Yet we cannot entirely condemn her—indeed, your family must be indebted to her, my dear." Charles then gave his wife a full account of Lucy Hamilton's elopement, which had ended with Miss Vernon's dismissal from school.

Catherine was shocked into silence.

"Even her benevolence is done poorly," Charles concluded. "If Sir James Martin is a man of any sense, he will not be in a hurry to marry her, unless he is as imprudent as Charles Smith. I daresay the Hamiltons must regret that *he* was ever introduced into the family."

Reginald was properly stung, as it had been he who had presented Mr. Smith to his relations. Catherine, however, was not so sharp, and she replied, "I quite agree with you, Mr. Vernon. We cannot be too quick to be introduced to new people, for we never can know what they are about."

chapter thirty-three

W HEN THEY WERE ALONE, FREDERICA'S SPIRITS, AGITATED by the recent events and her hasty removal from town, soon settled into equanimity.

Lady Vernon inquired of her journey. "What did your uncle say of Lucy Hamilton? Was he very angry?"

"I think he was, although I cannot say whether it was that his family must share in Lucy's folly or that *he* cannot share in Mr. Smith's good fortune. But I was not obliged to suffer his company all the way from town. Maria called upon me at the Johnsons' just after my uncle arrived, and Mr. Johnson inquired, 'Do you not go to visit the Parkers at Billingshurst, Miss Manwaring? I believe Mr. Lewis deCourcy told me that you do, for he is to go there himself in another week or so. Well, then, if Miss Vernon must leave us for Sussex, perhaps you would have the goodness to travel with her as far as your destination.' My uncle did not like this plan, and I was ashamed of his coldness toward Maria on the way to Billingshurst. When we arrived, the Parkers came out to meet us—they were all very civil and invited us to drink tea—but my uncle refused, and not with very good grace."

"And how do you like Mrs. Vernon?"

"Her greeting was more cordial than I expected."

"She believes that I do not want her to show you any affection, and so she is determined to like you in order to spite me. I advise you to accept what kindness you can get from her and not be too nice about the motive. And Reginald? What did you think of him?"

"He is very handsome. I daresay he thinks me quite foolish for running from the room as I did."

"That will not make him think less of you—the company of Hamiltons and deCourcys has accustomed him to foolishness. But what of his manner? Do you find him to be artificial and vain?"

Frederica blushed. "I regret that I had pronounced him so before I had any chance to meet him; science teaches us that insufficient observation will often lead us into error."

"And that the outward appearance may be a deceit or a camouflage," added Lady Vernon. "I give you leave to observe him as *scientifically* as you like. I think you will find him an interesting study. But there is another matter that concerns the natural order of things that I must make known to you." She then told Frederica of her own expectations and addressed the reversal of their own circumstances should her child be a son.

Frederica's reaction was one of astonishment, followed rapidly by concern for her mother's well-being.

"I have always been blessed with extraordinary good health," said Lady Vernon. "You need have no fear for me."

"But if you should have a son! My uncle will be very angry at the prospect that he might be deposed."

"Yes, but we will be in London before he can become aware of my situation. I have taken our Aunt Martin into my confidence. I think it will be sufficient to have her overcome her dislike of town and agree to stay with us at Portland Place. If your uncle should attempt to impose upon us, he will find us in the care of a very formidable guardian."

Their conversation was interrupted by the appearance of Miss Vernon's little cousins. They had always been kept to so close a family circle that anybody new was a great curiosity, and upon their cousin's arrival, they were possessed of such excitement that they ran away from their nursery maids and tumbled into Lady Vernon's apartments.

Frederica greeted them with a sweet and playful smile, which immediately secured their interest, and she shepherded them back to the nursery, entertained them with games and stories until their dinner was brought up, and sat with them while they dined.

CHAPTER THIRTY-FOUR

LADY MARTIN TO LADY VERNON

Ealing Park, Derbyshire
My dear niece,

I am both delighted and shocked at your news—it is what we have always wished for! But to come at such a time! I have given orders for my trunk to be packed in no more than a day—write at once to Mrs. Forrester, for I intend to be settled at Portland Place before you come to town. An "Elinor" would suit me very nicely, yet I cannot but wish for a "Frederick."

As far as the business at Miss Summers's, I commend my grand-niece for acting as she did. To run away from all protection in order to save a friend from an imprudent elopement! To contrive to get away from school and travel as far as two streets before she was overtaken! It is just the mixture of adventure and folly that I possessed before I married my husband and was obliged to be sensible. I am excessively pleased.

James, however, does not think it such a great joke as he once did to have everybody regard him as Frederica's suitor, now that all of London believes that she ran away from school to escape him! To my way of thinking, <u>that</u> could only raise her in anybody's esteem. I begin to fear that nobody would marry James unless dragged to the altar. Even Lady Hamilton's youngest daughter chose Mr. Charles Smith to my wastrel of a son. James does not like it at all when his character or his tailoring are called into question. He does not mind that people think him wanting in sense, but it grieves him to be thought wanting in appearance or kindness. It is all his own fault. If he does not wish to be the object of this sort of levity, he must marry somebody. He has dallied long enough.

I am anxious to know more of your opinion of Reginald deCourcy. There is a great deal of property and a large fortune, and though it would burden Frederica with Catherine Vernon for a sister and Lady deCourcy for a mother-in-law, perhaps they may settle somewhere distant until he comes into Parklands, and then he may send Lady deCourcy off to live with the Vernons. I confess that I like it very much. How long does young deCourcy continue at Churchill? You must throw them together as often as you can.

Your loving aunt,
Elinor Martin

Lady Vernon knew that Catherine's interest would be more difficult to secure than Reginald's—his *must* be won over by Frederica's beauty, her understanding, and her prepossessing manners, but Catherine's sympathy could only be roused by urging it in the opposite direction. In Catherine's presence, therefore, Lady Vernon adopted an attitude of sternness and detachment toward her daughter, which secured the forbearance of her sister-in-law more effectively than if she had made a show of maternal affection.

To be sure, even if Catherine were inclined to be strict, she could find no motive. Though Miss Vernon was the daughter of Sir Frederick Vernon and the cousin of Sir James Martin, she laid no claim to privilege and repaid her aunt's indifferent hospitality by arranging work boxes, mending purses, assisting the nursery maids, and keeping out of everyone's way, and Catherine could not but be pleased with one who did so much and required so little in return. As for the children, they were delighted with a cousin who was always good-humored when they slipped a frog into her pocket or tied her apron strings into a knot.

MRS. VERNON TO LADY DECOURCY

Churchill Manor, Sussex
My dear Madam,

On Thursday, Mr. Vernon returned from London and brought Miss Vernon with him, as Miss Summers absolutely refused to take her back. (I am sure that by now you have learned the motive of her conduct and cannot disapprove it, as it was done on behalf of our cousin Lucy.) They arrived just as we sat down to tea, and might have been with us earlier had my generous husband not undertaken to bring Miss Manwaring as far as Billingshurst.

When her daughter entered, Lady Vernon was the very picture of self-command, though earlier she had been shedding tears and pouring out her anxiety to Reginald. No doubt because the arrival of her daughter must expose him to all of her failures as a parent, which could not be evident while Miss Vernon was in London. She greeted her daughter with composure but without any tenderness of spirit. Miss Vernon's address was perfectly civil. She did not sit with us for ten minutes, however, before she burst into tears and ran from the room. Lady Vernon followed and reappeared again, only coming down to announce that Miss Vernon was very fatigued and that they would dine in their apartments. She made a pathetic show of concealing her misery, which tried my patience sorely, but fortunately we were not subjected to it for the entire evening.

I was able to see more of my niece on the following day. She is very pretty, but not at all like her mother. She has quite the Vernon cast of countenance, the oval face and mild dark eyes of her father. There had been a portrait of Sir Frederick somewhere in the gallery, which my dear husband was compelled to move in order to make way for a likeness of my grandfather. It had been done not long after Sir Frederick was knighted, and his age cannot have been much older than Miss Vernon is now, so the resemblance is rather striking.

I cannot think that a girl with so little in the way of fortune or accomplishment is truly the object of Sir James Martin, despite her mother's schemes, yet although she has had a wretched education and a poor example in her mother, she may not be too young to amend her defects. She is not entirely without merit, as she has made herself useful in any number of small tasks, and her little cousins have all grown very fond of her. I am persuaded that Mr. Vernon foresaw that her temperament would be suitable to tending to them (as we have yet to engage a governess) and elected to bring her to Churchill on that account. Mr. Vernon is always putting the children and me above anything—I do not think that there is a husband who is his equal!

When Lady Vernon departs Churchill for London, which I hope will take place very soon, perhaps the children and I may come to you in Kent, and I will contrive to bring Miss Vernon with me so that you may determine for yourself whether she would do for a governess. I assure you, my dear madam, that, though she is wanting something in elegance, there is nothing coarse about her, and she has the sort of modest and obliging disposition that would never presume upon your goodwill and notice.

Lady Vernon has said something of fixing herself in town. She retains the residence on Portland Place, and if her extravagance does not allow her to keep it up, I am certain that Mr. Vernon would take it off her hands, for the convenience of having an establishment when business obliges him to go to town. If, however, Lady Vernon regards his generosity with the same obstinacy that ruled her when she and Sir Frederick were obliged to get rid of Vernon Castle, I have no expectation that he will succeed.

I remind Reginald constantly that it is his duty to wait upon you and my father, and hope that when he comes to Kent you will be successful in keeping him there. When I asked how long he meant to be with you, and whether he would spend the entire season in town, he professed himself quite undetermined. Yet there was something in his look and voice that contradicted his words. I confess I do not like to see him go to London when I know that Lady Vernon means to be in town.

He has resumed his practice of walking up and down the shrubbery with her, and I suspect that she would like to fix him before he goes away—but of this I will say no more, for a great deal may happen

*between now and then. I can only hope that he will see in Miss
Vernon's want of elegance and sophistication all of the neglect and
selfishness of the mother.*

Your affectionate daughter,
Catherine Vernon

Reginald did not share his sister's opinion of their young guest.
Though he had not allowed her to be pretty when she first entered the
house, he now conceded that it was only the difference between Miss
Vernon and her mother that had biased his judgment. Indeed, she *was*
pretty, nay, beautiful, her figure and carriage were graceful, her manner unassuming, and her patience and good humor toward her young
cousins were highly to her credit. Once or twice, Reginald believed
that her pensive expression brightened when he approached, but she
invariably hurried on before he could utter anything beyond a "Good
morning." This piqued Reginald more than any outright flirtation
could have, and his remorse at having misjudged her developed into a
keen interest in knowing her better.

He resumed his habit of walking the grounds with Lady Vernon
solely to engage her in conversation on the subject of her daughter.
Lady Vernon did not spare herself in addressing Frederica's amiable
qualities, but always with such a tone of discouraging Reginald's interest so that, though once inclined to regard a union with Sir James
Martin as highly advantageous to Miss Vernon, he now began to
think that it was *she* who was too good for him.

When he ventured to give a hint of his opinion to Lady Vernon,
she would observe that a young woman's ability to attract a suitable
match would always be hindered by indigence, and that an offer of
marriage from any gentleman in possession of a good fortune was not
one that a poor young woman could easily dismiss. "The matter of our
poverty is one that I cannot address with equanimity—it is too closely
united with my husband's passing. Perhaps, after his injury, I ought to
have pressed Sir Frederick to make those amendments to his will that
would have confirmed his intentions regarding our fortune, but I always believed that Charles would honor them—no less than *you*

would if your sister's fortune had been left to your discretion—and at the time I was reluctant to introduce any subject that would suggest that I anticipated anything but my husband's complete recovery."

"But what of Miss Vernon's happiness?" he replied with some warmth. "Surely that must be a consideration in marriage?"

"Happiness will always be a consideration among those who can afford it," replied she, with a gentle smile. "But for a young woman who has been left with nothing, to be both unhappy and poor is far worse than to be unhappy and rich."

chapter thirty-five

ONE MORNING AT BREAKFAST, ABOUT A FORTNIGHT AFTER Miss Vernon's arrival, Catherine had been perusing a letter from her mother, which was a reply to her most recent communication.

I would be happy to think that the arrival of Miss Vernon will expose Reginald, at last, to all of Lady Vernon's failings and vanity, but I dare not be easy until he returns to us. Continue to urge him as much as you can and discourage Mr. Vernon from any sort of family feeling that would have Lady Vernon prolonging her visit. He must know that you cannot come to us while she is with you, and we are both very eager to see our dear grandchildren once more.

"Reginald," said Catherine as she laid down her letter. "Our mother expresses a wish to have you at Parklands. When you write to her next, you must assure her that you mean to go to them before you settle in town." She then recited several extracts from the letter, punctuating these with pointed observations that he had been with them "so very long" and that "it has been above six weeks since you came to us," which were meant to remind Lady Vernon of the duration of her own visit.

Reginald did not hear above two words; he was engaged in observing Miss Vernon's pensive countenance as she gazed out the window at the barren flower beds. "I think," he said to her in a low voice, "that you find Churchill Manor very much changed, Miss Vernon."

He was doubly rewarded, for not only did she turn her expressive eyes upon him but she replied as well, though only to say, "Yes, sir."

" 'Changed'?" Catherine exclaimed. "We have done nothing at all but put a carpet and some shelves in the nursery."

"I suspect that Miss Vernon does not address what has been altered but what has been neglected."

"Neglect?" cried Charles, with an uneasy glance that comprehended both Lady Vernon and her daughter.

"I refer to the greenhouses, Charles, which I think might be almost as fine as the ones at Parklands, if they were brought back to use."

"Oh, the greenhouses," rejoined Catherine. "Mr. Vernon's groundsman left us, and those who worked below him in the greenhouses are better off tending to their own fields and farms. Hothouses are good for nothing but growing melons and strawberries and the like, and Cook may get *those* from the village or the farms. I am not in favor of the current notion that everything put on the table must come from one's own orchards and gardens. To be sure, it is very useful to have a cook who can keep a kitchen garden and to grow a few herbs for one's own use, for one cannot forever be calling upon the apothecary. I daresay Mr. Lavery nearly poisoned little Charlie with his receipt when our dear boy had a congestion of the chest."

"Miss Vernon's interest goes beyond a few herbs." Reginald smiled. "I believe that she has made a serious study of botany. You might allow her to take a few liberties with the plant beds and the greenhouses, I think. Would you not like to look forward to a few plants and flowers in the spring?"

"Oh, I am as fond of plants and flowers as anybody who ever lived! Miss Vernon may explore the plant beds and the greenhouses as much as she likes. I am sure that no harm can come of it—there may be some way to turn the beds into sandboxes! And perhaps she may show the children how to make a few sachets or mosaics."

"Are you a *simpler*," Reginald inquired of Miss Vernon with a smile, "or a *sampler*?"

"I cannot lay claim to either talent," she replied. "My own handiwork might pass for that of a five-year-old child, and I have never poisoned anything beyond a rat. But that," she added, "was only out of some childish experimentation with woodruff and sweet-root. I do not *think* that I am inclined to poison anything now."

Lady Vernon checked a laugh. She perceived that Reginald was diverted by the reply, though Catherine declared that it was "a very odd subject for the table."

Frederica begged her aunt's pardon and asked if she might examine the greenhouses. Catherine readily gave her consent, and when Frederica withdrew, Lady Vernon said, "You must forgive Frederica. Her pursuits have always been solitary ones—gardening and books and music—excellent pastimes in themselves, but they do not promote ease of conversation."

"Miss Vernon is musical?" Reginald inquired. "Why does she not play? The instrument in the drawing room is a superior one and will likely go out of tune if it is not used, as Catherine does not play at all."

"Frederica always preferred the little pianoforte in the dressing room that Mrs. Vernon now occupies—I am certain that it will be a very convenient arrangement when the children begin to play."

"But as they do not play, I can see no reason why Miss Vernon may not use it for practice—Catherine is not always in her dressing room. You would not object, would you, Catherine?"

Catherine was not entirely happy with the proposal. She liked to have her mornings undisturbed so that she might write her letters and then proceed to do nothing in peace and quiet. "I shall have the instrument moved to your apartments," she said. "The furnishings in your dressing room can be arranged to make a place for it by the window. My niece may practice as much as she likes in that part of the house."

Lady Vernon thanked her sister-in-law, yet when she withdrew Catherine declared, "You are very generous with my instrument, Reginald."

"You would not deny her the occasional use of what had been hers," replied the brother. "She can do no more harm to the pianoforte than to the gardens, as both have been allowed to lie fallow. And while she is with you, you will have the enjoyment of a little music and Churchill will be free of rats."

chapter thirty-six

*U*PON ENTERING THE GREENHOUSE, FREDERICA EXPERI-
enced an equal measure of happiness and dejection; the place
must always hold happy associations for her, and yet she saw
at once how far five months of neglect and disuse had annulled all of
her effort.

The enclosure was still sound, and the rows of forcing beds in good
condition, though the earth was dried up and covered in desiccated
vines and leaves. Still, Frederica thought that something might be
done with it, that the leaves and dried vines could be cleared away
and the soil properly worked so that something might be planted. At
the end of one of the long enclosures, several bundles of herbs had
been hung to dry for the kitchen and for various *eaux de toilettes* and
balms, which Frederica had tied upon the very morning of her father's
death.

She took a dusty apron down from a peg and tied it round her
waist, and then sat upon one of the beds, to determine how it might
be worked.

She heard a quick step along the rows and looked up to see Reginald deCourcy advancing in her direction. She dropped a curtsy and
turned back to the beds, supposing that he meant to walk on.

To her surprise, he stopped and addressed her. "These were very
fine greenhouses. I cannot think why my brother allows them to fall
into decline unless his notion of landscape is for everything to grow in
a wild and random fashion."

"There is very little in nature that is random—even when neglected, there is some order to every growing thing."

"You reply as one who thinks first in a scientific manner. But take this plot, for example," he said, pointing to one of the beds where an irregular scattering of tendrils poked through the earth. "There is no system here."

"You must be patient, sir. I put the bulbs down myself last year, to force them here and then remove them to one of the plots in the spring. When they bloom, this row will be yellow tulips and those will be white crocuses. Plants, like people, are not always as they first appear—only in time will their nature be revealed."

"Yet there can be little deception in plants—a tulip is always a tulip, and a crocus cannot be other than a crocus."

"Yes, if you judge candor or deception only by the exterior. Then you see only the bloom and yet the roots that support it may be corrupt—and in such a way as may ruin the entire garden."

Reginald smiled in so warm and congenial a manner that Frederica felt emboldened and asked him to describe the grounds and gardens at Parklands. She listened raptly as he gave a comprehensive description of the deCourcy estate. "My father took a very active interest in the property when he was in health."

"Then I wish him a very speedy return to it," she said. She bound up two bundles of dried herbs. "This is agrimony and this one is dried peppermint. A strong brew of agrimony root and leaves is said to ease a congestion of the lungs, and peppermint tea will settle the stomach and promote digestion. I will write down the receipts for Sir Reginald, and directions for starting your own plants, if they are not grown at Parklands."

He thanked her and, eager to prolong the conversation, tried another subject. "You get on very well with my nieces and nephews."

"Yes. I am sorry to have not known them before now. It is fortunate that they have one another for companionship, as the move to Sussex must be a very great change for them. Mr. and Mrs. Vernon may live in as quiet a manner as they like, and the children will not be lonely."

"And were you lonely?"

"I never felt the want of companionship when I was a child, but now I do think it would be nice to have a sister or, even better, a brother."

"Better? I am not sure that Catherine would agree with you." He smiled.

"Oh, a sister is as pleasing as a brother, to be sure, but I cannot help thinking a brother would have been more useful to my mother in her situation."

"Though it gave Catherine the advantage of her own household, I am very sorry that her good fortune came at the expense of yours," he replied gravely. "Your father and mother have always been held in high regard by my Uncle deCourcy. His good opinion is always rooted in temperance and moderation."

"That makes his opinion more valuable than the sort of immoderate flattery that springs up everywhere."

Reginald wondered if she was thinking of Charles Smith. "Do you not think that flattery has its motive?"

"And so does censure."

"They are very different."

"Their language is very different, but can one's character not be equally misrepresented by excessive praise as by undeserved reproach?" she inquired.

Reginald smiled and fell into step with her as she completed her tour of the beds. Her conversation and opinions had elevated her even further in his esteem, and he began to think seriously of Catherine's urging him to return to Parklands—until he addressed his parents frankly, and put an end to all expectations that he would marry his cousin Lavinia, he could not be at liberty to make his addresses to a lady of his own choosing.

chapter thirty-seven

IN MOST CASES, A FORTNIGHT WOULD BE TOO SOON FOR any spirited young man to fix upon a marriage partner unless he possessed the sort of reckless nature that would stake all future happiness upon an infatuation; yet while Reginald deCourcy possessed a warm and occasionally headstrong temperament, he was no more inclined to offer his heart because he had been warned against it than to bestow his hand because it was urged upon him. His feelings for Frederica Vernon had been helped along by her mother's purposeful dissuasion and by his own compassion for her situation, but they might as easily have reversed if Miss Vernon had truly been ignorant, dull, or proud. Her beauty alone would not have secured him, but her accomplishments and her obliging manners bespoke a genuine superiority of mind, and her melancholy situation engaged his sympathy. While always attempting to be cheerful, particularly before the children, Miss Vernon must be unhappy, Reginald concluded. The loss of her father, her want of independence, the prospect of a union toward which she was disinclined, must make any sensitive young woman unhappy—and yet how could he object to her situation when he had allowed his family to anticipate his own marriage to Miss Hamilton? He had been very wrong to permit all of his family to presuppose a union that he knew would never take place.

Every day Catherine had made some mention of Parklands and how eager their parents were for a visit, but she had begun to despair of Reginald's spending any time in Kent before he settled in town. She was very surprised, therefore, when he came down to breakfast one morning and made a startling announcement.

"Catherine, I mean to go to Kent this week. I will send James ahead with the hunters this morning and be off myself in two days' time. As the journey must take me through London, if there is any commission that you, Charles, or any of the ladies would like for me to perform, have your petitions ready."

Both Catherine and Charles were astonished and excessively pleased, though for very different reasons; *she* supposed that Reginald's infatuation for Lady Vernon had run its course, while *he* was persuaded that Reginald meant to apply to his parents for their consent to marry her without delay.

Charles congratulated himself on the prospect of Lady Vernon's marriage to his brother. As Reginald's wife, she would be so rich and important that there would be no more musings and inquiries about why Sir Frederick had left her so poor. And yet he could not be entirely happy. Lady Vernon was so very lovely—much prettier than she had been when she first came to Churchill. Indeed, she was in such radiant good looks that she appeared almost young enough to be Miss Vernon's sister, and Charles could not but reflect what his happiness would have been if she had chosen him over Frederick. Then, left in his present situation, with an income that would not support his indulgences, and already weary of the quiet, country style of living, he would at least have got a more charming partner out of the bargain. But no, she had brought nothing into her marriage with Sir Frederick, and she possessed nothing that he had not got his hands on but for a house in town.

Lady Vernon, who suspected Reginald's motives, wished that he would remain at Churchill only a little longer. She did not doubt that Frederica had engaged his interest and sympathy; that he was in a fair way to being in love was evident, but Lady Vernon would have him *firmly* in love before he went away.

Catherine, for her part, was relieved that the affair that had given her so much anxiety was drawing to a happy conclusion. Her conviction that it had been her own influence with her brother that had affected his decision gave her such satisfaction that she was able to look upon his attentions toward Lady Vernon and her daughter as nothing more than polite indifference.

chapter thirty-eight

LADY VERNON TO MRS. JOHNSON

Churchill Manor
My dear Alicia,

This morning Reginald declared his intention to return to Park-lands. I must anticipate that once in Kent, he must succumb to his parents' wishes for his future. I am resigned. Even you, my dear friend, cannot flatter me into prosperity, and a jeune fille with thirty thousand must eclipse a widow who is some years Reginald's senior and who has no more than a modest jointure and a house in town.

Reginald will carry this letter to you himself, as he stops in town before going on to Kent. Allow this to serve as an introduction to you and Mr. Johnson. I think that you will be sufficiently impressed with his address and manners. If you are at leisure to have him spend an evening at Edward Street, I think that his conversation, and his love of books and reading, will ensure that even Mr. Johnson will not retreat from the acquaintance.

Lady Vernon was interrupted in her writing by the sound of a rapid footstep in the hallway.

Frederica burst into the room. "Forgive me, madam—our cousin has come! Mr. deCourcy and I saw his carriage turn down the avenue!"

"Surely you are mistaken!"

"He is this minute sitting in the drawing room! What are we to do?

What will *he* think! He takes my cousin James for a suitor! Why did we not undeceive everybody? It was wrong, very wrong."

"Your cousin was happy enough to encourage the gossip," Lady Vernon replied in great exasperation. "It was only when his suit was cast as *objectionable* and *unwanted* that he began to mind it. How provoking! He means to do mischief, to be sure!"

This remark put Frederica very near tears. "I do not like Mr. deCourcy to think that my cousin and I are to be married. What are we to do?"

"You and Wilson go down. Tell your cousin that I will join you directly. Your aunt is with the children, and I must inform her of what will be regarded as a most unwelcome imposition."

Lady Vernon knew that Catherine did not like any variation in her narrow routine, but she was always weak on the side of vanity. Lady Vernon, therefore, addressed this side when she said, "My cousin's unexpected visit requires some apology to you, my dear sister. I can only account for it by supposing that he means to join the Parkers' large party at Billingshurst and could not come into the neighborhood without waiting upon you and my brother."

"Billingshurst is ten miles off," remarked Catherine, who could not imagine going so far to pay her compliments to anyone.

"Sir James possesses the sort of affability and easy confidence that rejects the notion that such a visit might be unwelcome or that it might be an imposition upon the hospitality of equals, particularly when we are on such excellent terms."

For her own part, Catherine could only hope that the terms did not comprehend Lady Vernon hereafter becoming Reginald's wife, and though Catherine would not have gone a great distance to meet Sir James Martin, as he had come to Churchill, she was curious to see him.

"Cousin!" cried Sir James when the ladies entered the room, and he stepped forward to meet Lady Vernon. His merry glance met her cross one with equanimity.

Lady Vernon made the introductions, and Catherine bade them all sit down together.

"I take a great liberty in coming to Churchill," Sir James addressed Catherine. "I hope you will forgive it—I know you shall, for my cousin has written to me that your kindness and affection are very great, so great that it must extend to her kin."

"And how does my Aunt Martin fare now that she is left alone?" Lady Vernon inquired of her cousin.

"Very well, I trust. When I was with her last, she did complain of some trifling ailment or other, but she seemed to improve as my departure drew near, and now that I am gone I have no doubt but that she is entirely well."

"Then you are settled in town for the season?" Catherine asked.

"I am as settled as any poor bachelor ever is." Sir James laughed. "We settle ourselves wherever we are invited to stay. I hope that I do not take too great a liberty to impose myself upon your hospitality, Mrs. Vernon. If I do, you must take it to be the liberty of a relation."

Catherine was obliged to proffer an invitation for him to stay at Churchill for the present, "as you have no place else to go."

Sir James thanked her with a warmth that nearly provoked a laugh from Lady Vernon. "I called at Edward Street three evenings ago, and Mrs. Johnson urges me to tell you how happy she will be to have you in London once more and to convey to you both her very best love. I did protest that she could not possess better love for you than your nearest relation."

Frederica ventured to speak. "And Mr. Johnson? Is he well?"

"He commissioned me to bring you something from his library," Sir James replied as he took a packet from his coat. "And this is what I chose. *A Collection of Passion-Flowers from Nature*. I hope that you approve, cousin."

Frederica blushed and murmured her thanks, avoiding Reginald's gaze. He observed this exchange in perfect silence but with a heightened color that suggested that he was not pleased to have Sir James at Churchill Manor.

"I cannot think that Mr. Johnson knows anything of passion-flowers," Lady Vernon remarked.

"Perhaps that is why he is willing to part with it," Sir James replied. "And I am quite certain that Mrs. Johnson will not feel the

loss of it. I must offer my congratulations to you, madam," he addressed Catherine, "and to Mr. deCourcy on the marriage of your
cousin Miss Lucy Hamilton to Mr. Charles Smith. I hope that they are
very happy."

Reginald's expression assumed a greater shade of hauteur, but the
remark induced him to speak at last. "I have no reason to believe that
they are not."

"Nor have I. Smith has a frank and open disposition, and Miss
Lucy Hamilton has never possessed the convenient talent of affecting
sensations foreign to her heart. With nothing like artifice in her nature nor reserve in his, I think they have as fair a chance at happiness
as those whose unions were a sacrifice to policy or ambition."

"Your opinion of marriage does not sound entirely favorable, sir,"
Reginald deCourcy observed.

"I am always influenced by what is before me. Now that I am at
Churchill, I think there can be no better state."

"If you are so easily swayed, your opinion may reverse when you go
away again," Reginald observed.

"I hope that when I do go, it will be with an even happier view of
matrimony than when I came."

"Unfortunately, Mr. deCourcy will not be able to witness your
change of sentiment," Lady Vernon remarked. "He is to leave
Churchill before the end of the week."

"But not leave Sussex, I trust," Sir James said with a smile, "as I
understand that some of your relations will be at Billingshurst."

"I go directly to London and then on to Parklands."

"How regrettable! But Mrs. Vernon will have the pleasure of seeing them, I have no doubt."

Catherine was somewhat distressed at this assertion. If any of her
relations were to come as far as Billingshurst, she would indeed be
obliged to do something, though she did not know what. She could
not expect them to come ten miles to drink tea. They would have to
be asked to dine. Would she be obliged to invite Miss Maria Manwaring as well? She was a particular friend of Miss Vernon's, but of late
Charles had spoken of Manwaring with something like aversion.
Catherine sighed and wished that they were all back at Parklands,

where the matter of what was due to anybody had been left in her mother's capable hands.

"It has been a long time since I have seen anything of this part of the country and nothing suits me so well as a brisk walk after being confined to a carriage for many miles. We will excuse Mr. deCourcy, as he must have something better to attend to, but I think I can coax my cousins into a little walking party. And you will join us, will you not, Mrs. Vernon?"

Catherine was obliged to excuse herself, saying that she never walked and that she ought to return to the nursery. Sir James laughed and said that he hoped to be introduced to the little Vernons ere long, and what a wonderful thing it was to have such a family.

Sir James's cheerfulness seemed to provoke Reginald, who declared that he had no pressing matters to attend to and that he would indeed like to be one of the party, and Sir James, with his natural sense of mischief, offered his arm to Frederica and left Reginald to attend Lady Vernon.

The four of them set out across the front lawns and down the avenue, walking in the direction of the village.

"I am very happy to see you looking so well, Freddie," Sir James began. "Your ordeal in London cannot have been pleasant, but I was never persuaded that you ought to have been sent to school, and yet I do not like to see you back here at Churchill. I would much rather have had you remain in town, as your mother wished."

"I am sure that Mama would wish you there as well."

Sir James laughed. "I cannot recall a more chilly welcome than I have received just now! Is Mrs. Vernon generally so unequal to hospitality?"

"I have not had the opportunity to know her well. I think that she is very much a creature of routine, but so are we all in some manner or other."

"And what sort of person is Mr. deCourcy? Is he the same sort of creature as his sister?"

"He is intelligent and amiable."

"In other words, *nothing* like her. And yet there is nothing amiable in the stare that I feel directed at my back. He has heard that we are very near to being engaged and he does not like it. What shall we do? Are you still of the opinion that it is wrong to encourage discord? Will we turn back and undeceive him at once, or shall we have some fun at his expense?"

"I don't know what you mean, cousin!"

"Do you not? And yet you are a young lady of such extraordinary discernment. It is clear to *me* that Mr. deCourcy admires you and regards me as a rival. What will the Vernons say? Mrs. Vernon continues to hope that her brother will marry Miss Hamilton, and Mr. Vernon—"

Frederica drew her arm back and replied sharply, "I do not care what my uncle hopes for! *His* hopes cannot be accomplished unless someone else's are ruined!"

Sir James was startled at such an outburst from one whose temper was always so mild. He attempted something like an apology and she immediately begged his pardon and took her cousin's arm once more. The two continued on, and though Sir James endeavored to divert her, Frederica remained subdued, replying to his remarks with no more than a monosyllable or a nod.

Reginald, who walked with Lady Vernon many paces behind the pair, could not hear their exchange, but he observed enough to see that Sir James had said something to upset Frederica. He began to tally—with greater attention than the subject had ever produced heretofore—the many ills that might arise when a young woman was compelled to subordinate her happiness to a duty to marry well. By the time they had returned to the house, he had enumerated many arguments in favor of preference and was resolved to address them to Lady Vernon before he left Churchill.

chapter thirty-nine

*I*T IS A UNIVERSAL AMBITION TO PERSUADE AS MANY PEO-
ple as possible of one's understanding, intelligence, and wit
without having to cultivate any of them. In the case of Sir
James Martin, however, it was quite the reverse: his education had
been thorough and his understanding was sound, but an easy assurance and lively good humor had given rise to the impression of frivolity, and he did not trouble himself to contradict it.

His wit and complacency allowed him to keep up a steady stream
of pleasantries at the dinner table. Lady Vernon was too angry with
her cousin to speak to him, and Miss Vernon, who was afraid that any
interest in her cousin's conversation would be seen as a confirmation
of their betrothal, was silent as well. Reginald spoke when he could
not avoid it, and Mrs. Vernon, after pronouncing that the curried rab-
bit had turned out remarkably well, observed that the season for sport
was quite at an end and that she was afraid there was little else to
tempt Sir James to stay with them for *very* long.

Sir James smiled and replied, "My affection for this part of the
world is fixed on something more prepossessing than sport. But I will
not intrude upon your routine—none of your engagements need be
altered on my account."

Mrs. Vernon assured him that they did nothing and went nowhere.
"But do not stand on ceremony, sir. You have acquaintances in this
part of the country who will want a share of your company. Do not
put us above them. Spend as much time as you like with them. We
will not be offended."

Sir James thanked her with an emphasis that provoked Lady

Vernon to smile in spite of herself. "I will be happy to renew my acquaintance in this part of the world. But I am happier, of course, to
see my cousins, and in such good looks, for which I must give you and
Mr. Vernon credit. Your particular attentions to them seem to have
offset the melancholy sensations that must attend any visit to the
home that was lost to them in such a cruel fashion."

" 'Cruel'?" cried Vernon. "Do you say that my sister and niece have
been cruelly treated?"

Sir James was surprised at his vehemence and calmly replied, "Perhaps I should not have said 'cruel.' I should have said 'unfortunate'—
as the fortunes of those who survive such a loss are wont to decline."

Vernon murmured something about accidents and how terrible it
was when they resulted in a loss, how painful it was for them to be discussed at all.

Sir James apologized and changed the subject. "I honor your delicacy, Mrs. Vernon, for doing so little with Churchill Manor. There
were, no doubt, many alterations you wished to make, and to leave it
so unchanged must be a great comfort to my cousins."

"And yet," declared Reginald, "Miss Vernon remarked only this
morning how very much changed she found it to be."

"She *would* find it so," Sir James replied, directing an affectionate smile toward his young cousin. "Freddie is naturally observant—
nothing escapes her notice."

"There is nothing to notice," stammered Vernon. "Some changes
in the household staff . . . the rooms are much the same . . . nothing
whatsoever . . . !"

"Indeed," said his wife. "One cannot do everything. It is troublesome to know what ought to be done at all."

"I quite agree with you—it is troublesome, at least, to know what
must be done at *once* and what can wait until one is more settled. And
yet there have been some alterations that my young cousin must feel
deeply. There had been a portrait of Sir Frederick in the gallery. It had
been done when he was a very young man—not much older than
Freddie, I believe. To remove a portrait might not seem a great
change, but it is only natural that the absence of such a comforting
fixture must impress my young cousin very deeply."

"We were compelled to . . . it was necessary to make a place for my wife's grandfather," said Vernon uneasily.

"Undoubtedly. There is nothing like family feeling! That portrait now, of my cousins, was done when Freddie was only three years old," Sir James continued, pointing to a likeness of mother and daughter that hung upon the wall opposite Vernon. "It gave Sir Frederick a great deal of pleasure to look upon it when he sat in the chair that you now occupy, but it cannot inspire the same feeling in you. If I may be so bold as to suggest it, the portrait of Sir Frederick would go handsomely in its place. But perhaps you have already chosen another place for your brother's likeness."

"Oh, no," Mrs. Vernon chimed in. "It was put away in one of the attics."

Sir James was astonished. He had always known that Vernon's affection for Sir Frederick went no deeper than his enjoyment of the superior society of Churchill Manor and Portland Place, and the ease with which "my elder brother, Sir Frederick Vernon" got men of fortune to open their pocketbooks. Yet to remove his portrait from its rightful place among his forebears, a place moreover where it had hung for nearly thirty years, was more than indifference—there *was* something cruel about it.

The subject kindled Reginald's curiosity and he began to ask many questions about the age of the portrait and who had been the artist, and determining how far the dust and dampness of an attic might have injured the canvas. "The portrait of a former master must have its place," he declared. "That likeness of Lady Vernon and Miss Vernon is very pleasing, but you cannot have any particular attachment to it, Charles. May I not carry it to town and leave it with Lady Vernon's housekeeper at Portland Place, and then you may hang Sir Frederick's portrait here in the dining room if there is no place for it in the gallery? You would not object to that, Catherine?"

Mrs. Vernon was not at all unhappy to get rid of any likeness of Lady Vernon and declared that she could make no objection, and as Vernon's dumbfounded silence was taken for consent, the matter was considered settled.

When the ladies removed to the drawing room, the children

joined them and remained until the gentlemen appeared. They insisted that they would go to the nursery with nobody but their cousin Freddie, and Miss Vernon consented to take them upstairs.

Lady Vernon took out some embroidery while Mrs. Vernon poured tea and coffee and then sat down to look at the pages of a book. Sir James took a chair beside his cousin, and under the pretext of examining her handiwork, he said in a low voice, "Vernon does not appear to be very comfortable in his new situation."

"He does not want you here."

"Oh, nobody wants me here," Sir James persisted. "Except Mother, who is always glad to have me anywhere but where she is. But you are his brother's widow and entitled to a greater respect. To banish Frederick's portrait shows a wanton indifference to his brother's memory and to what is due to you and to Churchill."

Lady Vernon kept her eyes on her work. "James, I beg you to remember that we are *both* guests in my brother's house, and that Frederica and I are dependent upon his goodwill. We were not left so rich that we can take offense from those who take us in."

"If he does not wish you to take offense, he should not give it."

"Hush, James, they will hear you."

Sir James moderated his tone. "They would not be so likely to hear our conversation if they had any of their own. See how young de-Courcy looks in our direction. He believes that I plead with you for Freddie's hand. Let us have some fun with him, shall we?" he asked, and began to entertain his cousin with the latest London gossip in which "settlement" and "engagement" and "nuptials" were audible above their murmurs.

$\int$IR JAMES MARTIN'S NATURE, WHICH HE HAD TAKEN SOME
pains to conceal beneath a guise of frivolity, was one of keen
perception and kindness of heart. When he was provoked,
however, a propensity for mischief asserted itself. Though there was
not a hint of malice in his nature, he was often as likely to do more
damage from an act of caprice than another might do from outright
cruelty, and this was never more evident than in the havoc wrought
from his conduct on the following morning.

He rose with the memory of his cousins' reserve, Vernon's agitation, and Reginald's resentment fresh in his mind, and he had an
overwhelming desire to tease them all. Taking a sheet of paper, he
began to write a brief note, his penmanship a creditable imitation of
Frederica's straightforward and elegant hand.

Dear Sir,

*I hope you will excuse this liberty, but I am forced upon it by great
distress, or I should be ashamed to trouble you. I am forbidden from
ever speaking to my uncle or aunt on the subject. In applying to you,
I do perhaps attend only to the letter and not the spirit of Mama's com-
mands, but if you do not take my part, I know of no other way in the
world of helping myself.*

*I am very miserable about Sir James Martin. I have always dis-
liked him and thought him to be silly, impertinent, and disagreeable,
and now that I know how earnestly our marriage is contemplated, I
cannot bear him. I would rather work for my bread than marry him.*

*If you will have the unspeakable great kindness of taking my part with
Mama, and prevailing upon her to give Sir James an absolute refusal,
I shall be more than obliged to you.*

*I do not know how to apologize enough for this letter, and I am
aware how dreadfully angry it will make everybody at Churchill, but I
must run the risk.*

I am, sir, your most humble servant,
Frederica Susannah Vernon

He had read enough novels to think that he had written it in a
very high style and one that would do credit to any lovelorn young
lady. He folded the note over and wrote "Mr. Reginald deCourcy"
upon it, and slipped it under the door of the young man's chamber and
went down to the breakfast parlor. The family would not be down for
another half hour, which gave Sir James both the opportunity to eat
his breakfast in peace and occasion to feel something like remorse.

As he could not recover the note, he decided that the best thing
would be for him to take himself out of everybody's way, and sending
to the stables for his horse, he set off for Billingshurst.

Billingshurst had lately been taken by a family named Parker; the
elder branch of the family had made enough by way of trade to allow
the next two or three generations to forget it (provided the sons were
not too numerous and the daughters were pretty enough to find husbands). They were the sort of people whose fortune attracted a great
many friends and whose amiability kept nearly all of them. They
would have dearly loved to add the Vernons to their acquaintance,
but their recent arrival in the neighborhood, and a sense of their
humble origins, caused them to believe it was the Vernons' place to
make the overture. The manner in which Mr. Vernon had behaved
when he left Miss Manwaring at Billingshurst gave them little hope,
however—he had declined to come in and kept Lady Vernon's daughter sitting in the carriage.

In the village of Churchill, Sir James encountered a carriage bearing a familiar crest and was hailed by Mr. Lewis deCourcy, who had
been invited to pass a few days at Billingshurst. DeCourcy was very

surprised to hear that Sir James had come from Churchill Manor and persuaded him to turn over his horse to the groom and take a seat in the carriage.

"I hope," began Mr. deCourcy when they had set off, "that Lady Vernon's going to Churchill Manor is some indication that the concerns that she expressed to me on her way to Langford were resolved to her satisfaction. It would have pained me to think ill of Charles, as he is married to my niece."

Sir James did not know how to reply. If Lady Vernon had some source of distress beyond the loss of a beloved husband, she had not confided it to him. Of course, Sir James reflected ruefully, his conduct toward his cousin had not always inspired her confidence.

They were greeted at Billingshurst by Mr. and Mrs. Parker, who had bustled up from their table to meet the guests and ushered the gentlemen into the breakfast parlor without ceremony. Sir James was surprised to find Mr. and Mrs. Charles Smith among the party, as he had supposed that they would not be invited anywhere where there were deCourcys. To Lewis deCourcy's credit, he gave a kiss to his niece and shook her husband's hand and then took a seat beside Miss Maria Manwaring.

THE BREAKFAST TABLE at Churchill Manor was not as amiable. The party consisted only of Mr. and Mrs. Vernon, she engaged in reading a letter from Lady deCourcy and he looking up from his newspaper whenever his lady called upon him to listen to some extract of wisdom from her mother.

As Vernon was preparing to withdraw, a note was handed down to Mrs. Vernon and she read it with an exclamation of surprise. "Sir James has gone off to Billingshurst! He writes that we must not expect him until dinnertime. That is very strange conduct, do you not agree, my love? To take himself away for an entire day when he came here on our niece's account?"

"If he takes himself away for good, he may be as strange as he likes," he muttered.

Mrs. Vernon went up to the children and spent a quarter of an hour teaching them something, before sending them out in the care of a nursery maid for exercise. She then sat down to write a letter to her mother.

MRS. VERNON TO LADY deCOURCY

Churchill Manor, Sussex
My dear Madam,

I regret that I have not been able to write to you for some days. We have an unexpected guest with us. Sir James Martin arrived yesterday and took the very great liberty of inviting himself to remain with us as long as he liked! I thought it quite impertinent of him, and I do not think that Lady Vernon was happy to see him, either, though I cannot account for that, as she clearly means to forward a match between Sir James and her daughter.

Sir James is a very handsome and genteel sort of person, but he has a liveliness that borders on impudence. His manner is certainly the opposite of Miss Vernon's, and I confess that I see nothing in her conduct that suggests encouragement. It is all her mother's doing. She is absolutely determined to have them married. He is very rich, and Lady Vernon will not hesitate to sacrifice the poor girl in the cause of wealth and ambition. I would be very sorry to think that in years hence I would ever make either Kitty or Regina marry anyone toward whom they were violently opposed.

As for Reginald, I believe he does not know what to make of the matter. When Sir James first came, he appeared all astonishment and perplexity; the folly of Sir James and the confusion of Frederica entirely engrossed him and he is hurt, I am sure, at Lady Vernon allowing such a man's attentions to her daughter.

Have no fear that this turn of events will affect Reginald's plans. He still means to leave us tomorrow for London, and from there, on to Kent. How happy I will be when he is safely back at Parklands! I pray you may keep him there.

Lady Vernon will soon leave us, and (although my generous

husband, to the very last, urges her to extend her visit into the spring)
not even a desire to keep her from town and Reginald could compel me
to prolong her stay. Though I did not think that his attraction to her
was so pronounced in this last week as it had been when she first came
to us (as she could not conceal her failures as a mother once Miss Ver-
non arrived), she has been in such very good looks as to make any
young man's heart overrule his head.

I can only hope that the arrival of Sir James, while a very great
nuisance in all other respects, has given Reginald some insight into
Lady Vernon's coldness and ambition by her desire to force her daugh-
ter into a match with her cousin, for my brother's disposition is very
warm and it has been excited by compassion for Miss Vernon. I be-
lieve that he comes to see her as something like a heroine in distress, as
last night, after Sir James had retired (the ladies having gone upstairs
some time before), he remarked that our niece was "a sweet girl, and
she deserves a better fate than Sir James Martin."

While Catherine continued writing sheet upon sheet (as Reginald
would carry the letter, Lady deCourcy would not have to think of the
post), Reginald was given a very different sort of communication
when his servant handed him the note that had been found slipped
under the door.

Reginald read it with surprise and dismay. The latter sensation pre-
dominated; he was distressed by the impropriety of such an address
but was soon overcome by a feeling of pity for her plight and for the
evident desperation that had driven her to write the letter. These feelings were augmented by something like tenderness. "I would rather
work for my bread than marry him" was a particularly affecting sentiment, and one that made him smile at the thought of Miss Vernon,
who could not accommodate herself to the conventions of a ladies'
academy, going out into the world.

The closing sentences struck him with their conviction of Lady
Vernon's displeasure. If the violence of Miss Vernon's opposition to
Sir James were made known to her mother, surely Lady Vernon would
take her daughter's part despite the many advantages of such a match.

Miss Vernon was very wrong not to make a friend of her. Reginald, with letter in hand, went to Lady Vernon's apartments.

Lady Vernon had risen and dressed but did not wish to go down to breakfast until she was certain that Sir James had finished, and so was sitting at her writing desk when Reginald knocked. She invited him to sit and apologized for Miss Vernon's absence. "She and Wilson have gone to call upon Mrs. Chapman."

Reginald concluded that Miss Vernon had left right after slipping the letter under his door, in order to avoid any meeting with Sir James.

"I am glad that Miss Vernon is not here," he began without premise. "I wish to speak to you, Lady Vernon, on the impropriety—the unkindness—of allowing Sir James Martin to address your daughter. It is evident that Miss Vernon dislikes him. How can you, as her mother, not see how miserable she is?"

Lady Vernon did not know whether to protest or laugh at this declaration. "Can you think of no other motive for her misery, if she is indeed miserable?" she inquired. "Frederica has been deprived of her father, her home, and her fortune. Is that not sufficient to make her unhappy? And do you call it an unkindness to wish for an advantageous match for one's daughter?"

"It is not the matter of advantage—so superior a young lady as Miss Vernon ought to marry well. It is marriage to *Sir James* that is offensive."

"What, pray, compels you to speak in my daughter's defense? Does your sister commission you to reprimand me?"

"It is not Catherine but Miss Vernon who, by her own hand, asks me to speak on her behalf," he replied, and before she could protest, he produced the letter.

Lady Vernon took the sheet of paper and immediately recognized the counterfeit penmanship and the preposterous expressions that exposed the letter as one of her cousin's jokes. It affected her as Sir James's pranks so often did, leaving her with both a desire to laugh and to be angry. Only Reginald's grave and earnest countenance kept her from any display of emotion, and with great forbearance, she addressed him. "You know that my daughter is capable of impulse,

Mr. deCourcy, as she acted so in the matter of Miss Lucy Hamilton's elopement. Her dear father was inclined to spoil her, and I must often appear severe when contrasted with his indulgence. She is very young, and although she is a good-natured girl at heart, she is at an age when there must be opposition to one's parent in something."

"Can your ladyship wonder that she opposes a marriage with one who is so unequal to her in temperament? She writes that she cannot bear him."

"Please remember that you are speaking of my nearest relation," Lady Vernon reminded the young man. "You have only just been introduced to Sir James. His boyish manners often make him appear worse than he is, and in everything except common sense he would be a most desirable match."

"But he cannot be a desirable match for Miss Vernon if she does not love him."

Lady Vernon began to think that she ought to be grateful for her cousin's prank. Reginald's defense of Miss Vernon had excited a warmth and interest that he might not have come to so quickly without such inducement.

"What an opinion you must have of me! Can you possibly suppose that I wish for anything except her happiness? Do you think that I am destitute of every natural feeling?"

"I do *not* think so, but your daughter is not secure on this point. In her own hand, she writes that you are so insistent upon the match that you have forbidden her even from opening her heart to my sister and Charles."

Lady Vernon forced herself to remain calm in the face of his indignation and her own sense of the absurdity of the situation. "I admit that I did caution my daughter against troubling our relations with *any* of our concerns, as such complaints might be seen as a reproach for obliging us to leave Churchill Manor so soon after my husband's death or an insinuation that we meant to plead poverty and ask for money. If I have done wrong, it is only that in my own distressed state, I have not always known what will make Frederica happy. Although a prosperous marriage for her would be of material relief to us both, I assure you that I would never consign to everlasting misery the child whose welfare it is my duty to promote and whose happiness was always the first object of one whose memory will always be sacred to me." She was compelled to stop here and wipe away a tear. "I honor the discretion that you have shown in coming to me and I give you my word that before the day is out, I will address them both. If Sir James has any pretensions for my daughter, he must give them up."

Reginald took great pleasure in thinking that he had such influence with Lady Vernon, and a less creditable joy in the prospect of witnessing Sir James's disappointment. "Miss Vernon will be made happy before Sir James can be disappointed. He has gone to Billingshurst and does not plan to return until dinnertime, and perhaps later."

Lady Vernon, though quite out of patience with her cousin, was compelled to repress a smile at the sort of repentance that had him running away to Billingshurst. "I hope, Mr. deCourcy, that your determination to leave Churchill was not brought about by this situation. My own visit has already been too long, and it will not inconvenience us to depart at once. Whether Frederica and I are in Sussex or London is of no consequence to anyone, and I cannot in any way be instrumental in separating a family that is so well attached to one another."

Lady Vernon's willingness to sacrifice an advantageous match for her daughter, as well as the comforts and familiarity of Churchill, left Reginald satisfied with her generosity and affection; only the disturbing allusions to their poverty distressed him, for if they had indeed been left poor, might not Miss Vernon be pressed to take another rich suitor who was equally odious?

For her own part, Lady Vernon was delighted to see how easily Reginald's feelings were worked upon, and while his curiosity demanded an explanation in everything, very few words from her were necessary to render him tractable and satisfied. Nothing more could be wanted in a son-in-law than to be so accommodating to his wife's mother, and when he withdrew, Lady Vernon believed that if they could be kept from the interference of their families, she would, within a very few months, have a child come into the world and another one married.

chapter forty-one

WHEN REGINALD LEFT, LADY VERNON SAT DOWN TO WRITE
to her Aunt Martin.

LADY VERNON TO LADY MARTIN

Churchill Manor, Sussex
My dearest Aunt,

If you have not heard from James for some days, it is because he has taken it into his head to come down to Sussex and get himself into mischief. He came to us yesterday and set about teasing us all by behaving toward Frederica as a lover, so that Mr. deCourcy—who <u>has</u> come to feel something like interest in her—actually exhorted from me this morning a promise that I would put an end to all of James's expectations! The promise was given, and Mr. deCourcy delays his departure for Kent only long enough to have the pleasure of seeing my cousin's hopes dashed. I can only hope that James will gratify him by putting on as creditable a show of dejection as of ardor.

I do not think that Reginald will be in Kent for very long—only long enough, I suspect, to inform his parents that they must give up all expectations of a match between him and Miss Hamilton. The way will then be clear for him and Freddie; soon they will both be in London, which will always be the fairest field of action for a young couple to put the finishing touches to a romance.

Your affectionate niece,
Susan Vernon

While she was thus engaged, Reginald deCourcy was making some small preparations for his departure, which was to take place on the following day. He had no doubt that Lady Vernon intended to speak to Sir James that evening, and Reginald wanted only to remain long enough to see his rival's ambitions thwarted before he was gone. Reginald was not insensible of the fact that he would be bringing to Parklands a similar disappointment; he could no more marry *his* cousin than Frederica Vernon could marry *hers*, and he had come to understand that the brief pain that his parents must experience would be nothing to the prolonged anxiety of expectation.

In the business of arranging some small papers and letters, he found the sheet upon which Miss Vernon had written the receipts that she had promised to send to Sir Reginald. Reginald's keen perception was immediately aroused by the difference between this example of Miss Vernon's writing and the letter—there was a slight dissimilarity in the hand, and a pronounced distinction between the elevated expressions of the petition and the more sensible prose of the receipts. Some deception had been practiced, of that he was certain, and he resolved to speak to Frederica before her mother reprimanded her for a letter that she had not written.

He waited in the front hallway until he saw Frederica and Wilson turn down the avenue and then went out to meet them. He asked permission to speak to Frederica alone. Wilson withdrew with her customary discretion and Reginald waited only until she was out of earshot before he produced the letter and placed it in Frederica's hands.

Frederica's glance changed from one of puzzlement to deep embarrassment as she read the letter, and she immediately began to stammer something by way of explanation.

"Say nothing, Miss Vernon. I have proof that this letter is a counterfeit—I found a sample of your own hand, but not before acting upon this forgery with my usual haste. I was deceived so far as to confront your mother and plead your case."

Frederica was in considerable distress and would have run to the house immediately had he not caught her hand. "One moment, I beg you, Miss Vernon. This letter—no doubt the mischief of your cousin, who fled to Billingshurst right after he left it at my door—has been productive only of good. Depend upon it, if the *content* of this letter had not so distressed your mother, she would not have been deceived by the *hand*

and *then* she would never have agreed to relinquish all desire for a match between you and Sir James. I will not detain you. I know you will wish to hear this from her own lips. You will not be made unhappy any longer."

"I will go to her at once, but I beg you, sir," Frederica faltered, "do not think ill of my cousin. He is often so lively and teasing that those who do not know him well *will take* offense where he does not mean to *give* it."

"If he gives you up with as good grace as you have endured his foolishness," replied Reginald gravely, "I will think as well of him as you like."

"I have no doubt that he shall." Frederica found it hard to repress a smile as she said this. "I am certain that he is already very remorseful for what he has done."

Sir James was, in fact, so far from remorse that he had managed to persuade the party at Billingshurst that Mr. and Mrs. Vernon had quite depended upon his bringing them all to dine. Mrs. Smith, whose natural high spirits and delight in showing herself off as a married woman left her quite unembarrassed at meeting her dear cousins Catherine and Reginald, immediately supported the scheme. The Parkers declined to go, on account of Mr. Parker's having been up all the previous night nursing his favorite dog and Mrs. Parker's conviction that if Mrs. Vernon had wanted to know her, she would have waited upon her when they first came to Billingshurst. They were not averse to encouraging their guests, however, as their company included Mrs. Vernon's relations and Miss Vernon's particular friend Miss Manwaring and her brother. There was only the matter of what the ladies were to wear and how they were to be conveyed to be settled, and so they all set off, with Mr. and Mrs. Smith in their curricle, Claudia Hamilton, Lewis deCourcy, and Maria and Robert Manwaring in the Parkers' chaise-and-four, and Sir James on horseback.

This happy party appeared just before five o'clock. Lady Vernon and Frederica, who were sitting with the children, observed the party from an upper window that overlooked the avenue.

"Mama, there is my cousin—and there are two carriages with him!"

"Good heavens!" Lady Vernon cried, running to the window. "Is there no end to his mischief! He has brought them all from Billingshurst." The children were delighted with the appearance of the party, for there had been few visitors and no excitement or diversion since they had come to Churchill.

"What will my aunt and uncle say?" Frederica exclaimed.

What Mrs. Vernon was to say was very soon heard from the upper hallway, for there was a great bustle and exclamation from Mrs. Vernon's dressing room, and when Lady Vernon and Frederica emerged, they saw her in an animated exchange with her brother at the top of the stairs.

"What can Sir James mean! They cannot want to stay to dinner!" exclaimed Mrs. Vernon in horror. "Mr. Vernon is somewhere about the grounds, and I do not know when he is to be home, and I have got nothing but a shoulder of mutton for a family table!" Her distress was very great, and she was caught between her anger at Lady Vernon's cousin and her desire for that lady's opinion on how the business of unexpected visitors was to be managed.

Lady Vernon attempted to placate her sister. "My cousin thinks that every household follows the informality and liveliness of Ealing Park, but for the sake of these guests, we must endure his impertinence. Let us go down together to receive them while Mr. deCourcy sends for Mr. Vernon. Frederica can give orders to the kitchen—your table is such a superior one that it will be nothing for your cook to accommodate visitors."

Few could have been as calm as Frederica in the face of Cook's hysterics when informed that they would be twelve to dinner. "Twelve!" the good woman cried again and again, as though she might reduce the number by repeating it. "How am I to feed twelve people on what I have got in the larder?"

Frederica explained away all of the difficulty in a very systematic fashion, for she was inclined to undertake even a domestic problem with scientific precision. There was bouillon enough for a potage of julienne vegetables and a second of chestnut purée, which would do as well as a cream soup. The fishmonger, who kept a stew pond, had sent a supply of whitebait only that morning (Vernon having an insatiable appetite for delicacy), and Frederica repressed a smile as she determined that the portion of turbot was insufficient for twelve, so her uncle must sacrifice his private indulgence to hospitality. The haunch of mutton might be sliced and served *fricando* with some curried fowl, and there were peas and potatoes and cucumber and cabbage, which might be flavored with something like capers or bacon. Frederica's tranquillity appeased the cook so that even her objections to made-over dishes (though her mistress was willing to admit them at the children's table, or when she and Mr. Vernon dined alone) was overcome and she conceded that enough ham might be left on the bone to be turned into a bruet with the addition of some leeks, and that if something like *beaudinettes* with a cream sauce were made of the cold salmon and shrimp, nobody would suspect that they had been served the evening before. As for a dessert, if there was not cake and fruit enough, they might appeal to Mrs. Chapman, who would surely take pity upon them and send them something from her pantry and hothouse.

When the menu was fixed, Frederica went up to arrange her dress. Wilson urged her to change from her mourning to an evening dress of silver-gray crepe, to which Frederica was reconciled by the addition of a black sash.

The party had assembled in the saloon, and when Frederica entered, Lucy Smith jumped up at once and cried, "Ah, here you are! For shame—what would I have done if you had caught me! How miserable my dear Mr. Smith and I would have been if you had succeeded! You cannot be angry—you will shake hands in spite of it?"

Frederica could not but smile at such willful good nature, and she extended herself even so far as to shake hands with Mr. Smith, who looked somewhat abashed by the courtesy of a woman whom he had pronounced stupid and proud.

The conversation was awkward—nobody could be comfortable except for those whose conduct ought to have rendered them contrite and silent. Sir James was all ease and affability and Lucy Smith was delighted with everything. "What a sweet and natural spot your Churchill is! The woods appear quite wild! I do not like it at all when a property is laid out all orderly and trim! What do you think, Claudia, do you not think that Churchill is much prettier than Gisbourne?" she cried, naming the Hamiltons' country residence.

"I cannot think meanly of the home in which I was brought up," Claudia replied. Her younger sister's marriage had left her between the obligation to think ill of Lucy's elopement and the envy of a younger sister's nuptials occurring before her own.

"I think we all must have a particular attachment to the home in which we were raised," observed Mr. Lewis deCourcy in his easy fashion, "but circumstances will often oblige us to live elsewhere. My childhood was spent in Kent, and as a young man I lived primarily in town. I was fond of them both, and yet now that I have settled in Bath, I am perfectly happy—or very close to it."

"That is because you have the right disposition," Sir James answered with a smile. "But many of us are too unyielding. We do not want to settle anywhere but in familiar surroundings."

"Which often means that the *lady* must yield," was Lady Vernon's cool reply. "Unless her home and her husband's are in the same county. A gentleman can settle where he likes while his lady is often removed from all that is familiar to her."

"And yet you must agree, cousin," Sir James replied cheerfully, "that many marriages come out of a family connection, while the prospective couple are still children. Visiting each other's households and taking pleasure in each other's society must ensure that if a union should arise from it, there will be no feeling of unhappiness or sacrifice on the part of the lady."

"I think there must always be unhappiness when a lady is taken from her home," observed Mrs. Vernon. "I am sure that I cannot like Churchill Manor nearly so well as Parklands."

Even the Smiths, who were less sensible of what ought to give offense than anyone in the room, were uncomfortable at a declaration that slighted the family home of Lady Vernon and her daughter.

"La!" cried Mrs. Smith. "Then you would have us never marry!"

It was at this moment that Reginald came into the room with Vernon in tow. The latter could not conceal his agitation at the sight of the company, but he managed a few words of welcome and then, making his dress the excuse, hurried out of the room.

Sir James, in very high spirits, took up the conversation where it had left off, and moving his chair closer to Frederica's, he said, "I would have *everybody* marry. Let us all give up our claims to property and demands as to settlements that keep us single too long. I would marry this minute if the object of my affection would consent."

"Then you would marry too quickly for your own happiness," said Reginald, "and for the lady's, too."

"And yet if you wait too long, your opportunity to be happy may be lost forever," observed Lewis deCourcy, whose natural civility attempted to keep the conversation away from unpleasantness. "I should not be the old bachelor I am today if I had not thought too long and seriously over each prospect. Someone inevitably cut me out before I could bring myself to advance my suit."

"I cannot think that we disagree, Uncle," Reginald replied. "Where there is a genuine prospect of felicity, there is no need to delay from a want of fortune. We ought no more argue ourselves *out* of our happiness than we should allow ourselves to be argued *into* a union where there can be no promise of it. No gentleman can want a wife who finds him truly disagreeable and a woman of feeling would rather work for her bread than give her hand without her heart."

Frederica blushed deeply at this remark, and Miss Manwaring, sensing her friend's unease, hastened to observe, "I agree with Lady Vernon, sir. Your remarks are colored by the power of choice, which your sex enjoys. The prospect of working for one's bread is not a mean one, but it is not one that a lady is raised to. Marriage is the only situation for a gentlewoman of small fortune, and yet we cannot choose it, we must wait to be addressed. I daresay *you*, Mr. deCourcy, broke many hearts with your silence."

"My uncle cannot wish to marry," declared Claudia. "He is rich enough and happy enough to be single."

"And yet," replied her uncle with a smile that included Miss Manwaring, "those who have reached my age and are single are so because they have been too poor or too miserable to engage the affections of any lady."

Vernon did not come down again until the party was rising to go into the dining room, and they sat down to dinner with considerable discomfort on the part of both Vernon and his wife. She was in too much apprehension over her menu, and Vernon was oppressed by the benevolent gaze of Sir Frederick's portrait on the opposite wall (as Reginald, acting with his usual resolve, had removed the portrait of Lady Vernon and her daughter and ordered Sir Frederick's likeness brought down from the attic and hung in its place) and by the unhappy recollection that he had not had so many people at his table since Sir Frederick's death.

The conversation shifted from subject to subject until at last the weather and the roads and the excellence of a particular dish (which put Mrs. Vernon into a better humor, if it did not render her more talkative) were all gone over. Whenever there was a break in the conversation, Lucy Smith would inevitably say something to make one of the others blush or wince until, at the earliest possible moment, Mrs. Vernon rose and led the ladies from the table.

Frederica now had the opportunity to sit down with Maria Manwaring and enjoy a quiet *tête-à-tête*, while Lady Vernon took up some needlework and Mrs. Vernon inquired of her cousin Claudia how Lavinia did and whether she would accompany Lord and Lady Hamilton to London. "In town, Lavinia and Reginald will be at leisure to see one another on a more frequent footing."

"La!" cried Lucy, who had been roaming around the room and exclaiming over everything that caught her eye. "We will not want my cousin in town except to fix the date and then he may run away again until the wedding! Lavinia will need to buy her wedding clothes, and nobody wants a gentleman about for that! And we may buy ours together, as I had not time to get a stitch before my marriage."

This remark produced something like a flush of embarrassment to Mrs. Vernon. "Then perhaps you ought not have been so impetuous," she replied coolly.

Lucy, however, who heard nothing that she did not wish to hear, addressed Frederica. "We may all three go to the warehouses together, for I cannot believe your beau will be put off much longer! What a pleasant man Sir James is! How can you not like him!"

Frederica blushed at this remark, and Lady Vernon saved her from the obligation of making any reply by answering, "Sir James is our cousin, and I am sure that we both like him as much as we can—and sometimes more than he deserves. Our relations must claim a closer attachment than our friends and cannot be easily dropped from our acquaintance, though I believe many of us would divorce a cousin or a brother if we could."

Miss Manwaring said, "Indeed," almost too quietly to be heard, and Lucy exclaimed, "Oh, I daresay you are right! Claudia would not love me half so much if I were not her sister!"

Claudia Hamilton was spared the necessity of a reply by the appearance of the gentlemen, and the coffee and tea had no sooner been laid out than Lucy Smith cried, "Oh, what an excellent party we are—just so many gentlemen as there are ladies! And this room is such a fine size! Why, may we not have some dancing?"

Mrs. Vernon was dismayed at her young cousin's boldness, but Manwaring and Smith and even Sir James seemed to favor the proposal, and Vernon welcomed anything that might take the place of conversation.

The furniture was pushed away and the carpets rolled up so quickly that all was made ready before the musician was thought of. Lady Vernon immediately proceeded to the instrument, with more thought of escaping the attentions of Sir James and Manwaring than accommodating the company. Her powers were well suited to the occasion, as she could perform any number of country dances with spirit.

Reginald walked up to Frederica and made his petition, and to everyone's surprise, Lewis deCourcy claimed Miss Manwaring, who seemed not at all discomfited by the request. Smith would have nobody but his wife, and Manwaring, left to sit with the dull Mrs. Vernon or dance with the equally dull Claudia Hamilton, chose the latter.

Sir James put a chair beside the pianoforte and Lady Vernon attacked him at once, while her fingers danced over the keys. "You are a fine relation! What possessed you to write such a note! 'To work for my bread'! What would Mrs. Vernon think if it had fallen into her hands?"

"She would put poison in my teacup."

Lady Vernon replied to this with a toss of her head and fixed her eyes upon the keyboard once more.

"How pretty she looks! And young deCourcy is the picture of triumph. He knows that he has cut me out."

"Perhaps he only rejoices because he has got to your *teacup*."

Sir James laughed. "No, he will revenge himself upon me by marrying Freddie—that is as far as his imagination can take him. It will be an excellent match for them both—he will give her consequence and she will give him sense."

"I do not think that Mr. deCourcy is wanting in sense."

"Say rather that he does not want natural abilities. His education and understanding are good, but *sense* will always be vulnerable when those closest to us are weak-minded or prone to idleness or resentment or vice. In the company of a father who was too frail to exert his authority, a mother possessing neither education nor talents, and a sister whose fondness took the form of flattering his vanity, his understanding became susceptible, and he was encouraged to form opinions too hastily and express them with too little restraint. That is precisely what a prudent wife will guard against."

"You must not be severe upon him, James. All gentlemen do not possess your high degree of gravity and restraint."

"If I am to be grave, do not provoke me to laugh. I must look like one who has had his hopes dashed."

Lady Vernon made no reply, and after completing a reel, she complained of fatigue and withdrew from the instrument.

There was a pause as the ladies all considered whether one of them ought to take a turn at the instrument and each waited for another to surrender her enjoyment and her partner for the sake of the others. Vernon took advantage of this lull to observe how very cloudy a day it had been, and whether it boded rain or snow, and whether the drive back to Billingshurst was above an hour.

Mr. Lewis deCourcy immediately made the civil observation that the comfort of the ladies must be considered and that there were horses and servants who had been called out at very short notice for the sake of everyone's pleasure—they must be thought of as well. Another round of dancing was therefore forfeited in favor of a collation of fruit and cakes and tarts, which had been sent by Mrs. Chapman.

While the Vernons were bidding adieu to their guests, Sir James took the opportunity to walk up to Reginald. "I have played a mean trick on you—you must forgive it, for my cousins' sake. It will ease Lady Vernon's mind considerably if we attempt something like friendship. You cannot refuse to pardon one who asks for it so readily."

"I can only conclude that the readiness with which you ask for pardon comes from the number of occasions that have afforded you practice," Reginald replied.

"Far too many! Fortunately, my relations and friends are an exceptionally forgiving lot."

Mr. and Mrs. Vernon were both very surprised to walk back into the room to see Reginald and Sir James shaking hands. "Mrs. Vernon!" cried Sir James. "What an excellent party! I am delighted that my own taste for the impromptu did not inconvenience you—so excellent a dinner! I did not have one half so good at Lord Millbanke's last week, and he keeps three French cooks just for his large parties."

Before Mrs. Vernon could decide whether or not she ought to be mollified, Sir James continued. "I fear that I must end my visit prematurely and must leave for London very early tomorrow. You will none of you be down for breakfast, save for Mr. deCourcy—and I invite you, sir, to share my chaise, as it will be more suited to the weather and the state of the roads than your curricle. I will say good-bye to you, Vernon," he added, "and ask you to indulge me so far as to allow me to make my adieux to my fair cousins tonight so that they will not feel obliged to see me off tomorrow."

Mr. and Mrs. Vernon supposed that Sir James meant to make his offer for Miss Vernon and withdrew, she resolving never again to be caught without provisions for a dozen guests and he wondering how long it would be before the fishmonger had another such fine supply of whitebait.

Reginald bade them all a good night and expressed a wish that they might all meet in London very soon, then left them alone, his state of mind far more sanguine at the end of the day than at its beginning.

When he had gone, Frederica gave her cousin a kiss and advised him to depart from Churchill a better man than when he arrived, then allowed her mother and cousin to say their farewells in private.

"I hope that I shall be able to take Freddie's excellent advice," Sir James declared when the door had closed upon her. "I hope that I shall leave here a happier man, at least."

"You have never been unhappy, James."

"You are quite right. But I anticipate the particular satisfaction of taking my mother's advice. There is no triumph so complete as seeing the surprise of a parent who has got past expecting anything like compliance."

"I think that you can no more be compliant than my aunt can be surprised, unless her advice is of some consequence."

"It is. Mother has urged me to marry for so long that I am certain she has quite given up on the prospect."

Lady Vernon experienced something like sadness at his pronouncement. As the husband of another, the playfellow of her youth and her foil and confidant would be lost to her forever. "And who is the lady?" She affected something like her old playfulness of tone. "Not Miss Claudia Hamilton, surely. Or one of the Misses Millbanke?"

"Oh, no! I can allow for some shortcoming in my companions, but never in a wife—*there*, nothing less than perfection will do. I am such a good-for-nothing that I must have a wife who is exceptional in everything."

"I confess I am very curious, cousin. I can think of nobody in our range of acquaintance who is anywhere near perfection—save Freddie, perhaps, and you have resigned your role as her admirer."

"Yes, but there is someone *very near* Freddie who will suit me even better." To Lady Vernon's astonishment, her cousin became very grave. "My dear cousin—my dear Susan—I valued and esteemed Sir Frederick, you know that I did. I am acutely aware of what is due to his memory and I would never address you if to do so would be to trespass upon his wishes for your future happiness. I know that Freddie would approve, and Mother would be truly indebted to you for the very great honor you would confer upon her by taking me off her hands."

Here he paused and looked at her expression before deciding whether he should continue.

Lady Vernon was dumbfounded. She had always liked her cousin—nay, she loved him—with all of the warmth and affection of two people who have known each other since childhood. No match could suit either of them better, for she was inured to all of his faults and he was so in love as to be persuaded that she had almost none at all.

"I have forgot," Sir James continued, "the fervent assurances that I love you beyond expression. You will forgive me if I have overlooked what ought to be said at the outset. Though I have been said to be on the verge of marriage with every eligible young lady in England, I am quite a novice at the business of proposing—nor do I have any ambition to become a proficient."

Lady Vernon needed no such assurance. That Sir James loved her, she was certain. But would he have offered his hand if he knew that it would obligate him to Sir Frederick's unborn child? "I am not yet out of mourning."

"I am not proposing that we elope, Susan. That is for the likes of Charles Smith and Lucy Hamilton. I only ask for the permission to hope."

"I would be very wrong to encourage such a hope. My own prospects are so uncertain that yours may be injured by affixing your fortunes to mine. Did you not pronounce marriage to be a business transaction that one should not enter without a promise of a return? I encourage you, as a cousin who has loved you all her life, to aspire to a happier and richer union than I can offer."

"I do not look to be enriched by marriage, only to be happy. I entirely comprehend your hesitation, but you need have no anxiety on Freddie's account," he hastened to assure her. "Tomorrow I journey to London with deCourcy and I will impress upon him any of Freddie's perfections that have escaped his notice—it will take far less than thirty miles to accomplish. They will be married in six months."

"A great deal may change in six months," Lady Vernon replied. "Your nature and inclinations are such that in half a year's time you may regret your offer to me."

Sir James was affronted and almost angry. "When have I ever wavered in my devotion to you? When have I ever given you cause to think that I would tender my proposals to *anyone* without sincerity? I do not deserve such censure."

Lady Vernon had never seen him so carried away by emotion. "I beg your pardon, cousin. I do not censure you—indeed, I have always relied upon your devotion."

"And you may continue to rely upon it. If six months' time should bring about any change in me, it will be that of a more determined attachment."

"If that is true, you will not object to postponing your addresses. In six months' time, if your attachment is not what you declare it to be today—if some circumstance should arise that would make you unwilling to renew your proposals—you will suffer neither reproach nor blame from me."

"I assure you that in six months the only regret I will feel is the loss of so much time to suspense and anxiety when I might have been happy and secure. But it is no sacrifice—indeed, as Frederick has been gone barely six months, it is no more than is due to his memory."

Lady Vernon was resigned to her cousin's determination to be happy and decided that it was better to let the passage of time, and the event that it would bring about, test the depth of his fidelity. She extended her hand and he kissed it, both perfectly satisfied that the matter was resolved.

VOLUME III

London and Kent

LONDON

WHILE THEIR CONDUCT AND COMPANIONS HAD BEEN very different, Sir James Martin and Sir Frederick Vernon had shared many qualities in common, and chief among them was optimism. No problem was insoluble, no obstacle insurmountable, nor was any misery permanent.

Sir James, therefore, woke on the following morning certain that time would resolve all in his favor. It had been unfeeling of him to address his cousin in a place that must recall both her happiest and unhappiest days, and there were other considerations that made her hesitation perfectly natural. In making so early a second marriage, she would certainly incur the censure of the world (which he had once advised her to heed), and she could not think of marrying before a match for Frederica might be secured. His efforts would better be directed toward bringing Frederica and Reginald deCourcy together— once their attachment was a settled thing, Susan would have only her own future to think about.

He wrote a handsome note to Mrs. Vernon thanking her for her hospitality and expressing his desire to reciprocate it should she ever come to London, and another more affectionate one to his cousins, apologizing once more for his mischief and insisting that they must always regard him as one who had only their best interests at heart.

The gentlemen had an early breakfast, their baggage was secured, and the carriage set off at nine o'clock. The weather was favorable to Sir James—that is, there was just enough drizzle and fog to slow their journey, and Sir James had ample time to promote Miss Vernon's beauty, refinement, and accomplishment.

"She is superior in every way, and I may speak as one who has known her since her birth, though not"—Sir James smiled—"as one who was ever a suitor. Lady Vernon and I were brought up almost as brother and sister, and our families were always on very intimate footing, which, I suppose, began the gossip that I had not married because I was waiting for my young cousin to come of age. I was very wrong to let it go on as long as it did, as it only added to speculation. A gentleman of fortune *must* be married—his friends and neighbors will have no peace until he is."

"But if you never meant to make a proposal for Miss Vernon, why, when I addressed Lady Vernon on the subject, did she not contradict me?"

"I suspect that my cousin was so very shocked that you believed the gossip that she did not know what to say. And supposing that the rumor had come to you by way of Mrs. Vernon, she did not wish to impugn your good sister's information. I am quite certain that when addressed on the subject, Lady Vernon thought only to defend Miss Vernon as *deserving* of the addresses of a gentleman in my situation and not to deliberately suggest that I was her object."

Reginald could not clearly recall what had been said and, after a moment, decided that this had indeed been the case.

"But so it is with parents," Sir James continued. "By them we are taught, from the moment we think of marrying at all, that we cannot marry without some attention to money. And yet if they might only consider the unequal matches that are the result of it— the years of unhappiness that follow a union fashioned out of a parent's ambition—perhaps they might consider the very great advantage of a son- or daughter-in-law whose character and abilities may be superior to wealth."

"You speak with a great feeling for the subject."

"There was someone I liked," Sir James replied gravely, "who suited me in every regard. But her fortune was not what my father— an excellent parent in every other respect, and a gentleman always worthy of the highest regard—wished for me, and I allowed his desires, if not to rule me, at least to cause me to hesitate just long enough for another to win her heart and her hand. I have not found anybody I liked quite as well ever since."

Reginald was struck by the unexpected sincerity of Sir James's manner.

"It is a lesson," Sir James continued, "not to let ourselves be ruled by others in the matter of our happiness, nor to place fortune above true felicity."

"But that is spoken like a rich man, who may do as he likes." Reginald smiled.

"All the more reason that I ought to have done as I liked when the opportunity was before me."

"You cannot reproach yourself for honoring your father's wishes."

"I *can* reproach myself for giving so little credit to his affection by supposing that he would feel a lasting resentment if I married against his ambition. I allowed myself to think that he would prefer me to be rich rather than happy. If I had spoken at once, if I had made my feelings plain, he might have attempted to argue me out of them—he might have attributed them to youth, as I was very young at the time—but I believe that he would have yielded in the end."

"There was no objection to the lady's character?"

"None at all. She was unexceptionable in every regard."

After a few moments, Sir James continued with a smile, "The result is that I have made myself the fodder of the gossipmongers and the matchmakers. The rumors of an engagement to my young cousin came out of it, and will not end until she comes to London and engages the attention of some young man or other. Not all young men can be the fool that I was, nor can every father be so ambitious. A young lady of Frederica's beauty and accomplishment, of such excellent disposition and character, will not be disregarded for a want of fortune."

Reginald could say no more than "Indeed, no."

As REGINALD WAS only to stay in London until the following morning, Sir James invited him to pass the night at his house in town, and Reginald accepted with pleasure. The journey gave Reginald an opportunity to understand that Sir James was very different from what gossip had pronounced him to be; he had been said to be thoughtless and giddy, and yet every expression had shown him to be civil, intelligent, and amiable.

They decided to stop at Portland Place in order to turn over Lady Vernon's portrait to her housekeeper. The door was answered by this woman, who greeted Sir James with genuine warmth and commissioned the footman to take charge of the parcel.

Then, to their very great surprise, the housekeeper declared, "Lady Martin has been awaiting you in the front parlor. She would have you join her."

"Mother!" Sir James cried, throwing open the door to the parlor. Lady Martin was sitting beside the fire, needlework on her lap and two plump cats at her feet.

"Well, you have got here! You may kiss me—I cannot get up. Do not tease Kit! You are Mr. deCourcy," she addressed Reginald. "There, the bother of deciding which of us must request an introduction is done with. I have some slight acquaintance with your father and mother, sir, and I hope that they were in health when you saw them last."

Reginald was surprised, but not displeased, with the lady's address, which despite her easy manner retained an air of elegance.

"My father has not been as strong as I would like, but Miss Vernon was kind enough to send a few receipts, which I hope will give him some improvement."

"Excellent! She is an excellent girl—but a superior mother will invariably produce a superior daughter. If I had a daughter, she should have been a very superior girl, and nothing at all like this reprobate whose company you have been compelled to suffer all the way from Sussex. Sit down—why do you stand there? I will give you some tea. Do you stop at my son's house?"

"Yes, ma'am, Sir James has been kind enough to ask me to stay for the night. Tomorrow I proceed to Parklands."

"Well, one night in his company can do you no harm."

"I am very surprised to see you here, Mother," said Sir James. "I cannot account for it."

"Why may I not come to town if I like?"

"But you do not like it—you haven't come to town for ten years."

"But I *meant* to come," she maintained, and addressed Reginald once more. "But for her father's accident, Frederica would have been presented. Sir Frederick would have been so delighted, the proudest father who ever lived. A very great loss to her. There are some who will say that a father is never of great consequence to a daughter, that so long as she has been left comfortably off, it is of no matter whether he is present or absent, as they have no interests in common, but that was not true of Sir Frederick and my niece. He would not have wished her away for a son."

"But you do not say why you come to London, ma'am."

"To stand up with Frederica if she likes to go out and keep the nuisances from imposing upon Susan when *she* likes to stay at home. I do not mean to suggest that *you* are among the nuisances, sir." She addressed Reginald. "*You* may call as often as you like when you are in town."

Reginald thanked her.

"Such an accomplished girl. She plays and sings so charmingly, and as for her drawing! Look at those watercolors upon the wall—that is a crocus border she put in at Vernon Castle, and there, too, is the laurel hedge round the lodge. Do you not think they are very nicely done?"

Reginald walked over to examine the sketches. "Yes, they are very well done."

"It is a great pity she was obliged to leave Vernon Castle. Ah, here is our tea! You must be very tired after your journey."

When they had drunk their tea and Lady Martin had asked their opinion of whether the portrait ought to be hung in the sitting room or the library, and then deciding the matter for herself, she invited Reginald to dine at Portland Place upon his return to London.

The gentlemen left shortly afterward, and although Sir James felt obliged to beg for some small allowance of his mother's outspoken manner, Reginald assured him that he had found Lady Martin to be delightful.

chapter forty-three

TWO DAYS AFTER REGINALD'S DEPARTURE, MR. LEWIS deCourcy called at Churchill Manor, bringing Miss Manwaring with him. "Manwaring left for town this morning, but Miss Manwaring and I are to remain a few days longer, and then I escort her to London. The Parkers have expressed a desire to meet Miss Vernon. May we not bring her to Billingshurst with us until Lady Vernon is ready to quit Churchill?"

"I think that Frederica will be delighted to know the Parkers," declared Lady Vernon. "Indeed, it is a scheme that will suit everyone. Mrs. Vernon has long desired to go to Parklands, and now that her brother is gone, I will not suspend her pleasure by prolonging my visit. Frederica may go with you, and I will make my own preparations for town, which can be accomplished in two days' time."

"Oh, no!" protested Charles, who had no desire to have his wife get to Parklands before Reginald had left it. If Reginald did mean to ask his parents' consent to a marriage with Lady Vernon, he might well withstand a confrontation with Lady deCourcy, but Catherine and her mother together could wear him down. "Lady Vernon was to be with us another week at least and I am certain that Catherine and the children cannot be ready to travel with only two days to prepare."

"Indeed, I *can*," cried Catherine with more feeling than civility.

"I will write to Mrs. Forrester at once, and I invite you, my dear sister, to stop the night at Portland Place before going on to Kent—it is a very modest return for all of the hospitality you have shown me."

"If Frederica is to leave us, and travels with my uncle to London," said Catherine to Lady Vernon, "I will take this opportunity of asking now what I meant to ask upon her departure. I hope that I may persuade you to allow Frederica to accompany me to Parklands. You may spare her for a few weeks, I think, and her presence will recompense the children for their father's absence, as Charles will be obliged to spend many weeks in town."

Lady Vernon did not remark that Charles spent so little time with the children and took so little interest in their concerns as to make it of no consequence to them whether he was in London or Kent, and she suspected that Catherine's invitation was given solely to have someone at hand who was so useful in managing the children and so accommodating to *her*. The opportunity to let her daughter become known to the deCourcys, however, was one that Lady Vernon could not refuse—Frederica might easily be spared for a few weeks before she would be wanted at her mother's side in London.

She gave her consent, therefore, and Mr. deCourcy suggested that the plan be adapted to include Miss Manwaring. "I will write to Sir Reginald myself, which will secure her welcome to Parklands, and it will give Miss Vernon a companion on those occasions when you, Catherine, will be occupied with your mother or the children."

Catherine did not approve of her uncle's proposal at once. It was certainly a very forward thing to expect Miss Manwaring, a person of no consequence, to be admitted to Parklands Manor. She would not have to exert herself, however, so far as to petition her father, nor to accommodate Miss Manwaring in any way—to be at Parklands would be honor enough for *her*.

All was speedily arranged, and when the young ladies and Mr. deCourcy departed for Billingshurst, Lady Vernon retired to her rooms to write to her aunt in London.

LADY VERNON TO LADY MARTIN

Churchill Manor, Sussex
My dear Aunt,

I will be in London in three days' time. I am obliged to have the Vernons stop at Portland Place; for that, I beg your pardon, but it will only be for the night. Mrs. Vernon will not stay longer, as she is eager to get to Parklands, no doubt hoping to join her mother in attempting to keep Reginald from returning to London.

How did you like him? Do you not think they are well suited? I have every expectation that he goes to Kent on purpose to disappoint his parents in regard to Miss Hamilton, and then it will only be a matter of time—a very short time, I hope—before he declares himself to Frederica. I think that event might be reasonably looked for in the course of a twelvemonth, but as Reginald's nature is equally impulsive and resolute, it might as easily be accomplished in less than half the time.

Mrs. Vernon has asked that Freddie accompany her to Kent, and while the motive for the invitation must be for her own convenience, I am happy for Freddie to have the opportunity to secure the good opinion of those who hereinafter may become her in-laws.

I hope that the prospect of <u>that</u>, my dear Aunt, will offset your disappointment in another matter. James has made his proposals to me. How far you ever considered the possibility of this, I cannot tell, but I was taken entirely by surprise. The honor of this application cannot be measured, and in different circumstances the prospect of a proposal from James would have been gratifying beyond expression; under <u>these</u> circumstances, however, I am persuaded that the expectation of a first husband's child must lessen my appeal were James aware of it.

I have said nothing to Frederica of this. All thoughts of marriage must be directed toward her future.

We will all be at Portland Place by dinnertime. The party will include not only the Vernons but also Miss Manwaring and Mr. Lewis deCourcy.

Yours, etc.,
Susan V.

chapter forty-four

EGINALD DECOURCY'S ARRIVAL AT PARKLANDS MANOR was greeted with extravagant delight by his mother and with a more temperate and genuine pleasure by his father. He handed over Catherine's letter immediately, and Lady deCourcy hurried away to her dressing room so that she might peruse it in private and immediately write her reply.

She passed quickly over the description of Sir James Martin and fixed her attention on Catherine's anxiety for Reginald.

> Unless, my dear Mother, you and my father can contrive to keep Reginald at Parklands until his infatuation with Lady Vernon has subsided, I must think of their eventual marriage as a possibility. Use every persuasion in your power, and if, after all exertion, he is still resolved upon settling in town for the coming months, I fear that it may be that there is already an arrangement between them.
>
> As for Miss Vernon, I am of half a mind to prevail upon Lady Vernon to keep her with me. I am convinced that she must be happier with us than in town with her mother, where she will be compelled to be in the company of Lady Vernon's friends—a very bad set, I doubt not. I do not say that Miss Vernon is so weak that her mother's companions can injure her, but in London she must mix with them or be left in solitude, where at Parklands she might make herself useful. I begin to think more and more of engaging her as a governess until a more suitable match than Sir James Martin may be found for her. My Aunt Hamilton had spoke of the likelihood that the Reverend Mr. Heywood might soon be in want of a wife and I am certain that Miss

Vernon would do for him. He is in possession of such a good living that he cannot be very particular as to fortune, and Charles once mentioned that she has no more than the two or three thousand pounds left to her by her grandparents. As for Sir James Martin, he would be much better suited to someone like my cousin Claudia, who is his equal in birth and fortune.

Charles will be obliged to remain in town for many weeks, so we shall have a very good, long visit in Kent. Pray heaven that I may quit Sussex as soon as possible and that you may keep Reginald at Parklands until that time so that we may all work upon him together.

Your affectionate daughter,
Catherine Vernon

While Lady deCourcy was preoccupied with penning her response, Reginald sat down to a quiet interview with his father, and to answer all of Sir Reginald's inquiries as to how Catherine and the children did and how his time had been spent at Churchill Manor.

The subject of Lady Vernon was not directly introduced, but Reginald spoke of her by way of her relations, declaring that his opinion of Sir James Martin had been very much improved and that his introduction to Lady Martin had been very agreeable. "She expressed nothing but affection and regard for Lady Vernon, and my Uncle deCourcy likewise holds her in very high esteem—and they are, sir, the commendations of people who have known her since childhood."

"And so do you now discredit *all* of the accounts of her unbecoming conduct, not only at Langford but also during her marriage?"

"I do now what I ought to have done at first, sir—what your principles ought to have compelled me to do sooner. I disallow all that cannot be supported by any particular examples of that lady's profligacy or any unmitigated proof of impropriety. By all the neighbors and tenants, she is held up as a model of respectability and generosity, and I was myself a daily witness to the deference she paid to Catherine, however difficult it must have been to see her post assumed by another and be reduced to a visitor and a dependent in the home where she had once been mistress."

"And yet her going to Langford—the look of it was so very bad. My sister was quite shocked by her conduct, which was very gay for a widow."

"We forget that she was obliged to go *somewhere*, sir, as she could not stay on at Churchill, and that perhaps it was Langford, and not Lady Vernon, that was too gay."

"Yet she was not so friendless that Langford was her only refuge. She might have chosen more prudently."

"Yes, but it may have been done for her daughter's sake. Miss Vernon's spirits were quite depressed and Lady Vernon might have hoped to revive them by bringing her daughter among other young people."

"And what sort of person is Miss Vernon?"

Reginald spoke with great feeling of Miss Vernon's superior character and understanding, reminding his father of the generous impulse that had overtaken prudence so much as to cause Miss Vernon to lose her place at school and enumerating the many ways in which she had made herself useful at Churchill.

Although Reginald did not hesitate in his praise of Lady Vernon's respectability, an incident had occurred, while he passed through London, which gave him some concern for her reputation.

MR. deCOURCY TO LADY VERNON

Parklands Manor, Kent
Dear Madam,

Forgive any indelicacy of writing to you in this manner and allow me to assure you that the portrait that you entrusted to me has been safely delivered to Portland Place. There I had the very great pleasure of being introduced to Lady Martin.

I wish, madam, that I could express an equal pleasure with my experience at Edward Street. When I was admitted and ushered into the drawing room, a dispute between a lady and a gentleman was clearly audible from the other side of the door, and the name "Manwaring" was unmistakable.

Mrs. Johnson hurried into the room and I presented her your letter. She welcomed me in a civil fashion, though she was very much embarrassed by what was overheard. "You must forgive the state in which you find us," she said to me. "My husband's ward has called upon him very unexpectedly."

She then bade me sit down and asked a great many questions about your coming to town. She had learned that Lady Martin had taken residence at Portland Place and seemed to take this as evidence that a marriage between Sir James and Miss Vernon was imminent. I did not think that it was my place to undeceive her, and before the subject might be continued, the library door was thrown open and a lady and gentleman entered the room. The gentleman was Mr. Johnson and the lady was introduced as Mrs. Manwaring, and as it was evident that she wished to speak privately with Mrs. Johnson, I was invited by Mr. Johnson into his library, so that the ladies might have their tête-à-tête.

I found Mr. Johnson, though abrupt in his manner, to be a very gentlemanlike man. He asked most particularly after Miss Vernon. I made some mention of her friendship with Miss Manwaring and my recent introduction to her and her brother, and Mr. Johnson replied, "It is no secret that I was not pleased with Eliza's choice of a husband, but I am not so pitiless as to rejoice that I had been right. She seeks my aid in effecting a separation, and if you have any influence with Lady Vernon, I would advise you to caution her of the imprudence of admitting Manwaring to her household when she comes to London. Toward _her_, I will not think as ill as I once did—she cannot have produced as excellent a daughter as Miss Vernon if she had been truly bad. But an ill-chosen acquaintance may give one the appearance of impropriety, which, for the sake of Miss Vernon, I hope her mother will avoid."

I assured Mr. Johnson that I would heed his advice, and as Mrs. Manwaring and I left together, I offered to escort her to her lodgings in town.

We had no sooner settled in my carriage than Mrs. Manwaring began to importune me on the subject of your time in Sussex and whether Mr. Manwaring had frequently been a visitor to Churchill

Manor. I was struck with the impropriety of such forwardness to a stranger and replied that though I had been many weeks at Churchill Manor, I had seen her husband only once, when he had dined with the party from Billingshurst. However Mrs. Manwaring's jealousy must mislead her in regard to you, madam, it was very clear from her expressions that she and Manwaring are to part and that her visit to Edward Street was an attempt—one of many, I infer—to secure the interest of her former guardian.

I write this so that when you come to London, you will know how things stand. I hope that Mr. Manwaring will not use his sister's intimacy with Miss Vernon to gain admittance to Portland Place.

I remain,
Reginald deCourcy

As Charles Vernon and his groom drove along Portland Place in Reginald's curricle (which Charles had agreed to convey to town), he looked at the elegant residences as if for the first time and noted the number of crests upon the passing vehicles and wondered how his sister could keep such a fine address on her modest income. In his mind, he rehearsed a few remarks about how much must be attended to in a house that Lady Vernon had not occupied for nearly two years and how far the presence of a male relation and his family might hold off the gossip that would be stirred up when a lady was living alone.

His hopes lasted only until the front door was opened. Two liveried footmen hurried down to the carriages, and in the doorway stood Lady Martin. Charles was very surprised, for he had heard that Lady Martin liked town even less than Lady deCourcy. She would not have come so far unless there was a very particular reason, and that reason must be the desire of the mothers to see the daughter of one married to the son of the other.

The evening was just long enough for everyone to dine and talk about nothing; for the children to run up and down the staircases and exclaim over the variety of curious vehicles that passed by the front-facing windows; and for Catherine to wonder whether she was obliged to buy her mother a present, and how (as Miss Manwaring and Miss Vernon had come to town with her uncle and would continue to Parklands with *her*) their party might be crammed into a single carriage, or whether the two nursery maids, who each had sat from Sussex to London with a child on her lap, might be sent by stage.

On the following morning, however, she found that Lady Martin had arranged for the young ladies to travel by postchaise, assigning a footman to accompany them, and paying the fare herself. Catherine was happy to have this settled at no trouble or expense to herself, and Charles resolved that, though his expectations of residing at Portland Place must be over, the goodwill of a woman who could send two young ladies to Kent by postchaise was worth retaining.

The passengers were off, and the girls settled comfortably together with no one to interrupt an unreserved conversation. Maria Manwaring *was* reserved, however, and made only the briefest of replies to her friend's remarks until at last Frederica asked Maria if she was unwell.

"No, quite the reverse. I am well—very well—but very far from being myself. I hardly know where to begin."

"In science, we always begin at the very root of the matter, which ensures that nothing will be overlooked."

"That will not do. I do not know where it *did* begin, so I must begin at the end instead. But you must not say anything until my brother is applied to for his consent—which he will not fail to give. I am to be married to Mr. Lewis deCourcy."

Frederica could not conceal her surprise, nor prevent herself from exclaiming, "Mr. Lewis deCourcy! I cannot believe it!"

"Then I have no hope that anyone else shall, until we are married," Maria replied with a blush. "My fortune is so little and the disparity in our ages so great that everyone will dismiss it as gossip. And when they are persuaded it is true, everyone will think that his suit is foolish and my consent is grossly mercenary."

"I do not think so; I know you too well. When I look back, I do recall signs of his preference—he was certainly very attentive to you when we were all together after my father's passing. But it was not an occasion where any of us were disposed to be curious. You must tell me all: How did it come about?"

"It came upon me very gradually. I have always known Mr. deCourcy through my brother and have always thought very highly of his abilities and character. In the past year, many situations have thrown us together a great deal and he declares that he came to Billingshurst on purpose to determine whether I could ever regard him as a suitor. He tells me that only a conviction that my brother and Eliza wished me to marry much higher prevented him from declaring himself sooner. But what do you think? Am I very foolish for abiding by my heart?"

"No, how could I think so? My own parents' marriage was one where there was a disparity in age and fortune, but in taste and disposition they were so well suited as to make everyone forget it."

"I hope that the deCourcys can forget it. Mr. deCourcy told me privately that he seized upon the idea of having me accompany you to Parklands Manor in order to have me known to his family."

"When does he intend to tell them of your engagement?"

"He will speak to my brother first—very soon, I hope—and then he will come to Parklands. Will it not be amusing to have me the aunt of the Hamilton girls?"

The girls indulged in some mirth at the notion of Lavinia and Claudia Hamilton compelled to address Maria as "my Aunt deCourcy," though it was agreed between them that Lucy would think it was great fun.

chapter forty-six

THE FIRST VIEW OF PARKLANDS MANOR CAME FROM THE west, where an expanse of cherry and walnut trees gave way to a wooded area that formed the beginning of a park. At the road's highest point, a clearing presented the traveler with a commanding view of the deCourcy estate. In its beauty and aspect, it reminded Frederica of Vernon Castle, although Parklands Manor was far more imposing than what her family had owned in either Staffordshire or Sussex.

Their carriage made a winding descent into a valley with a broad stream at its lowest point, and passing over a wooden bridge, it ascended once more to the lodge, where the travelers were obliged to depart from the public road. As they approached the main house, the span of valleys behind, dotted with copses and fields, came into view, and Frederica exclaimed over the great variety of flora, naming each tree and shrub with awe. How, she wondered, could Reginald deCourcy ever wish to be anywhere else!

The party was ushered into a vast entryway, calculated to impress upon the visitor the owners' wealth. The young ladies were suitably impressed, although the children, released from the tedium of the journey from town, immediately began to slide upon the polished marble and dash in and out of the many rooms until the nursery maids collected their charges and shepherded them away.

Mrs. Vernon then directed their attention to the many doors that opened from the hallway to the saloons and drawing rooms, the parlors for music and billiards and breakfast, and the grand dining room and the "main library, as there is a second, devoted entirely to my father's particular volumes."

They were left to collect around the fire in the larger of the drawing rooms while Mrs. Vernon inquired of her mother and father.

"Lady deCourcy is indisposed and has confined herself to her dressing room, but Sir Reginald is somewhere upon the grounds with Mr. deCourcy."

"Reginald has not gone back to London?" said Mrs. Vernon with great pleasure.

"No, ma'am."

Mrs. Vernon announced her intention to go immediately to her mother and instructed the housekeeper to have Miss Vernon and Miss Manwaring shown to their apartments.

When Mrs. Vernon entered her mother's dressing room, she found the lady in great distress. "Oh, I am so glad you have come!" cried Lady deCourcy. "Reginald is resolved upon leaving tomorrow—he will not be persuaded otherwise. You must talk him out of it. He has made us so very wretched—he vows that he cannot marry Lavinia. Oh, my poor sister Hamilton—to have Lucy marry so imprudently and now to have Lavinia's hopes dashed! Your father has been scarcely able to rise from his bed."

Mrs. Vernon did not think to observe that her father's *scarcely* rising from his bed was a considerable improvement over his *never* rising from it.

"Sit down, my dear girl. What can we do? How are the dear children? I made every argument I could think of—the obligation to his family, the expectations of Lavinia, and the slight to Lord and Lady Hamilton. Nothing will sway him. 'We would not suit' was all he would say to defend himself. 'You would not wish me to marry without any thought to my happiness.' How can he put his *happiness* above his duty to all of us? I am certain that if I had not been guided by my parents and had only my own *happiness* to consult, I should never have married your father. And where am I to go *now* when your father dies? Lavinia would not object to keeping me here—indeed, there are several apartments in the west wing that would do very well for me. But Lady Vernon would send me away—and yet even *that* might be borne if she were not ever to be addressed as 'Lady deCourcy.' How am I to endure it? Indeed, there is no mother fonder of her children than I have been, but I would almost rather survive my son than see him marry ill!"

"But what has he told you of Lady Vernon? Has he asked your consent to their marriage?"

"He has said nothing of her at all, but I am convinced that he is bewitched by her, for I gave him a very broad hint—I asked him if he had succumbed to another attachment while he was with you, and he would neither confirm nor deny it. And he spoke so favorably of his time with you, even praising Lady Vernon's daughter and making her out to be quite a paragon of beauty and accomplishment! Ah, you know what they say—to court the mother, you must flatter the child! So, you have brought the girl with you? And her friend as well—Manwaring's sister! After all that was said of Lady Vernon's conduct at Langford, to think of a friendship between them! It is a very inconstant world—very inconstant—and I do not know how we are to abide it if people *will* not keep to their own sphere. But perhaps if Mr. Manwaring does not have to look after his sister in London, he will pursue Lady Vernon as he did at Langford—and if *she* had so little restraint in the country, she will have none at all in town—*then*, perhaps, Reginald's eyes will be opened to what she is."

While they were engaged in hopes for Reginald's being disillusioned and made miserable, Miss Vernon and Miss Manwaring were ushered up the gleaming oak staircase and through a maze of lesser flights and landings until they were brought to a wing that had a series of doors on one side and a series of windows on the other.

The apartments that the friends were to share were well proportioned, the furniture was handsome, the walls prettily papered, and the aspect pleasing, but with the sort of simplicity and want of ornamentation that suggested that the room was reserved for inferior guests.

The two girls decided to take a turn in the open air, and after donning sturdier shoes, they struck out across one of the lawns toward a high hedge that formed a border between the small park and the greenhouses. Two gentlemen stepped into their path, one leaning upon the arm of another. Miss Vernon recognized Reginald deCourcy by his form, and as the gentlemen approached, she saw in the other a similarity of countenance and figure (though the countenance was pale and the figure bowed and wasted), which pronounced him to be Sir Reginald deCourcy.

The ladies dropped a curtsy, and the elder gentleman, seeing the look of recognition upon his son's face, immediately applied to him to make the introductions.

"Miss Frederica Vernon," he pronounced, and if Sir Reginald was surprised to see that the beautiful young lady in half-mourning was the daughter of a woman against whom he had been so prejudiced, he gave no indication of it. He bowed politely and said, "Cook has brewed me tea according to your receipts every day."

"I hope they have served you well, sir."

"Indeed they have. I have been able to get out again and enjoy my grounds. The house is a grand one—I know it is, for everybody says so, and I cannot think that so universal an opinion on any one subject can err—but I much prefer the out-of-doors. And your friend, I think, is Miss Manwaring?"

Miss Vernon said that she was.

"My brother has spoken very highly of you, Miss Manwaring, and his commendation is never bestowed idly," the gentleman said.

"It has the advantage of consensus with the world in general," added Reginald with great civility, "and therefore cannot err."

Miss Manwaring blushed, and as the path that took them toward the house narrowed, they were obliged to walk in pairs. Sir Reginald offered Miss Vernon his arm, and she concluded from his son's look of surprise (as he offered his own arm to Miss Manwaring) that it had been some time since his father had been the provider, rather than the recipient, of such support.

"January and February are too early in the year to see the true beauty of the place," said Sir Reginald. "When all is in bloom, it is a remarkable sight, but you will get some notion of the excellence of the forcing gardens and the size of the orchards, and tomorrow, in the light, I will take you to the summer house, where we drink tea in fine weather. But I will not confine you to Parklands. We keep a handsome phaeton that gets too little use. You ladies must take advantage of it on any day that is fine, for even in the winter Kent is full of beauties. It is quite the garden of England, do you not think so?"

"I do. And I thought the same of Staffordshire and Sussex, sir— indeed, when I was first taken to the apothecary gardens in town, I was quite ready to call London the garden of England as well."

Sir Reginald laughed and proceeded to inquire, with genuine interest, about her knowledge of plants and flowers. Had she studied Latin? Had she read Withering? Had the fuchsia been introduced to Churchill Manor?

Miss Vernon felt all of the compliment of his inquiries, which went beyond casual civility. She was equally pleased to understand, from the little of their conversation she overheard, that Reginald addressed Miss Manwaring with equal courtesy, and that her replies conveyed her taste, her understanding, and her superior manners. However he might regard Robert Manwaring, Reginald deCourcy must conclude that his sister was a very intelligent young woman.

They were six to dinner, and yet there were thirty covers and an array of silver plate and a great many attendants. If the two country girls were inclined to overlook some particular symptom of privilege, Lady deCourcy did not hesitate to call it to their attention, and her conversation consisted principally of remarks such as "I daresay you have not seen such superior cos lettuce," or "I would be very surprised if Mrs. Manwaring can ever get her hands upon such crayfish as these."

Reginald often blushed for her, but her daughter and husband felt no embarrassment; *she* had no consciousness of her mother's incivility and he had ceased to listen to her for many years.

If the elder gentleman's remarks were less frequent, they were more civil. He had always been fond of society, but a spell of ill health, which his wife had encouraged along to infirmity, had kept him from the sort of company that he had enjoyed in earlier years. He found Miss Vernon to be a beautiful girl, her manners refined, her conversation thoughtful and fresh, and her knowledge of growing and groundskeeping profound.

The desserts were laid and Sir Reginald deferred to Miss Vernon, whose receipts had aided his digestion so well as to enable him to eat a handsome dinner for the first time in a year. Miss Vernon smiled at the compliment and, expressing admiration for the yield of his pinery, suggested, "There is nothing so good for the digestion as pineapple, except perhaps for the extract of *carica papaya* before it ripens."

Sir Reginald took a slice of the pineapple and began to recount a few tales of the West Indies. The young ladies listened with intense interest, though Lady deCourcy seemed impatient to withdraw and once or twice seemed about to rise when a question from one of the girls or from Reginald (who was astonished at his father's excellent appetite and spirits) delayed her. At last she stood, and the other ladies followed her to the drawing room.

The party was made lively and noisy by the entrance of the children, and Lady deCourcy turned her attention entirely to them and her daughter.

"How very tall our Charlie has got in the months since you left for Sussex. Lady Penrice called on her way to Ramsgate and told the wildest tales of how tall her grandson Frank had got—six months younger than Charlie and she vows he was half a head taller! She has got a house at Ramsgate and means to have them all with her until summer, as she says London is full of influenza. How long does Charles stay in town? Nobody can remain in health very long in London. The air is so bad! He must, on no account, bring the influenza here among the children. How is the air in Sussex? Is it a very dirty place?"

Miss Vernon, who was showing little Kitty how to cut some gold paper, felt a warm blush overspread her cheeks.

"It is not as fine as Parklands," her daughter replied.

"And the people? They are a very yeomanlike set, I gather?"

"There is no society. The Parkers are ten miles off, which is too far to go to mix with people who are only moderately genteel. Mr. Parker was in trade."

"Trade is a terrible thing," declared Lady deCourcy. "It encourages those who engage in it to be ambitious above their class."

The gentlemen entered as she uttered this remark, and she called immediately for their opinion. "Catherine tells me that there is nobody in her neighborhood but for the Parkers, who made a great deal of money in trade. Do you not agree that she is very poorly situated? Would it not be best to have her and the children home again with us?"

Reginald glanced at Miss Vernon, who was bent over her work. "You forget, madam, that the hospitality of the Parkers was acceptable to my cousins and my uncle."

It was not in Lady deCourcy's nature to feel embarrassment. "Perhaps, and yet Billingshurst cannot be as pleasant as Parklands."

"I agree with you, madam," said Reginald with a smile. "I cannot wish to be anywhere else at present, and indeed I very much regret that I must leave you all tomorrow."

"If you regret it, then you ought to stay," his mother replied. "There is nobody in town."

"My sister's husband is in town. If, Catherine, you have a letter for Charles, I will bring it, and I will be happy to do the same for Miss Vernon, if she desires to send any message to her mother."

Lady deCourcy declared that neither Catherine nor Miss Vernon could have anything to write, and that it would be enough for Reginald to tell Charles that they had all got safely to Parklands, which Charles could report to Lady Vernon whenever he happened to call.

"Catherine need not write," Reginald replied, "but we must let Miss Vernon decide for herself."

Miss Vernon favored him with a grateful smile and, consigning the amusement of the children to Maria, went to a little desk in the corner to compose her letter.

Miss Vernon to Lady Vernon

Parklands Manor, Kent
My dear Madam,

> We have arrived safely in Kent to find Mr. deCourcy still at home, though he will stay only until tomorrow.
> You will want to know something of Parklands. It is very beautifully situated, and as far as the grounds are concerned, nothing has

been transformed that ought to have been left alone, and nothing has been neglected that ought to have been improved. The interior is the work of Lady deCourcy, however, and it is Langford all over again, with three items crammed where one would do and everything for show. The apartment that I share with Maria appears to be a chamber reserved for her inferior company and therefore has only such furnishings as are necessary for comfort without needless embellishment and display.

We were introduced to Sir Reginald, and he is not the fearsome object that I expected to find. In his person, he gives every appearance of having been a very commanding figure when in health, but illness has made him frail—this decline, however, appears to be reversing, as he has been able to take some exercise and to dine with the family, which I understand has not been his custom.

His manners are formal and old-fashioned but without any condescension. His welcome to Maria and me did not make me feel such an intruder as Lady deCourcy has—she does not want anybody but her daughter and the children, but if the weather is fine enough for walking, we will not be in her way.

Be assured, my dear Mother, that even if all were as it should be, were my aunt affectionate and her mother's welcome effusive, I could never be happy if I had not left you in the very capable and obliging hands of my Aunt Martin and Miss Wilson.

Please give my love to both, and write to me as often as you can.

Your affectionate daughter,
Frederica Vernon

EGINALD CALLED AT PORTLAND PLACE IMMEDIATELY upon his arrival in town and was admitted to the drawing room, where Lady Vernon reclined upon a sofa, wrapped in shawls and with an open book on her lap. She extended her hand to him, and he bowed and gave her Miss Vernon's letter, urging her not to delay the pleasure of reading it on his account.

Reginald studied Lady Vernon while she read her letter. She was pale and her movements languid. He recalled some remarks of his mother's about influenza and inquired after her health as she folded the letter.

"I am quite well. I hope that you left Sir Reginald and Lady deCourcy and Catherine in good health."

"I did, though I cannot say that I left them entirely tranquil," he replied. "I can no longer allow them to hope that I will ever address my cousin—they might have been spared a great deal of anxiety if I had been frank from the first."

"I am very glad that you were frank with them *at last*." Lady Vernon smiled.

"And my frankness with you? You may have cause to resent my advice regarding Mr. Manwaring."

"Indeed, I have no cause. Manwaring's marriage is the sort that ought to be a caution to everybody against marrying for the wrong motives. Our mutual acquaintance and Miss Manwaring's friendship with Frederica must give him some claim upon my hospitality, but I assure you, I will not have my character at the mercy of a man whose conduct has been so inconstant."

Lady Martin, having heard that Reginald deCourcy was in the house, immediately came away from her writing desk to greet him. "How did you travel? Did these terrible rains make the roads very dirty? And what of my dear niece—how does she fare at Parklands? Is she in good looks? The country air will always bring out the best in looks."

"Miss Vernon's beauty is of that superior type that makes improvement unnecessary and injury impossible."

"Ah, and if she had only been presented, she would have been universally admired. Did I tell you," she added, addressing her niece, "that Lord Whitby called yesterday? I am certain that I did. And he asked most particularly after my niece and seemed quite downcast when he learned that she had gone to Kent. Such a handsome, good-humored man," she added, turning to Reginald once more.

Lady Vernon repressed a smile and a shake of her head, as her aunt continued, "I told him that he must not hope to meet with Frederica again for a fortnight at least."

"A fortnight?" cried Reginald. "I am certain that Catherine said Miss Vernon was to be with her for three or four weeks."

"Ah, then I must be mistaken. A person of my age never makes much distinction between two weeks or three. It is only of importance to young people and to those in love."

Reginald had no opportunity to reply, as the door was thrown open and Mrs. Johnson entered the room. The spell of heavy rains had kept Lady Vernon and her aunt from being troubled by many callers, but Mrs. Johnson would not be put off by dirty weather. The distinction of being received by Lady Martin and collecting a few scraps of gossip to scatter through London was one that not even the ruin of six inches of hem could suppress.

She was delighted to meet Reginald again, particularly at Portland Place—it supported her conviction that the young man meant to make Lady Vernon an offer of marriage, and this was confirmed by Lady Vernon's pale and languid appearance, which must be the result of waiting for him to speak.

"Are you settled in town for the season, sir?" inquired Mrs. Johnson.

"I cannot say. There is an interest that brings me to London and another that may call me back to Kent."

"Well, you have got to that time of life when everybody will want a share of your company, and it will be difficult to know how to please them and do your duty to your parents as well."

"Indeed," observed Lady Martin, "I tell my son that he must not concern himself with duty—he may keep away from me as long as he likes without ever offending me or thinking me neglected. There will be time enough to settle when you marry. Then your friends and relations may come to you, and I can only hope that the occasion will see such an improvement in Sir Reginald that you will be obliged to find a property of your own when you settle."

"Oh, yes, indeed!" chimed in Mrs. Johnson. "For entails can be very awkward arrangements."

"I think the purpose of an entail is an excellent one," replied Reginald.

"Yes," Lady Vernon observed, "but the *purpose* is not always borne out in practice. Not every heir can administer the property entrusted to him, and when an inheritance is neglected or driven into debt, I think that family feeling must suffer."

"Yes, indeed," agreed her aunt. "And only think of all the daughters and wives who are cast adrift when property goes from one hand to another. What is to be done with *them* ought to be laid out in the entail as well. And where do you go now?" she inquired as Reginald rose to take his leave. "To your club, I expect—which is it, White's? Clubs are very treacherous places when the weather is so wet. It keeps the members too long at wagering and cards. Many a fortune has been lost at a comfortable club on a rainy day, and *that* is even harder on the wives and daughters, as it brings disgrace upon them as well as poverty."

"That is one advantage of an entail." Reginald smiled. "I cannot lose Parklands Manor at cards."

"A gentleman of property will see that as an advantage," replied Lady Vernon gravely as she extended her hand, "because he will always be left with something to fall back upon, but a woman whose livelihood is in the custody of a gamester must always tremble when a reckless husband or brother goes to his club."

"Oh, yes!" declared Mrs. Johnson. "If Mr. Johnson were affable enough to sit down to cards, he might have lost Eliza Manwaring's fortune, as it was all left in his charge. You are left better off than Eliza," she said to her friend, "for one brother will not breach the trust of another, but friendship often does not survive a lifetime, much less beyond it."

Lady Vernon was grateful for Mrs. Johnson's useful vulgarity, as it often caused her to put forth ideas that a more genteel person would be loath to express. At her allusion to Charles Vernon, Reginald became very sober and, soon after, took his leave.

"How very handsome of him to visit you so immediately upon his coming from Kent!" declared Mrs. Johnson when he was gone. "Such extraordinary attention cannot be without motive!"

She then made her adieux and hurried to call upon Lady Millbanke, Mrs. Crosby, and Eliza Manwaring and relate all that had passed between Lady Vernon and Reginald deCourcy while their looks and words were still fresh in her head. They would make a match of it, she declared, as soon as Lady Vernon was able to exert, for she had looked very fatigued and sat upon the sofa covered up with shawls for the entire visit.

As for Reginald, he went directly to his club, where he asked of the more seasoned habitués whether his brother Vernon had been often seen in the card room and if Lord Whitby had been exhibiting any symptoms of being in love.

chapter forty-eight

LADY VERNON TO MISS VERNON

Portland Place, London
My dear Frederica,

I am very happy that you are so pleased with Parklands. To be
warmly received by Lady deCourcy was perhaps too much to hope
for, but the civility of Sir Reginald and the companionship of Maria
will be ample compensation, particularly in so delightful a setting.

We have been confined to Portland Place by the weather—or
rather, confined by our country habits, which have us content with
needlework and books and conversation when it rains. Those who
prefer the town to the country are not put off by the wet. Lucy Smith
called, wearing blue peacock feathers upon her head and her pink husband on her arm—she expressed great surprise over your being in
Kent, great disappointment at your not being here, and great delight to
be introduced to Lady Martin. Indeed, every expression and emotion
and exclamation was very great—she makes no allowance for shade
or degree. The Smiths are inoffensive and silly, but it is the silliness
that might easily make them prey to contrivance and double dealing.

Mr. Manwaring has called every day, but I do not think it is wise
to admit him unless my aunt is at leisure to sit with us. He has grown
very incautious in a manner that has raised the estrangement with his
wife to the level of scandal, yet he is still received everywhere—his
manners remain so affable and high-spirited that he cannot be
shunned. It is no difficult thing to find good people to put at one's

dinner table or saloon, but the clever and entertaining ones are harder to come by, and relief from dullness is purchased at the cost of a little impropriety.

Eliza Manwaring is so far reconciled to her guardian as to have continual admission at Edward Street. Alicia Johnson declares that he is inclined to consign the whole of Eliza's fortune to her and be done with it, and so poor Alicia does not know which Manwaring to befriend—the privilege of visiting Langford must be weighed against keeping up an acquaintance who may have thirty thousand. I honor your sense, my dear Freddie, in choosing the best of the three, as Maria is superior to both her brother and his wife, and am very pleased to learn that she will soon be removed to a situation that will ensure her happiness.

This information—which must have been confided to you by Maria, as it is of the sort that young ladies will never keep from a bosom friend—has been disclosed to me by Mr. Lewis deCourcy. I think the news, when it is generally known, will surprise many at first, but I am so persuaded of Mr. deCourcy's sound character and good judgment that I think he would never choose rashly or ill. I hope that Sir Reginald is pleased with her—pleased enough that the news of their engagement will meet with no coldness or opposition from him. How well Lady deCourcy will like to have a girl younger than her own son as her sister, I cannot say, but I do not think that Mr. Lewis de-Courcy will be held back in anything because Lady deCourcy does not like it. His brother's good opinion may have more influence, and therefore, if you may effect anything on your friend's behalf, I hope that you will do it, as it would be for the best if Maria were not to ever return to either Eliza or Manwaring. I have never been an advocate for long engagements, nor an opponent of marriages where there is some disparity in age or fortune. My own marriage to your honored father came about within months of our introduction and produced so many years of happiness that I cannot think anybody now remembers that it was regarded as a very unequal match.

My aunt takes Dr. Driggs's visits in very good humor, and all of her pronouncements upon the charlatanry of London attendants are made out of his hearing, but I fear that the residents of Portland Place have put a very dire construction upon his regular attendance (as my situation is so well concealed that only my aunt, Wilson, and Mrs. Forrester know of it). If, therefore, you should receive word of my imminent demise, do not be alarmed.

I am very interested in your portrait of Sir Reginald. Write to me faithfully to tell me how you get on with him.

My aunt bids me send you her love, and Sir James, who is a very faithful visitor, likewise instructs me to close no letter to you without assuring you of his affection.

Your mother,
S. Vernon

Sir James Martin was very much entertained by the gossip making its way through fashionable circles, that Lady Vernon was the object of Reginald deCourcy. He imagined what great fun it would be when his engagement to Lady Vernon was made public. Of that prospect, he had not the least doubt—had he any rival, his cousin would have refused him outright and not asked only that he postpone his addresses.

He called very regularly at Portland Place, always making a grand bow in the direction of the upper window of the Misses Millbanke across the way before he stepped into the house.

"He must be impatient to advance his marriage with Miss Vernon," declared Mrs. Johnson to these young ladies. "If he were a poor man, I would advise him to delay, for if Lady Vernon marries Reginald deCourcy, she will be very rich, and in a position to settle a great deal more upon her daughter than she can at present."

It was not until a morning near the middle of February, however, that Sir James spied the bowed form of Dr. Driggs as the latter was departing from Portland Place and alighted from his carriage in great haste, afraid that his mother or cousin had been taken ill. To his relief, he saw Lady Martin with her workbasket at her feet and her sewing on her lap, and Lady Vernon reclining by the fire, covered with shawls. She smiled with her customary pleasure when he entered and held out her hand, though she did not stir from her position.

"You are not ill?" he asked at once, looking earnestly into her face.

"Illness is too dangerous an indulgence for any woman past the age of nineteen or twenty," said Lady Vernon with a smile. "It wears down the looks of the sufferer and the patience of those who attend her."

"It is the rain, nothing more," declared Lady Martin. "It is of great use in the country, as it keeps everyone at home. I daresay I never got so much carpet work done as one spring when it rained for a fortnight without a day's relief. But here in town a lady who lives very near her neighbor may run over and gossip and a gentleman who lives a street or two from his club will fall into hard play."

"Particularly if he does not possess a conscience or a wife—which are very much the same. It is an easy thing for a man who is on his own in London to succumb to vice."

"I am sure that there are many married men whose wives have *driven* them to vice." Lady Vernon smiled.

"Married or single, a man will always look to someone else to blame for his frailties," declared Lady Martin.

"I did not mean to suggest that vice is the inevitable consequence of living in London," replied Sir James. "Only that those who are inclined toward it will find greater opportunity. At any rate, the rain does not keep the postboy away, and I have got several nice letters from Freddie. She gets on superbly with Sir Reginald—the son will not want for the father's consent when he makes up his mind to speak. I am so convinced of it that I have made up *my* mind. I mean to give a ball in Freddie's honor when she returns to London, and a ball will always be the best means of hurrying a romance on to a proposal."

"A ball!" exclaimed Lady Martin. "What do you say to it, Susan? It will be quite as handsome as if she had been presented, James, for I know you do nothing by halves. But much of London still believes that she is *your* object. To have young deCourcy engage her interest under your very roof would make you a laughingstock!"

"But that ridicule would not extend to you, Mother, nor to you, Susan—and I think that neither of you would mind very much if I were made to look foolish."

"How could we mind anything to which we are so well accustomed?" Lady Vernon replied with a grave smile.

"And when the proposals are made and the wedding date is fixed, I mean to settle Vernon Castle on Freddie as a wedding present, what do you think? Nobody else will take it off my hands and I cannot see them installed in Parklands Cottage."

"Such a gesture may injure Mr. deCourcy's pride."

"Yes, but when he is made to understand Freddie's affection for the place, his pride will be overcome by his love for her and that will be the end of it. I will write to Freddie at once and allow her to name the date for the ball, so that she and Miss Manwaring may begin to engage in that frenzy of decision over what each will wear, and whether they ought to dress their hair alike or in contrasting styles, and if artificial flowers are now more *à la mode* than fresh ones."

He made several more remarks in this lighthearted tone, but when he took his leave, he made some excuse to get his mother to accompany him to the hallway and said in a low voice, "Do not trifle with me, ma'am, I beg you. Is my cousin well?"

"She is only a little pale, which comes from having no opportunity to get a good airing."

"There is talk of influenza."

"There is always talk of influenza—a spell of dirty weather will always bring about talk of influenza. Indeed, Miss Sophia Millbanke had almost decided upon taking it when Miss Elliot invited her to pass a fortnight at Kellynch. Miss Elliot's father has a dread of anything like contagion, and Miss Elliot began to think that Miss Claudia Hamilton would suit her better, and *that* brought Miss Sophia around to health once more."

chapter forty-nine

LADY DECOURCY AND HER DAUGHTER HAD GOT VERY fond of Miss Vernon and Miss Manwaring. The young ladies were never idle; they were always teaching and playing with the children, or making up a table for whist in the evening, or writing the letters and lists according to Lady deCourcy's dictation, or reading aloud, or playing on the pianoforte. Before the first week of their visit had concluded, Lady deCourcy declared her guests to be very good, pretty girls. "If Miss Vernon *should* marry Sir James," she said to her daughter, "I think Miss Manwaring would do as well for my sister Hamilton's clergyman. And if she will not have him, you might do well to engage *her* as governess. She is a clever, patient sort of person, her manners are good, and she reads aloud very nicely. But there is no need to hurry anything along, as I am not imposed upon in the least by having them here."

Lady deCourcy was particularly pleased with Miss Vernon for taking Sir Reginald off her hands. She had never had very much to say to him and *that* had all been said in the early years of their marriage— afterward, her remarks were confined to "How tall our Reginald has got!" or "Catherine must have some new gowns for the winter," to which Sir Reginald would reply, "I daresay you are right."

His infirmity relieved her of even these inconvenient attentions, as they often had him confined to his own apartments, and Lady deCourcy had got into the habit of doing as she liked without consulting her husband's opinion or making any accommodation for his wishes, while at the same time enjoying the expediency of Sir Reginald's ill health when she did not like to do anything at all. She had settled into the comfortable conviction that she would not be troubled by him at all until his demise compelled her to order her mourning—and, indeed, she had already laid aside one or two things to have ready so as not to be caught up short.

Much to his wife's dismay, Sir Reginald had improved so far as to spend much of his day with his family and young guests, and to join in their interests and conversation. Miss Vernon prevented Lady deCourcy from being imposed upon by taking Sir Reginald out of their way. They often breakfasted before the family had come down and then went out to examine the grounds and succession houses, calculating how many more pineapples might be got with just a little change in the soil and enumerating what remedies for poor digestion and sleeplessness and ill health might be cultivated in the kitchen garden. They sat down to dinner full of conversation, and if Lady deCourcy did not think that the table was a suitable place for terms such as *mulching* and *bile*, at least she was not troubled for her opinion of either.

Sir Reginald found Miss Vernon very different from the wretchedly educated young woman described in his daughter's letters to his wife. It was only Miss Vernon's natural diffidence and a disinclination toward show that prevented her accomplishments from being more generally known. Her nature was not so inscrutable, however, as to conceal a certain look of pensive admiration whenever Reginald's name was spoken, and Sir Reginald began to think that it would be no hardship at all to regard her as a daughter.

He began to want to know more of her history, and as a means of encouraging her to speak, he would direct her attention to some feature of the grounds and inquire whether there was any similarity to Churchill Manor.

"It is more like Vernon Castle than Churchill Manor," Miss Vernon would reply, and by inviting her to describe the similarities of the two estates, he obtained a description of the Staffordshire property and her own understanding (related with gentle candor that was careful to lay no blame upon her father) of how it had been lost.

"I am very sorry, for your own sake," said he, "as the property might have been settled on you and the loss of your home in Sussex would have been less."

"There are some losses that can never be lessened—and there is no advantage to myself that can compensate me for the loss of a most beloved parent."

He was touched by the sincerity of expression; he did not believe that his own passing would produce such a response from Catherine. "I do not speak of the grief that the death of an excellent husband and father, friend and landlord, must produce, but of the material alteration in your circumstances."

"Very few of my sex are so independent that they will never experience a material alteration in their fortunes. We are often impoverished when we lose a parent and sometimes enriched when we acquire a husband. One plight is certain to bring misery and the other is no assurance of happiness."

"An advantageous match does not ensure happiness, it is true," observed Sir Reginald, "and yet happiness must have something to live upon."

"Yes, sir, but I am of the opinion that only women who are left with *nothing* to live upon can be so desperate as to put that *something* before all other considerations."

"Then it is fortunate that you are not left desperate," said he with a smile. "Sir Frederick was always spoken of as the most affectionate and generous of fathers, and Catherine has often written to us of Charles's generosity toward your mother and yourself. I confess that I have not always had confidence in my son-in-law's better nature, but perhaps it is that he has never had occasion to put it into practice."

"I have always found nature to be remarkably consistent," replied Frederica gravely.

The old gentleman detected Miss Vernon's uneasiness, and after one or two attempts to encourage her to say something of her uncle's conduct toward herself and Lady Vernon, he abandoned the subject and asked instead how far a spray of lemon water and clove oil would ward off beetles and ants.

When they parted in the hallway, however, Sir Reginald went immediately to his chamber and sat down to write a letter to his son.

SIR REGINALD deCOURCY TO MR. deCOURCY

Parklands Manor, Kent
My dear Reginald,

You know that prevarication is not in my nature, and I cannot begin a subject with all of the prelude and nicety that often serves only to give anxiety to the object. I must therefore lay my concerns before you without vacillation.

At the time of your sister's marriage, there appeared no objection to Mr. Vernon other than some anxiety for the difference in age, as Catherine was three and twenty and Mr. Vernon a dozen or more years older. The disparity in itself was not greater than is often met with, and indeed in temperament they did appear to suit—yet for a gentleman who is a second son to come to the age of five and thirty with no profession and no residence beyond his set of rooms in town displayed a character wanting in proper ambition, one that looked entirely to a fortunate marriage or to the acquisition of the Vernon entail to provide for his comfort.

That your sister's fortune was a significant inducement for him to marry her, I did not doubt; that efforts were made to shield me from the many rumors of his extravagance, I also cannot gainsay, but it was not until after their marriage that I heard anything of wretched companions and wasteful habits, and I continued to hope that the influence of a wife and family would prevail over temptation, and that my good brother's giving Charles a profession would instill in him a sense of responsibility.

I knew very little of the relationship between Charles and his elder brother, and most of that came from Charles himself, as Catherine had no wish to know them—this may have been influenced by the jealousy a woman will feel when she is not a first choice (for I had heard *that Charles had sought the hand of his sister-in-law). I had also heard (though I did not know how to credit it at the time) that Charles had enticed his brother into the speculation that had compelled Sir Frederick to sell Vernon Castle in order to reconcile his debts.*

In forwarding an acquaintance with Miss Vernon, I have observed that any discussion of Vernon Castle or, more particularly, her uncle is steadily avoided and with an aversion for the latter subject that is very unusual from one who is, in all other respects, genteel, prudent, and self-possessed.

It would grieve me exceedingly to think that Charles may have used Lady Vernon and her daughter ill in any way, and yet it would grieve me more to know that such was the case and I had done nothing to repair it. Your Uncle deCourcy may be of some service to you in this—he was acquainted not only with Sir Frederick Vernon but with Lady Vernon's father.

I will say in closing that I like Miss Vernon very much, but I am compelled to close my letter—there is no room to express the extent of my regard for her. She and Miss Manwaring talk of their visit ending inside a fortnight, and my brother writes to say that he means to travel to Parklands in order to bring them to town himself.

I am, etc.,
Reginald deCourcy

chapter fifty

REGINALD HAD ALWAYS BEEN A FAITHFUL CORRESPONDENT
to both of his parents; letters from Parklands, however, came
more frequently from his mother than from his father. Upon
receiving word from her son, Lady deCourcy would immediately take
up her pen, and having hurried her letter to the post, she would recall
one or two more words of advice or caution and dispatch a second or
even third reply; her husband, on the other hand, wrote only when a
particular item of news, or a matter of grave urgency, warranted.

Reginald, therefore, opened his father's letter with some apprehension and read it so eagerly that he scarcely took all of it in on
the first perusal. Indeed, it was the closing paragraph that impressed
him—*there is no room to express the extent of my regard for her*. He read
it over many times before he returned his attention to the rest of the
letter.

He was struck by his father's words; at the time of Catherine's marriage, Reginald had supposed that his father's *consent* to the union had
implied his *approval*. The apprehension expressed in his father's letter
recalled conversations and incidents from Reginald's visit to Churchill
that had not perturbed him individually but that now collected into a
troublesome whole.

He immediately took up his pen to write to his father.

Mr. deCourcy to Sir Reginald deCourcy

Wimpole Street, London
My dear Sir,

I have this moment received your letter. I must confess that it compels me to look back upon incidents that (as they were intermingled with so many pleasant interludes) I can only view as ominous in light of your inquiry. These I will lay before you.

I had not been long in Sussex when I learned that my friendship with Lady Vernon had given rise to a rumor that I meant to make her an offer of marriage and also that her daughter was on the verge of an engagement to her cousin, Sir James Martin. Such rumors are not uncommon—the world has little patience for people who do not marry when they are free to do so—and yet they often spoke of poverty as Lady Vernon's motive for wishing an advantageous union for herself and her daughter. That the survivors of Sir Frederick Vernon should be distressed for money did not seem likely, and yet more than once did Catherine suggest that Lady Vernon had come to Sussex on purpose to beg Charles for his financial assistance and that Miss Vernon was being urged upon Sir James because Sir Frederick had left her with nothing. Of Sir Frederick's will, I know nothing, yet however improbable were Lady Vernon's <u>designs</u>, sir, I gradually became convinced that her <u>distress</u> was very real, and though she is in possession of a very handsome house in town, <u>that</u> was settled on her by Lady Martin. I cannot find that anything of significance was left to her by her husband.

Several days after Miss Vernon's arrival, Sir James Martin came to Churchill Manor. One evening at dinner he inquired after a portrait of Sir Frederick, which had hung in the gallery for many years beside those of Churchill's previous masters, and it was revealed that Charles had ordered this portrait removed to one of the attics! Such an affront to his brother and his line! Lady Vernon must have felt the insult, and yet in all the time I was at Churchill, I never heard her utter a word of protest or reproach.

There are other incidents that, while not rising to the level of reprehensible conduct, do not speak well for the master of an estate. There seemed a callousness in the dismissal of many old family retainers; the property is poorly maintained; and the neighbors and tenants, to whom my brother, as master, owes some attention and hospitality, are neglected as well.

I wish, for my sister's sake, that I could express a firm conviction that such lapses and omissions rise from my brother's new and unfamiliar responsibilities as master of Churchill Manor; and yet, as my own circle of acquaintance has increased (for I was but seventeen at the time of Catherine's marriage) and more of my time is spent among our mutual associates, I see how far his imprudence—his indiscretions—are known. I know that these have often embraced money matters, but can you believe—as you suggest in your letter—that my brother may have taken license with a trust that was meant to benefit Lady Vernon and her daughter? I wish, for the sake of Catherine and the children, that I could protest it at once. All I can say is that I do not know how such a thing can be easily proved and that any attempt at redress may only reveal that any fortune has been lost to my brother's extravagance.

For Lady Vernon's sake, I wish that something material might be done, but for Miss Vernon I think that a want of fortune will be no obstacle to her happiness. She is such a superior young lady that no gentleman of discernment would seek anything but her person in applying for her hand.

I am very happy to hear that she has secured your affection and your regard. Lady Vernon depends upon her returning to town in the early part of March, and I hope by that time you, sir, will part from her on such terms as will make you look favorably on the possibility of a more lasting connection.

I am, etc.,
R deC

chapter fifty-one

LONDON PROVED TO BE LESS DISAGREEABLE THAN LADY Martin had feared, save for the necessity of leaving her cards at the houses of some connections whom she had not dropped, as *their* coming to London every season and *her* staying in Derbyshire had kept acquaintance at bay. She would read the newspapers or *The Lady's Magazine* at the breakfast table and declare that there was no taste in politics nor sense in fashion. She was never without some kind of handiwork, and her fingers were so adept that they did not slow when her eyes wandered to the window and she exclaimed, "Only look at that muff that Miss Millbanke carries! I declare it goes to her knees!"—"Why, there is Mrs. Ferrars driving by, and both she and her pug in bottle-green velvet! I declare it suits the pup's complexion better than her own!"—"There goes Mrs. Mapleton, as big as life, when I had every reason to suppose that she was dead!"

The honor of being received by Lady Martin and the opportunity of getting a look at Lady Vernon had many of these curiosities calling at Portland Place and coming away with gossip that was as excessively delightful as it was inaccurate; Sir James Martin was such a regular visitor that his engagement to Miss Vernon must be very close to being made public, and Mr. Reginald deCourcy was likewise so frequently at Portland Place that his intention to marry Lady Vernon was a certainty. Even the visits of Mr. Lewis deCourcy were attributed by some to matrimonial design—was it not possible that his long friendship with Lady Martin had ripened into love? To be sure, his visits might have no other purpose than to advise Lady Vernon on how she might invest the very great legacy left to her by Sir Frederick, and yet it was more delightful to think that aunt, niece, and grand-niece might all be bound for the altar.

By Dr. Driggs's calculation, it would be another ten weeks before Lady Vernon's confinement, and he did not object to her taking the air so long as she was neither compelled to sit in one attitude for more than an hour nor to climb in and out of the carriage too frequently, and provided the wind was not too brisk, nor the coach too warm, nor the air too wet, nor her shoes too thin. Lady Martin regarded all such decrees with patient disdain—*some* were too apt to forget that babies had come into the world long before anybody had thought to make a profession of writing receipts for dyspepsia and occasionally taking a pulse—but she was determined that nothing should be overlooked in providing for her niece.

The spell of rain ended, and one particularly mild morning Lady Martin announced that she had given orders for her carriage. "We both want an airing, and there is no better way of avoiding callers than being elsewhere when they arrive. I have it in mind to go to Rundell's to purchase a pair of nice bracelets for Frederica to wear to the ball. Ah, me! My first season, when I was sixteen, I went to fifty balls and an equal number of musical parties and concerts and picnics. So many lively young men, and yet"—she sighed—"I settled upon your uncle. But he was a very good man, for all his gravity."

Lady Martin had been so long from London that every change intrigued her. "How many more shops there are than when I was here last! Stop. I must see the ostrich plumes upon that bonnet!"—"Ah, just see those caricatures! Why, I daresay I know who *that* is without getting down to have a closer look!"

They made their way to Ludgate Hill at last, and Lady Vernon elected to sit in the carriage while her aunt went in to give her order for the bracelets. The part of town was very near to where she had lived as a girl, and she was absorbed in looking round the street and indulging in some pleasing memories when a rap at the carriage door brought her back to the present.

Lady Vernon was startled to see Manwaring standing beside the carriage, and pulling her lap robe higher upon her, she rolled down the glass to bid him good morning.

"What an excellent piece of luck to meet with you here! I would have called upon you today for I have the most astonishing piece of news. I think you will like to have the advantage of Alicia Johnson— for once, you will be able to surprise her."

"It must be something very particular."

"It is, indeed. I have been applied to for Maria's hand—can you believe my good fortune? To have her out for five seasons at least, and thinking that I should have her on my hands forever! And you will never guess who the gentleman is!"

"I think it is Mr. Lewis deCourcy."

The look of dejection upon his face brought her very near to laughing.

"Yes," he said. "I confess that when the gentleman addressed me, I thought it was all a great joke! He was so very solemn! But he laid out his reasons for wishing to marry her very soundly, and what is more, he asks not a penny for her and will settle on her very handsomely. Of course, I gave my consent at once, though it is a very unequal match, but felicity in even the most equal matches is a matter of luck. And it will be a great comfort to me to have her so rich, for he is rolling in money and has never done more than purchase a very pretty house in Bath and some nice horses and carriages. And Maria asks for so little that they will not spend a quarter of what he brings in."

"I am very happy to think that your sister will be so well settled."

"And may I say that I am equally happy for Miss Vernon? It will be a great relief to you when her engagement to Sir James is announced—once she and Maria are married, we will both be at liberty to do as we like."

Lady Vernon evaded this approach to familiarity by inquiring whether it was the business of Maria's engagement that brought him into the city.

"Yes, indeed. There is a very fine diamond brooch that our mother had entrusted to me for Maria and it needs to be properly cleaned. I saw no occasion to present it to her before this, and I daresay there were times when I gave some thought to changing it for paste!" He laughed. "And in this part of the city, and Rundell being as discreet as he is, I have no doubt that I might have got away with it!"

"Save for those not infrequent pangs of conscience when your sister wore a brooch that your mother had entrusted to you and that you exchanged for paste."

"Yes," he replied, "and yet, if I could be assured that they were *very* infrequent, and the intervals between excessively delightful, I think that I could bear the inconvenience."

"Your notion of conscience is a strange one! An inconvenience! And I suppose you would call it a blessing, then, to have no conscience at all?"

"To be entirely without one? Oh, yes! For when conscience has not kept a fellow from doing wrong, it may yet awaken afterward and subject him forever to the fear of discovery. It is better to do without."

It was at this moment that Lady Martin bustled from the shop, amid bows and smiles from the shop owner, which signified that she had made a very costly purchase. She greeted Manwaring and they exchanged the usual civilities, which resolved that the weather was fine, the roads were well dried up, and that it was a very great coincidence to find each other in the same part of the city.

She then congratulated him upon Maria's engagement. "I am certain that everyone will rejoice in their good fortune and that they are most certainly equals in everything that contributes to happiness."

"I daresay there will be *one* party who will not be happy to have his uncle married," said he with a knowing smile, and with a bow he bade the ladies good morning.

"What can he mean?" inquired Lady Martin of her niece. " 'Not be happy to have his uncle married'? Surely Mr. Reginald deCourcy will not begrudge his uncle any happiness."

"I do not think that Mr. Manwaring was speaking of Reginald deCourcy, Aunt. I think that he must mean Charles."

"Oh, I had not thought of that. I suppose Charles Vernon is also a nephew in a manner of speaking—and yet why would he care whether or not his wife's uncle marries?"

"After Reginald deCourcy, his uncle is next to the entail, before it passes to the female line—and it is not unlike Charles to think first in terms of advantage to himself."

"Yes, but to anticipate something so improbable as getting his hands on the deCourcy property! It is a very grasping and selfish manner of looking at things. How I should like to see Churchill Manor restored to a son of yours! James tells me that it has got run down, and it is not seven months since dear Frederick has gone! I would be very happy to give up the prospect of a namesake to have you get back all that you are due."

"I do not think there is any prospect of getting it all back, Aunt," Lady Vernon remarked with a sigh.

"Why, what do you mean?" demanded Lady Martin with a very penetrating look. "You must not be inscrutable and you know that I do not like to be kept in the dark about anything save for how James spends his time and money when he is out of my sight—the less I know about *that*, the better."

Lady Vernon, with some hesitation, unburdened herself to her aunt regarding her situation, explaining the particulars of her husband's will and repeating her conversation with Charles in which he had made it clear that her house in London and her modest income were all that she had a right to claim. "I beg you, Aunt, do not judge poor Frederick too harshly."

"Aye, poor man. He was so content with the present. Too many men think that tomorrow will always be soon enough to provide for their wives and daughters."

"I must take some share of the blame. I never addressed Frederick when I might have."

"You did not wish to press your husband when his health was in a precarious state. But Frederick's wishes for you and Frederica must have been very clear—no man of honor could dispute it. I have never liked Charles Vernon, but I did not think him lost to all obligation to his family. Oh, if I were but a man, I would call him out in an instant!"

"I beg you, Aunt, you must say nothing to James."

Lady Martin nodded sagely. "Yes, yes. James is very slow to mind an insult to himself, but he will avenge an insult to family with no thought to the consequence. Yet what can be done? It is too much to hope that Vernon is a miserly sort and has spent nothing! To think of him running through *your* money at the card tables! Why, I recall how

Admiral Harvey lost a hundred thousand pounds in an evening! It will be another two months before you are confined—even if you should have a son, there may not be a shilling left." Then perceiving how the subject gave her niece pain, she attempted something like consolation. "There must be some comfort in the expectation that Reginald deCourcy will ask for nothing when he applies to you for Frederica, and so I think our best effort now must be directed toward that. There is nothing like a ball to bring about a proposal of marriage—I daresay I received three proposals the morning after Lord Murray's ball. Let us run over to the warehouses. A nice white embroidered silk gauze over satin—we must do nothing by halves."

chapter fifty-two

MR. VERNON TO MRS. VERNON

Bond Street, London
My dear wife,

If I have not been a very regular correspondent, it is because I must suppose that anything of note has already been communicated by Reginald, whose range of acquaintance affords him society and engagements more extensive and varied than my own—even those invitations that come to a gentleman in my profession must often be declined as my modest rooms put it out of my power to reciprocate in the same style. I often think it a great pity that your parents had never thought it prudent to take a house in town, if not for their own pleasure, then for the pleasure and convenience of Reginald and ourselves. Even if I were to leave the banking house (as it is no longer necessary for me to have an occupation), my new situation must require that part of the year be spent in town. To do otherwise would be to deprive our children of the society from which the very best matches will proceed. How such an establishment is to be managed must wait upon a better understanding of how far the income of Churchill Manor will allow it—and yet it would be a great pity not to have an establishment sooner.

I am very glad to hear that my father-in-law is in improved health, and it occurs to me that if he is fit enough to travel, he may well wish to consult with one of the superior physicians in town. There are several very fine houses to let, and I am certain that I could find one that would suit Sir Reginald in every way. I know that my uncle goes to Parklands very soon to fetch your two young visitors back to London, and I think very little persuasion on your part will be wanted to have your father return with them. Lady deCourcy, I know, does not like London and will wish to continue with you and the children at Parklands—you may both be assured that if Sir Reginald does come to town, I will be very happy to attend him in any way he likes.

I think that our Uncle deCourcy would also like to have his brother in town for a reason that will come as a very great surprise to you—here *is* a bit of news! It is being said that he has come to an understanding with Lady Martin! I have this from Mrs. Johnson—I dined with the Carrs two nights ago and she was of the party—and it was declared to be a settled thing that our uncle is to marry. As this is news that cannot be withheld indefinitely from his family, I believe that Mr. deCourcy means to surprise you all with the news when he comes to Kent—you may have the advantage of him now, as I now know that we are both of the opinion that such surprises are very disagreeable things. Indeed, this news would be a most unpleasant surprise if it were to have an injurious effect upon our own fortunes—the deCourcy family can only benefit, however, as it is said that Lady Martin has something in her own right, which, if it does not come to a husband, would likely be settled upon Lady Vernon or her daughter. Indeed, the house in town that Lady Vernon now occupies was settled upon her by Lady Martin, thus putting it out of Sir Frederick's power to direct that *all* of his property pass to his heir (which, I am certain, would have been his wish). Indeed, I think it is Lady Vernon who could do well with a comfortable set of rooms more easily than I, as she does not give any parties or dinners and leaves it entirely to her aunt to repay all of their calls.

I have, on occasion, stopped at Portland Place, but spoken only to Lady Martin, who said that Lady Vernon was unwell and could not receive visitors. I have heard that she is visited very regularly by a prominent physician, and, my dear wife, though I would not indulge your hopes prematurely, who is to say what may come of *that*? The influenza is not nearly so widespread as it is rumored—nobody of consequence has died of it—but if she were to be the first, we can hope for no better outcome of her inevitable marriage to Reginald, as it might leave him in possession of the Portland Place residence yet without the encumbrance of such a wife. The loss would, of course, take its toll upon such a sensitive nature as Reginald's and likely keep him from ever marrying imprudently again. I must write no more, for to do so would unreasonably excite our hopes by fixing them upon an event that may not come to pass.

Of Reginald, I can write very little. In town our obligations and associates take us into very different circles. I see him occasionally at White's.

I have taken your rings to Rundell's, and the stones have all been reset as you have directed.

Your devoted husband,
Charles Vernon

Catherine Vernon read this letter more certain than ever of her husband's solicitous and accommodating nature. To think of Sir Reginald's health, to offer to attend to him in town, and even to offer her the hope that the wretchedness of Reginald's union with Lady Vernon might be short-lived, exceeded all of her former notions of her husband's benevolence.

She was very surprised, however, to hear that her Uncle deCourcy might think of marrying at so comfortable and settled a stage of his life, a feeling that was shared by Lady deCourcy, to whom she read her letter.

"I am quite shocked," she declared. "There were one or two very eligible young ladies whom he might have married, though I do not think that Elinor Metcalfe was ever among them. Well, I cannot blame your uncle. If an opportunity to increase his wealth should come his way, it is his duty to take it, for the sake of you and Reginald, who inherit his money and property when he goes. Her motives are more incomprehensible to me, for being so comfortable a widow, what reason can she have to marry again? Could she be so fond of your uncle that she would sacrifice every worldly advantage to feeling? Your father will be quite shocked—I daresay it will set him back a great deal. He does not bear anything like a surprise as well as you and I do."

Lady deCourcy was very soon called upon to suffer a surprise, however, when, from her dressing-room window, she saw her son alight from Lewis deCourcy's carriage. She ran straightaway to Catherine's apartments, crying out, "Reginald is come! What can have compelled him to come away from town with his uncle? Can it be that he and Lady Vernon have parted? It is too much to hope for! I must go down directly—you must hurry and dress. Miss Vernon is somewhere about the grounds with your father! Call Miss Manwaring to help with the children."

She then ran downstairs and out the door to meet the two gentlemen. "My dear boy! You have come back again! Oh, how will your father bear the pleasure of seeing you home again so soon! I fear it will send him back to his bed! But how long do you stay—you must not hurry back to town."

"I am afraid that we stay only a very short time, Mother. We are charged to bring Miss Vernon and Miss Manwaring back to town." He then inquired after Sir Reginald and was told that he was somewhere on the grounds with Miss Vernon, whereupon Reginald walked out to find them while Lady deCourcy hurried back upstairs to Catherine.

"How does Reginald appear?" inquired Catherine. "How are his spirits? Is he very low? Can Lady Vernon's spell over him be broken?"

"It is almost too much to hope for—and yet there was no need for him to accompany your uncle unless he wished to get away from London. Your uncle's prudent decision to marry Lady Martin must have awakened Reginald to the necessity of choosing dispassionately and with regard to his family—perhaps I may write to my dear sister Hamilton that all is not lost."

Reginald, meanwhile, had been directed by the groundskeepers toward the summerhouse. There he spied his father and Miss Vernon examining some of the water plants upon one of the ornamental ponds. He was delighted to see his father in such improved health, for his color was robust and when he spoke his voice was clear and strong.

The elder gentleman was attending to Miss Vernon as she pronounced one of the plants to be a water hawthorn, "as there are very few pond plants that will show any bloom this early—the scent of vanilla, too, pronounces it most certainly to be water hawthorn."

Sir Reginald began to inquire whether the plant was known to have any curative properties when he spied his son. He greeted him warmly and said, "I trust that your journey was easy and that I will find my brother well."

"In health and in spirit, I have never seen him better," replied Reginald. "And," he added, addressing Miss Vernon with a knowing smile, "I hope the same may be said for your friend, Miss Manwaring?"

"I think that the very same may be said for her, sir."

Mr. deCourcy then told Miss Vernon that he had seen her mother and aunt only the day before and was gratified to hear his father inquire, "I hope that you left them both in very good health—and I hope that you, Miss Vernon, will convey my thanks to them for giving up your company these four weeks so that you might study the curiosities of Kent."

They found the rest of the party in the sitting room, and for half an hour Lady deCourcy kept them from anything like conversation by declaring again and again that the month had gone by very fast and that if the young ladies were of a mind to stay another fortnight, they would not at all be in the way. "Lady Vernon can certainly spare her daughter, and Miss Manwaring has only her brother and Mrs. Manwaring in town—and sisters and brothers are more often apart unless some unfortunate circumstance of economy should compel them to live together."

"I cannot say whether you are right in the general sense," replied Reginald with a smile, "but I think that in this particular case, we must yield to Mr. Manwaring's affection for his sister and Lady Vernon's for her daughter. In any case, when there is to be such a private ball in London as Sir James Martin means to give, I cannot think that even Miss Vernon's delight in the curiosities of Kent would have her prefer the country over town."

Miss Vernon's blush was understood only by Reginald; Lady deCourcy supposed that it was a mark of chagrin at the mention of Sir James Martin, and she declared that Miss Vernon was of an age when the loss of one ball was of no consequence. "If she should stay another month, she may accompany Catherine to town, as there are some small errands and purchases that I wish her to make, and if at the end of that, Miss Vernon does not like to be left in town, she may come with me to my sister Hamilton's at Gisbourne—I am certain that she would find it very picturesque. Indeed, the parsonage is one of the prettiest cottages in all of England, do you not think so, Reginald?"

"I think that everybody will always think cottages to be pretty and charming, save for those who are compelled to live in them."

"Nonsense," declared Catherine. "I am very sorry that I have been compelled to leave Parklands Cottage—though it is so spacious and well appointed that it is an affront to call it a cottage at all—and Kent is much more to my liking than Sussex."

Sir Reginald saw a pained look pass over Miss Vernon's countenance. "I must think that it is your fondness for your mother and me that influences your attachment, Catherine, and Miss Vernon can feel no less for Churchill Manor. Affection will always make a castle even of a cottage. But even if Gisbourne's parsonage were a palace, I do not think that Miss Vernon can put off her return to London, as I understand that the ball Sir James Martin gives is in her honor."

"And it is an honor that is not undeserved," added Lewis deCourcy.

Lady deCourcy and her daughter said no more, and soon afterward the party broke up to allow the gentlemen to rest and refresh themselves after their journey and the young ladies to attend to packing their belongings for the return to London.

chapter fifty-three

Sir Reginald repaired to his son's apartments and asked his brother to join them. "I think, brother, that I may be frank with you. I have laid my misgivings before Reginald and your long-standing acquaintance with Lady Vernon must make you a party to them. Many things that Miss Vernon has said—but more particularly what she has *not* said—have made me uncomfortable with Charles's manner of dealing with her and Lady Vernon after Sir Frederick's death."

Lewis deCourcy looked very grave and gave a brief account of his interview with Lady Vernon on the subject when she had stopped at Bath. "Charles may not have done wrong in doing *less* than was stipulated by Sir Frederick's will—I am only surprised that he has not done more. I know that the terms of the will were such as made sense at the time it was drawn, and indeed there is some merit in keeping fortune and property together."

"Yes," agreed Sir Reginald. "I would be remiss if I did not leave a good portion of money with Parklands, as I wish always for Reginald to keep it in proper style. But if the residue should be insufficient for Lady deCourcy's comfort, I know that you, Reginald, would need no written document to compel you to do right."

"I would not wish to remove any advantage from my niece and her children," said Lewis deCourcy, "but I have often thought that it was a great pity that Sir Frederick and Lady Vernon did not have a son. If only Miss Vernon had been a boy—"

"I am sure that my son cannot agree with you *there*," said Sir Reginald, smiling. "Charles has written to Catherine and suggested that I come to town for the benefit of a London practitioner, which I am inclined to do."

"That cannot be necessary, brother. I have not seen you in such excellent health for some time."

"For that, I credit Miss Vernon. Indeed, I do not think that I have ever been less in need of doctoring than in this past month. Charles's invitation is given only with the object of securing a more comfortable situation at my expense—but he does not anticipate the price I mean to exact for his convenience."

chapter fifty-four

THE PARTY DID NOT REASSEMBLE AGAIN UNTIL DINNER, and Sir Reginald immediately announced his intention of accompanying his son and brother to town.

Lady deCourcy endeavored to express something like concern and protest—"You are not in health to stand the journey, I think" and "There is talk of the influenza in London"—but after one or two more attempts, she decided that having Sir Reginald go to town would entail no difficulty or sacrifice on her own part, and that her time with Catherine might be even more pleasant when free of those inescapable attentions one is obliged to direct toward one's husband.

The remainder of the dinner passed in pleasant conversation. Sir Reginald and Miss Vernon engaged in a spirited discussion of one or two projects that they had begun in the hothouses, and Lewis deCourcy joined his brother in recollections of some youthful incidents that the young people found highly diverting.

When Lady deCourcy made a move to rise, her husband's brother rose and bade her wait. "I have some information that I think—I hope—will bring as much joy to my family as it has to me." And taking the hand of Miss Manwaring, who was seated beside him, he continued, "Miss Manwaring has done me the very great honor to accept my hand in marriage, and as her brother has given his consent, I hope that I may persuade you all to wish us well."

Lady deCourcy was far too surprised to express anything like joy and yet not so surprised as to be shocked into silence. "Engaged?" she cried. "Engaged to Miss Manwaring? Why, what do you mean, brother? If you mean to have a joke at our expense, it is a very poor one! Surely you mean to tell us that you have got engaged to Lady Martin!"

Reginald was compelled to smile at Miss Vernon's attempt to conceal her diversion at the notion of a union between his uncle and her aunt.

"I assure you, sister," said Lewis deCourcy with greater civility and forbearance than the lady deserved, "that my inexperience with the decorums which are part of the practice is not so great that it would lead me to mistake the object."

Reginald now put himself forward to announce his prior intelligence and express his pleasure in the connection. "Though if I cannot bring myself to call you 'Aunt' you will forgive me," he said to the young lady with a smile. "I hope that when the happy event takes place, you will consent to have me address you by your Christian name."

Lady deCourcy was not quite ready to relinquish her protests. "You do not know what you are about. How can you think so little of your brother's health? He cannot bear anything so shocking. A marriage to Lady Martin could be withstood well enough, but such a proposal as this will send him straight to his bed."

"My dear, how could my brother's happiness have anything but a most favorable effect upon me?" declared Sir Reginald. "I can think of only one *other* announcement that would make me happier than the prospect of my brother's union."

Then, rising from his chair, he went over to Miss Manwaring, took her hand and kissed it with great formality, then expressed his delight at the prospect of calling her "sister."

Catherine, who had sat speechless throughout, suggested to her mother that it was time for the ladies to withdraw, and Lady de-Courcy, with a reproachful look at them all, strode into the drawing room and took the chair closest to the fire.

Reginald accompanied the ladies in order to keep his mother from importuning Miss Manwaring. Fortunately for the young ladies, it was the custom for the children to be called down after dinner, and in entertaining them with some books and puzzles, Miss Vernon and Miss Manwaring were able to avoid Lady deCourcy's disapproving glances.

"I think I have been very ill used for Miss Manwaring to have presented herself as an unattached young lady!" maintained Lady de-Courcy to her son and daughter. "Catherine and I had quite settled upon her as the children's governess—they must have a governess and Miss Vernon will not do, for once she is in town, she will not be allowed to quit her mother's house again until she marries Sir James Martin. I cannot blame Miss Manwaring—it is a very great step up for her to be a deCourcy, but I pity your uncle—to have got so foolish in his stage of life. I think your uncle is very much to be pitied, do you not agree, Reginald?"

"I think I shall reserve my pity for the Reverend Mr. Heywood, who has seen two excellent prospects come to nothing. A gentleman's joy of surviving his wife must be considerably lessened if his second choice marries before circumstances allow him to make her an offer."

"Reginald, do not run on in the manner that you do in town—I cannot bear such levity when I have been thwarted in everything."

"How can you think yourself thwarted in anything, madam? You have a daughter married and four handsome grandchildren, a husband whose health is remarkably improved, and a brother-in-law engaged to a charming young lady. That is a very strange notion of ill treatment."

"You delight in provoking me."

"Indeed, I do not—but it is a provocation that you will not have to endure for very long. Tomorrow I return to town and you may be at peace once more."

"I cannot be at peace while you are in town—I will imagine you in all sorts of mischief!"

"Then at least you will never want for something to think about."

"I would rather you stayed with us in Kent—then I would not have to think about anything at all!"

"I would not for anything deprive you of the pleasures of imagination. As for mischief, I can only promise to get in as little as any gentleman can when in town, and to assure you that there will be those who put their mothers' imaginations to the task, and with far greater cause than I."

This was no consolation for Lady deCourcy, however, and she passed the rest of the evening in grievances and whist.

chapter fifty-five

MRS. JOHNSON TO LADY VERNON

Edward Street, London
My dear creature,

How unlucky that you should have been from home when I last
called at Portland Place—it is so provoking, for I have had such a tale
to tell! The rumors of Miss Manwaring and Mr. Lewis deCourcy
marrying are quite true, but it was not until just now that I have
learned that they are to be married to <u>each other</u>! This I have on the
indisputable authority of Eliza Manwaring, who has this moment
left us.

I had gone to Bedford Square, to call upon Lady Hamilton and her
daughters. Miss Hamilton and Miss Claudia were with their mantua
maker, having their gowns for Sir James's ball finished, but Lady
Hamilton was sitting with her youngest daughter and her husband.
Mr. Smith has learned that forgiveness for his conduct is very easily
come by—he has only to flatter Lady Hamilton and agree with her
every opinion and pronouncement to be declared "a very agreeable
sort of young man."

I returned to find Eliza sitting with Mr. Johnson, and I had no
sooner stepped into the room when Eliza demanded my congratulations upon Maria's engagement and added, "They have both been so
cautious—I do not call it a real courtship at all! Mr. Johnson has already heard the news, as he and Mr. deCourcy are such good friends,
but you must confess yourself surprised, Alicia."

"Mr. deCourcy!" I cried. I quite naturally supposed that she spoke of Mr. Reginald deCourcy—for he and Mr. Johnson are the greatest friends in the world since their introduction—and yet I could not believe that he would desert you for Maria Manwaring.

I cannot describe my shock when I was undeceived, and I shall never forgive Mr. Johnson, for he must have known this for a fortnight at least! Maria Manwaring and Lewis deCourcy! He must be thirty or more years her senior! He is very rich, of course, and Manwaring will be very happy to have her off his hands—indeed, you will have to be very prudent, as this is likely to make Manwaring more indiscreet than ever in his attentions toward you. I fear he is capable of some great imprudence and may act in such a way as to excite deCourcy's jealousy and to make you miserable. I advise you, therefore, not to put off your marriage until Miss Vernon's is a settled thing. You must think more of yourself and less of your daughter.

Mr. Johnson has reconciled himself to Eliza so far as to invite her and Maria to stay with us at Edward Street for the present. Such a reversal in feeling, such goodwill where there was once censure! Men are such inconstant creatures!

I am not disinclined to have Maria here. She will want a great deal of looking after now that she is to be married, and Eliza has been so little in town that she will not know where the best shops and warehouses are. And while she and Manwaring will not see each other, I am on such terms with Manwaring that I must necessarily be the proxy—I am certain that I can get him to spend more than he will be inclined to for Maria's wedding clothes.

It is my understanding that Mr. deCourcy and his nephew have gone to Parklands to bring Maria and Miss Vernon back to town, and perhaps when they are settled, we may all make a little party of going around to the warehouses together?

Yours, &c.,
Alicia Johnson

Lady Vernon had received a note from her daughter announcing the day and time when she might be expected back at Portland Place.

She was very surprised, however, when Lady Martin ran into her dressing room at the appointed hour, crying out, "My dear, the whole party from Kent has just this minute drawn up to the house in a barouche, and Frederica rides in the box with Reginald deCourcy! And what do you think? His father is among them!"

"He will not come in."

"I daresay not, but it is a great compliment to Miss Manwaring and Frederica that he should accompany them."

The eager footstep of Frederica was heard upon the stair and a moment later, she was in her mother's embrace and then gave an equally affectionate greeting to her aunt and Wilson. "But you must come down to the drawing room, for Sir Reginald deCourcy most particularly wishes to be introduced to you."

Lady Vernon was all astonishment—that the gentleman who only months earlier had written of her in such critical terms should call upon her immediately upon his arrival in town was a great compliment—and sending her aunt and daughter down to their guests, she asked Wilson to arrange her gown and shawls in order to conceal her condition as well as possible, before she joined the party.

The formidable introduction was made, and Reginald, who had watched with some apprehension as his father was presented to Lady Vernon, was relieved to see that the gentleman's conduct was courteous and civil and that the lady's every word revealed her superiority of taste and manner. Her warmth toward his brother and Miss Manwaring, her unreserved happiness in their engagement, advanced Sir Reginald's good opinion of her.

For her part, Lady Vernon was pleased that Frederica was the subject of so much of Sir Reginald's discourse (and with very little prodding from Lady Martin upon her niece's looks and accomplishments); in recalling the many pleasant hours they had spent at Parklands, the old gentleman gave every indication of his regard for Frederica, and Lady Vernon was convinced that when Reginald did ask for her hand (as his looks and words toward Frederica gave every indication that he would) his father would not object to the match.

Their visitors stayed with them above half an hour, and when they walked out to their carriage, the shades upon many upper windows fluttered, and it was whispered in several drawing rooms that the appearance of Sir Reginald deCourcy at Portland Place must mean that he had relented and given his consent to his son's marrying Lady Vernon at last.

chapter fifty-six

CHARLES VERNON HAD NOT BEEN PLEASED WHEN HE learned of Lewis deCourcy's engagement to Maria Manwaring. Although it was not likely that the union would produce any future claimants upon Parklands, it was hard to think that the considerable fortune of his uncle would go to a penniless girl, for Lewis deCourcy was the sort of gentleman who would not think of marrying anybody without first settling how she was to be provided for upon his demise. His sympathies might still be played upon—he might be persuaded to settle something upon the children—but Charles must give over all hope of having any of Lewis deCourcy's fortune come to him.

His disappointment was offset, to some degree, by the satisfying news that Sir Reginald had come to town. Charles rehearsed a proposal to relinquish his rooms in order to reside with his father-in-law, an offer that began with an earnest desire to be of use to Sir Reginald and concluded with a list of residences that were suitably quiet, convenient, and grand. He determined that the arrangement would entail no more than occasionally writing letters of business or performing some commission in the city, a small sacrifice for securing a handsome address in town.

Charles received word of his father-in-law's arrival and immediately waited upon him at Reginald's address in very sanguine spirits, which supported him until he was ushered into the gentleman's presence. Then his confidence weakened, for Sir Reginald's appearance and demeanor were no longer fragile and retiring; instead of losing ground since they had last parted, Sir Reginald now appeared to be in very good health—his complexion was ruddy, his eye sharp, and his voice clear and resolute.

Charles stammered out a greeting and could not help adding, "I am surprised to see you looking so well, sir."

"I *am* well, which I must attribute to the advantage of good company—of Miss Vernon and Miss Manwaring I cannot speak too highly, and I am always happy to see Catherine and the children. But you appear more *surprised* to see me in health than *pleased* about it."

Charles's protests were cut short by Sir Reginald, who added, "You can, however, be no more displeased than I, as I hear accounts of your conduct that disappoint me exceedingly."

"I cannot imagine. What can you allude to?"

"Churchill. Churchill—that word should be sufficient."

Charles first went white and then colored deeply. "Churchill?" he stammered. "How can the single word 'Churchill' be interpreted to my discredit?"

Sir Reginald needed nothing more than the look of guilty apprehension upon his son-in-law's countenance to confirm that his suspicions, which he hoped had imputed too much to Charles, had instead assigned too little. "Do you require particulars?"

"Sir, to simply utter the name of my family home—and the home of your daughter and grandchildren—conveys nothing that supersedes the necessity for more."

"Then, however much it pains me to speak so to the husband of my daughter and the father of my grandchildren, I must be frank. If even I, living in seclusion, with so little company and correspondence, have come to hear accounts of your misconduct during the life and since the death of your brother, can you think that the world in general is ignorant of it?"

" 'Misconduct'?"

"To have abused the trust of your brother and robbed Lady Vernon and her daughter of all peace and security."

"I have acted in no way that contradicted the directions laid down in my brother's will. You may apply to his attorney in Sussex, Mr. Barrett, if you have any doubt."

"I have no doubt as to Sir Frederick's instructions, nor do I doubt that they were faithfully carried out by Mr. Barrett, but that does not excuse your want of regard. To be so often at Sir Frederick's side during his infirmity left him susceptible to your persuasion, which *might* have been employed in encouraging your brother to better provide for his wife and daughter."

"If I did not exert as much as I ought, it was only to spare my brother the anxiety and activity that might have sent him into a decline—and if the worst did come to pass, would you have me argue in favor of Lady Vernon and her daughter, who will always have the protection of the Martins, at the expense of Catherine and your grandchildren? My brother's fortune must substantially benefit *them*."

"Nobody can benefit from a legacy if it is squandered in high living," replied Sir Reginald coldly.

"Sir, I have lived in town more modestly than most gentlemen of my station—indeed, much lower than I ought, as Lady Vernon's settlement entitled *her* to the house on Portland Place."

Sir Reginald endeavored to conceal his disgust at the self-interest that could not even comprehend a sense of wrongdoing—yet he could not accuse his son-in-law without feeling the full measure of his own neglect. He ought not to have allowed the marriage. Catherine's sentiments had been guided only by the belief that at three and twenty she ought to have a husband, and Lady deCourcy had promoted the match as one that would allow her daughter the distinction of being married while placing her in a situation that would (as Charles Vernon had no property, nor the immediate means of securing any) support their settling where the relationship of mother and daughter might continue uninterrupted. Governed by expedience and ease, and his brother's efforts to secure Charles Vernon some respectable means of employment, Sir Reginald had given his consent to the match. The ability to have his daughter and son take up residence on the property gave Sir Reginald some measure of satisfaction as he might—if he wished to exert it—oversee his son-in-law's conduct. That he did *not* exert to correct in Charles the want of principle that might have spared Miss Vernon and her mother such misery made him now sensible of something like responsibility—refusing his consent to a marriage with Catherine would likely not have reversed the course Charles had taken, but had Sir Reginald been more conscientious, it might have instilled in Charles something like conscience.

"You have no immediate need of a house in town," replied Sir Reginald. "Colonel Beresford's house on Berkeley Square is put up to let and I have taken it for two months—you may give up your quarters and take up residence there. You cannot want to be away from Churchill Manor beyond two months, as I understand it is in need of the sort of supervision that cannot be done from town. As for your decision to give up your position at the banking house, I support it. You must devote yourself to putting your own house in order. Churchill Manor cannot be properly managed if your interests are divided by an occupation that draws you so often to town."

The arrangement that Charles had hoped for was beginning to lose some of its luster. He was persuaded that he was over the worst of it, but there was a parting shot, which was very hard upon him. "You will give up your clubs. They will no longer be necessary to keep up business associations and are a poor place to be idle, for they will draw one into debts of honor, which may erase many years' independence. I will excuse you now, as you will have some arrangements to make in quitting your rooms."

Charles took leave of his father-in-law with as much poise as he could summon. He was relieved that the subject of how much of his brother's legacy was left at his disposal had been avoided, and decided that a respite from his clubs and associates (until the next quarter came due and Catherine was persuaded to cajole something from her father) would not be a great inconvenience.

chapter fifty-seven

SIR REGINALD DID NOT WAIT UNTIL HE WAS INSTALLED AT Berkeley Square to call upon Miss Manwaring's brother. Manwaring received him with informality and giddy spirits, which caused Sir Reginald to wonder that anyone could think that Lady Vernon had invited the attentions of such a frivolous creature. Manwaring's congratulations were directed toward himself as often as toward the engaged couple. He expressed his relief that Lewis deCourcy would take Maria for nothing—"for our father provided her with little, and I am sure that it was costly enough for me to keep a roof over her head and buy her three or four new gowns every winter."

In working his way around the subject of money (in order that his sister's future relations clearly understood how little he could do for her), Manwaring lapsed into several anecdotes of those speculations that accounted for his having nothing at all to give Maria. Sir Frederick Vernon was a minor player in one of his tales, and Sir Reginald asked just enough, and deduced just enough, to think that rather than being too harsh with his son-in-law, he had been too liberal.

He followed this visit with a call upon Miss Manwaring. The lady had gone out in the company of Mrs. Johnson, and Sir Reginald meant only to leave his card, but when Mr. Johnson understood who the caller was, he came out from his library and greeted the gentleman. The reticence of one and the formality of the other were rapidly overcome—Mr. Johnson's high opinion of Miss Vernon and Reginald deCourcy ensured the old gentleman's regard and drew them into a conversation that centered around their mutual acquaintance and ended with an engagement to dine the following week.

NOT EVEN THE satisfaction of accompanying Miss Manwaring and Eliza on a round of shopping and calls could console Alicia Johnson for not being at home to receive Sir Reginald deCourcy. She coaxed from her husband as much as she could, which involved too much conversation for him yet too little to satisfy her.

MRS. JOHNSON TO LADY VERNON

Edward Street, London
My dear friend,

I fully meant to call yesterday, but it was absolutely necessary to take Maria to the mantua maker, where she was fit for her gown, and today we were obliged to go around with Eliza, and then we were all to drink tea with Mrs. Carr. And you cannot think—it is too provoking! Sir Reginald deCourcy called while we were out! He did not merely leave his card but was a half hour talking to Mr. Johnson— Mr. Johnson was not at all displeased by having been taken away from his books. Indeed, he was so very far from being displeased that he invited Sir Reginald to dine with us next week! We will have his brother and son as well, and I hope that when the date is fixed, you will consent to make up the party. Indeed, I thought to call upon you today, but we had not been home a half hour when Manwaring called. Mr. Johnson will not receive him, of course, but concedes that he must be admitted now and again until Maria marries, and that will be so soon that she will be married from Edward Street.

I assure you, I did not expect anything more from Manwaring than congratulating himself upon Maria's engagement and talk of you—but upon the latter subject, he was very strange! He told us that Sir Reginald deCourcy had waited upon him, and that something was dropped in the conversation of your having nothing at all—not so much as a penny! Manwaring said that Sir Reginald led him to believe that your husband left all of his money to Charles Vernon!

Are you not diverted? The old gentleman is very sly, for this little falsehood must be calculated to drive off his son's rival. You will certainly not be troubled anymore with Manwaring's attentions if he thinks you have nothing! I congratulate you, my dear friend, for it seems that Sir Reginald has capitulated entirely! Manwaring says that he is to take the Beresfords' house for two months, and so I must conclude that you will be a married woman before the season is out.

As you cannot mean to marry before Miss Vernon, I expect that she has overcome her aversion to Sir James—their wedding must be the grandest of the three, but I will be as happy to attend your nuptials quite as well as Maria's.

Your devoted friend,
Alicia Johnson

chapter fifty-eight

THE DAY OF SIR JAMES'S BALL ARRIVED, AND IT WAS DE-
cided that Miss Manwaring would come to Portland Place
to dine and spend the night. They barely tasted the meal
and excused themselves from the table as soon as they could to hurry
to Miss Vernon's apartments. Their gowns were donned, their hair
was arranged, their gloves and fans and shawls gathered up, and then
they went to show themselves to Lady Martin, who was to accompany
them, and to Lady Vernon, who was to remain at home.

Lady Martin entertained the young ladies with tales of the many
balls she had attended as a girl: "The table for dinner was three hundred feet long with a centerpiece of white orchids and green fern all
entwined with a riband of crimson satin from one end of the table to
the other—and the entire thing was not fabric and flowers at all, but
fashioned out of spun sugar!"—"Five or six full chandeliers, and each
one was said to cost eight thousand pounds!"—"White velvet from
head to toe—even to her slippers! And she came out of the evening
with scarcely a spot upon it, for she danced only one dance and would
eat and drink nothing at all."

The effect upon the young ladies was to amaze Maria Manwaring,
who began to think that all the time she had been out had been
squandered attending very inferior balls, and to frighten Frederica,
who had never been to a ball in all her life.

When their carriage turned along Cavendish Square, a sensation of
awe overwhelmed any remaining feelings of delightful anticipation.
The carriage was forced to settle into a queue of three dozen vehicles.

"Good heavens!" cried Lady Martin. "He has invited all of London!

Look how Lady Millbanke hurries her girls down from the carriage, as she is eager that one of them will get Sir James for the first dance. I will not have *us* scramble down the street in such a common fashion!"

The progression of the carriage to the door took a full half hour, and when their destination was at last in view, they were very happy to see Mr. Lewis deCourcy step ahead of the footmen to hand the ladies down, claiming Miss Manwaring with that particular confidence of a successful lover.

Frederica began to feel the effect of her appearance in the whispers and glances that attended her party as they ascended the stairs. In town, private balls varied from one another only in the setting, but the company was very much the same—anybody new was an object of great curiosity, and Frederica had the advantage of her adventure at Miss Summers's, her connection with the Martins, and her elegance of dress to provoke audible murmurs of "She is every bit the beauty that her mother is!" and "Her gown cannot have cost her less than a hundred guineas!"

The room they entered was splendidly appointed and ablaze with light; the effect upon Frederica was quite overpowering and she would have turned away into one of the quieter passages when her cousin approached and took her hand. "And where is your mother? I know that she cannot be dancing, but it would have been quite allowable for her to come as your chaperone."

"My mother was certain that my aunt would do as well and that her presence would not be missed."

"I can agree with the first sentiment, but I protest the second. But, come, you must attend to your office—as the guest of honor, you must receive with me."

"Oh, no—you must take my Aunt Martin!" cried Frederica in horror.

"Nonsense!" declared Lady Martin, who had come up behind them. "I see a fine chair in the corner, if Lady Millbanke does not claim it, where I can watch the dancing. You have said nothing of the girls' dress, James, and they both took most particular care. I must have some compliments to bring back with me to Portland Place."

"I cannot hope to be more eloquent than their own mirrors, Mother. Miss Manwaring has a very particular bloom that must be attributed to more than the becoming shade of her gown. I cannot hope to interest you in any of the first dances, Miss Manwaring, as there is one who has the greater claim, but I would be very honored if you would oblige me later in the evening."

The lady gave him a very pretty smile.

He then attended his cousin to her post, where she was obliged to curtsy and shake hands with a great many people and think of some answer to their pleasantries that at least gave the impression of ease and interest. There was only a moment of coolness when Lady Hamilton appeared with her eldest daughters. The Hamiltons could not bring themselves to decline an invitation to so superior a gathering, and yet they were deeply humiliated to see Frederica at her cousin's side and to think of her making such a fine match, when her mother had stolen Reginald from Lavinia.

When the company was well assembled, Frederica had hoped to be released from her cousin's side and go to her aunt, where she might sit and observe in silence. Her knowledge of how everything was to proceed had come only from conversation and books, and she was discomfited, therefore, to learn that she was to open the ball with her cousin. The artlessness that had preserved her from any fear of not having a partner was unequal to this discovery. "Oh, but, cousin— surely it cannot be my place! There are so many young ladies who are higher—who have a right to expect the distinction!"

"Yes, there are too many of them who *expect* it, but none who *deserves* it more," he said as he conducted her to the top of the room. "Have no fear, cousin, I will claim only the two first—it was quite settled between young deCourcy and myself that I should have you open the dance and then he may have as much of your company as he likes."

Frederica replied with a blush and a toss of her head, and began the dance with more elegance and composure than she was feeling. It was her nature to learn everything thoroughly, and when impressed with the fact that young ladies *must* dance, she had applied herself to the process with as much dedication as to science, and with as much success. The attention of everyone was engaged by their host and his partner as they went down the dance; they saw nothing that suggested an aversion to her cousin on Miss Vernon's part and yet nothing that

indicated anything like infatuation on his. The rumors of their engagement had everyone on his side—he was handsome, amiable, and
rich, and Miss Vernon was a very great fool if she did not like him;
yet *that* had been resolved before she was seen very much at all. Indeed,
she was everything that was lovely and elegant, and many of the young
men who had precipitately engaged other partners for every dance
began to regret their haste, while those who had saved a dance or two
readied themselves to petition her in the course of the evening.

Sir James would have escorted her to his mother, but Lucy Smith
caught Frederica's hand as soon as she had finished dancing and
whisked her to the side of the room. "How exquisite your gown is! I
have such a good bit of gossip! You will die of laughter when I tell
you! They are all so angry that Lavinia could not sit still to have her
hair dressed! Only look how it has frizzed all over! My uncle has written to my mother and told her that Reginald does not mean to marry
Livvy! Only think of all the gentlemen she took no notice of because
she was secure of him! My uncle's letter was so solemn—'We erred,
my dear sister, in substituting our own wishes for theirs, and supposing
that filial obligation must include a surrender of all inclination. Reginald's heart, I believe, has been fixed elsewhere'!" Here, Lucy broke
into a fit of giggles. "Ah, you look so conscious! And to have Sir Reginald call upon your mother so immediately upon coming to town—so,
is it all settled between them?"

The color rushed into Frederica's cheeks. The journey from Kent
to London had increased her and Reginald's admiration of each
other—Reginald was captivated by her thoughtful conversation and
her beauty, and she was very pleased with his opinions and manners.
The engagement of Maria and Lewis deCourcy, moreover, had put
them both in a frame of mind to think and talk of marriage, and the
length of the journey was just enough for them to understand that
their views on the subject were very much the same.

Still, Lucy spoke as though Reginald or his father had already addressed Lady Vernon and Frederica was undecided whether to be
pleased at Lucy's conviction that Reginald had declared himself or to
be offended that he had not declared himself to *her* before speaking to
her mother.

"Ah, here comes my dear Smith again," declared Lucy, "plaguing me to dance—to have him importune me so when he sought my hand was well and good, but a husband does not need to court his wife."

Mr. Smith claimed her, and Frederica began to make her way around the room toward Lady Martin, when a group of people standing together to comment upon the dancing and the company barred her path, and she happened to catch some of their conversation. "Lady Vernon has quite captivated young deCourcy, I understand, and Sir Reginald has come to London on purpose to give them his blessing. They must wait until Miss Vernon weds Sir James, of course—it would not be suitable for the mother to marry before the daughter."

Can that have been Lucy's meaning? Frederica wondered. She did not know whether to laugh or to cry—she had come to be inured to the belief that she was to marry Sir James and was content that such a rumor must die out in time—but to think that Reginald was to wed her mother!

She went and sat down beside her aunt.

"Why, what is the matter, child? You are quite pale. One dance cannot have done you in, for here comes young deCourcy to claim you."

"Oh, Aunt, I cannot—do make some excuse! What significance will everyone put upon our dancing together?"

"What do you mean?"

Reginald came up to the ladies and bowed, and after exchanging a few words with Lady Martin, he petitioned Frederica for the next set.

Frederica could not refuse. She danced the first dance with more diligence than feeling, and as the second was to begin, Reginald looked at her closely and said in a low voice, "I think that you would rather sit down—may we not go up to the conservatory? It will be cooler there."

Frederica took his arm and they went up to the conservatory, which was arranged with an elegance and discrimination that would have surprised those who believed Sir James to be thoughtless and shallow.

"These occasions so often take on the importance of a debut—a newly engaged couple or a lady's being out will always make someone or other the object of attention. Miss Manwaring bears the discomfort of being stared at very well, and as my uncle sees no one save for her, he is equally free of distress. You feel for them more than they feel for themselves, I think."

"I feel nothing but joy for them, I assure you," replied Frederica. "But my weeks at Parklands had put everything unpleasant very far from my thoughts, and I had forgotten how many had convinced themselves that I was to marry my cousin."

"It cannot be disconcerting to be admired by Sir James—*he* cannot distress you. Is it, then, the notion of marrying *anybody* that you find to be unpleasant?"

"Oh, no!" she replied with a blush. "I have known more happy marriages than unhappy ones. It is not the *prospect* of marriage but the *rumors* that distress me—not of a union between Sir James and myself, but between my mother and—and you."

She observed his reaction to her words carefully. If his response to the rumor of a marriage to her mother was either laughter or indignation, she was convinced that she could not like him.

He did not laugh, however, nor did he recoil. He smiled gravely and said, "Such rumors began when I arrived at Churchill Manor, and your mother was good enough not to ridicule the notion. She, very sensibly, accounted for the gossip by saying that when a single gentleman and lady are under one roof, everybody will want to have them married. I do not deny that I admire Lady Vernon. Her superior company helped my leisure hours at Churchill Manor pass very pleasantly, and after your arrival we developed a greater rapport, as we had an interest in common."

Her attentive expression and sweet smile gave him all of the encouragement he needed to continue. "Miss Vernon, I am confident in my own sentiments—my gratitude for the very material improvement in my father, which I must attribute entirely to you, would itself be a sensible foundation for affection—and I know you to be a young lady who ranks sense very highly. But I have other grounds for regard—I assure you I have a dozen speeches ready in praise of your kindness, your accomplishments, and your excellent understanding, if you will hear them."

Frederica had not the advantage of romantic novels, which would have taught her how to simper and waver and hold him in suspense.

"Indeed, I need not hear them," she replied. "For if you are too excessive in your commendation, it may stir up my vanity, and if you are too moderate, it will injure my pride."

"Even the most extravagant praise of you must fall short of the truth," he replied. "And any expression of my own admiration and love, however eloquent, will be less than you deserve." He then proceeded to declare himself in as warm and rational a manner as a young lady of scientific disposition could wish, and asked for her hand in marriage.

Frederica hesitated, not from any reluctance to accept the offer but from an understanding of the enormity of the honor—but sense overcame her reticence and, in language that gave him no doubt of her affection, she accepted him.

"We will now have the happy task of undeceiving everyone who had us marry elsewhere." He smiled. "But I think there will be at least as many who are happy for us as those who are disappointed."

Frederica, imagining that he might immediately go down and proclaim his successful love to all the company, reminded him of their obligation to seek their parents' consent before a more general announcement was made. "I would not have anyone happy before Mother and Sir Reginald," she declared.

They joined the company once more, and although Reginald was obliged to yield Frederica to a succession of partners and to offer himself to several young ladies who would otherwise have had to sit out a dance, when they were together, they appeared so cheerful and animated as to persuade everyone that young deCourcy had reconciled Frederica to his union with her mother and that she had at last resigned herself to marrying Sir James.

While Sir James was seeing his mother to the carriage, Reginald drew Frederica aside, and they decided that their parents' consent must be asked as soon as possible. "I think—I *hope*—that Sir Reginald will be happy," said Frederica. "But I am afraid that the joy of Lady deCourcy and the Hamiltons will not be so easily won."

"Whether or not they will approve, they must be resigned to what is inevitable," declared Reginald. "I have left everyone else to cultivate my happiness too long, and they have been very poor gardeners—I must attend to it myself."

chapter fifty-nine

REDERICA WAS TOO HAPPY TO WAIT FOR DAYLIGHT TO make her important communication to her mother. Lady Vernon laughed, wept, and said, "Your father would have been so very pleased with your choice," then wiped away her tears and smiled once more. Upon Frederica's urging, she rang for Wilson, who hurried from her bed, fearing some change in her mistress's condition; her congratulations were asked for and enthusiastically given, and their expressions of joy were so great that they drew Lady Martin from her own quarters.

"What? Are you still up, Susan? Are you ill?"

Her anxiety for Lady Vernon was immediately set right and her delight at Frederica's news could barely be contained. "Oh, Lord bless me! Did I not tell you? Did I not say how well they were suited to each other? Oh, what a handsome couple you will make—and Miss Manwaring being married to his uncle! Oh, but it is not right that we should all celebrate and Miss Manwaring be left out!" she insisted, whereupon Miss Manwaring was called from her quarters to share in their joy.

Nearly an hour was spent in talking, until at last Lady Martin determined, "We must all get ourselves to bed. There will be enough time for talking tomorrow when we are refreshed—then we can go over the entire ball. I daresay I never saw anything as curious as Miss Hamilton's hair! Why, I recall that I was proposed to at a ball myself— it was not your uncle, for a ball is a very romantic place to propose and your uncle did not have a romantic bone in his body—though he was a very good man, for all that. Come, we must get to bed."

The morning hours of Portland Place were not late as a rule, but on the morrow, the girls and Lady Vernon were still in bed when Lady Martin came down to breakfast. She had just poured out her coffee and put a saucer of cream down for her cats when the door was thrown open and Sir James was ushered into the room.

"Good morning, Mother! Is no one else down? I had hoped that I might find all of you together so that I might be properly congratulated. Have no fear, nothing has got around yet, for half of respectable London and *all* of the scoundrels and gossips are still in bed, but I needed no confirmation other than deCourcy's looks and Freddie's smiles last night as the dancing progressed. Did I not tell you that the ball would do the trick? I take all the credit for the engagement that can be spared from Freddie—I will allow generously for her beauty and cleverness and the gracefulness of her dancing, but I must have my share of praise for bringing young deCourcy to the point."

"And what did you do?" scoffed Lady Martin. "Frederica's beauty comes from her mother's side, for *her* mother was an Osbourne, and her cleverness was helped on by her parents and Miss Wilson, and the gracefulness of her dancing must be attributed to her own application to the process!"

"Well, then—I have sharpened her wits."

"A girl needs very little wit to say 'I will' when a gentleman asks her."

"You are determined not to flatter me at all—it is a pity that Susan is not up. *She* would not be so miserly with her praise. I must wait until tonight, for we are all to dine with the Johnsons. I am in such good spirits that I do not even mind that Charles Vernon is to be of the party."

Sir Reginald and Mr. Lewis deCourcy called some time later, the former to address Lady Vernon and the latter to escort Miss Manwaring back to Edward Street.

Lady Vernon, whose natural fatigue had been increased by very little sleep, received Sir Reginald in her dressing room. He thought her very pale and languid, though she held out her hand in welcome, and her eyes glowed with pleasure when he told her how very pleased he was with his son's choice and assured her that he gave his hearty consent to the union of their children. "Miss Vernon is everything I could wish in a daughter, and her disposition will complement Reginald's in every regard. As to the date and the particulars, it must be arranged with respect to your situation; I would not impose upon your mourning and I hope that seeing your daughter to the altar will bring you a little happiness to lighten your sorrow."

Lady Vernon thanked him, for his present kindness and for the many kindnesses he had shown Frederica while she was at Parklands. "Your son's offer does credit to his heart, but with you I may be frank—it must be an offer that is entirely disinterested. My daughter has no fortune—certainly nothing like what would have been settled upon Miss Hamilton can be settled upon Frederica."

"I am very sorry for Miss Vernon that such is the case—sorrier, indeed, because I must think that it would be otherwise but for the interference of my son-in-law. If I could compel him to make amends, I would do so. As it is, I can only give you my assurances that no claim to any entitlement save for Miss Vernon herself is sought."

He then rose to take leave, as she did not seem to be equal to a prolonged conversation. He asked permission to call upon her again and assured her that she might very soon expect to receive a letter from Lady deCourcy giving her blessing and approval to the engagement.

Maria proposed that Frederica accompany her to Edward Street to spend the day, and Lady Vernon decided that she would just as soon be spared the paroxysms of astonishment and agitation when her dear friend Alicia Johnson learned of Frederica's engagement.

Mrs. Johnson's emotions were indeed thrown into turmoil by the announcement—Miss Vernon engaged to Reginald deCourcy! How could he have proposed to the daughter when everybody had him all but married to the mother? And yet how much more exciting to have Miss Vernon, rather than her mother, as Reginald deCourcy's object. Lady Vernon was not quite eight months a widow—if she were to marry now, everything must be delayed and done in a very modest fashion, but Miss Vernon's engagement must entail a great deal of shopping and visiting. And what a round of parties and balls and receptions there would be!

Mrs. Johnson was well into a reverie that had her looking through

pattern books and overseeing the selection of laces and veils when she
was struck with another thought. What of Sir James Martin now that
Miss Vernon was *not* to marry Sir James! The notion that he was unattached roused her to action—she must immediately call upon Lady
Hamilton and Lady Millbanke and Mrs. Carr and tell them that Sir
James Martin was eligible once more, and leaving the two girls to the
company of Mr. Johnson—which was to leave him alone in his library
and the girls to a happy *tête-à-tête* in the sitting room—she hurried out
the door.

chapter sixty

As Miss Manwaring and Miss Vernon were arrang-ing their dress for dinner, a note was handed up to the latter.

Lady Martin to Miss Vernon

Portland Place
My dear girl,

> *I send this with another note to Mrs. Johnson asking her to excuse your mother and me from dining tonight. I have said only that your mother is not well—it is many, many hours before anything more in the way of explanation will be required. I would not have you stay to dine at Edward Street if you would rather be at home, but you can do nothing here, while there you may keep up such appearances as will prevent James from hurrying to Portland Place and making a nuisance of himself. It is a part that will require some presence of mind, but I have every confidence in your abilities and assure you that Wilson's and mine are equal to the present state of affairs.*

> *Yours, etc.,*
> *E. Martin*

Mrs. Johnson was excessively displeased by her letter. "Why, it was to have been very evenly laid out—six ladies and six gentlemen!" she expostulated to Eliza Manwaring. "If I had been given more notice, I might have invited somebody else. I do not think that Miss Hamilton and Miss Claudia would have come, as they must be very angry at their cousin, but I owe something in the way of a dinner to Mrs. Younge, who might have brought her niece."

"At least it will not be an odd party," consoled Eliza. She was all contentment, for she was to dine in the company of Sir Reginald de-Courcy and his son, which was a mark of distinction she had never enjoyed when at Langford.

Sir James was more displeased than Mrs. Johnson at the absence of his mother and cousin. He was inclined to excuse himself at once and go directly to Portland Place, but Frederica's presence reassured him that she would not stay to dine if her mother were ill.

The remainder of the party arrived and Frederica was quite surprised to see the change in her Uncle Vernon. His countenance was wan and tense, and when he congratulated the young ladies upon their good fortune, he did not know where to look. Toward Frederica he was particularly ill at ease, and he retreated to the company of gentlemen, though he seemed to have little to say to any of them. At dinner, he was seated between Mrs. Johnson and Eliza, where he was principally occupied in repeating to one the remarks the other had not heard.

During a change in the courses, there was just such a lull in the conversation that allowed Sir James to address the entire party. "My young cousin's engagement compels me to think of my obligation as her nearest male relation—from her mother's branch of the family," he added with a nod in Vernon's direction. "I have decided upon my wedding present, which I know will please Freddie and I hope will please you, deCourcy."

"If it pleases Frederica, then it will please me," said Reginald with a smile.

"But you must tell us what it is," urged Mrs. Johnson.

"It is a garden—indeed, several gardens—laid out in some of the finest property in Staffordshire."

"Staffordshire!"

"Yes, what a wonderful opportunity your engagement presents, for I may get Vernon Castle off my hands at last."

"Sir, I must protest," declared Reginald.

"Yes, indeed you must." Sir James laughed. "You must protest that you have asked nothing to take Freddie off our hands—I would think less of you if you did not. But it was always to have been Freddie's property, and I have never intended it for any other purpose than to be settled on her. You must be on my side, Sir Reginald. Surely you see no impropriety in my offer."

"None at all. Certainly Miss Vernon is deserving of no less."

"Indeed, she deserves much more. Do you not agree, Vernon?"

Charles Vernon started. Sir James's announcement had left him speechless; to have Vernon Castle given away in such an offhand fashion—the property he had once coveted and got so close to possessing!

Sir James repeated his question, and Vernon, not knowing what to say, muttered something like assent.

"I am delighted to hear it, for we must be together in this. I will settle the property and I will leave the dowry to you—whatever Sir Frederick confided to you that he *meant* to give her—there will be no occasion for anything more." He then turned the subject aside to Vernon Castle, and in describing the countryside, for the gentlemen's benefit, and the appointment of the rooms, for the ladies', he entertained them until the ladies withdrew.

Frederica was not insensible of the philanthropy of Sir James's gift, though she also recognized the practicality of it—she and Reginald must live somewhere when they married, and she neither wished for Parklands to come to them in the near future nor to be in an everyday proximity to Lady deCourcy.

Alicia Johnson and Eliza Manwaring thought the gesture a very handsome one—extraordinarily handsome—and Eliza, in particular, addressed Frederica with a greater desire to make herself agreeable than she ever had before. Her resentment of Lady Vernon, the misery occasioned by her husband's conduct at Langford, must be set aside if the privilege of being invited to Vernon Castle was to be cultivated, for though she had visited innumerable manors and parks and halls and lodges, she had yet to enjoy the distinction of being asked to a castle.

Maria's selfishness was very moderate by comparison—she was

only sorry that she and Frederica would be settled so far from each other. "It is more than a hundred miles," she lamented.

Eliza protested, "A hundred miles is only a great distance when the conditions of travel are inferior, but that is not the case here. Your husbands possess such handsome carriages, and they will always have the best horses that you may travel with such ease and comfort—I daresay you would not think yourselves far at twice the distance!"

The gentlemen stayed somewhat longer than usual in the dining room, and when they appeared, Frederica noticed Vernon's ashen face and silent manner. He took some coffee from Mrs. Johnson solely, it seemed, to have something to do with his hands, and he sat because it seemed that his legs would not support him.

Sir James took a chair beside his cousin and smiled. "I know that your uncle has made you unhappy—how far, and from what cause, you have not chosen to confide—but I think that I have gotten satisfaction."

"I am sorry that you have found me reserved, cousin, but I will not be sparing in my thanks."

"You must spare some of your thanks for Sir Reginald. Gentlemen will be very direct when the ladies have left the table. 'I quite agree that it is for Miss Vernon's male relations to act in the place of her father,' said he. 'Sir James has settled very handsomely upon her in the matter of property, and so I think it is for you, Charles, to name the dowry.' Vernon gave a sort of sickly smile and protested, 'I think that Reginald's pride will not allow it,' and young deCourcy replied, 'My pride will always give way before any gesture of respect for Miss Vernon.' There was nothing to be done. Eight thousand pounds—what do you think? I would have liked ten better than eight, but Vernon does have a second son and two daughters to provide for in time, so under the circumstances, I think it is very handsome."

Frederica was astonished. She had given up all hope that her uncle would concede to any of Sir Frederick's *promises* regarding her and her mother—to have agreed to particulars was unbelievable!

She expressed her misgivings to her cousin. "He is like many false-hearted men who will say one thing in the evening and retract it on the following day."

"He will not be given the opportunity," replied her cousin, "for once he named the amount, Sir Reginald declared that there was nothing to prevent the terms from being drawn up immediately, and Johnson even offered to act as witness. Ah, here comes your young man, and I must give way. He is an excellent fellow and as sensible as a man who is violently in love can be—you must not hope for anything more."

The evening passed away; if Charles Vernon was morose and silent, *that* was offset by Mr. Johnson's uncommon affability. His friendship with Lewis deCourcy was long-standing, but now he took pains to know Sir Reginald better, and in their mutual esteem of Frederica, there was something to promote conversation. He was even cordial toward Eliza and went so far as to throw any praise of the house or the dinner in Mrs. Johnson's direction.

Sir Reginald's habits were regular and he kept early hours, and soon after they had taken their coffee and tea, he called for his carriage. Reginald and Vernon departed with him, and Sir James and Mr. Lewis deCourcy left not long after. Frederica waited only for her cousin to be gone before she asked Mr. Johnson if she might trouble him to be conveyed back to Portland Place.

"Indeed, yes, for you will have a great deal to tell Lady Vernon. It will be a great relief—when she is better, I hope that I may be permitted to call upon her—if there was any misunderstanding—any feeling that I did not wish for the acquaintance—you will smooth things over, to be sure."

Frederica assured him that both her mother and Lady Martin would be happy to know him, and after a round of thanks and promises and engagements that must prolong any parting for an additional fifteen minutes, Frederica departed.

She found her mother so well attended by her aunt, Miss Wilson, and Mrs. Forrester that *her* presence would have given rise to confusion rather than comfort. As the night progressed into morning, however, all four women had a part to play; and though it was frequently to obey some order of Dr. Driggs's or to assure each other that Lady Vernon was in no great distress or in any danger, they were diligent, capable, and tireless.

The morning brought the fulfillment of all of Lady Vernon's hopes and the end of Charles Vernon's expectations, and though making his arrival well before it had been anticipated, the child gave no indication of being the worse for it. Lady Martin, too overcome with exhaustion and relief, said, "When no ill effects come of it, it is just as well to have a child come early as not," though she could not help adding that it was the good doctor's calculations that might have been amiss.

She then declared that he had the Vernon forehead and the Martin chin, while Lady Vernon was content to reassure herself that he had the proper number of limbs and pronounced his name to be James Frederick Vernon.

chapter sixty-one

CHARLES VERNON WOKE THE NEXT MORNING, LOOKING toward his tenure as master of Churchill Manor with renewed interest. The quarter was due in a matter of weeks, and while it might not be what he would like (as he had done nothing to increase the property's yield or rents), it would put his creditors off a little longer and help to settle the sort of debts of honor that must be reconciled without delay.

The news of Reginald's engagement to Frederica was a wretched turn of events, but to see her mistress of Vernon Castle and to have his vague concurrence that he ought to do something for her turned into a fixed sum—eight thousand pounds!—was not to be borne. Still, the sum was not yet surrendered—he must act to repair the damage before it was irrevocable.

MR. VERNON TO MRS. VERNON

Berkeley Square, London
My dear wife,

I have some very surprising news that I do not doubt will reach your mother by way of Sir Reginald. Your brother has proposed to our niece! After appearances had convinced all of London that she was reconciled to a marriage with her cousin—indeed, she received with him at Cavendish Square and opened the ball in such a manner (so I have heard, as I was not present) as persuaded everyone that the announcement of their engagement was imminent. I begin to wonder if all of the rumors of our niece's engagement to her cousin were circulated by herself, and if her show of distress while she was with us at Churchill was a charade to pique Reginald's interest, for you know that a gentleman will always find a woman who is promised to another more appealing than one who is thrown at his head.

This news can please my mother-in-law in only one regard—Reginald does not marry Lady Vernon—and yet, for your sake, I would almost prefer _that_ marriage to _this_ one. Even if Lady Vernon were in health to make the marriage a long one (which I doubt, as reports have her becoming increasingly frail), a wife toward whom his father was so decidedly opposed would always ensure that you remain first with Sir Reginald—now I fear that the distinction of "daughter" is one that you must share with our niece, who, it appears, has now set herself toward securing your father's affections with the same slyness that allowed her to play upon Reginald's heart.

I now reside at Berkeley Square with Sir Reginald and have done my part to ensure his comfort, yet one thing is wanting and that is to have you here. You know that your father's spirits are always at their best and most generous when our children are present, and I fear that if his liberality does not have a proper object, he will be inclined to squander it—and we will be comprehended in his imprudence. Already he has coerced from me a promise that I will provide our niece's dowry! As this was brought up in company, and before Reginald, I could not protest the injury such a loss would do to our children and was even compelled to agree to a sum—nearly a third of my brother's legacy! This, when added to some other expenses that my situation must incur (and with no income from the banking house, as that position has been given up), is not insignificant—I can only hope that when the quarter comes due from Churchill Manor, it may be, in some part, offset.

The irony is that our niece has no need for a dowry; not only can marriage to Reginald make it unnecessary, but Sir James Martin has resolved to settle Vernon Castle upon her! To wring an additional eight thousand pounds from me is very unreasonable. Had you been here, I am certain that you might have talked your father out of it—

this may yet be possible; your presence and those mild and disinter-
ested arguments that have always prevailed with your father (when
added to the company of our dear children) may persuade him to re-
tract this extravagant gesture. If you cannot come at once, an express
to your father may do as well, but I think you had better come.

Your devoted husband,
Charles Vernon

Sir Reginald's letter to his wife was more to the point; they had so
little to say to each other that even the most significant communication did not extend beyond a concise disclosure of the facts.

SIR DECOURCY TO LADY DECOURCY

Berkeley Square, London
My dear wife,

You have long looked toward the prospect of Reginald's marriage
and you will be pleased to know that all of the prudent encouragement
has not been given in vain. Reginald has made an offer to Miss Ver-
non and she has accepted him. I have given my consent, and Lady
Vernon has likewise given her blessing. I will leave it to Reginald to so-
licit yours, and will trouble you for a few lines to Miss Vernon and her
mother.

Your devoted husband, etc.,
Reginald deCourcy

Charles Vernon had spent so freely that the portion he agreed to
settle on his niece represented more than half of what remained of
the money bequeathed by his brother. His desire to preserve it long
enough for Catherine to come to London and coax her father back
into prudence and sense had him fabricating some urgent business at
Churchill Manor. He could not meet with Sir Reginald's agents and

attorneys while he was in Sussex, and so immediately after dispatch-ing his letter to Catherine, he made some remarks about a matter of business at the family estate that could not be resolved by correspon-dence and required his immediate attention. He promised to return in three or four days' time, which, he calculated, was all that would be al-lowed for Catherine to receive his letter, apprehend the urgency of their situation, and come to town.

Reginald arrived at Berkeley Square to find Charles gone and his father engaged with his uncle, so he decided to call at Portland Place. His carriage drew up beside Sir James's and the two gentlemen greeted each other and were admitted together.

Sir James was at once aware of some disruption in the household, for the footman's livery was half-buttoned and his wig askew, and Miss Wilson appeared from below with a shawl thrown over her nightdress and a tea tray in her hands.

"Miss Wilson!" Sir James cried. "What is the matter?"

She immediately handed her tray to the footman with orders that he take it up and ask Lady Martin to come down, then showed the gentlemen into the drawing room. She bade them sit, in a manner that did credit to her self-command.

"What is the matter?" Sir James demanded once more, with more feeling than civility. "Why is there no fire? Why are the drapes still drawn? Has someone been taken ill?"

Lady Martin bustled into the room, her dress disordered and her hair hastily tucked under a cap. Her face revealed her exhaustion, but her eyes were bright and her expression joyful. "What do you mean by coming upon us so early—it is only eleven o'clock! Why do you not stay in bed until noon anymore? You mean to become steady and sen-sible just to plague me. If it is *your* influence, Mr. deCourcy, I cannot protest. Come, sir, and we will have a comfortable chat—for my Fred-erica has only just got to sleep and I do not think you would have me wake her. As for you, James, you may go to Susan—she is very com-fortable now, and when she heard that you had come, she decided that she would as soon see you now as later—but you must not keep her long, for she is very weak and will not stand much conversation."

Sir James, filled with notions of influenza and putrid fever, hurried to his cousin's apartments, not even stopping to knock on the door before he entered. He found Frederica fast asleep upon the sofa and Susan sitting up in her bed, her beautiful face very pale, and holding a bundle in her arms.

Sir James's shock cannot be described, but his self-command, always concealed by his facade of merriment and nonsense, rose to support him, and drawing a chair beside her, he looked at her searchingly, assuring himself that she was not in danger, and then turned his gaze upon the child.

"Well!" he declared, attempting to affect his old buoyancy of tone. "Who is this? I beg you to introduce me, cousin."

"May I present you to your cousin, James Frederick Vernon."

"Excellent! You must let me hold him—have no fear, I will not break him—there! You are surprised, no doubt, that I know how to hold an infant—it is a delightful thing to have everyone think one so trifling and silly, their expression of surprise when one says or does anything in a sensible fashion is excessively diverting. What an excellent little fellow! I declare, he has the Martin forehead and the Vernon chin! Why, what will this mean for Frederick's line? The little fellow must precede Vernon—and do you know what that means?"

"I do." Lady Vernon smiled.

" 'I do'—an excellent phrase. And as you, young man, are now the head of the family, I would be very happy to hear it from you. I ask your consent to marry your mother. I have asked once, but your mother—for some unaccountable reason—put me off. She seemed to think that some mysterious and unacceptable circumstance might come to pass that would make me regret my offer! But if *you* approve me, she cannot refuse. See how he grasps my finger! He has given his blessing—it is how an infant will express his consent, I am quite sure of it. What a perceptive little fellow he is! I declare, he can all but talk, but if he could I am certain that when I asked him if he would consent to our marriage, he would say 'I do.' "

chapter sixty-two

CHARLES VERNON HAD GONE TO CHURCHILL MANOR WITH every intention of wringing from it all the income he could, and a sincere desire to apply himself, at this late date, toward the administration of the family property. The desire was stronger than the sincerity, and had he behaved as he ought, and come into his inheritance honorably, he would nonetheless have been ill equipped for the responsibility.

He returned to London full of plans for exploiting his last resource to find Sir Reginald gone to call upon Lady Vernon, and a letter from Catherine.

MRS. CHARLES VERNON TO MR. VERNON

Parklands Manor, Kent
My dear husband,

Your letter surprised me beyond measure. Can it be true that Reginald and Frederica are engaged? Perhaps Lady Vernon's ill health has been the result of her parting with Reginald—yet while it is far better than if Reginald had married Lady Vernon, I am equally confounded by his credulity and her pretense, for I must think that her eagerness to come to Parklands was only to understand precisely how rich the wife of Reginald deCourcy must be—and having succeeded in ingratiating herself with Reginald's parents, she set out to steal him away from her mother. It seems that she is Lady Vernon's daughter after all.

My mother is very angry that you have provided our niece with a dowry—she is quite of your opinion that it is unnecessary, and a very great imposition, as she is enriched at the expense of little Frederick, Kitty, and Regina. In fact, she is so angry as to insist that we think of changing Frederick's name to something else, as she does not wish to hear anything like "Frederica."

In her present state, she cannot think of coming to town—even in her happiest disposition, London is odious to her, and with all of the talk of influenza, I do not think it would be a fit place for the children. In any case, we should likely no sooner be settled than my father's spell of good health would give way, and we would all be compelled to return to Kent—but as you are no longer with the banking house, why may you not come to us?

Your devoted wife,
C. Vernon

This blow was a very mild one when compared to the next, for Sir Reginald's valet, having emboldened himself to wish Mr. Vernon joy, was required to explain himself, which he did by providing the newspapers that proclaimed Lady Vernon, widow of Sir Frederick Vernon, had been safely delivered of a son and heir, and added a few lines about the alteration in the succession that this very interesting sequence of events must bring about.

Vernon's response was utter disbelief. To have nothing, nothing at all—the heirs to Parklands both to marry—the surrender of his position at the banking house—the loss of Churchill Manor! To evade this responsibility became uppermost in his mind, and he immediately quit the house and made his way back to Parklands Manor, to throw himself upon the mercy of his wife and her mother.

The recent fluctuation in their family left them both vulnerable and eager to cling to anything like stability. Vernon had little difficulty in convincing them that they had been used very ill by Lady Vernon and her daughter, and to agree that the loss of eight thousand pounds would place a very great burden upon Kitty, Regina, and Frederick, when Lady deCourcy, who was very quick to understand anything in the way of profit or loss to her family, asked, "But will even that be theirs? Will you not be compelled to give back the whole sum to Sir Frederick's heir? Unless some childhood illness or other carries him off, you will be obliged to restore all to him, will you not?"

$\mathscr{I}$T IS BEST, FOR ALL PARTIES WHO SUFFER FROM A TRAGEDY, to not look too deeply into how far that misfortune came to be the source of a new happiness; thus, Lady Vernon did not dwell upon the *circumstance* that left her free to marry a second time. Sir Frederick was not forgotten—he could not be forgotten by those who had esteemed him so highly, nor could his memory fade in the presence of little James Frederick, whom Lady Martin declared the possessor of the Vernon forehead while Sir James maintained that he had the Vernon chin.

The devotion of Sir James and the steadiness and counsel of his mother persuaded Lady Vernon to amend the answer she had given to her cousin at Churchill. She did not oblige him to wait out the year, and three weeks after the birth of James Frederick, she and Sir James were quietly married. A month later, Miss Manwaring was wed to Lewis deCourcy in a modest ceremony, and before the season was out, the marriage of Frederica Susannah Vernon to Reginald Hamilton de-Courcy was celebrated in a fashion that Alicia Johnson declared was "quite the jewel of the season."

Mr. and Mrs. Reginald deCourcy settled happily in Staffordshire, where Frederica had the particular pleasure of renewing her acquaintance with the Clarkes and residing a very easy distance from the Martins at Ealing Park. Her intimacy with Maria did not suffer for the hundred miles between Vernon Castle and Bath—superior conveyances, excellent roads, and an affection between uncle and nephew, which had them always ready to promote the closeness of their wives, brought them together as often as they could wish.

In time, Frederica ceased to dwell with pain upon her father's death, and though she must tolerate the occasional encounter with Charles Vernon in town or at Parklands, she beseeched her husband to support her in never having him at Vernon Castle.

In the coming year, Charles Vernon was to suffer a final humiliation: having lost Churchill Manor for himself, his line was further divided from Parklands when the Mrs. deCourcies were delivered of a young Reginald and a young Lewis, respectively. The two boys, born only a month apart, grew up to be the best of friends.

It is, perhaps, too indulgent to describe the course of Vernon's mortification any further, but to spare his daughter from the effects of it as far as he could, Sir Reginald pledged himself to all that had been promised to Frederica and bequeathed to Churchill's heir. Vernon's reputation was restored as far as it could be, but all of his claims to money and property were gone, and he was obliged to return to Parklands Cottage with no hope of ever leaving it for those pleasant country visits or lively occasions in town that he had taken for granted while Sir Frederick had lived. Catherine and her mother were as little distressed by this turn of events as anybody could be—they mixed no more with the world than they had done in the early years of Catherine's marriage, and so were spared the distress of hearing anything to Vernon's discredit. They kept little company, went nowhere, and returned to a routine that was without variety or diversion and that seldom had them going beyond the lane that separated Parklands Manor from Parklands Cottage.

Sir Reginald could not think well of his son-in-law, and although he must maintain him at Parklands, he reserved his liberality for the children, and for Reginald and Frederica.

The necessity for someone to hold Churchill Manor back from a slide into serious neglect before the heir could come into possession of it was a matter of some discussion, and Lady Martin finally decided that she might yield the management of Ealing Park to her daughter-in-law and withdraw to Churchill Manor, where she resumed her usefulness, coaxing the farmers into productiveness and the neighbors into harmony and hurrying to the bedside of anyone who fell ill before they could summon the apothecary or the surgeon.

Miss Hamilton and her mother were deeply mortified by Reginald's marriage, but as the word got round of Vernon Castle's stateliness and beauty, they made a gesture of rapprochement in order to gain admission to the estate and kept up their friendship with Mrs. Lewis deCourcy so as to widen their acquaintance among the eligible gentlemen at Bath. Yet, despite all of Lady Hamilton's determination to get them husbands, and her daughters' thirty thousand apiece, many years were to pass before any offers of consequence came their way.

Lucy Smith and her husband were frequent visitors at Vernon Castle and Bath; they were always cheerful and affectionate, possessing the sort of good-natured exuberance that might settle into contentment or sink into imprudence and misfortune; the latter was to be their fate, but not for many years.

As for Manwaring, he drew a harder lot than mere folly merited, for having pursued every woman but his wife, he now came to think that only Eliza had suited him after all; she had been a capable mistress of Langford and the possessor of a fortune that brought him fifteen hundred pounds per annum without having to do anything much for it. She had no sooner won over Mr. Johnson and installed herself at Edward Street when Manwaring set about courting her, as energetically as he had done before their marriage.

LADY SUSAN is the title character of an untitled epistolary novella written by Jane Austen in the early to mid-1790s when she was "not one and twenty." The narrative is composed of a series of letters, exchanged principally between Lady Susan and her London friend Alicia Johnson, and Lady Susan's sister-in-law, Catherine Vernon, and Catherine's mother, Lady deCourcy. In Austen's original work, Lady Susan Vernon is a beautiful widow who is rumored to be a "dangerous creature" and "the most accomplished coquette in England," not unlike the calculating Marquise de Merteuil in the sensational French novel *Les Liaisons Dangereuses.* That novel was published in England a decade before *Lady Susan* was written, and it is very likely, from their pronounced similarities, that the character of Lady Susan was influenced by the marquise.

Austen laid this work aside and began to work on the early novels in her canon; in 1805, she made a clean, legible duplicate—a "fair copy"—of *Lady Susan,* then abandoned it once more. Perhaps a thirty-year-old Austen recognized that, as the centerpiece of a novel, the intrigues and infidelities of racy aristocrats had become passé.

In converting *Lady Susan* to *Lady Vernon and Her Daughter,* we decided that Austen's six mature works were the most appropriate template, and that required two modifications in the character of Lady Susan. In Austen's work, Lady Susan is "wanting Maternal tenderness," and is often regarded as the worst of Austen's mothers (though whether she is worse than a controlling Mrs. Ferrars, an indolent Lady Bertram, or a suffocating Lady Catherine deBourgh might be a subject for lively debate); her cold-bloodedness is vain—"There is exquisite pleasure in subduing an insolent spirit, in making a person predetermined to dislike, acknowledge one's superiority"—rather than acquisitive.

But while Austen's heroines are flawed, they are not malicious, and marriage and money, treated rather dismissively in *Lady Susan*, are essential to a gentlewoman's happiness and respectability in Austen's later works. So to take the backdrop provided by Austen—that Lady Susan Vernon has lost the provider and protector of herself and her daughter and is compelled to provide for their security on her own—and to bring marriage, with the economic security and respectability it provides, to the forefront was a modification that brought Lady Susan Vernon and Frederica into a more sympathetic, and authentically Austen, framework. Her conduct is not radically altered, but it is motivated by economy, rather than "exquisite pleasure."

With that premise, "Lady Susan" (which implies a woman of high rank) became Lady Vernon, the wife of a knight. As a woman of rank, even if her husband had died and her brother-in-law had ignored his duties, it is unlikely that Lady Susan would have had to shift for herself. While there are a few widows of independent means in Austen—Lady Catherine deBourgh, Lady Russell, Mrs. Rushworth—her widows are more likely to range anywhere from women of modest means to the downright indigent—Mrs. Dashwood, Mrs. Bates, Mrs. Smith, Mrs. Norris, Mrs. Thorpe. Only one of Austen's heroines—Emma Woodhouse—is wealthy, and none of them are women of rank. To elevate Susan Vernon to the level of an earl's daughter would have taken her out of the sphere from which Austen's heroines are drawn.

While these changes do mean there is a significant difference between Lady Susan and Lady Vernon, we believe that they are true to the spirit of Austen, in keeping with her later works and what she might have done had she ever returned to this forgotten gem.

Acknowledgments

We are deeply grateful for the energy and commitment of those who helped bring this book to life: to Marly Rusoff, who was a tireless advocate, and to the team at Marly Rusoff & Associates, whose enthusiasm got it to her desk; to our excellent editor, Heather Lazare, whose guidance and skill made it a better book; to Cristina Concepcion and Lauren Galit, who provided a much-needed second look; to Aileen Schumacher whose advice was always tempered with good humor and common sense; to Bronwyn and Nick for their imaginative input; and to Eric Diehl for his illustrations. And, of course, to Bill (aka Dad), the "founder of the feast."

An excerpt from Jane Austen's *Lady Susan*

Letter 1

Lady Susan Vernon to Mr Vernon

Langford, December
My dear brother,

I can no longer refuse myself the pleasure of profiting by your kind invitation when we last parted, of spending some weeks with you at Churchill, and therefore if quite convenient to you and Mrs Vernon to receive me at present, I shall hope within a few days to be introduced to a sister whom I have so long desired to be acquainted with. My kind friends here are most affectionately urgent with me to prolong my stay, but their hospitable and cheerful dispositions lead them too much into society for my present situation and state of mind; and I impatiently look forward to the hour when I shall be admitted into your delightful retirement. I long to be made known to your dear little children, in whose hearts I shall be very eager to secure an interest. I shall soon have occasion for all my fortitude, as I am on the point of separation from my own daughter. The long illness of her dear father prevented my paying her that attention which duty and affection equally dictated, and I have but too much reason to fear that the governess to whose care I consigned her, was unequal to the charge. I have therefore resolved on placing her at one of the best private schools in town, where I shall have an opportunity of leaving her myself, in my way to you. I am determined you see, not to be denied admittance at Churchill. It would indeed give me most painful sensations to know that it were not in your power to receive me.

Your most obliged and affectionate sister
Susan Vernon

Letter 2

❧

LADY SUSAN TO MRS JOHNSON

Langford

You were mistaken my dear Alicia, in supposing me fixed at this place for the rest of the winter. It grieves me to say how greatly you were mistaken, for I have seldom spent three months more agreably than those which have just flown away. At present nothing goes smoothly. The females of the family are united against me. You foretold how it would be, when I first came to Langford; and Manwaring is so uncommonly pleasing that I was not without apprehensions myself. I remember saying to myself as I drove to the house, 'I like this man; pray Heaven no harm come of it!' But I was determined to be discreet, to bear in mind my being only four months a widow, and to be as quiet as possible,—and I have been so; my dear creature, I have admitted no one's attentions but Manwaring's, I have avoided all general flirtation whatever, I have distinguished no creature besides of all the numbers resorting hither, except Sir James Martin, on whom I bestowed a little notice in order to detach him from Miss Manwaring. But if the world could know my motive *there*, they would honour me. I have been called an unkind mother, but it was the sacred impulse of maternal affection, it was the advantage of my daughter that led me on; and if that daughter were not the greatest simpleton on earth, I might have been rewarded for my exertions as I ought.—Sir James did make proposals to me for Frederica—but Frederica, who was born to be the torment of my life, chose to set herself so violently against the match, that I thought it better to lay aside the scheme for the present. I have more than once repented that I did not marry him myself, and were he but one degree less contemptibly weak I certainly should, but I must own myself rather romantic in that respect, and that riches only, will not satisfy me. The event of all this is very provoking. Sir James is gone, Maria highly incensed, and Mrs Manwaring insupportably jealous; so jealous in short, and so enraged against me, that in the fury of her temper I should not be surprised at her appealing to her guardian if she had the liberty of addressing him—but there your husband stands my friend, and the kindest, most amiable action of his life was throwing her off forever on her marriage. Keep up his resentment therefore I charge you. We are now in a sad state; no house was ever more altered; the whole family are at war, and Manwaring scarcely dares speak to me. It is time for me to be gone; I have therefore determined on leaving them, and shall spend I hope a comfortable day with you in town within this week. If I am as little in favour with Mr Johnson as ever, you must come to me at No. 10, Wigmore St—but I hope this may not be the case, for as Mr Johnson with all his faults is a man to whom that great word 'Respectable' is always given, and I am known to be so intimate with his wife, his slighting me has an awkward look. I take town in my way to that insupportable spot, a country village, for I am really going to Churchill. Forgive me my dear friend, it is my last resource. Were there another place in England open to me, I would prefer it. Charles Vernon is my aversion, and I am afraid of his wife. At Churchill however I must remain till I have something better in view. My young lady accompanies me to town, where I shall deposit her under the care of Miss Summers in Wigmore Street, till she becomes a little more reasonable. She will make good connections there, as the girls are all of the best families. The price is immense, and much beyond what I can ever attempt to pay.

Adeiu. I will send you a line, as soon as I arrive in town.

Yours ever,
Susan Vernon

Letter 3

~~

MRS VERNON TO LADY DE COURCY

Churchill
My *dear mother*,

I am very sorry to tell you that it will not be in our power to keep our promise of spending the Christmas with you; and we are prevented that happiness by a circumstance which is not likely to make us any amends. Lady Susan in a letter to her brother, has declared her intention of visiting us almost immediately—and as such a visit is in all probability merely an affair of convenience, it is impossible to conjecture its length. I was by no means prepared for such an event, nor can I now account for her ladyship's conduct. Langford appeared so exactly the place for her in every respect, as well from the elegant and expensive style of living there, as from her particular attachment to Mrs Manwaring, that I was very far from expecting so speedy a distinction, though I always imagined from her increasing friendship for us since her husband's death, that we should at some future period be obliged to receive her. Mr Vernon I think was a great deal too kind to her, when he was in Staffordshire. Her behaviour to him, independent of her general character, has been so inexcusably artful and ungenerous since our marriage was first in agitation, that no one less amiable and mild than himself could have overlooked it at all; and though as his brother's widow and in narrow circumstances it was proper to render her pecuniary assistance, I cannot help thinking his pressing invitation to her to visit us at Churchill perfectly unnecessary. Disposed however as he always is to think the best of every one, her display of grief, and professions of regret, and general resolutions of prudence were sufficient to soften his heart, and make him really confide in her sincerity. But as for myself, I am still unconvinced; and plausibly as her ladyship has now written, I cannot make up my mind, till I better understand her real meaning in coming to us you may guess therefore my dear Madam, with what feelings I look forward to her arrival. She will have occasion for all those attractive powers for which she is celebrated, to gain any share of my regard; and I shall certainly endeavour to guard myself against their influence, if not accompanied by something more substantial. She expresses a most eager desire of being acquainted with me, and makes very generous mention of my children, but I am not quite weak enough to suppose a woman who has behaved with inattention if not unkindness to her own child, should be attached to any of mine. Miss Vernon is to be placed at a school in town before her mother comes to us, which I am glad of, for her sake and my own. It must be to her advantage to be separated from her mother; and a girl of sixteen who has received so wretched an education would not be a very desirable companion here. Reginald has long wished I know to see this captivating Lady Susan, and we shall depend on his joining our party soon. I am glad to hear that my father continues so well, and am, with best love etc.,

Catherine Vernon

Letter 4

MR DE COURCY TO MRS VERNON

Parklands
My *dear sister*,

I congratulate you and Mr Vernon on being about to receive into your family, the most accomplished coquette in England. As a very distinguished flirt, I have always been taught to consider her; but it has lately fallen in my way to hear some particulars of her conduct at Langford, which prove that she does not confine herself to that sort of honest flirtation which satisfies most people, but aspires to the more delicious gratification of making a whole family miserable. By her behaviour to Mr Manwaring, she gave jealousy and wretchedness to his wife, and by her attentions to a young man previously attached to Mr Manwaring's sister, deprived an amiable girl of her lover. I learnt all this from a Mr Smith now in this neighbourhood—(I have dined with him at Hurst and Wilford)—who is just come from Langford, where he was a fortnight in the house with her ladyship, and who is therefore well qualified to make the communication.

What a woman she must be! I long to see her, and shall certainly accept your kind invitation, that I may form some idea of those bewitching powers which can do so much—engaging at the same time and in the same house the affections of two men who were neither of them at liberty to bestow them—and all this, without the charm of youth. I am glad to find that Miss Vernon does not come with her mother to Churchill, as she has not even manners to recommend her, and according to Mr Smith's account, is equally dull and proud. Where pride and stupidity unite, there can be no dissimulation worthy notice, and Miss Vernon shall be consigned to unrelenting contempt; but by all that I can gather, Lady Susan possesses a degree of captivating deceit which must be pleasing to witness and detect. I shall be with you very soon, and am

your affectionate brother
Reginald De Courcy

Letter 5

∽⚬∼

LADY SUSAN TO MRS JOHNSON

Churchill

I received your note my dear Alicia, just before I left town, and rejoice to be assured that Mr Johnson suspected nothing of your engagement the evening before; it is undoubtedly better to deceive him entirely; since he will be stubborn, he must be tricked. I arrived here in safety, and have no reason to complain of my reception from Mr Vernon; but I confess myself not equally satisfied with the conduct of his lady. She is perfectly well bred indeed, and has the air of a woman of fashion, but her manners are not such as can persuade me of her being prepossessed in my favour. I wanted her to be delighted at seeing me—I was as amiable as possible on the occasion—but all in vain—she does not like me. To be sure, when we consider that I *did* take some pains to prevent my brother-in-law's marrying her, this want of cordiality is not very surprising—and yet it shows an illiberal and vindictive spirit to resent a project which influenced me six years ago, and which never succeeded at last. I am sometimes half disposed to repent that I did not let Charles buy Vernon Castle when we were obliged to sell it, but it was a trying circumstance, especially as the sale took place exactly at the time of his marriage—and everybody ought to respect the delicacy of those feelings, which could not endure that my husband's dignity should be lessened by his younger brother's having possession of the family estate. Could matters have been so arranged as to prevent the necessity of our leaving the Castle, could we have lived with Charles and kept him single, I should have been very far from persuading my husband to dispose of it elsewhere; but Charles was then on the point of marrying Miss De Courcy, and the event has justified me. Here are children in abundance, and what benefit could have accrued to me from his purchasing Vernon? My having prevented it, may perhaps have given his wife an unfavourable impression—but where there is a disposition to dislike a motive will never be wanting; and as to money-matters, it has not with-held him from being very useful to me. I really have a regard for him, he is so easily imposed on!

The house is a good one, the furniture fashionable, and everything announces plenty and elegance. Charles is very rich I am sure; when a man has once got his name in a banking house he rolls in money. But they do not know what to do with their fortune, keep very little company, and never go to town but on business. We shall be as stupid as possible. I mean to win my sister-in-law's heart through her children; I know all their names already, and am going to attach myself with the greatest sensibility to one in particular, a young Frederic, whom I take on my lap and sigh over for his dear uncle's sake.

Poor Manwaring!—I need not tell you how much I miss him—how perpetually he is in my thoughts. I found a dismal letter from him on my arrival here, full of complaints of his wife and sister, and lamentations on the cruelty of his fate. I passed off the letter as his wife's, to the Vernons, and when I write to him, it must be under cover to you.

Yours ever,
S.V.

Letter 6

∽✦∾

MRS VERNON TO MR DE COURCY

Churchill

Well my dear Reginald, I have seen this dangerous creature, and must give you some description of her, though I hope you will soon be able to form your own judgement. She is really excessively pretty. However you may choose to question the allurements of a lady no longer young, I must for my own part declare that I have seldom seen so lovely a woman as Lady Susan. She is delicately fair, with fine grey eyes and dark eyelashes; and from her appearance one would not suppose her more than five and twenty, though she must in fact be ten years older. I was certainly not disposed to admire her, though always hearing she was beautiful; but I cannot help feeling that she possesses an uncommon union of symmetry, brilliancy and grace. Her address to me was so gentle, frank and even affectionate, that if I had not known how much she has always disliked me for marrying Mr Vernon, and that we had never met before, I should have imagined her an attached friend. One is apt I believe to connect assurance of manner with coquetry, and to expect that an impudent address will necessarily attend an impudent mind; at least I was myself prepared for an improper degree of confidence in Lady Susan; but her countenance is absolutely sweet, and her voice and manner winningly mild. I am sorry it is so, for what is this but deceit? Unfortunately one knows her too well. She is clever and agreable, has all that knowledge of the world which makes conversation easy, and talks very well, with a happy command of language, which is too often used I believe to make black appear white. She has already almost persuaded me of her being warmly attached to her daughter, though I have so long been convinced of the contrary. She speaks of her with so much tenderness and anxiety, lamenting so bitterly the neglect of her education, which she represents however as wholly unavoidable, that I am forced to recollect how many successive springs her ladyship spent in town, while her daughter was left in Staffordshire to the care of servants or a governess very little better, to prevent my believing whatever she says.

If her manners have so great an influence on my resentful heart, you may guess how much more strongly they operate on Mr Vernon's generous temper. I wish I could be as well satisfied as he is, that it was really her choice to leave Langford for Churchill; and if she had not stayed three months there before she discovered that her friends' manner of living did not suit her situation or feelings, I might have believed that concern for the loss of such a husband as Mr Vernon, to whom her own behaviour was far from unexceptionable, might for a time make her wish for retirement. But I cannot forget the length of her visit to the Manwarings, and when I reflect on the different mode of life which she led with them, from that of which she must now submit, I can only suppose that the wish of establishing her reputation by following, though late, the path of propriety, occasioned her removal from a family where she must in reality have been particularly happy. Your friend Mr Smith's story however cannot be quite true, as she corresponds regularly with Mrs Manwaring; at any rate it must be exaggerated; it is scarcely possible that two men should be so grossly deceived by her at once.

Yours etc.,
Catherine Vernon

Letter 7

∽⁊∾

LADY SUSAN TO MRS JOHNSON

Churchill
My *dear Alicia,*

You are very good in taking notice of Frederica, and I am grateful for it as a mark of your friendship; but as I cannot have a doubt of the warmth of that friendship, I am far from exacting so heavy a sacrifice. She is a stupid girl, and has nothing to recommend her. I would not therefore on any account have you encumber one moment of your precious time by sending her to Edward St, especially as every visit is so many hours deducted from the grand affair of education, which I really wish to be attended to, while she remains with Miss Summers. I want her to play and sing with some portion of taste, and a good deal of assurance, as she has my hand and arm, and a tolerable voice. I was so much indulged in my infant years that I was never obliged to attend to anything, and consequently am without those accomplishments which are necessary to finish a pretty woman. Not that I am an advocate for the prevailing fashion of acquiring a perfect knowledge in all the languages arts and sciences; it is throwing time away; to be mistress of French, Italian, German, music, singing, drawing etc., will gain a woman some applause, but will not add one lover to her list. Grace and manner after all are of the greatest importance. I do not mean therefore that Frederica's acquirements should be more than superficial, and I flatter myself that she will not remain long enough at school to understand anything thoroughly. I hope to see her the wife of Sir James within a twelvemonth. You know on what I ground my hope, and it is certainly a good foundation, for school must be very humiliating to a girl of Frederica's age; and by the bye, you had better not invite her any more on that account, as I wish her to find her situation as unpleasant as possible. I am sure of Sir James at any time, and could make him renew his application by a line.

I shall trouble you meanwhile to prevent his forming any other attachment when he comes to town; ask him to your house occasionally, and talk to him about Frederica that he may not forget her.

Upon the whole I commend my own conduct in this affair extremely, and regard it as a very happy mixture of circumspection and tenderness. Some mothers would have insisted on their daughter's accepting so great an offer on the first overture, but I could not answer it to myself to force Frederica into a marriage from which her heart revolted; and instead of adopting so harsh a measure, merely propose to make it her own choice by rendering her life thoroughly uncomfortable till she does accept him. But enough of this tiresome girl.

You may well wonder how I contrive to pass my time here—and for the first week, it was most insufferably dull. Now however, we begin to mend; our party is enlarged by Mrs Vernon's brother, a handsome young man, who promises me some amusement. There is something about him that rather interests me, a sort of sauciness, of familiarity which I shall teach him to correct. He is lively and seems clever, and when I have inspired him with greater respect for me than his sister's kind offices have implanted, he may be an agreable flirt. There is exquisite pleasure in subduing an insolent spirit, in making a person pre-determined to dislike, acknowledge one's superiority. I have disconcerted him already by my calm reserve; and it shall be my endeavour to humble the pride of these self-important De Courcies still lower, to convince Mrs Vernon that her sisterly cautions have been bestowed in vain, and to persuade Reginald that she has scandalously belied me. This project will serve at least to amuse me, and prevent my feeling so acutely this dreadful separation from you and all whom I love. Adeiu.

Yours ever
S. Vernon

Letter 8

∼⁓∽

MRS VERNON TO LADY DE COURCY

Churchill
My *dear mother,*

You must not expect Reginald back again for some time. He desires me to tell you that the present open weather induces him to accept Mr Vernon's invitation to prolong his stay in Sussex that they may have some hunting together. He means to send for his horses immediately, and it is impossible to say when you may see him in Kent. I will not disguise my sentiments on this change from you my dear Madam, though I think you had better not communicate them to my father, whose excessive anxiety about Reginald would subject him to an alarm which might seriously affect his health and spirits. Lady Susan has certainly contrived in the space of a fortnight to make my brother like her. In short, I am persuaded that his continuing here beyond the time originally fixed for his return, is occasioned as much by a degree of fascination towards her, as by the wish of hunting with Mr Vernon, and of course I cannot receive that pleasure from the length of his visit which my brother's company would otherwise give me. I am indeed provoked at the artifice of this unprincipled woman. What stronger proof of her dangerous abilities can be given, than this perversion of Reginald's judgement, which when he entered the house was so decidedly against her? In his last letter he actually gave me some particulars of her behaviour at Langford, such as he received from a gentleman who knew her perfectly well, which if true must raise abhorrence against her, and which Reginald himself was entirely disposed to credit. His opinion of her I am sure, was as low as of any woman in England, and when he first came it was evident that he considered her as one entitled neither to delicacy nor respect, and that he felt she would be delighted with the attentions of any man inclined to flirt with her.

Her behaviour I confess has been calculated to do away with such an idea, I have not detected the smallest impropriety in it,—nothing of vanity, of pretension, of levity—and she is altogether so attractive, that I should not wonder at his being delighted with her, had he known nothing of her previous to this personal acquaintance; but against reason, against conviction, to be so well pleased with her as I am sure he is, does really astonish me. His admiration was at first very strong, but no more than was natural; and I did not wonder at his being struck by the gentleness and delicacy of her manners; but when he has mentioned her of late, it has been in terms of more extraordinary praise, and yesterday he actually said, that he could not be surprised at any effect produced on the heart of man by such loveliness and such abilities; and when I lamented in reply the badness of her disposition, he observed that whatever might have been her errors, they were to be imputed to her neglected education and early marriage, and that she was altogether a wonderful woman.

This tendency to excuse her conduct, or to forget it in the warmth of admiration vexes me; and if I did not know that Reginald is too much at home at Churchill to need an invitation for lengthening his visit, I should regret Mr Vernon's giving him any.

Lady Susan's intentions are of course those of absolute coquetry, or a desire of universal admiration. I cannot for a moment imagine that she has anything more serious in view, but it mortifies me to see a young man of Reginald's sense duped by her at all. I am etc.

Catherine Vernon

Letter 9

❧

MRS JOHNSON TO LADY SUSAN

Edward St
My *dearest friend,*

I congratulate you on Mr De Courcy's arrival, and advise you by all means to marry him; his father's estate is we know considerable, and I believe certainly entailed. Sir Reginald is very infirm, and not likely to stand in your way long. I hear the young man well spoken of, and though no one can really deserve you my dearest Susan, Mr De Courcy may be worth having. Manwaring will storm of course, but you may easily pacify him. Besides, the most scrupulous point of honour could not require you to wait for *his* emancipation. I have seen Sir James,—he came to town for a few days last week, and called several times in Edward Street. I talked to him about you and your daughter, and he is so far from having forgotten you, that I am sure he would marry either of you with pleasure. I gave him hopes of Frederica's relenting, and told him a great deal of her improvements. I scolded him for making love to Maria Manwaring; he protested that he had been only in joke, and we both laughed heartily at her disappointment, and in short were very agreable. He is as silly as ever.—

Yours faithfully
Alicia

Letter 10

∾

LADY SUSAN TO MRS JOHNSON

Churchill

I am much obliged to you my dear friend, for your advice respecting Mr De Courcy, which I know was given with the fullest conviction of its expediency, though I am not quite determined on following it. I cannot easily resolve on anything so serious as marriage, especially as I am not at present in want of money, and might perhaps till the old gentleman's death, be very little benefited by the match. It is true that I am vain enough to believe it within my reach. I have made him sensible of my power, and can now enjoy the pleasure of triumphing over a mind prepared to dislike me, and prejudiced against all my past actions. His sister too, is I hope convinced how little the ungenerous representations of any one to the disadvantage of another will avail, when opposed to the immediate influence of intellect and manner. I see plainly that she is uneasy at my progress in the good opinion of her brother, and conclude that nothing will be wanting on her part to counteract me; but having once made him doubt the justice of her opinion of me, I think I may defy her.

It has been delightful to me to watch his advances towards intimacy, especially to observe his altered manner in consequence of my repressing by the calm dignity of my deportment, his insolent approach to direct familiarity. My conduct has been equally guarded from the first, and I never behaved less like a coquette in the whole course of my life, though perhaps my desire of dominion was never more decided. I have subdued him entirely by sentiment and sérious conversation, and made him I may venture to say *half* in love with me, without the semblance of the most common-place flirtation. Mrs Vernon's consciousness of deserving every sort of revenge that it can be in my power to inflict, for her ill-offices, could alone enable her to perceive that I am actuated by any design in behaviour so gentle and unpretending. Let her think and act as she chooses however; I have never yet found that the advice of a sister could prevent a young man's being in love if he chose it. We are advancing now towards some kind of confidence, and in short are likely to be engaged in a kind of platonic friendship. On my side, you may be sure of its never being more, for if I were not already as much attached to another person as I can be to any one, I should make a point of not bestowing my affection on a man who had dared to think so meanly of me.

Reginald has a good figure, and is not unworthy the praise you have heard given him, but is still greatly inferior to our friend at Langford. He is less polished, less insinuating than Manwaring, and is comparatively deficient in the power of saying those delightful things which put one in good humour with oneself and all the world. He is quite agreable enough however, to afford me amusement, and to make many of those hours pass very pleasantly which would be otherwise spent in endeavouring to overcome my sister-in-law's reserve, and listen to her husband's insipid talk.

Your account of Sir James is most satisfactory, and I mean to give Miss Frederica a hint of my intentions very soon.—Yours etc.

S. *Vernon*

Letter 11

~~~

MRS VERNON TO LADY DE COURCY

I really grow quite uneasy my dearest mother about Reginald, from witnessing the very rapid increase of Lady Susan's influence. They are now on terms of the most particular friendship, frequently engaged in long conversations together, and she has contrived by the most artful coquetry to subdue his judgement to her own purposes. It is impossible to see the intimacy between them, so very soon established, without some alarm, though I can hardly suppose that Lady Susan's views extend to marriage. I wish you could get Reginald home again, under any plausible pretence. He is not at all disposed to leave us, and I have given him as many hints of my father's precarious state of health, as common decency will allow me to do in my own house. Her power over him must now be boundless, as she has entirely effaced all his former ill-opinion, and persuaded him not merely to forget, but to justify her conduct. Mr Smith's account of her proceedings at Langford, where he accused her of having made Mr Manwaring and a young man engaged to Miss Manwaring distractedly in love with her, which Reginald firmly believed when he came to Churchill, is now he is persuaded only a scandalous invention. He has told me so in a warmth of manner which spoke his regret at having ever believed the contrary himself.

How sincerely do I grieve that she ever entered this house! I always looked forward to her coming with uneasiness—but very far was it, from originating in anxiety for Reginald. I expected a most disagreable companion to myself, but could not imagine that my brother would be in the smallest danger of being captivated by a woman with whose principles he was so well acquainted, and whose character he so heartily despised. If you can get him away, it will be a good thing.

Yours affectionately
Catherine Vernon

Letter 12

SIR REGINALD DE COURCY TO HIS SON

Parklands

I know that young men in general do not admit of any enquiry even from their nearest relations, into affairs of the heart; but I hope my dear Reginald that you will be superior to such as allow nothing for a father's anxiety, and think themselves privileged to refuse him their confidence and slight his advice. You must be sensible that as an only son and the representative of an ancient family, your conduct in life is most interesting to your connections. In the very important concern of marriage especially, there is everything at stake; your own happiness, that of your parents, and the credit of your name. I do not suppose that you would deliberately form an absolute engagement of that nature without acquainting your mother and myself, or at least without being convinced that we should approve your choice; but I cannot help fearing that you may be drawn in by the lady who has lately attached you, to a marriage, which the whole of your family, far and near, must highly reprobate.

Lady Susan's age is itself a material objection, but her want of character is one so much more serious, that the difference of even twelve years becomes in comparison of small account. Were you not blinded by a sort of fascination, it would be ridiculous in me to repeat the instances of great misconduct on her side, so very generally known. Her neglect of her husband, her encouragement of other men, her extravagance and dissipation were so gross and notorious, that no one could be ignorant of them at the time, nor can now have forgotten them. To our family, she has always been represented in softened colours by the benevolence of Mr Charles Vernon; and yet in spite of his generous endeavours to excuse her, we know that she did, from the most selfish motives, take all possible pains to prevent his marrying Catherine.

My years and increasing infirmities make me very desirous my dear

Reginald, of seeing you settled in the world. To the fortune of your wife, the goodness of my own, will make me indifferent; but her family and character must be equally unexceptionable. When your choice is so fixed as that no objection can be made to either, I can promise you a ready and cheerful consent; but it is my duty to oppose a match, which deep art only could render probable, and must in the end make wretched.

It is possible that her behaviour may arise only from vanity, or a wish of gaining the admiration of a man whom she must imagine to be particularly prejudiced against her; but it is more likely that she should aim at something farther. She is poor, and may naturally seek an alliance which may be advantageous to herself. You know your own rights, and that it is out of my power to prevent your inheriting the family estate. My ability of distressing you during my life, would be a species of revenge to which I should hardly stoop under any circumstances. I honestly tell you my sentiments and intentions. I do not wish to work on your fears, but on your sense and affection. It would destroy every comfort of my life, to know that you were married to Lady Susan Vernon. It would be the death of that honest pride with which I have hitherto considered my son, I should blush to see him, to hear of him, to think of him.

I may perhaps do no good, but that of relieving my own mind, by this letter; but I felt it my duty to tell you that your partiality for Lady Susan is no secret to your friends, and to warn you against her. I should be glad to hear your reasons for disbelieving Mr Smith's intelligence; you had no doubt of its authenticity a month ago.

If you can give me your assurance of having no design beyond enjoying the conversation of a clever woman for a short period, and of yielding admiration only to her beauty and abilities without being blinded by them to her faults, you will restore me to happiness; but if you cannot do this, explain to me at least what has occasioned so great an alteration in your opinion of her.

I am etc.
Reginald De Courcy

1. Throughout Austen's works, we have examples of fathers who are inattentive, or who neglect the welfare of the family. How does Sir Frederick Vernon compare to other Austen fathers, such as Mr. Bennet, Sir Thomas Bertram, or Sir Walter Elliot? Is he better or worse?

2. Austen often reveals characters by way of appearance versus principles—for example, Elizabeth Bennet says of Darcy and Wickham, "One has got all the goodness, and the other all the appearance of it." How do the appearance and conduct of Sir James Martin contradict his true character?

3. *Lady Susan* began as an epistolary novel. While Austen abandoned this format, she still used letters to advance the plot in all of her major novels. How does the use of letters advance the plot of *Lady Vernon and Her Daughter*?

4. In Austen's novels, principle characters frequently become the subject of gossip. Sometimes this only leads to misunderstanding, as when Mrs. Jennings believes that Colonel Brandon has proposed to Elinor Dashwood. Sometimes it is intentionally spiteful, as when Wickham deliberately maligns Darcy. How do Lady Vernon and Frederica become the subject of gossip and how does this impact the plot?

5. In *Lady Susan*, Frederica's appeal to Reginald is written in her own hand. In *Lady Vernon and Her Daughter*, it is written by Sir James as a

prank. Discuss how this alteration redefines the characters of Lady Vernon, Frederica, Reginald, and Sir James.

6. In R. W. Chapman's *Jane Austen: Facts and Problems*, he notes that as a general rule, Austen never has two young men in conversation without a woman present. We broke this rule with the carriage scene between Sir James and Reginald. Are the revelations and insights into character worth deviating from Austen's established structure?

7. Generally, Austen's heroines either have none of the usual female accomplishments (Catharine Morland, Fanny Price) or do little to acquire proficiency (Elizabeth Bennet, Emma Woodhouse). The Dashwood sisters—Elinor is an artist, Marianne is a musician—are the exception, as is Frederica Vernon, who is a botanist. What other correlations are there between the Dashwood girls and Frederica?

8. In an earlier draft of *Lady Susan*, it was made clear that Charles Vernon deliberately caused Sir Frederick's death. In *Lady Vernon and Her Daughter*, there is only a suggestion of some culpability. How much responsibility do you assign to Charles's conduct? What do you think happened in Churchill Wood?

9. *Lady Susan* begins with Susan Vernon leaving Langford to go to Churchill. In *Lady Vernon and Her Daughter*, we created an entire backstory (beyond that she has made herself unwelcome at Langford) to illustrate what motivates this decision. Do you agree with the dimension this adds to the plight of the Vernon ladies, or do you think that our novel should have begun where Austen's did?

10. In *Lady Susan*, Charles Smith and the Hamiltons are merely mentioned. In *Lady Vernon and Her Daughter*, we developed these characters and used them to create a connection with Austen's *Persuasion*. Do you think it adds a provocative episode to the story, or does it draw the focus away from Lady Vernon and Frederica?